THE QUIET TENANT

CLÉMENCE MICHALLON

THE QUIET TENANT

abacus
books

ABACUS

First published in the United States in 2023 by Knopf
First published in the United Kingdom in 2023 by Abacus

1 3 5 7 9 10 8 6 4 2

A CIP catalogue record for this book
is available from the British Library.

HB ISBN: 978-1-408-71686-1
TPB ISBN: 978-1-408-71687-8

Printed and bound in Great Britain by
Clays Ltd, Elcograf S.p.A.

Papers used by Abacus are from well-managed forests
and other responsible sources.

Abacus
An imprint of
Little, Brown Book Group
Carmelite House
50 Victoria Embankment
London EC4Y 0DZ

An Hachette UK Company
www.hachette.co.uk

www.littlebrown.co.uk

FOR TYLER

Alas! Who does not know that these gentle wolves
Are of all such creatures the most dangerous!

—CHARLES PERRAULT, *LITTLE RED RIDING HOOD*

THE
QUIET
TENANT

CHAPTER 1

The woman in the shed

You like to think every woman has one, and he just happens to be yours.

It's easier this way. If no one's free. There is no room in your world for the ones still outside. No love for the wind in their hair, no patience for the sun on their skin.

He comes at night. Unlocks the door. Drags his boots through a trail of dead leaves. Shuts the door behind him, slides the deadbolt into place.

This man: young, strong, groomed. You think back to the day you met, to that brief moment before he revealed his true nature, and here's what you see: A man who knows his neighbors. Who always takes out the recycling on time. Who stood in the delivery room the day his child was born, a steady presence against the evils of the world. Mothers see him in line at the grocery store and shove their babies into his arms: *Can you hold her for a minute, I forgot the formula, be right back.*

And now he's here. Now he's yours.

There is an order to what you do.

He glances at you, a look that serves as an inventory. You are here. All two arms, two legs, one torso, and one head of you.

Then comes the sigh. A softening in the muscles of his back as he settles into your shared moment. He bends to adjust the electric heater or the fan, depending on the season.

You put out your hand and receive a Tupperware box. Steam rises from the lasagna, the shepherd's pie, the tuna casserole, whatever else it might be. The food, piping hot, leaves blisters on the roof of your mouth.

He hands you water. Never in a glass. Always in a canteen. Nothing that can be broken and sharpened. The cold liquid sends electric shocks through your teeth. But you drink, because the time to drink is now. A metallic taste lingers in your mouth afterward.

He gives you the bucket, and you do what you have to do. You stopped feeling ashamed a long time ago.

He takes your waste and leaves you for a minute or so. You hear him right outside, the padding of his boots against the ground, the spray of the hose. When he comes back, the bucket is clean, full of soapy water.

He watches as you clean yourself. In the hierarchy of your body, you are the tenant and he is the landlord. He hands you your tools: a bar of soap, a plastic comb, a toothbrush, a small tube of toothpaste. Once a month, the anti-lice shampoo. Your body: always brewing trouble, and him, keeping it at bay. Every three weeks, he pulls the nail clippers out of his back pocket. He waits while you snip yourself back to presentableness, then takes them back. Always, he takes them back. You have done this for years.

You put your clothes back on. It seems pointless to you, given what follows, but this is what he's decided. It doesn't work, you think, if you do it yourself. He has to be the one to pull down the zippers, undo the buttons, peel off the layers.

The geography of his flesh: things you didn't want to learn, but learned anyway. A mole on his shoulder. The trail of hair down his abdomen. His hands: the grip of his fingers. The hot pressure of his palm on your neck.

Through it all, he never looks at you. This isn't about you. This is about all the women and all the girls. This is about him and all the things boiling inside his head.

When it's over, he never lingers. He's a man in the world, with responsibilities calling out to him. A family, a household to run. Homework to check. Movies to watch. A wife to keep happy and a daughter to cradle. There are items on his to-do list beyond you and your little existence, all demanding to be crossed out.

Except tonight.

Tonight, everything changes.

Tonight is the night you see this man—this very careful man, known to take only calculated steps—violate his own rules.

He pushes himself up, palms flat on the wooden floor. His fingers are miraculously splinter-free. He secures the belt buckle underneath his belly button, pushes the metal against the tight skin of his midsection.

"Listen," he says.

Something sharpens, the most essential part of you rising to attention.

"You've been here long enough."

You search his face. Nothing. He's a man of few words, of muted facial expressions.

"What do you mean?" you ask.

He shrugs his fleece back on, zips it up to his chin.

"I have to move," he says.

Again, you must ask: "What?"

A vein pulses at the base of his forehead. You have annoyed him.

"To a new house."

"Why?"

He frowns. Opens his mouth as if to say something, then thinks better of it.

Not tonight.

You make sure his gaze catches yours on his way out. You want him to drink in your confusion, all the questions left unaddressed. You want him to feel the satisfaction of leaving you hanging.

Rule number one of staying alive in the shed: He always wins. For five years, you have made sure of it.

CHAPTER 2

Emily

I have no idea if Aidan Thomas knows my name. I wouldn't hold a grudge if he didn't. He has more important things to remember than the name of the girl who pours his Cherry Coke twice a week.

Aidan Thomas doesn't drink. Not liquor. A beautiful man who doesn't drink could be a problem for a bartender, but my love language isn't booze; it's people sitting at my bar and putting themselves in my care for an hour or two.

This isn't a language Aidan Thomas speaks fluently. He's a deer on the side of the road, keeping still until you drive by, ready to bolt if you show too much interest. So I let him come to me. Tuesdays and Thursdays. In a sea of regulars, he's the only one I want to see.

Today is a Tuesday.

At seven o'clock, I start glancing at the door. Keep one eye out for him and the other on the kitchen—my lead waitress, my sommelier, my absolute prick of a head chef. My hands move on autopilot. One sidecar, one Sprite, one Jack and Coke. The door opens. It's not him. It's the lady from the four-top by the door who had to go move her car to a new spot. One bitters and soda. A new straw for the kid at the back. A report from my lead waitress: the four-top didn't like the pasta. It was cold or it wasn't spicy enough. Their grievances are unclear, but they are here, and Cora isn't losing her tips because the kitchen can't work a food warmer. Placate Cora. Tell her to tell the cooks to redo the pasta, with a free side of something as an apology. Or have Sophie, our baker, send out a dessert if the four-top look like they have a sweet tooth. Whatever it takes to shut them up.

The restaurant is a black hole of needs, a monster that can never be sated. My father never asked me; he just assumed I would step in. And then he went ahead and died, because that's what chefs do—exist in a blur of heat and chaos only to leave you to pick up the pieces.

I pinch my temples between two fingers, try to fend off the dread.

Maybe it's the weather—it's the first week of October, still early fall, but the days are getting shorter, the air colder. Maybe it's something else. But tonight, every failure feels especially mine.

The door opens.

It's him.

Something lightens inside of me. A joy bubbles up, the kind that leaves me feeling small and a little bit dirty and possibly quite dumb, but it's the sweetest sensation the restaurant has to offer, and I'll take it. Twice a week, I'll take it.

Aidan Thomas sits at my bar in silence. He and I don't talk except for the usual pleasantries. This is a dance, and we know our steps by heart. Glass, ice cubes, soda gun, paper coaster. *Amandine* written in vintage cursive across the cardboard. One Cherry Coke. One satisfied man.

"Thank you."

I give him a quick smile and keep my hands busy. In between tasks—rinsing a shaker, organizing jars of olives and lemon slices—I sneak glances at him. Like a poem I know by heart but never tire of: blue eyes, dark-blond hair, neat beard. Lines under his eyes, because he has lived. Because he has loved and lost. And then, his hands: one resting on the counter, the other wrapped around his glass. Steady. Strong. Hands that tell a story.

"Emily."

Cora's leaning against the bar.

"What now?"

"Nick says we need to eighty-six the sirloin."

I hold in a sigh. Nick's tantrums are not Cora's fault.

"And why would we need to do that?"

"He says the cut isn't right and the cooking times are off."

I tear my eyes away from Aidan to face Cora.

"I'm not saying he's right," she says. "He just . . . asked me to tell you."

At any other time, I would leave the bar and deal with Nick myself. But he's not going to take this moment from me.

"Tell him message received."

Cora waits for the rest. She knows as well as I do that "message received" won't get Nick off anyone's back.

"Tell him that if we get any complaints about the sirloin, I'll handle them personally. I promise. I'll shoulder all the blame. Sirloingate will be my legacy. Tell him the food has been raved about tonight. And tell him he should worry less about the sirloin and more about his pickup station, if his guys are sending out cold food."

Cora raises her hands, like *All right, all right*. She heads back toward the kitchen.

This time, I allow myself a sigh. I'm about to turn my attention to a couple of martini glasses in need of a shine when I feel a gaze on me.

Aidan.

He's looking up from the counter, giving me a half smile.

"Sirloingate, eh?"

Shit. He heard.

I force myself to chuckle. "Sorry about that."

He shakes his head, takes a sip from his Cherry Coke.

"No need to apologize," he says.

I smile back and focus on my martini glasses, for real this time. In the corner of my eye, Aidan finishes his Coke. Our choreography resumes: A tilt of the head to ask for his check. A hand raised briefly as a goodbye.

And just like that, the best part of my day is over.

I collect Aidan's receipt—two-dollar tip, as always—and his empty cup. It's not until I wipe the bar that I notice it: a hitch, a change in our well-rehearsed pas de deux.

His coaster. The paper one I slipped under his drink. Now would be the time for me to throw it in the recycling bin, but I can't find it.

Maybe it fell? I step on the other side of the counter, look at the foot of the barstool he was sitting on just a few minutes ago. Nothing.

It's the weirdest thing, but undeniable. The coaster is gone.

CHAPTER 3

The woman in the shed

He brought you here.

His home revealed itself to you in flashes, quick glances when he wasn't looking. Over the years, you have gone over those images, clung to every detail: the house at the center of a patch of land. Green grass, willow trees. Every plant trimmed, every leaf tended to. Smaller buildings scattered around the property like tea cakes on a platter. A detached garage, a barn, a bike rack. Power lines snaking through branches. This man, you learned, lived somewhere soft and beautiful. A place for children to run, for flowers to bloom.

He walked fast, down a dirt path and up a hill. The house faded into the distance, replaced by a litany of trees. He stopped. There was nothing to grab onto, no one to call out to. You stood in front of a shed. Four gray walls, a slanted roof. Windowless. He held the metallic padlock, separated a key from the rest of the bunch.

Inside, he taught you the new rules of the world.

"Your name," he said. He was kneeling, yet still towering above you, hands on each side of your face so that your vision began and ended with his fingers. "Your name is Rachel."

Your name was not Rachel. He knew your real one. He had seen it on your driver's license after taking your wallet.

But he told you your name was Rachel, and it was vital for you to accept this fact. The way he said it, the growl of the *r* and the definitiveness of the *l*. Rachel was a blank slate. Rachel didn't have a past or a life to get back to. Rachel could survive in the shed.

"Your name is Rachel," he said, "and no one knows who you are."

You nodded. Not eagerly enough. His hands left your face and grabbed onto your sweater. He pushed you into the wall, arm lodged against your neck, wrist bones embedded into your trachea. There was no air, no oxygen at all.

"I said," he said, and the world started slipping from you, but not hearing him wasn't an option, "no one knows who you are. No one is looking for you. Do you fucking understand?"

He let go. Before you coughed, before you wheezed, before you did anything else, you nodded. Like you meant it. You nodded for dear life.

You became Rachel.

You have been Rachel for years.

She has kept you alive. You have kept you alive.

BOOTS, DEAD LEAVES, deadbolt. Sigh. Heater. Everything as usual, except him. Tonight, he rushes through his ritual as though he's left water boiling on the stove. You're still chewing your last bite of chicken pot pie when he takes the Tupperware from you.

"Come on," he says. "I don't have all night."

It's not eagerness, this haste of his. More like you're a song and he's fast-forwarding through the boring parts.

He keeps his clothes on. The zipper of his fleece digs a crevice into your abdomen. A strand of your hair lodges itself in the clasp of his watch. He pulls his wrist away, wrestles himself free of you. You hear a tear. Your scalp burns. Everything palpable, everything real, even as he hovers over you like a ghost.

You need him here. With you. You need him relaxed and comfortable.

You need him to talk.

You wait until after. Your clothes back on for good.

As he prepares to leave, you run a hand through your hair. A gesture you used to deploy on dates, the elbow of your biker jacket on a restaurant table, your white T-shirt livened up by a cluster of silver pendants.

This happens. You remember bits of yourself, and sometimes they help you.

"You know," you tell him, "I worry about you."

He scoffs.

"It's true. I mean—I just wonder. That's all."

He sniffs, stuffs his hands into his pockets.

"Maybe I could help," you try. "Find a way for you to stay."

He snorts but makes no move toward the door. You have to hold on to that. You have to believe this is the beginning of a victory.

He talks to you, sometimes. Not often, and always reluctantly, but he does. Some nights, it's bragging. Other nights, it's a confession. Perhaps this is why he has bothered keeping you alive at all: there are things in his life he needs to share, and you're the only one who can hear them.

"If you tell me what happened, maybe I could figure it out," you say.

He bends his knees, brings his face in front of yours. His breath, minty fresh. His palm, warm and rugged against your cheekbone. The tip of his thumb digs into your eye socket.

"You think if I tell you, you'll figure it out?"

His gaze trails from your face to your feet. Repelled. Scornful. But always—this is important—a little bit curious. About the things he can do to you, the things he can get away with.

"What could you possibly know?" He traces the outline of your jaw, his nail grazing against your chin. "Do you even know who you are?"

You do. Like a prayer, like a mantra. *You are Rachel. He found you. All you know is what he has taught you. All you have is what he has given you.* A chain around your ankle, nailed to the wall. A sleeping bag. On an upturned crate, the items he has brought you over the years: three paperbacks, a wallet (empty), a stress ball (really). Random and mismatched. Taken, you inferred, by this magpie of a man from other women.

"I found you," he says. "You were lost. I gave you a roof. I keep you alive." He points to the empty Tupperware. "Know what you'd be, without me? Nothing. You'd be dead."

He gets up again. Cracks his knuckles, each finger a distinct pop.

You are not much. You know that. But in the shed, in this part of his life, you're all he's got.

"She's dead," he says. He tries it on for size and says again: "She's dead."

You have no idea who he's talking about until he adds: "Her parents are selling the house."

And then you get it.

His wife.

You try to think all the thoughts at once. You want to say what people say in polite society: *I'm so sorry to hear.* You want to ask, *When? How?* You wonder, *Did he do it? Did he finally snap?*

"So we have to move."

He paces, as much as one can pace in the shed. Rattled, which is unlike him. But you have no time for his emotions. No time to waste figuring out whether he did it. Who cares if he did? He kills. You know that.

What you need to do is think. Search the atrophied folds of your brain, the ones that used to solve the problems of daily life. The part of you that helped your friends, your family. But the only thing your brain screams is that if he moves—if he leaves this house, this property—you die. Unless you can convince him to bring you along.

"I'm sorry," you tell him.

You are so sorry, all the time. You are sorry his wife is dead. You are sorry, truly so, about the injustices of the world, the way they've befallen him. You are sorry he's stuck with you, such a needy woman, always hungry and thirsty and cold, and so nosy at that.

Rule number two of staying alive in the shed: He's always right, and you're always sorry.

CHAPTER 4

Emily

He's back. Tuesdays and Thursdays. As reliable as an eighty-six-proof whiskey, brimming with promises.

Aidan Thomas removes his gray trapper hat, his hair like ruffled feathers underneath. Tonight, he's carrying a duffel bag—green nylon, like something out of an army surplus store. It hangs heavily at his side, the strap tugging at his shoulder.

The door slams behind him. I startle. He usually shuts it in one cautious gesture, one hand on the handle and the other on the frame.

He keeps his head down as he walks to the bar. There's a heaviness to his step, and it's not just the duffel's fault.

Something is weighing on him.

He stuffs the hat in his pocket, smooths his hair, drops the duffel at his feet.

"Do you have my Manhattans?"

With a distracted glance, I slide two drinks in Cora's direction. She skitters away. Aidan waits until she's gone to gaze up at me.

"What can I get you?"

He gives me a tired smile.

I pick up the soda gun. "I have your usual." An idea comes to me. "Or I could make you something, if you need a little pick-me-up."

He lets out a breathy laugh. "That obvious, huh?"

A cool shrug, as if none of this matters all that much. "It's my job to notice."

His eyes go vacant. In the background, Eric gesticulates. He's describing the specials to a four-top. His customers drink him in, wide-eyed. Eric's so good at it, the showmanship. He knows how to earn his tables' affection, how to inflate his tips by two to five percent in a few sentences.

Sweet Eric. A friend who remained my friend when I became his boss. Who has my back. Who somehow believes in me, in my ability to run this place.

"Let's try something."

I pick up a rocks glass, give it a quick shine. Aidan Thomas raises his eyebrows at me. Something is happening, new, different. He's not sure he likes it. It kills me to do this to him, when all he wanted was his usual Cherry Coke.

"I'll be right back."

I do my best to keep my stride casual. Behind the swing doors, Nick is hunched over four plates of tonight's special—breaded pork chop with cheesy mashed potatoes and bacon-scallion gravy. *Simple, but flavorful,* he told me. *Folks want to know what's on their plate, but they don't come here to eat stuff they could have made at home.* Like it was his idea, and not what my father started drilling into my head before I could even walk. *Real food, at good prices, too,* my dad used to say. *We don't want to cater only to the city crowd. They show up on weekends, but it's the locals who carry us through the week. We're here for them first.*

Eric passes me on his way out of the kitchen, three plates balanced on his left arm. Through the swing door, he sees Aidan at the bar. He pauses and turns back to give me a half grin. I pretend not to notice and step toward the walk-in.

"Is there any more of that elderflower tea we brewed at lunch?"

Silence. Everyone is either working or ignoring me. Yuwanda, the third musketeer of my trio with Eric, would know, but she's in the dining room, probably reciting the pros and cons of Gewürztraminer versus Riesling. I keep looking until I locate the pitcher behind a vat of buttermilk ranch. There's about a cup left.

Perfect.

I hurry back out. Aidan is waiting, hands on the counter. Unlike most of us, he doesn't reach for his phone the second he's alone. He knows how to be by himself, how to stretch into a moment to find stillness, if not comfort.

"Sorry about the wait."

With his gaze on me, I drop a sugar cube into the glass. Orange slice, dash of Angostura bitters. I add an ice cube, then the tea, and stir. With a spoon—nothing cramps a bartender's style as tragically as plastic gloves—I fish a Maraschino cherry out of a Mason jar.

"*Voilà.*"

He smiles at my exaggerated French inflection. A warmth pools in my stomach. I nudge the glass in front of him. He brings it up to his face, takes a whiff. It occurs to me, with blinding obviousness, that I have no idea what this man likes to drink aside from Cherry Coke.

"What am I having?" he asks.

"Virgin old-fashioned."

He grins. "Old-fashioned *and* a virgin? I suppose that makes sense."

Heat percolates under my cheeks. Immediately I want to disavow my body, my cheekbones reddening at the mere suggestion of sex, my hands leaving damp imprints on the counter.

He takes a sip and spares me from having to think of a witty retort, smacks his lips as he sets the glass down.

"Good."

My knees give in for an instant. I hope he can't see my shoulders, my face, my fingers, every muscle in my body loosen with relief.

"Glad you like it."

Fingernails tap the left side of the bar. Cora. She needs a vodka martini and a Bellini. I fill a martini glass with ice, turn around to search for an open bottle of Champagne.

Aidan Thomas swirls the ice cube at the bottom of his drink. Takes a quick sip and swirls again. Here is this beautiful man, who has done so much for our town. Who lost his wife a month ago. Sitting at my bar, alone, even though he doesn't drink. I have to think that if there is a gaping hole at the center of his life, then maybe maintaining this habit has brought him some form of solace. I have to think this—our shared silences, our silent routine—means something to him, too.

Everyone in town has an Aidan Thomas story. If you're a kid, he saved your ass moments before the Christmas parade. He showed up when you needed him, tool belt cinched around his hips, to fix your wobbly sleigh, right your reindeer's antlers.

Two years ago, when that terrible storm hit and a tree fell on old Mr. McMillan's house, Aidan drove up and set up a generator while he worked on the power line. He returned every weekend the following month to mend the roof. Mr. McMillan tried to pay him, but Aidan wouldn't take the money.

My family's Aidan Thomas story took place when I was thirteen. My father was in the middle of dinner service when the walk-in fried. I forget the details, or maybe I never bothered learning them. It was always the same thing—a faulty motor, a bad circuit. My dad was losing his mind, trying to figure out how to fix it while running the kitchen. A lovely man, who was there having dinner with his wife, overheard and offered to help. My father hesitated. Then, in a rare, *oh-what-the-hell* moment, he led the man into his kitchen. Aidan Thomas spent the better part of the evening on his knees, politely asking for tools and appeasing the frazzled staff.

By the time service ended, the fridge was cooling off. So was my father. In the kitchen, he offered Aidan Thomas and his wife glasses of pear brandy. They both declined: he didn't drink, and she was newly pregnant.

I was helping out that night, as children of restaurant owners do. When I went to refill the bowl of mints on the hostess stand, I found Aidan Thomas in the dining room. He was searching his coat pockets the way customers do at the end of a meal, hoping to locate wallets and cell phones and car keys. My father's laugh trickled from the kitchen over to us. My father, a great chef with an even greater temper, whose perfectionism so often devolved into anger. Relaxed. Enjoying a rare moment of reprieve in the restaurant he had built. As close to happy as he would ever get.

"Thank you for that."

Aidan Thomas looked up as if he had just noticed my presence. I wanted to catch my words, still hanging in the air between us, and swallow them back. You learn to hate the sound of your own voice at an early age, when you're a girl.

I waited for him to give me a distracted nod and hurry back to the kitchen, to humor me as most adults did. But Aidan Thomas wasn't like other adults. He wasn't like anyone.

Aidan Thomas smiled. He winked. And he said in a low, gravelly voice that hit me somewhere deep, a part of my body I hadn't known existed until that moment: "You're very welcome."

It was nothing and it was everything. It was basic politeness and it was endless kindness. A halo of light landing on a hidden girl, plucking her out of the shadows, allowing her to be seen.

The thing I needed the most. Something it hadn't even occurred to me to crave.

NOW I WATCH as Aidan Thomas is frozen mid-sip, gazing at me through his glass. I am no longer the hidden girl, waiting for men to cast a light on her. I am a woman who has just walked into a halo of her own making.

He reaches over. Something shifts. A disturbance in the world, tectonic plates bumping against each other, miles below the Hudson River. His fingers brush against mine and his thumb grazes the inside of my wrist, and my heart—my heart, it's not even pounding at this point, it's just gone gone gone gone gone, can't handle it.

"Thank you," he says. "This was very . . . Thank you." A squeeze, a jolt of something indecipherable and priceless, from him to me.

He lets go of my hand, tilts his head back to empty his drink. His neck, his whole body lean, muscular, a smooth confidence.

"How much do I owe you?"

I take the empty glass and rinse it behind the bar. Keep my hands occupied so he can't see them shake.

"You know what? Don't worry about it. This one's on the house."

He takes out his wallet. "Come on."

"It's fine. I promise. You can . . ."

You can buy me one soon and we'll call it even is what I'd say if his wife hadn't died like five minutes ago. Instead, I unfold a clean bar mop and begin shining his glass.

"Next time."

He smiles and returns the wallet to his pocket, then gets up to put on his parka. I turn to set the glass on the shelf behind me. My arm stops halfway. Yes, I am jittery and my face is burning, but something just happened. I took a chance and it worked. I spoke and no disaster ensued.

Maybe I dare, just a little bit more.

I turn around, lean against the counter, pretend to tighten the lid on a jar of pickled onions.

"Where are you headed next?" I ask, as if small talk were a staple of our shared vocabulary.

Aidan Thomas zips up his parka, puts the trapper hat back on, and picks up his duffel bag. It settles against his hip with a metallic clink.

"Just somewhere I can get some thinking done."

CHAPTER 5

The woman in the shed

You wait for dinner, for splashes of tepid water. For anything. Even the groan of zippers being pulled up and down.

He doesn't show.

You picture the shed, hidden in the trees. It has to be fall by now. He took away the fan and brought in the heater a couple of weeks ago. You close your eyes. What you remember of this time of the year: short days, the sun setting at six o'clock. Naked branches against the turning sky. What you picture: In the distance, hidden from you, his house. Yellow squares of light at the windows, orange leaves scattered across the yard. Maybe hot tea. Maybe apple cider doughnuts.

In the distance, the purr of his truck. He is here, on the property. Living his life. Tending to his needs. Not yours, though. You wait and you wait and still he doesn't come.

You try to meditate the hunger pangs away. You flip through the books he brought you, taken to the shed in no particular order. Stephen King's *It*. A tired paperback of *A Tree Grows in Brooklyn*. Mary Higgins Clark's *Loves Music, Loves to Dance*. The books came used. Dog-eared pages, notes in the margins. You asked him one day, a long time ago, if they were his. He shook his head. More trinkets, you figured. Things he took from the ones who weren't as lucky as you.

You squat in a corner of the shed. Without him to bring you the bucket, you have no other choice. He'll be furious, if he gets back. He'll wrinkle his nose, throw a bottle of bleach in your direction. *Start scrubbing and don't stop until I can't smell it anymore.*

You try not to worry, because worrying gets in the way of staying alive.

HE HAS LEFT you before. Not like this, though. Nine months into the first year, the man who kept you in the shed told you he was going somewhere. He brought you the bucket, a box of granola bars, and a pack of small water bottles.

"I need to leave," he said. Not *I want*. Not *I have to*. *I need*.

"You will not," he said, "do anything. You will not move. You will not scream. I know you won't."

He grabbed you by the shoulders. You felt the urge to wrap your hands around his. To hold on to him, just a little bit. *You are Rachel. He found you. All you know is what he has taught you. All you have is what he has given you.*

He shook you. You allowed the tremor to rock you. "If you try anything," he said, "I will find out. And it won't be good for you. Do you understand?"

You nodded. By then, you knew how to nod so that he'd believe you.

He was gone for three days and returned the happiest man on earth. A pep in his step, something like static buzzing through his limbs. He took deep, gluttonous breaths, like the air had never tasted so sweet to him.

This wasn't the man you knew. A man of duties and responsibilities.

He did what he came to do to you. Buzzing. A little wild.

Then he told you. He didn't say much. Just that she went along with it. That she was *perfect*. That she didn't know, until she knew, but by then it was too late.

It happened again. Right before last Thanksgiving. You knew because he brought you leftovers. Has done so every year. You don't know if he knows that's how you keep track of time. You suspect he hasn't thought about it.

That's two, total. Two he killed while he let you live. Two now added to the rule while you remained the exception.

Each time he left you, he prepped. This time, he gave you nothing. Did he forget about you? Did he find another project to devote himself to?

WITHOUT HIS VISITS, it's hard to count the days. You think his truck signals when he leaves in the morning and when he returns at night, but you can't be sure. Your body tells you when to sleep and when to wake up. Palm against the wall, you try to feel the warmth of the sun and the cold of the night. Based on your estimates, one day goes by, then another.

By the end of what feels like day two, your mouth is lined with sandpaper. Bats zoom around your brain. You suck on your fingers to make saliva, lick the wall of the shed in search of condensation, anything to relieve the thirst. Soon you are just a body, a skull and a spine and a pelvis and feet lying flat on the wooden slats, your skin clammy, your breath labored.

Maybe he overestimated your resilience. Maybe he'll kill you without meaning to. He'll return, open the shed, and find you cold and unresponsive, as you were always meant to be.

On what you tell yourself is day three, the padlock rattles. He's a silhouette in the doorframe, bucket in one hand, a bottle in the other. You should sit up, snatch the water away, unscrew the cap, and drink, drink, drink until the world comes back into focus. But you can't. He has to come to you, kneel at your side, position the neck of the bottle against your lips.

You swallow. Wipe your lips with the back of your hand. He doesn't look like himself. Most days, he's a man who takes care of his appearance. Nicks from a manual razor turn up on his cheekbones and down his neck. His hair smells of lemongrass. His teeth are white, his gums healthy. You've never seen him do it, but you can tell he flosses assiduously, every morning or every night, a swish of mouthwash to finish the job. But tonight, he looks rough. His beard is unkempt. His gaze bounces, unfocused, from one end of the shed to the other.

"Food?"

Your voice comes out raspy. He shakes his head no.

"She's still up. Packing."

You assume he means his daughter.

"So there's nothing? Nothing at all?"

You're pushing your luck, you know, but it's been three days, and without the thirst numbing your body, you feel it all, the hollowness of hunger below your rib cage, the soreness in your back, a thousand alarm bells pointing to the broken parts of you.

He holds up his hands. "What? You think I can microwave a TV dinner and walk out the door and she won't ask any questions?"

The food he brings you is always one part of a whole. A portion of lasagna, a bowl of stew, the center square of a casserole. Meals that can go missing unnoticed. Much more discreet than a slice of pizza, a whole cheeseburger, the leg of a roasted chicken. For all this time he's been cooking in bulk, squirreling away parts of his dishes and bringing them to you. It's one of the ways he's found to keep you a secret.

He sits next to you with a groan. You wait for him to pull at the zipper on your jacket, wrap his hands around your neck. Instead, he reaches around his waistband. There is a glimmer, a flash of metal.

You recognize the gun. It's the same one he pointed at you five years ago, a black pistol and the glossy length of a silencer.

Your toes twitch as if to prepare for a sprint. The chain tightens, cold and heavy against your ankle. Dragging you down as if to suck you into the ground, first your foot and then the rest of you.

Focus. Stay with him.

His chest moves up and down, one deep breath after the other. Without the fuzz of dehydration, you read him more clearly. Tired but not weary. Dizzy but not sick. He's a mess, yes, but he's happy. Like after an exhausting task, a long run or a steep hike.

Like after a kill.

He reaches into his pocket and drops something on your lap, a cat offering up a dead mouse.

Sunglasses. Designer, judging by the heavy frame and the logo on the side. Entirely worthless inside the shed, but the sunglasses aren't the point. The point is these used to belong to someone, and she doesn't need them anymore.

You feel it on him now. The triumph. The boundless thrill of a successful hunting trip.

She calls out to you. What kind of a job did she have to be able to afford sunglasses like these? What did her fingers look like when she slid them up her nose? Did she ever use them to hold her hair back? Did she wear them one summer afternoon in the passenger seat of a convertible with the top down, loose hair whipping at her cheeks?

You can't go there. You can't think about her. You do not have time to be shocked or devastated.

This is a chance. His hubris. Tonight, he will believe himself capable of anything.

"So, listen," you say.

He takes the sunglasses back. Probably second-guessing his choice. You could break the lenses, turn them into weapons.

"I've been thinking. About your move."

His hands go still. You are in danger of ruining his fun. You are pulling him back to the annoyances of daily life, when all he wants is to ride his high for as long as it will go.

"You could take me with you."

He looks up, lets out a chuckle.

"Come on," he says. "I don't think you understand."

But you do. You know his light and his shadow. You know that he comes to see you almost every night, certainly every night he's here. You know he's become used to certain things. It's not you he likes, not exactly, but you at his disposal. What he wants, whenever he wants.

What will he do without you?

"I'm just saying," you tell him. "We could still see each other. It wouldn't have to end. It doesn't have to."

He folds his arms across his chest.

"I could be right there," you tell him. You tilt your head toward the door. Toward the outside, the world he took you from and its myriad of people. "And no one would know."

He smiles. Brings his hand to the back of your head. Strokes your hair with the soft, poised gesture of a man who knows himself to be safe, then tugs. Just enough to hurt.

"And of course," he says, "you're just looking out for me."

You freeze under his touch.

He slips away, releases the deadbolt, invites the cold air of the night into the shed. Outside, the padlock clicks into place. He's heading back to the house, to his daughter, to whatever is left of light and warmth inside their home.

Rule number three of staying alive in the shed: In his world, you are the purest thing. Everything that happens must happen to the two of you.

CHAPTER 6

Number one

He was young. I could tell immediately it was his first time. He wasn't good at it. Not good at all.

It happened on campus, in his dorm. The way he did it—botched. Blood everywhere. My DNA on him, his on me. Prints, too.

He didn't know me. But I had noticed him in the weeks before. If you hung around the university long enough, especially on Saturday nights, you could be sure a shy undergrad would eventually walk up to you. Unsure how to ask, when to pay.

Most of them snapped out of it after they handed me the money. Then they carried themselves with the arrogance the world had taught them. They were respectable young men, and I was the woman charging fifteen dollars for a blow job.

I did not expect it from him. He was too young, too frail. He had no idea what he was doing.

He was surprised, I think, that I liked to read. The guys never thought of me as someone who might have liked to read. But I did. I wrote notes next to the passages that made me think, dog-eared the pages that made me feel. That night, I had two paperbacks on the dashboard of my truck: *It* and a thriller called *Loves Music, Loves to Dance.* I remember them both because I never got to find out how they ended.

He waited until I went to put my top back on. His hand shot out to my neck. Like a dare with himself. Like he knew that if he didn't do it then, he might chicken out forever.

His eyes widened as mine shut. The air of amazement on his face: Shock that he was actually doing this, and that my body responded in the correct manner. Shock that it was a real thing—that if you squeezed someone's throat hard enough, they would in fact stop moving.

I remember realizing, while he killed me: if he gets away with this, he'll think he can get away with anything.

CHAPTER 7

The woman in the shed

You remember bits of yourself, and sometimes they help you.

Like Matt.

Matt was the closest thing you had to a boyfriend when you went missing. He was like everything else, a promise that never came true.

The thing you remember the best about Matt: he knew how to pick locks.

In the shed, you have thought about Matt a lot. You have tried a few times. Pried a splinter off the floor, made a discreet dent in a wall. The wood was no match for the large lock on the chain. You worried it would break, and then what?

Then you would have been fucked.

You remember bits of yourself, and sometimes, they help you. Only sometimes.

THE MAN WHO keeps you returns the next day with hot food and a fork. You stuff five giant bites into your mouth before you can even think of trying to identify what you are eating—spaghetti and meatballs. It takes you three more bites to realize he's talking, two more to find the strength to put down the fork. What he's saying matters more for your survival than a single meal.

"Tell me your name."

Your ears are buzzing. You place the lid back on the food container, the leftover meatball calling out to you.

"Hey."

He walks over from the other end of the shed, catches your chin to force your gaze up.

You cannot afford to piss him off. Not ever, but especially not now.

"Sorry," you say. "I'm listening."

"No you're not. I said tell me your fucking name."

You put the Tupperware on the floor and sit on your hands to keep them from massaging your face where his fingers pressed. Take a long breath in. When you say this, he has to believe you. It has to be a spell, a reading from a sacred text. It has to be the truth.

"Rachel," you tell him. "My name is Rachel."

"What else?"

You lower the pitch of your voice, enrich it with the round inflections of fervor. He needs something from you, and he has taught you, time and time again, how to give it to him.

"You found me." You offer up the rest without him having to ask. "All I know is what you have taught me. All I have is what you have given me."

He shifts his weight from one foot to the other.

"I was lost," you recite. "You found me. You gave me a roof." The next sentence is a gamble. If you lean in too hard, he will see the strings behind your magic trick. But if you hold back, he will remain out of your reach.

"You keep me alive." You pick up the Tupperware again as evidence. "I'd be dead without you."

He traces the outline of his wedding band, twists it around his finger a couple of times. Takes it off and puts it back on.

A man free to roam the world, locked in a garden shed. A man who met a woman, held her hand, got down on one knee, convinced her to marry him. A man so determined to control the elements, and still he lost her. Now his world has fallen apart, but in the rubble of his life, he still has you.

And he still has a daughter.

"What's her name?"

He looks at you like *What are you talking about?* You point toward the house.

"Why do you care?"

If telling the truth were an option in the shed, you'd say, *You wouldn't get it. It's embedded in you, once you've been a girl. You pass them on the street. You hear their laughs. You feel their pain. You want to lift them into your arms and carry them over to the end point, sparing their feet from the thorns that drew blood from your own.*

Every girl in the world is a little bit me, and every girl in the world is a little bit mine. Even yours. Even the one that's half you.

I care, you would tell him, *because I need the part of you that made her. You would never kill your own daughter, would you?*

You sit in silence. Let him believe what he needs to believe.

His left hand curls into a fist. He presses it against his forehead, squeezes his eyes shut for a moment.

You watch, unable to take another breath. Whatever he sees at the back of his eyelids, your life depends on it.

His eyes open.

He's with you again.

"She can't start asking questions because of you."

You blink. With an impatient sigh, he tilts his head in the direction of the outside world—in the direction of the house.

His kid. He's talking about his kid.

You try to resume breathing, but you've forgotten how.

"I'll tell her you're an acquaintance. A friend of friends. Renting out a spare room."

His speech ramps up as he explains. This is him: Hesitant, until he convinces himself of his own invincibility. Then he commits and never looks back.

He tells it to you like it was all his idea. Like you never planted a seed, never made a suggestion. He'll move you to the new house in the middle of the night. No one will see. You will have a room. You will spend most of your time in that room. You will be handcuffed to a radiator, except to eat, shower, and sleep. There will be breakfast most mornings, lunch on some weekends, dinner most nights. You will have to skip a meal here and there. No tenant, no matter how friendly or needy, would eat with her landlord and his daughter all of the time.

At night, you will sleep handcuffed to the bed. He will visit you, as always. That part won't change.

You will be quiet. Through it all, you will be very quiet.

You will speak to his daughter only at mealtimes, just enough to ward off suspicion. This is what the meals are for: he will make you accessible to her, so you will lose your allure. She will not be intrigued by you. You will become a part of her life—a boring one, one she won't even think to question.

Above all, you are to act normally. He stresses this point several times, between the shower rules and the sleeping rules and the eating rules. You cannot give away any sign of the truth. If you do, you will get hurt.

You nod. It is all you can do. You try to picture it—you, him, and his kid, all in one place. A bed. A mattress. A pillow. Blankets. Furniture. Breakfast and lunch. Food served on a plate. An actual shower. Hot water. Conversations. A window onto the world. A third person. For the first time in five years, someone other than him.

He stops pacing and crouches in front of you. The skin around his fingernails is raw, freshly bitten. He lifts your chin again, brings your face up to his. The whole world, right here in his eyes.

His fingers travel down to your neck, his thumb against your throat. He could do it. Now. It would be so easy, like crumpling a piece of paper.

"No one will know." His face flushes in the glow of the camping lantern. "That's the whole point. Do you understand? Just me. And Cecilia."

Cecilia.

You go to say it out loud, but the name catches in your vocal cords. You swallow it back. His daughter, his child. There's something so organic about it. So noble. Him in a hospital, wrapped in a paper gown, holding up a bloody newborn with trembling hands. A man becoming a father. Did he get up at two, three, five in the morning to feed her? Did he warm bottles in the dark, his brain fuzzy from sleep deprivation? Did he take her on a carousel, help her blow out her first birthday candle? Did he sleep on the floor next to her bed when she was sick?

It's just the two of them now. Does he let her have a phone? When she cries, if she cries, does he find the right words? At her mom's funeral, did he know to put a hand on her shoulder? To tell her things like *Those we love are never really gone, our memories keep them alive, all you have to do is live a life that would have made her proud?*

"It's a beautiful name," you say.

But you should never have let me know it.

CHAPTER 8

Emily

He knows my name.

Thursday comes and he doesn't show. I think I have lost him. But then, a delightful surprise: on Friday evening, when I'm not expecting him, he materializes at the bar.

"Emily," he calls out, and it's my name in his mouth, a stream of familiarity linking him to me.

I tell him hi and—before I can stop myself—that I didn't see him yesterday. He smiles. Tells me sorry. A work emergency out of town, he says. But he's back now.

And all is right in the world, I tell myself. Silently this time.

I keep it with me. His surprise visit, the sound of my name on his breath. I allow it to carry me through the night, through the next day, all the way into Saturday evening.

At the restaurant, Saturdays are a battlefield. Folks drive up from the city, compete with the locals for reservations. They're happy until they're not. Food flies out of the kitchen—hot, cold, it doesn't matter. What we need is plates on tables, plates on tables. Behind the bar, I grow a second pair of arms. Everyone wants mixed drinks on a Saturday. It's one martini after the other, an endless streak of twists and olives. I peel the back of my thumb along with the skin of a lemon. My wrists protest each time I raise the shaker, carpal tunnel settling in my joints with each clatter of ice cubes.

A rare good thing about the restaurant: when it's that busy, it numbs me. There is no time to think, no time to care that Nick ignores most of my orders, that he's a dick to everyone, including me, that I should have fired him a long time ago but worry a different chef would be even worse. It's just me and the bar until the last customers leave and Cora locks the door behind them.

When it's all over, we go out. It doesn't make sense, but it must be done, even if we've all had enough of one another for the evening.

Because if Saturday nights are a battlefield, then we are soldiers, and we must be able to exist together. And the way to do that is to drink.

By the time I show up, everyone is already sitting at our usual table. I wave to Ryan, the owner—not a bad guy, just someone who thinks naming a dive the Hairy Spider is a good idea—and pull up a chair between Eric and Yuwanda.

"They say it was an accident, but I don't buy it," Cora's saying. "Have you seen the trails over there? It would be really hard to fall."

Ryan brings me his beer of the week, a pumpkin sour. I take a sip and give him what I hope passes for an appreciative nod.

"What are we talking about?"

Yuwanda fills me in. "That woman who went missing last week."

I read about her in the local weekly: mid-thirties, no history of mental illness or drug use. A painter with a little workshop about forty miles north of here. Disappeared overnight and hasn't been seen since. No activity on her phone or credit cards.

"One of the cops told my sister they think she went for a hike and fell down a ravine," Sophie says. "Apparently she liked the trails."

Yuwanda cuts in: "But don't they have surveillance video of her at some convenience store around seven that night?"

Sophie nods.

"So, what," Yuwanda continues, "she stopped at the store and then went for a hike? Who goes hiking that late?"

Eric takes a sip of his beer. "Maybe she wanted to watch the sunset?"

Cora shakes her head. "Nah. First of all, the sun sets earlier than that now. At seven, she would've had nothing left to watch. And why bother going to the trails? I know that town. You can see the sunset from just about anywhere."

I go to take another sip of Ryan's pumpkin sour, then settle for a whiff and set my glass down. There's something I can't make sense of. "Why are they even focusing on the trails?"

Cora looks down, a slight admission of defeat. "They found her shoe in the brush," she concedes. "But I don't know. It's just a shoe. It doesn't explain why she'd go on a hike that late in the day, and by herself, too."

Eric pats her arm. "People do weird stuff all the time," he tells her softly. "It happens."

"Eric's not wrong," I say. "Accidents do happen."

No one challenges me. People look down at their drinks, at the rings of condensation they've left on Ryan's table. You don't argue with an orphan who tells you accidents happen. My father: a heart attack on a sunny Saturday morning two years ago; my mother: a car crash in the haze that followed.

"Anyway," Nick says after a few beats. "I heard some chef from the city bought the building where Mulligan's used to be. He's turning it into a steakhouse, apparently." He turns to me with what could pass for an air of gentle ribbing: "Maybe he'll tell you where he gets his sirloin, if you ask nicely."

I sigh. "You know, Nick, I think it's really healthy how you don't sweat the small stuff. When people ask me what I love most about my head chef, I always tell them he's a real big-picture guy."

The line gets smiles from Eric and Yuwanda. Everyone else chooses to sit this one out. I would, too, if I had to spend fifty hours a week in a kitchen with Nick and a wide array of butcher knives.

A couple of hours later, Eric drives us back to the house that used to be my parents', which I now share with him and Yuwanda. It was one of those arrangements that fell into place because it had to. They both showed up the day after the car crash and took care of me the way only childhood friends can. They kept the fridge full, made sure I ate and slept, at least a little. They helped me plan two funerals at once. They kept me company when I couldn't be alone and gave me space when I needed it. Somewhere along the way, we agreed it would be better if they never left. The house was too big for just me. Selling it would have required some remodeling, which was out of the question. So we moved my parents' stuff into storage one weekend and collapsed on the couch at the end of the day, our new equilibrium sealed. Imperfect and slightly unusual. The only thing that made sense.

Tonight, I toss and turn, exhausted but unable to fall asleep. I think about the missing woman. Melissa. All that's left of her: a first name, a job, the name of a town, a shoe found near a trail. Like the eulogies people gave for my parents, accurate but desperately lacking.

My father's life pared down to a few words: he was a chef, he was a dad, he worked hard. The pieces of my mother's existence, like the other half of a puzzle: she ran the business, she was the hostess, she was the bookkeeper, she was the glue that kept it all together. All true, but nothing that captured them as people. Nothing about my father's smile, my mother's perfume. Nothing about what it felt like to live with them, to be raised by them, to be loved and abandoned by them in equal measures.

I go back to the missing woman, try filling in the gaps in her narrative. It feels treacherous, using her as a blank canvas to make her up the way I want to, but something about her story has a hold on my brain.

Maybe she was a bit like me. *Was*—look at me, thinking of her in the past when we don't know yet. Maybe she, too, grew up at once captivated and terrified by the world. Maybe she was made to wear dresses when she preferred pants. Maybe she was made to say hi to the grown-ups when she wanted to be alone. Maybe she learned to always feel a little uncomfortable, always a little sorry. Maybe she grew up and waited for a teenage rebellion that never came, and maybe when she reached her mid-twenties she regretted never getting the angst out of her system.

This is the story I tell myself. No one's around to tell me it doesn't make sense. It starts out as a tribute and ends in selfishness. It isn't about her. Not really. It's about me and the parts of my life that find me in the dark. It's about me and my younger self and the way she looks at me, the way she keeps calling out to me, demanding answers I don't have.

CHAPTER 9

The woman in the shed, when she was still a girl

The warning signs come in 2001, the year of your tenth birthday. Your best friend's mom gets cancer. Your cousin's apartment is ransacked, her priciest possessions gone overnight. Your aunt dies. Each time, the lesson becomes a little clearer: bad things happen to people you know.

You start suspecting that bad things might, one day, happen to you. Somewhere in a corner of your heart, you hope to be exempt. Until now, you've had a blessed life. Loving parents who taught you how to ride your bike in Riverside Park, an older brother who doesn't treat you like an idiot. Fairies leaned over your crib and gave you these beautiful things. Why should your good fortune run out?

Your childhood ends with the hope pretty much intact. Then, the teenage years begin, and the journey gets rockier. Your brother takes the pills. A first time, a second time. You learn to feel sad. You learn to occupy the hole in your parents' heart, the one that yearns for a golden child. You turn fifteen. You are ready for someone to see who you really are. You are ready for someone to love the true you.

At a ski resort, you kiss a boy for the first time. What you remember from this moment: his heart beating against yours, the smell of his hair gel, the glow of snowplows making shapes on the walls of your rented room. After you go home, it becomes apparent that the boy has no intention of calling you, ever. You learn heartbreak. It will take you longer to recover from this than from actual breakups as an adult. Summer comes. You begin to heal.

Two years later, you meet your first boyfriend. He's perfect. If they marketed mail-order-boyfriend services to teens, you would have picked him. If a witch had gifted you a lump of clay with the ability to come to life, you would have molded him.

You take the work of being a girlfriend seriously. This is your first chance to prove yourself in this area, and you want to do everything right. You take him to see Duke Ellington's grave at Woodlawn Cemetery. For his birthday, you buy a multitude of tiny presents—a music box that plays the *Love Story* theme, a weed lollipop, the *Catcher in the Rye* paperback with the horse on the cover—and hide them on your body, stuffed in your back pockets and tucked into the waistband of your jeans. When the time comes to give him his gifts, you tell him to search. He puts his hands on you.

You've never had sex. He has. He's six months older than you. You're in no rush to grow up. You know this is something you should feel ashamed of, but you aren't. Not enough to change your mind.

But you do the other stuff, and it's good to be with a guy who knows what to do. You let him slip his hands underneath your shirt. You let him unclasp your bra with two fingers. You let him pop open the button of your jeans. After that, you tense up, and he can tell. He stops. He always stops.

Around the two-month mark, you think about ending it. Instead, you let yourself fall in love. One sunny afternoon in July, you lie beneath the trees on the Columbia campus and realize it's been six months. People tell you how lucky you are, that a guy like him has stayed with a girl like you for this long without pressuring you into sex. You smile and say you know.

And you do know. You can't believe he's yours. Sometimes, he falls asleep, or maybe he pretends to. All you know is he's here and his eyes are closed and even though your arm is numb you can't imagine removing it from underneath his head. You're seventeen. Love tastes even sweeter than you expected.

One night, your parents drive to New Jersey for a fundraiser. He comes over. You "watch a movie," code for making out. Two weeks ago, the two of you "watched" *Requiem for a Dream*. You couldn't quote a line from that movie if your life depended on it.

That night, it's *Fight Club*. You've never seen it. He, like all the boys, says it's his favorite. It doesn't matter. Nothing about *Fight Club* matters. What matters is his skin against your skin and the warmth of his breath on your face. His fingers in your hair, on your thighs, between your legs. You feel so adventurous, so happy you've found him to guide you. This is what the magazines told you to look for: Someone you like and who likes you back. A boy you can trust.

You're wearing a skirt. Edward Norton mourns his sofa, his stereo, his nice wardrobe, and your boyfriend pushes two fingers inside your underwear, then quickly, before you can even realize, inside you. Something you have never thought of until now: skirts mean easy access, especially in the summer, without tights and layers of wool weaving boundaries between you and the world.

Your boyfriend's fingers get to work. You can deal. You take a breath and tell yourself to relax.

Brad Pitt is in a basement, explaining the first rule of Fight Club. Your boyfriend pulls your underwear down your legs. You have never felt so naked in your life. A laugh comes out of your chest like a cough. Your boyfriend responds by kissing you harder.

There is an escalation here that you can't quite process. Edward Norton's face splits open against the concrete floor. You and your boyfriend are both naked from the waist down.

People told you to say no. They never said how. They made it very clear that the world wouldn't stop for you and that it was your responsibility to make it slow down, but no one ever gave instructions beyond that. No one told you how to look into the eyes of the person you love and say you want to stop.

Ideally, your sweet boyfriend would understand without you having to say it. He'd notice that your arms have gone limp, that your teeth are chattering. But Edward Norton emails poems to his coworkers and your boyfriend reaches for a condom. You had no idea he kept them in the inside pocket of his backpack. No idea he had a system for those things.

Brad Pitt delivers a monologue about how advertising destroys the soul. You watch as your boyfriend enters you. It's your first time, and it happens because you were too afraid to say no. Because the boy who did it forgot to look into your eyes.

The following week, you leave him a voice mail. You tell him you've thought about it and it's better if you two end things. You hang up and cry.

Years later, you will type his name in the Facebook search bar. His profile will be locked, a gray square where his picture should be. You will not friend him.

In the meantime, you survive. Of course you do.

You have sex again. Sometimes bad sex. Sometimes boring sex. More often than you would like, you find yourself coming back to that moment.

You don't forget your first. You never forget the boy who taught you how to survive as a stranger in your own body.

CHAPTER 10

The woman in transit

Every night, you ask him when, and every night he refuses to tell you. "You'll know soon enough," he says. "What's the rush, anyway? It's not like you have anywhere to be."

He says they're not done packing. How much stuff can they possibly have? He's not a wealthy man. His clothes are neat but worn. He has mentioned chores in the past, the floors he has to mop, the laundry he needs to hang. The weight of the world on his shoulders, and no one, certainly no paid help, to provide relief. But they have lived in this house for years, and now they have to excavate the contents of their family history, every scrap of paper, every gadget tossed aside. They are going on a journey, and they need to decide what's staying and what's coming with them. They need to leave and settle somewhere else.

Then, one night, he walks in and says, "Let's go."

It takes you a second. When you understand, you freeze. He yanks you to your feet and starts to work on the chain. There's a key—there was a key all along—and a couple of tugs. The chain slips off your foot with a thud. You feel impossibly light.

Without the chain, your balance is thrown off. You steady yourself against the wall. Already he's pulling at your arm, trying to get you outside as fast as possible.

"Come on," he says. "Move it."

In a few seconds there will be grass underneath your feet and no walls around you.

"Wait."

You take a step toward the back of the shed. His hand almost slides off you. His grip finds you again, tight, the strength of a man who will never, ever let go. Your left arm twists so suddenly your vision blurs. His weight presses into your back.

"Are you fucking kidding me?"

You gasp and, with your free hand, point to the books. He brought you a plastic bag a long time ago, to protect them from humidity. He wanted to show you, you figure, that he knows how to take care of the things he owns. There are also the trinkets on the crate, all the things he took from others and passed on to you.

"I just wanted to get my stuff," you say through gritted teeth. "I promise. I'm sorry."

"Fuck's sake."

He walks you over to the stack of books, your left arm nudged against your hip. His feet get caught in yours. You trip. He catches you, sets you upright.

"Go."

His body moves with yours as you crouch to retrieve the plastic bag. You drop it inside the crate, along with the rest of your things.

"Ready now?"

You nod. He guides you to the door. No time to say goodbye. Just grab at whatever memories you can, days meshing into one another, five years turning into mud. One long stretch of the shed. A place of despair, of devastation, but in the end, it became what you knew.

Here, you learned how to survive. This new house he's taking you to, it's full of uncertainty, the possibility of a mistake lurking in every corner.

He stops you once you reach the door. There's a glimmer of metal, something cold and hard against your wrist. Handcuffs. He secures one end around you, loops the other around his own arm.

"Let's move."

His free hand reaches up to the deadbolt. He brings his face close to yours.

"Don't try anything outside. I mean it. If you run or scream—if you do anything other than walk with me to the car, there will be consequences."

He lets go of the deadbolt, wraps his hand around the back of your head, and makes you look down. The gun. Hanging at his hip in a holster.

"I understand," you say.

He releases your head. There's a click and a tug, and—it's too sudden, over before you can welcome it—the miracle of wind on your face.

"Come on."

He pulls you forward. You take your first step, then a second one. You are outside. Standing up and breathing. Strands of your hair graze against your cheeks. So much happening, nature demanding to be heard, felt. The whirl of the wind against tree leaves, soil swarming underneath your bare feet. Insects buzzing and twigs creaking. The wetness of dew on your ankles.

Another tug. You are marching toward his parked truck. For the second time ever, you see the outside of the shed: vertical slats painted gray, white trim around the door. Well maintained and orderly. He's not a man who lets weeds grow on his property, or one for change. If someone saw it, they would never have suspected.

On your left, if you squint, you can make out the distant contours of the house. Tall, wide, empty. A house where, you imagine, a family was once happy, light glowing from the ceilings, laughs echoing down hallways, bouncing off shiny appliances. Now the windows are dark, the door shut. Memories gone. Scorched earth, a collective life erased from its walls.

Onward you go. A busy, eager man rushing you to your destination. Tonight is not for you. None of this is for you.

Above you, you know, is the sky. Maybe stars. Maybe the moon.

You have to look.

It could cost you a lot, craning your neck up to take a peek. He wouldn't like it. But it's been five years, and if it's going to happen, it has to be now.

He's in front of you, head bent down, eyes on his feet. Wouldn't want to stumble. The last thing this man wants to do is fall.

You keep up with his cadence, careful not to fall behind, and—slowly, like someone stepping on the wobbly end of a suspended bridge—tilt your head back.

It's here, like it's been waiting for you. A black sky and dozens of stars. You keep marching, one step after another, as you let the sky drink you in. You and the darkness. You, the bottomless ocean, and the promise of tiny icebergs speckled all around. You, black ink, brought to life by glimmers of white paint.

There is something else. A tug in your chest, a devastating bitterness. You, and all the people gazing up at the same sky as you. Women like you and children like you and men like you and old people like you and babies like you and pets like you.

This is what the sky tells you: you used to have people. You had a mother and a father and a brother. You had a roommate. You had a blood family and a chosen family. People you went to concerts with, people you met for drinks. People you shared food with. People who held you in their arms, lifted you up to the world.

You went searching for it, and now you have it. A silent communion tearing you apart.

A pinch in your calves. Something rising from the depths of you. You have to find them again, the people he took you from. One day, you will have to run to them.

"What are you doing?"

He has stopped and turned around. He's looking at you looking at the sky. Your neck snaps back to its natural angle.

"Nothing," you tell him. "Sorry."

He shakes his head and pulls you forward.

The sky has unnerved you. You want to scream and claw at your chest and run, run, run, even though you know, you damn well know, it would be the end of you.

Stupid. This is what happens when you think about the people outside.

Rule number one of staying alive outside the shed: You don't run unless you're sure.

He stops again. You stumble to a halt, just in time to avoid ramming into him. You are standing next to the passenger door of his truck. He pulls it open and you place the crate onto the backseat. One last flash of green leaves, one stealthy breath of fresh air. You lower yourself onto the polyester seat at the front. His end of the handcuffs clicks open. He brings both of your hands behind your back and cuffs them into place.

"Don't move."

He leans over, secures your seat belt. Not the kind of man who risks getting pulled over for minor traffic violations. He stays out of trouble and the world thanks him for it.

After double-checking the seat belt, he stands upright again. Fumbles with the waistband of his jeans, pulls the gun out of the holster. Waves it in front of your face. Your skin melts to nothingness in front of a gun. Your body offers no help, no protection—just parts to be broken. Only the endless promise of pain.

"Don't move. I won't be happy if you move."

You nod. *I believe you,* you want to tell him like a pledge, like a sermon. *I always believe you.*

He slams the passenger door and crosses over to the driver's side, gun pointed at the windshield, his gaze never leaving yours. His door opens. He slides onto his seat. Drops the gun onto the dashboard, buckles his own seat belt. A sharp outtake of breath.

"Let's go."

He says it to himself more than you.

He switches on the ignition. Returns the gun to the holster. You wait for him to press the gas pedal, but he turns to face you instead. Your jaw contracts. He could change his mind. At the very last minute, he could decide that this isn't going to work. That it would be easier, better, if you disappeared for good.

"When we get there . . . It's late. She's asleep. You will be very quiet. I don't want her to get up in the middle of the night and start asking questions."

You nod.

"Okay. Now close your eyes."

You can't help but frown.

"I said, close your eyes."

You close your eyes. The explanation comes to you as the truck rumbles to life under your thighs: he doesn't want you to see where you are or where you are going. Same as five years ago, when he took you, except that time, he blindfolded you. Handed you a bandanna and made you wrap it over your eyes while he brought you to his property. But that was then, and this is now. He knows you now. He knows you do what he tells you to.

In any other circumstances, you'd risk it. You'd open your eyes and take a quick look. But not tonight. Tonight, all that matters is staying alive.

You focus on the sways and jerks of the truck. It bumps across what you imagine is the driveway before reaching a smooth surface—asphalt, presumably. A road. You feel dizzy, not with motion sickness but with possibility. What if you leaned over, as much as the seat belt allows, and disturbed his posture? Made him turn the wheel? What if you turned it yourself, with your knee or your foot or any other part of your body? What if the both of you went careening toward a guardrail or a ravine? He wouldn't have time to grab the gun. Maybe. Or maybe he'd get the truck back on the road in a matter of seconds, drive to a secluded area, pull out the pistol, and deal with you.

So you stay still. There's only the purr of the engine, the occasional tapping of his fingers on the steering wheel. It's hard to say how long he drives for. Ten minutes? Twenty-five? Eventually, the truck slows, then stops. You hear the jingle of a key getting pulled out of the ignition.

You don't move. You don't open your eyes. There are things you don't do unless he tells you to. But already you know. You have arrived. You can feel it. The house, calling out to you. Yearning.

CHAPTER 11

The woman in the house

The driver's door opens and shuts. A few seconds later, he's at your side. He reaches for your hands, still tucked between your back and the passenger seat. The handcuff slides off your left wrist. A fumble, a click. When he tells you to open your eyes, you're chained to each other again.

"Let's go."

You make no move to step off the truck. He sighs, then leans over to undo your seat belt.

"Couldn't have done that yourself?"

So you could freak out? Pistol-whip me from behind? I don't think so.

He gives you a tug. You step onto a patch of grass. He leans to retrieve your crate from the backseat. Your chance to look: You are standing at the edge of a tiny front yard, a border between his world and the sidewalk. The truck parked to one side in a small graveled driveway, tire tracks you have to assume were made when he parked just now. Roads in two directions: the one you came from, and the unknown. A tree and a door with a doorbell and a welcome mat. Trash bins with wheels, one green, one black. Tucked underneath the ground floor, wedged at the foot of a hill, a garage door. On the other side of the house, a tiny patio, metallic chairs, and the matching table.

All so normal. The tidy accoutrements of suburban life.

He guides you right up to it—the house, an actual house within your reach. Walls and windows and wooden slats, like the shed but larger, taller, and then a roof. On the front door, a lock and a key that comes out of his pocket and fits inside that lock, and before you can comprehend it, before the echo of the key turning inside the lock fully reaches your eardrums, you are inside.

"Come on."

He hurries you toward a flight of stairs. The house offers itself up to you in brief, elusive visions—a couch, a TV, picture frames on a bookshelf. An open kitchen, the thin buzz of appliances.

"Let's go."

You follow him. Climb one step, then two, and then—your body tips forward. You catch yourself on the railing before your chin can hit the ground. You look down at your feet. You tripped: the steps are carpeted, and you're no longer used to soft ground.

He turns to shoot you a look. Your stomach tightens.

But he resumes climbing the stairs, pulling you forward with renewed eagerness. He wants you in the room he has assigned you. He wants control. All he has ever wanted is for life to go according to his plans.

You reach the second floor. You spot it in the dark at the end of the hallway, a poster taped to the door. You focus, try to make out the image—a faceless figure cradling another, smaller one, spots of orange and blue glowing in the dark. Your eyes scan all of it and your brain—you can barely believe it—your brain says *Keith Haring*. A bolt of recognition flashing through a pile of rubble. The parts of you the shed couldn't erase.

It has to be his daughter's room. His must be the one to your left, on this end of the hallway. He stands in front of the bare door, shut, quietly holding in his secrets. Like he doesn't even want you to see it. Like it conceals a world entirely separate from yours.

To your right is another door. Blank. Bland. He takes out another key, inserts it in the lock at the center of the round doorknob, and turns it. Smooth, silent. So deadly agile, even in the dark.

THE ROOM IS small and bare. A twin bed immediately to your right, with one of those old, wiry iron frames. A small desk and the matching stool in a corner, a chest of drawers next to it. The radiator on the opposite end of the space. A window, obscured by blackout shades. It is the most amazing room you have ever laid eyes on. It is everything and nothing, yours and not yours, home and not home.

He shuts the door. A light fixture hangs from the ceiling but he makes no move to switch it on. Instead, he drops the crate onto the floor, undoes his end of the handcuffs, and gestures toward the bed.

"Go."

He waits for you to lie down. That was the deal: handcuffed to the radiator by day, to the bed at night. You sit on the mattress. Springs groan underneath your body. For the first time in five years, you sink into something soft and bouncy. You bring both legs up onto the mattress, extend them, lower your torso, and let your head touch the pillow.

This is supposed to feel good. After more than a thousand nights in a sleeping bag on wooden slats, you should be hearing angels sing. But it's all wrong. The mattress sags like it's trying to swallow you. Like you'll keep sinking and sinking until there's nothing left, no trace of you on this earth, nothing to let people know you were ever here.

You sit back up, searching for your breath.

"I'm sorry."

His hand springs to your shoulder. He pushes you back down, his fingers digging under your clavicle.

"What. The fuck. Are you doing?"

"I'm not . . . I'm sorry. I just don't . . . I don't think this is going to work."

His grip hardens. You want to appease him, but your chest tightens. A stabbing sensation sets your rib cage on fire. He needs to know you're not going to try anything, that you couldn't run even if you thought you had a chance. You try and fail to inhale.

"Just . . . sorry."

You bring your hands up, hoping your body will tell him what you can't verbalize. That you are innocent, that you have nothing to hide. He's still holding the pistol. The silencer grazes the side of your knee. You focus on your breath. A long time ago, in your former life, you downloaded a meditation app. An Englishman prompted you in prerecorded sessions to breathe in through the nose, out through the mouth. Again, and again, and again.

Just as you think your chest is beginning to settle, a wheeze rises from your throat. Or is that a ringing in your ears? In through the nose. Out through the mouth. Hands up. Eyes on the gun.

"Would it be okay . . . if I slept on the floor?"

He lifts an eyebrow.

"It's just . . . the mattress . . . It's very different from the shed. I know it's stupid. Sorry. I'm sorry. But could I? It won't change anything. I swear."

He sighs. Scratches his temple with the barrel of the gun. Does that mean the safety's on? Or is he that confident in his own marksmanship?

Finally, he shrugs.

"Suit yourself."

You slide off the mattress. With the slow, delicate gestures of a bomb disposal expert, you lie down on the floor. A knot unspools inside your chest. This is what you know. This is like the shed. You know how to stay alive in the shed. You can learn to do the same here.

He kneels at your side and grabs your handcuffed wrist. He extends your arm above your head, slides the free end of the handcuffs between two iron curves at the bottom of the bed frame. Flecks of paint peel off as he jerks the mechanism left and right, testing it.

When he's certain you won't be able to wriggle free, he gets up.

"If I hear anything—anything at all—I won't be happy. Understand?"

You nod as best as you can with your head on the floor.

"My room is across the hallway. If you try anything, I'll know."

Another nod.

"I'll be back tomorrow morning. I expect to see you in the same spot. Same position. Same everything."

Again, you nod. He takes a couple of steps, puts his hand on the doorknob, and goes still.

"I promise," you say. "I won't move."

He squints at you. It never ends, the uncertainty of his gaze on you. Can he trust you? What about now? What about in an hour? What about in a week?

"I mean it," you add. "I'm so tired. I'm going to be out cold the second you step out."

With your free hand, you twirl your index finger around the room.

"This is nice. Thank you."

He's turning the doorknob when it happens. A rasp on the other side of the wall, a floorboard creaking. A call from the other end of the hallway: "Dad?"

Something like terror flashes in his eyes. He looks at you as if you're dead, a body and blood on his hands and his daughter walking in your direction.

Just as quickly, he composes himself. His face relaxes. His gaze sharpens. He raises a hand in your direction. *Stay out of this. Be very quiet.*

In one lithe movement, he slips out of the room. Does she see him? Or is it too dark, and is she too far away? It's the hardest thing you've ever had to do, not looking. Not lifting your head, not craning your neck. Keeping your mouth shut as the door closes behind him. A swift gust of air brushes against your face. You suck your lips in, chew on the inside of your cheeks.

Muffled noises seep through the wall: "Is everything okay" and "Yes" and "It's so late" and "I know, I know" and "I tried to text you" and "I didn't hear" and eventually "Go back to bed." She must listen to him, because soon the sounds fade away and it's just you. You in a room. You in a real house with furniture and heat and so many walls and doors. You and him, and somewhere down the hallway, someone else.

You can almost feel her. Cecilia. Like a force field. A glowing ember in the dark. For the first time in five years, a small hurricane. The infinite promise of a new person.

CHAPTER 12

Number two

He was engaged.

That's the first thing he told me. After I closed down the store. After he demanded the cash from the register. After I realized money wasn't the only thing he was after.

He said it while he took my ring. He had jewelry on his mind, because he had recently gotten engaged.

To a wonderful woman, he said.

The other thing about him: he was good at knots. "See this?" he told me after tying my hands together in front of me. "It's a figure-eight loop. It won't come apart if you pull. Pressure only makes it tighter. So don't try. Don't even fucking try."

I tried, when he wasn't looking. But the thing with that man was, he was not a liar. His knot never came apart.

The last thing I learned: he was prepared. I think he had done it before. There was a confidence to him, a determination. Calm, even when I didn't go along with his plan. Because he knew I would, eventually. He knew the world would bend to his will.

He was—that's the last thing I ever thought—like a warrior. Like someone who knows it's not over until the other side stops squirming.

CHAPTER 13

The woman in the house

A tremor in your shoulder. He's leaning over you, shaking you awake. When did you fall asleep? All you remember is lying on the hardwood floor, trying to find a decent position for your handcuffed arm.

You wait for him to free you. He pulls you up to your feet. You rub your eyes, shake out your legs. In the shed, you were always awake by the time he came in. Your throat closes at the idea that he was able to slip in unnoticed—that he hovered over you as you lay, eyes closed, mouth slightly open, oblivious to the world around you. Unaware of him.

"Let's go."

He grabs your arm, opens the door, guides you across the hallway. Under his other elbow, he has tucked a bath towel and a set of clothes. He opens another door to your left—one you didn't notice last night—and pulls you in. You conduct a quick assessment: bathtub, shower curtain, sink, toilet. He puts a finger on his lips as he turns on the shower. "She's still asleep," he says, his voice low, drowned out by the stream. "But be quick. And be quiet."

Cecilia. The memory of last night floats between the two of you, his daughter's inquiring voice and the panic in his eyes. All three of you, standing, hands linked, on the edge of a cliff.

You slide your jeans and your underwear down your legs. Take off your sweater, your T-shirt, the cheap sports bra he got you when the hooks on your original one finally gave out.

You lift the toilet lid. You're so busy being stunned by the reality of the experience that you forget, for a moment or two, that he's watching. All you know is there's a cotton mat grazing the arches of your feet, a cold rim of enamel digging into the back of your thighs. A roll of toilet paper to your right, white, two-ply. He keeps his gaze on you, as indifferent as if you were a dog relieving itself on a walk.

To your left, water splashes against the tub. You don't ask about

Cecilia, whether the sound of someone showering might wake her up. He's a father, and he knows what interrupts his child's sleep. Your guess: she's used to it. For all you know, he's been getting up before her for years, shaving and brushing his teeth before her first yawn.

From the toilet, you examine him. Bingo. He's dressed—jeans and a clean fleece and work boots laced up. Hair combed, beard freshly trimmed. He got up early, made time for his own ablutions before tending to yours. If she hears anything, his kid will think that the new tenant is just like her dad, an early riser.

You get up to flush. You're about to step into the bathtub when something stops you. A shape in the mirror. A woman. New and unknown. You.

You need a few seconds. To look at your hair, long and dark as it used to be, but the roots graying, a couple of white skunk stripes streaking past your shoulders. Ribs protruding, rolling under your skin as if threatening to poke through. The outline of your face.

"Come on."

Before you can get a better look, he grabs your arm, slides the shower curtain to the side, and hurries you under the water.

It's so hot. You used to take showers like this every morning. You stood for long moments, water ricocheting down your chest. You tilted your head back and let it fill your ears, fill your mouth, possess you. You gave yourself to the moment fully, with finality, grasping for a sort of sublime that never materialized. Now, after five years of splashing yourself with water from the bucket, you can't tell what part of this experience—water scalding your back, streaming over your face, steam filling your lungs—was supposed to be enjoyable.

You keep your eyes open, try to breathe through the fog. Do you remember how to do this? You go to grab the soap. Your feet slip. He catches you, rolls his eyes. The shower curtain is still drawn to the side. There's no razor, nothing you could use to harm him or yourself—not even a bottle of shampoo you could squirt into his eyes. Just you, your naked body, and a bar of soap.

You hold it under the stream. Rub the foam on your arms, your chest, between your legs, all the way down to your toes.

"You done yet?"

You tell him almost. You go back for more soap and wash your face and hair. Then you switch off the water and turn to him. He hands you the towel. You dry yourself. Your body is so present, so real under the yellow lighting. In the shed, in the gleam of the camping lantern, you couldn't see its details—stretch marks like lightning bolts on the inside of your thighs, dark hairs on your forearms and calves, tufts in your armpits. Bruises on your arms, stagnating pools of purple and blue in the crooks of your elbows. On your chest, a smattering of scars. Brutal years written across your skin.

You hand him the towel. He points to a hook on the door, where you hang it to dry. He gestures to the pile of clothes he has set on the floor. You kneel to find new, supermarket-issue underwear. A sports bra cut out of the same black cotton. Clean jeans, a white T-shirt, a gray hoodie with a zipper. Everything cheap, neutral, boring. Everything new. Everything yours.

As you slip on the clothes, you remind yourself of the details of your new identity. *You are Rachel. You moved into town recently. You needed a place to stay, and you heard that a friend of a friend was subletting a room.* He hands you a new toothbrush and points to the toothpaste on the rim of the sink—his, presumably.

This isn't kindness. The basic hygiene, a chance to clean yourself up. It's easier for him if you don't get sick, if your teeth don't fall out, if your body doesn't fuss itself into an infection. In the shed, he needed you healthy enough that you wouldn't create additional work for him. Now he needs you to look as normal as possible for his daughter.

"Come here."

He positions you in front of the mirror and wipes off the fog with a washcloth. This is your chance to take a closer look at yourself. You were never pretty, not exactly, but on the right day, from the right angles, you were able to see the appeal of you. Your jet-black hair, your short bangs. Good skin, save for a monthly breakout announcing your period. Defined lips. You could pull off red lipstick. You taught yourself winged eyeliner, white pencil on the rim of your lower lid. Eyes as large and round as possible.

The woman in the mirror doesn't have bangs. They grew out a long time ago. Your skin feels, somehow, dry and oily at once. There are new creases on your forehead, between your eyebrows, around your mouth. Pinhead bumps from your temples to your jawline. The weight loss has transformed your face, too. Your cheeks are hollow, permanently sucked in.

You used to be muscular and healthy. A runner who ate oatmeal and stretched on Sundays, an occasional yogi with a Pilates subscription. You walked as much as you could, ate when you were hungry, stopped when you were full. Your metabolism whirred, undisturbed. It was a miracle to you, this obedient little machine, this organism that rewarded you for taking care of it. And now he's ruined it. Ravaged it, like he does everything.

"Stand still."

He's holding a pair of scissors. You freeze.

"It's too long." With the scissors, he points at your hair. It hasn't grown as much as you imagined it would. After the first twelve months—twelve months of one meal a day—your body decided to use its resources for more pressing matters. Your ends thinned out, forever hovering underneath your shoulder blades.

He needs you neater than this. He needs you to look like someone who never lost access to haircuts.

"Don't move," he tells you. "Be a shame if you made my hand slip."

You keep still as he runs the blades across your back, repress a shiver as the metal bounces against your skin. In a couple of snips, he brings your hair back to shoulder length.

He stuffs the scissors in his back pocket and tugs at your arm.

It's all he ever does, jerking you this way and that, hurrying you up, never the right amount of time for anything. You turn to face him. His blue eyes, the ones you swear turn dark at times. His carefully groomed facial hair, his cheekbones, shockingly delicate, almost fragile.

There is probably nice shampoo hidden in the drawers under the sink. Aloe vera aftershave and pomade in the mirrored cabinet. Nothing expensive, just enough to feel clean and put together.

Anger rises, hot, up your spine. Your eyes dart around the room in search of things to grab and throw. Perhaps the soap dish could crack his skull. Or you could use your hands, and how good would it feel, for a few seconds, to hit his chest with your closed fists again and again and again, perhaps land a punch on his face, hit the bone just above the eye, split his lip, turn his teeth red, push his nose right into his brain? But his grip on your arm tightens. This well-fed, well-rested man who knows where the weapons are hidden. The master in his domain.

"Sorry," you say, and you zip up your hoodie. "I'm ready."

He picks up your old clothes and tells you to follow him. Swiftly, he opens the door to the bedroom, throws your stuff inside. In the daylight, you get a better look at the door: the round knob with a lock at the center, the kind that latches from inside, like you had when you lived with roommates. This one isn't meant to keep you in. It's for Cecilia, here to make sure she stays out. Only her father has the key. Only he can come in.

You step back into the room. He handcuffs you to the bed again. At the end of the hallway, an alarm chirps. Right on time.

You sit and wait, your hair damp against your back. It's not long until he returns and uncuffs you again. This time, he shuts the door behind you and grabs your wrist. You follow him downstairs. The house comes alive underneath your feet. Gray carpet on the steps, walls painted white, ditto the banister. You make a left and walk into the open kitchen. *Your name is Rachel; you are Rachel.* To your right is the living area. No foyer. Just the front door, beckoning to you. A couch, an armchair, a decently sized television screen. A coffee table with a couple of magazines. Photo frames on the walls and that bookshelf in the corner, lined with paperbacks. Underneath the staircase, a door.

You want to inspect it all. You want to turn drawers upside down, empty all the closets, open all the doors. But he pulls you toward the kitchen table—wooden, a few scratches, but freshly shined. Not too far from it, a back door. The entire house is clean and devoid of personality, like it's afraid that if it starts talking, it will say too much.

He points to a chair, also wooden, the farthest away from the back door. You sit. The table is set with three plates, two empty mugs, three kitchen knives. A Mr. Coffee sputters on the counter. He puts his hand on your shoulder, gives you a shake. You glance at his waist. No holster.

"Remember."

You are Rachel. You are a friend of a friend. You will not take a knife to his throat. You will act naturally.

He opens the silver fridge, takes out a bag of white bread, places slices inside the toaster. The breakfasts of your childhood come back to you: Pop-Tarts pinched between two paper towels, still hot, eaten on the way to school. Later on, a similar routine, but with scrambled-egg sandwiches and paper cups of coffee from a cart. As far back as you can remember, you didn't sit down to breakfast with your parents. Certainly not on weekdays.

From your chair, you make a note of everything you see: a block of knives on the counter, tongs on the drying rack. Ladle, can opener, a long pair of scissors. A kitchen towel draped over the oven handle. Everything clean, every element in its allocated spot. He has unpacked his boxes. Made himself at home in this new space. It is his now, under his control.

He goes to lean against the banister, tips his head in the direction of the first floor.

"Cecilia!" he calls out.

He shuffles back to the Mr. Coffee to check whether it's done brewing. A dad on breakfast duty, going about his morning routine.

THE FIRST YOU see of her is her feet. Two light-blue socks padding down the stairs. Skinny black pants, a fuzzy mauve sweater. Halfway down the staircase, she leans over to peer into the kitchen.

"Hi," you say.

Your voice startles her, him, and most of all you. His gaze bounces from you to his daughter. You worry you've done it wrong. One word, and already you've ruined everything. But Cecilia makes her way to the table and sits across from you.

"Hi," she says.

You can't say hi again, so you give her a little wave. You're trying not to stare, but you can't help it, devouring her face, feasting on the details of her features.

You scan her for any trace of her father, search for the story of her upbringing. There is some resemblance to her dad—a stranger on the street would assume they're related—but she is her own person, her face rounder than his, softer. Dotted with freckles and framed by wavy red hair. Her eyes, however, are his—the same blue-gray, same glimmers of yellow around the irises.

He sets a plate of toast on the table. With his back to his daughter, he raises his eyebrows at you. *Don't fuck up.*

You're trying, but you have no idea how to do this. Nothing could have prepared you to sit in this man's kitchen, dredge up the friendly parts of you, and offer them to his daughter.

"I'm Rachel," you tell her.

She nods. "Cecilia."

"Nice to meet you."

She smiles briefly. Her dad walks to the kitchen counter, picks up the coffee carafe, and returns to sit at the table. He turns to her.

"Sleep well?"

She nods, eyes on her empty plate. Dimly, you remember what you were like in the mornings at her age: always tired, never hungry, certainly never in the mood to talk. Her father pours himself a cup of coffee, then sets the pot at the edge of your place mat. Telling you, directing you to help yourself. You fill the mug in front of you. It's only when you bring it up to your lips that you notice the words printed on the other side of the ceramic: BEST DAD EVER in large black letters.

At the breakfast table, the best dad ever reaches for a strand of his daughter's hair. He brings it up to her nose and moves it up and down, poking at her nostril. At first, she doesn't react. Around the third poke, she swats him away gently, laughs as if against her better judgment.

"Stop it!"

He smiles, partly to her and partly to himself. A father and his daughter, comfortable around each other.

He loves her. It's obvious, even to you.

The thing with love: it can make people weak.

While they're distracted, you close your eyes and swallow your first sip of coffee in years. The taste knocks you back in time to your last morning, the day he took you. Before that, a summer internship in a newsroom, tired employees inserting pods into a machine well into the afternoon. And through it all, every visit at a coffee shop. When it came to coffee, you remember now, you were never faithful. You tried every drink imaginable, plain drip, flat white with an extra shot, latte with hazelnut syrup, cappuccino with extra foam. Refusing to commit. Wanting to try everything the world had to offer.

When you open your eyes again, the kid is reading the back of the butter container. *Act normally.* You reach for a slice of toast, drop it onto your plate. Glance at the best dad ever, wait for his wordless approval before you pick up a dull knife. His daughter relinquishes her reading material and you spread butter on your bread. You add a layer of jelly like it's nothing, like this isn't the first time in five years that you get to decide how much you're going to have of a given food. As ceremoniously as you can without raising suspicion, you take a bite.

A sharp pain bites at the edges of your gums. The jelly is so sweet it sticks to the back of your throat. You haven't seen a dentist in ages. You don't want to think about the mess inside. Cavities, gingivitis, a mouth that would ooze blood if you were to floss. The toast hurts, but it's also warm and crunchy and the butter is partially melted and you are so fucking ravenous, so hungry you forgot what it feels like to be sated. Maybe you've been storing hunger, somewhere between your hollow stomach and the knots of your hip bones, and you won't be able to stop eating until you've made up for every calorie you missed out on in the shed.

"Do you have that note for Ms. Newman?"

A father's voice brings you back to the kitchen. To your hands on the table, to your feet on the floor, to this man and his daughter and their perfectly nice morning routine. Cecilia confirms that she does, in fact, have that note for Ms. Newman. There's more chitchat between the two of them, inquiries about an upcoming test, confirmation that Cecilia will go to art class tonight and that he will pick her up at five-thirty.

You didn't know fathers could act this way. No matter how far back you search, you can't remember yours ever making you breakfast, playing with your hair, knowing your teachers' names and your class schedule. Your father left for work early and came back after dinner wearing a nice suit, briefcase in hand, tired but happy. He made time for you and your brother, for game days and school plays, for Sunday afternoons in the park. But you were an item on a to-do list. Even as a child, you sensed that if no one reminded him of this particular mission, fatherhood might slip his mind, your childhood like a dry-cleaning item no one had bothered to pick up.

The best dad ever empties his coffee mug. His daughter gives up on the slice of toast she tried to munch on. They get up. He tells her, "Five minutes," and she tells him she knows and disappears upstairs. As soon as the sound of the bathroom door shutting reaches the kitchen, he turns to you.

"Come. Now."

He signals for you to walk in front of him and up the stairs. He follows closely, his body brushing against yours. You make your way back to the bedroom. He doesn't have to tell you to position yourself near the radiator. You sit on the floor and lift your right hand. He retrieves the handcuffs from his pocket, secures one loop around your wrist, the other around the metallic pipe. He slides it up and down, makes sure the mechanism is secure.

"I have to take her to school, and then I have to go to work. Now, look."

He takes out his phone. You've never seen it before. It has a much larger screen than the ones you remember from five years ago.

"I have cameras. In this room, at the front door, everywhere. Hidden. They link to an app in here." He gives the screen a few taps, then turns it in your direction. It's not the camera feed—he won't show that to you. That would give too much away. It's an online video. A demo.

He plays it with just a whisper of sound. It shows the entrance to a house. A woman opens and shuts the door. You see it, you hear it. A red icon pops up in the bottom right corner of the screen.

You absorb the house and the door and the woman hired to walk into a home that's not really hers. The technology. The menace of his eyes and ears on you.

Your jaw tightens. The shed. He didn't have eyes in the shed. Not while he was away. You could read, in the shed. You could lie down.

You could sit up. You could do these things, and he didn't know when or how you did them. It wasn't much but it was something, and that something belonged to you.

This was supposed to be better, you want to say, and immediately you want to curse yourself for thinking that way. *Better* isn't something he lets you have. *Better* is a fairy tale.

The screen goes dark. He locks it again.

"If you do anything—if you scream or move and I see anyone coming over to check things out, I'll get a notification. And I won't be happy." He glances at the bedroom window, obscured by a drawn shade. "I work close to here. Do you understand?"

You tell him you do, but something holds him back. He kneels at your side. Brings a hand to your face and forces you to look up. He needs to see it in your eyes. That you believe him, and he can believe you in return.

"Do you know what I do for a living?"

Is he really asking? Does he really not remember that he never told you?

You try to shake your head no.

"I'm a lineman." You give him what must be a blank stare, because he rolls his eyes and adds, "Do you know what that means?"

You think you do, but he asks with such intensity it makes you think you don't.

"Kind of," you say.

"I fix and maintain power lines. Never saw any of us up there, working on the overhead cables?"

You tell him yeah, that's what you thought. It makes sense to you, this job for him. All day perched on a utility pole, only a layer of rubber between him and a deadly power.

"This is a small town," he continues. "And when I'm working, well, it's pretty incredible how far you can see from up there."

He lets go of your face, gazes up, like he can see through the ceiling. You picture him, treetops in the background, birds flying past. He goes back to his phone.

This time, he shows you the results of a Google Images search. Men hanging from cables, one foot resting at the top of a forty-foot pole, the other hovering in the air. Hard hats and thick gloves. A mess of pulleys and hooks. You feel his stare on you as you take it all in. He gives you a few moments, then puts the phone away.

"You can see everything, when you're up there." His eyes dart to the window again. "Every street. Every house. Every road. Every person." His gaze travels back to you. "I see it all. Do you understand? Even when people can't tell. I'm watching. I'll always be watching."

"I understand," you tell him. If your voice had hands, they'd be joined in prayer right now. "I get it."

He stares you down for a few seconds, then walks to the door. "Wait!"

His finger flies up to his lips. You lower your voice. "My stuff." You tug at the handcuffs to emphasize the fact that you are here and your books are over there, out of reach. He picks them up, tosses them in a pile next to you.

"Thank you."

He checks his watch and hurries out. You hear footsteps, then his voice coming from downstairs. "Ready?"

Cecilia must nod her head yes. The front door opens and shuts. The truck starts, then the hum of the engine melts away.

Without them, the house is quiet. Not a peaceful kind of quiet. A blank silence, oppressive, as uncomfortable as sitting in a stranger's lap. The room feels enormous and tiny at once. It's as if its walls are sliding toward one another, the surface shrinking, the structure shutting around you.

You close your eyes. Think back to the shed, to the hardwood floor underneath your head, to your world of wooden slats. You press your palms against your eyes and move them to cover your ears. You can hear the current of air passing through you, like the rush inside a conch shell.

You are here.

You are breathing.

This morning was a test and you passed. As far as you can tell, you passed.

CHAPTER 14

Emily

After Aidan's wife died, and her parents, for reasons unknown, kicked him out of their home, Judge Byrne offered to rent him that small house he owns in the hamlet, near the Hudson. It's not big. From what I heard, the judge cut him a great deal on rent, the kind you can't refuse. Classic Judge Byrne.

Judge Byrne thinks of himself as the glue that holds the town together. He has performed every wedding in a ten-mile radius since before I was born. When the going gets tough, Judge Byrne finds you. He always makes time to talk. He has your back, even when you wish he didn't.

Which is why Judge Byrne suggested the 5K fundraiser on the town's Facebook page three days ago. "Aidan—everyone's favorite handyman and general good guy around town—has just lost his home and his wife, and he is still facing staggering medical bills for her care while raising a daughter by himself," he wrote. "He's far too proud to admit it or complain, but I know the man could use some help."

People loved the idea. One of the volunteer firefighters drew the course, starting and ending in the town center. In the comments section, the Garcías offered up supplies from their organic grocery store—paper bags filled with raisins, orange segments. Kids from my former school signed up to hand out cups of water. Dads rallied as course marshals. Everyone was so eager to help that we almost lost sight of the endgame: registration for the race costs a minimum of five dollars, additional donations encouraged. The total will go to Aidan and his daughter to cover bills, rent, remaining funeral expenses, and whatever else.

Meanwhile, Aidan Thomas remained silent. I imagined him watching as our town tripped over itself to help him. Not wanting to sound rude, but hating the attention.

Until this afternoon.

I know Aidan's profile, although we're not Facebook friends. He only has something like three contacts on there, including what used to be his wife's account. But I immediately recognized his picture—not a photo of himself, of course not. Just a scenic image of the Hudson, frozen, taken from the hill by the inn.

"Thank you so much, everyone," he wrote under the judge's post. "Cecilia and I are so grateful for this community."

The comment was shared two hours ago, and more than fifty people have liked it already. Some have gone as far as responding with hearts or caring emoji, their little cartoon arms joined in a virtual embrace.

I sit in my bedroom, my index finger hovering over the trackpad on my laptop.

In the multiplex of my brain, the same movie has been playing on a loop: Aidan's blue eyes watching me through his glass the night of the virgin old-fashioned. Something that belongs only to the two of us.

On Facebook, I click "comment" and start typing. Stop. Start again. Stop again.

The last thing I want is to appear overeager.

No, that's not true.

The last thing I want is to look like I don't care.

"Amandine would love to support all runners (and their cheerleaders). I'd be happy to set up a hot-cocoa station at the finish line?"

The restaurant does the hot-cocoa thing every year for the Christmas parade. I don't mind setting up the dispenser a little early this year. Come race day, it'll give me something to do and a reason to be around.

I proofread my comment and hit "send."

As I get ready for dinner service, I return to the screen to check for updates. Just when I'm about to leave, a notification pops up in the top-right corner.

Two comments.

One is from Mrs. Cooper, who moved here with her husband and their two kids a few years ago. "What a wonderful idea!" she wrote. Mrs. Cooper. Always a bit too enthusiastic. Always worried she and her family won't fit in.

The second comment is from him. I read it too fast, a panicky feeling compressing my rib cage (*what if he thinks it's dumb, what if it's too much, what if it's not enough*). Then, I go again, taking my time. Savoring every word.

"How kind of you."

Here, he pressed the shift and return keys together to start a new paragraph.

"I think that sounds delicious."

CHAPTER 15

The woman in the house

You shift next to the radiator, try to find the least uncomfortable position. If you rest your back against the wall, you can stretch your legs out.

You close your eyes and listen. Outside, a woodpecker pecks. A different kind of bird sings. Before he took you, you had started learning about birdsong. You had found a book with a list of species and descriptions of the corresponding melodies. It all sounded so clear in theory, but you have never managed to match a bird to its sound with certainty, not even after years of practice in the shed. To your city ears, a bird is a bird is a bird is a bird.

By the time the truck returns, the squares of light around the shades have dimmed. Doors open and shut. Voices rise from the kitchen. You catch bits of sentences—"homework," "dinner," "jeopardy." Someone climbs the staircase. The toilet flushes; the bathroom sink makes the pipes sing. The smell of food wafts through the house, rich and hot and—if you remember correctly—buttery.

He has warned you: Dinner won't be every night. Breakfast won't be every morning. He will come and get you at appropriate times. But tonight is the first night. So tonight, he shows up.

Already, you know the dance. He frees you from the handcuffs and tells you to hurry. You get up, bend your knees a couple of times, rub your feet back to life. Downstairs, the table is set like it was in the morning, with glasses of water in lieu of coffee mugs. He opens the oven and checks whatever's cooking inside.

"Cecilia!"

A man in his house, putting food on the table. Feeding his child. *A father.*

He nudges you, like *What are you waiting for?* You sit at the same spot he assigned you at breakfast.

Cecilia comes down the stairs. She suppresses a yawn. You remember being her age, how exhausting it was, having everything to learn, all those books to read, all those math formulas to memorize. The world at your fingertips, and the all-consuming task of figuring out—in between classes, at recess—what kind of person you wanted to be and the best path to get there.

She stops by the living area and points a remote at the television. A jingle fills the room, brass instruments, a singsongy refrain, then a booming voice. "This iiiiis *Jeopardy!*" Contestants flash up on the screen, names and locations, Holly from Silver Springs and Jasper from Park City and Benjamin from Buffalo. A man in a suit and tie walks onto the set.

"And here is the host of *Jeopardy!*, Alex Trebek."

Your arms go numb. Your legs and feet tingle. The house, you can manage. Even Cecilia, you can handle, the energy of one extra person in the room, her youth, the mysteries of her life. But TV, people answering questions for money, Alex greeting Holly and Jasper and Benjamin like old friends—it's too much. Too much outside. Too much evidence that the world has kept going without you.

Inside the house, a father walks over to his daughter, wraps an arm around her shoulder. *Like your dad used to do,* your brain whispers, *when he nudged you close to him and reminded you that you were his buddy.*

"Dinner's ready."

Cecilia looks up at him with pleading eyes.

"Just the first round? Please?"

A father sighs. He glances at you. Maybe he decides a distraction wouldn't be the worst thing in the world. Keep the girl focused on the TV, not on the new woman at the table.

"Lower the volume and we'll leave it on in the background."

Cecilia raises her eyebrows. For a second, she looks like him, the same air of suspicion, always on the lookout for a trick, a deception. Not wanting to press her luck, she aims the remote at the TV until Alex's voice fades into a faint buzz. She fiddles with the buttons some more. Closed captions appear at the bottom of the screen. Smart girl.

With his fingers wrapped in a kitchen towel, a father sets a ceramic dish down at the center of the table, next to a cut-up loaf of garlic bread. Cecilia leans over to take a whiff.

"What's this?"

He tells her it's veggie lasagna and to sit down. She serves him, then herself, then looks at you, spoon raised like a question mark. You bring your plate to her and help yourself to a piece of garlic bread. Cecilia studies you for a few moments, until her father points to the television. The category is "Matters of the Heart." Eight hundred dollars are at stake. Closed captions flash up as Alex reads from a card. "This is what happens when a life-threatening amount of fluid accumulates around the heart."

A father answers out loud, "What's tamponade." He doesn't say it like a question, just a statement of fact.

Benjamin from Buffalo gives the same answer. Eight hundred dollars are added to his total.

"That's not fair," the kid says. "You studied that stuff."

You know that the man with the key to the shed—with the key to your bedroom—isn't a doctor. There is a story here that eludes you. Ambitions unfulfilled, changes of plans. Before you can think of a smart way to probe, Benjamin from Buffalo picks the category "Nicknames" for two hundred. Alex delivers the clue: "He was also known as the 'quiet Beatle.'"

Something stirs within you. Knowledge from the past. Songs you used to sing. CDs plucked from your father's shelf in his home office. The first chords of "It's All Too Much," the whine of a distorted electric guitar.

A father and his daughter exchange clueless looks. Then, your voice. "Who was George Harrison?"

Benjamin from Buffalo guesses John Lennon and strikes out. Jasper from Park City goes for Ringo. Holly from Silver Springs declines to try until the clock runs out. Alex makes a sorry face. "Not John, not Ringo," he says in closed captions. "The correct answer is . . . Who was George Harrison?"

Cecilia gives you a little smile, like *Well done.* Her dad waits until her eyes are on the screen again to gaze at you. You raise your shoulders slightly. *What? You said to keep it normal.* He turns back to the

TV, where Benjamin has picked the category "Nicknames" again, this time for four hundred.

"This iconic Briton, born in Brixton, London, was known among other things as the 'Thin White Duke.' His real name is this."

Holly from Silver Springs clicks her buzzer and purses her lips. More memories find you: A lightning bolt across your face one Halloween night. A fluttering in your chest as you fell in love with a skinny silhouette, thin lips, hypnotic eyes. You swallow a mouthful of lasagna quickly enough to answer: "Who's David Jones?"

On the screen, Holly hesitates until she's out of time. She smiles apologetically at Alex, who waits for the other two to try their chance, then explains: "The answer is David Jones . . . Who was also known as David Bowie."

Cecilia turns to you again.

"How did you know that?"

You can't think of a reason not to tell her the truth.

"I really like music."

She squirms a little in her seat. "Oh. Me, too."

Her father has stopped eating, his fork balanced on the edge of his plate. His eyes toggle from you to Cecilia like he's watching a tennis match.

Something else you remember: How exciting it felt, at her age, when a teacher let you do a presentation on Cher. When someone else's eyes widened with excitement at the mention of Bob Dylan. How music was a shortcut to kinship, to ending the devastating loneliness that came with being thirteen.

You smile at her. The girl who's half him, the girl who mustn't know what her father does in the shadows. "Who do you listen to?" you ask.

She thinks. You used to love and hate that question in equal measures. Love, because you never tired of tasting those names on your tongue—Pink Floyd and Bowie and Patti Smith and Jimi Hendrix and the Stones and Aerosmith and the Beatles and Deep Purple and Fleetwood Mac and Dylan. Hate, because you were terrified of saying the wrong name, the one that would unmask you not as a rock connoisseur, but just another teenage girl.

Cecilia names a few artists, Taylor Swift and Selena Gomez and Harry Styles. People who were just getting started when you disappeared. Talents that blossomed in your absence.

"Nice," you tell her. How hard you found it, back when you were still out in the world, meeting people, making new friends, trying to sound appreciative but not condescending.

She nods. "You?"

You feel a father's burning stare. *This is what people do,* you'll tell him later, if he asks. *They speak. They share the things they love the most.*

You tell her some names. "The Rolling Stones—I saw them live in 2012, actually. The Beach Boys. The Pointer Sisters. Elvis, but I guess everyone loves Elvis. And Dolly Parton. I loved Dolly so much, when I was growing up. Begged my parents to take me to Dollywood every s—"

Like a curse word in a church. A stutter in an incantation. It stops you in your tracks. *My parents.* It's the first time you've acknowledged them in his presence, the people he took you from.

You had your own life. A college student, weeks away from graduation. You had papers to write, things to do, friends, a job. But you were still theirs. Whether you liked it or not. You were still owed weekly dinners together. Texts and phone calls. A life to share.

Cecilia clears her throat. She reaches for the serving spoon, gives you time to collect yourself. You try again. ". . . every summer. Never worked, though."

She dumps a spoonful of lasagna on her plate. When she lifts her gaze up to you again, it destroys you. It's been so long since anyone looked at you like this. With kindness. With the idea that you and your feelings matter.

You don't know what she's thinking. Probably that you and your folks had a falling out, or that they died before they got a chance to take you to Dollywood. Whatever story she's telling herself, she wants you to know that she gets it.

"Well," she says. "Now you can go whenever you want."

You stare down at what's left on your plate. "Right. Whenever I want."

Later on, when her dad tells her to go brush her teeth, she sneaks

a glance at you. She has the eyes of a new intern who just found someone to sit next to on her first day of work. Of a lost cousin at a funeral,
relieved to find a conversation partner during the reception.

You know these eyes. You've seen them before. They're the eyes of
someone who's been lonely, and hurt.

CHAPTER 16

Cecilia

Sometimes I feel this terrible pressure at the back of my throat. It makes me want to scream or punch something. Not someone, never someone. Just something.

If my dad knew, he'd shake his head in that way that makes me want to die a little. My mom used to tell him, *You can't hold everyone to such high standards. Let her be a kid. She has her whole life to be like you.*

When I can't take it anymore, I go into the wooded area by the cemetery up the hill. I find a tree and kick it a few times with my shoe. Soft at first, then harder with each kick. My dad doesn't know. Obviously. I do it between school and my art class so he doesn't see me. He has enough on his plate right now.

First there was my mom, and then there was Rachel.

He told me about her before we moved. A friend of a friend of a friend is what he said. Whatever. I didn't really care who she was, only that she was going to live with us in this new house I already didn't love all that much.

Rachel needed help, he said. Bad things had happened to her. I asked what bad things, exactly. He said he didn't want to go into details, but that she had gotten hurt and she didn't have anyone else to help. So we were going to sublet the extra room in the judge's house, and we were going to have her share our meals and things like that.

What I didn't tell my dad: I've hit a rough patch, too, and I'm not crazy about sharing my meals with strangers, but sure.

"She's been through a lot," he told me. "So don't crowd her. Don't ask questions. Just be nice and polite and give her some space."

I wanted to tell him that wouldn't be a problem, that I wasn't dying to make friends with some random woman anyway. But that wouldn't have been nice. And my dad, he's a nice person. What he's doing right now, helping out Rachel, that's a nice thing, especially right after my mom—his wife—died. So I told him okay. I told him I'd do my best.

I'm not stupid. I know it's not exactly normal to move a stranger into your house the minute your spouse dies. So at first, I thought for sure Rachel must have been his girlfriend or something. I've seen movies. I watch a good amount of TV. I know what husbands do after their wives die. They move on. Granted, I didn't expect my dad to move on that fast, but it's not like I had a say.

But then I saw how they acted around each other, and I realized I had it all wrong. I remember how my parents used to hold hands, how she called him "honey," how they would look at each other, even after a fight. There's none of that between my dad and Rachel. No sparks. No butterflies. Nothing.

It was unfair of me to think those things about my dad in the first place. He would never forget my mom so fast, move someone in to replace her. He loved her. We still love her so much.

The most surprising thing about Rachel so far is that I kind of like her. She's a weirdo, for sure, but that's not a bad thing. I'm kind of a weirdo, too, to be honest. But Rachel doesn't talk to me the way other adults do. She asks about me and the things I like. She never mentions my mom. It's refreshing, having someone who doesn't treat me like a broken thing.

Before she moved in, my dad promised me her arrival wouldn't change anything for us. Obviously, it has. Not in a bad way. But she lives with us. She eats with us. Of course things have changed. I don't know how he could have expected them not to. He likes to think he can control those things, freeze time into place. But things are always changing.

Take this, for example: after my mom died, I had trouble eating for a while. Now, my appetite is back. Even worse: I've started enjoying dinner again. The three of us sit together and watch *Jeopardy!* and for a few moments things are sort of okay.

And ever since she arrived, I haven't felt the need to kick that poor tree as often as I used to.

I'm sure the tree's thrilled, but me? It kills me to say that. My mom's been dead for only a couple of months. What kind of daughter does that make me?

I'm not supposed to be done feeling sad. I'm supposed to be hurting still.

I like her, the woman in our house, but I also hate her a little bit for pulling me out of my funk.

Mainly, though, I'm just relieved she and my dad aren't doing it.

CHAPTER 17

The woman in the house

When the house is dark, he finds you.

His process here is almost identical to what it was in the shed. He sighs. He scans you from head to toe. He doesn't need to wait until you're done eating or until you've used the bucket now. Instead, he uncuffs you, gestures for you to get onto the bed. Then, he thinks better of it and tells you to get back on the floor. You're confused, but you obey.

A little later, you get it. He doesn't want his daughter to hear springs creaking, the telltale thump of the bed frame against the wall.

The woman in the house

The days are yours.

You read your paperbacks. You know them by heart now, almost entirely. You challenge yourself to recite the first chapter of *A Tree Grows in Brooklyn* from memory. You try to remember meditation sequences from your previous life, how your mind could compress the time or let it stretch.

The house is so silent without them that you sometimes hum just to make sure your ears still work.

Your life as a runner taught you skills. The key to a marathon: You do not think about the end. You do not picture the finish line. You keep moving. You exist in the present. The only way to do it: one stride at a time. It doesn't have to be pretty. It certainly doesn't have to be enjoyable. All that matters is that you are still alive at the end of it.

YOU LOOK AROUND for the cameras. Alone in the bedroom, and from the kitchen at mealtimes. You can't know for sure whether he was telling the truth or making them up. You can't see anything, but how easy would it be to hide them between two books, in the corner of a dropped ceiling, behind a kitchen cabinet? You believe he can see everything.

On weekend mornings, they depart, packed lunches in stuffed backpacks. You hear nothing but birdsong until the evening. Cecilia returns exhausted but willing to share tales of an afternoon spent hiking, exploring, wandering around a library, a museum. You mine each of her sentences for information. Cold hikes: you must be near mountains, maybe still upstate. Impossible to know for sure. Some days, she mentions the names of nearby towns. Nothing rings a bell. You could be anywhere.

She quizzes you. Cecilia. Wants to know what you're up to when she's not around. You recite the lie her father cooked up: you work remotely, doing customer service for a tech company. Around it, you make up a life for Rachel, for the person Cecilia believes you to be. Afternoons spent reading—not exactly a lie. Vague excursions to stores, the same ones you've heard her father mention. You stop short of giving Rachel friends or a family. You do not trust your brain to hold a cast of made-up characters, to keep up with the full stories of their lives. She's smart. If you make a mistake, she'll notice.

YOU ARE NOT allowed to touch anything, but your eyes have powers. They can travel anywhere. Like when you were a kid and your mom took you shopping: *Touch with your eyes only.* You let your gaze bounce around the kitchen, peer into the living room. On the bookshelf, a row of medical thrillers. You sit on the couch, head tilted, trying to decipher the titles. What are you looking for? A pattern? A theme? An explanation for who he is and what he does, tucked between *Postmortem* and *The Andromeda Strain*?

It is right here, pulsing through the walls, like a quiet roar underneath the hardwood floors. The truth of him, encased in the very heart of this house.

Every item tells a story that may or may not be true. The medical thrillers: a dead wife's paperback collection, left over from a string of summer vacations, or a warning sign of a dark obsession with the human body? Childhood photos of Cecilia learning to swim in a motel's pool, "graduating" third grade, lost under a witch hat for Halloween: the usual tokens of family life, or props in the theater of his existence, placed here to keep up appearances?

This house—does it know him? Or is it a movie set, an alternative world, built piece by piece, to hide his true self?

There are the things you see, and there are the things you notice for their absence: No landline. No desktop computer. You assume there is a laptop somewhere, locked in a drawer and password-protected, taken out only for administrative tasks and homework. Their cell phones live tucked away in their respective pockets. Cecilia doesn't even get to keep hers: she has it for school and for art class, whenever she's away from him. As soon as she gets home, he holds out his hand and she gives it to him. She is thirteen. On the rare occasions she complains about his phone rules, he says he doesn't want her to waste her time on social media, swears that she'll thank him later. She sighs but doesn't challenge him.

Your eyes return to the paperbacks, to the photos, to the neatly stacked nature magazines on the coffee table. Looking for answers. For a man, for a sign of life. Searching for his story.

At night, you dream. Visions that have followed you from the shed: You, running hard on a country road lined with trees. Behind you, the sound of his breath, the menace of his stride catching up with yours.

You startle awake. Even in your dreams, he chases you. But you run, and for a few moments it feels real to you. You hold on to those sensations as long as you can in the dark, the momentum of your body, the whipping of your arms at your sides, the delicious burn of the air up and down your throat.

YOU MAKE YOUR most startling discovery one night, over a plate of veggie pot pie. Cecilia's eyes are on the TV. Nick from Arkansas has picked "Mottos" for four hundred.

"These two Latin words symbolize the ethos of the U.S. Marines," Alex Trebek says.

"Semper fidelis."

You speak at the same time. You and the perfect father. He turns his head slowly. For the first time in his daughter's presence, he looks straight into your eyes.

"How did you know?"

His tone is purposeful, focused. Something here means a lot to him.

You do not want to tell him the real reason. You want to keep your memories of the 2012 Marine Corps Marathon to yourself. An evening train from Penn Station to Union Station, one night at a hotel, and a wake-up call at four in the morning. A bus packed with nylon silhouettes, a hazy walk to the Pentagon before sunrise. Men in uniform searching your running belt, browsing through pouches of caffeinated gel, single packs of Advil, nutrition bars. The national anthem, then a gun start. Thirty thousand runners. Four hours and twenty minutes. The Virginia woods on each side of the course, an unending stretch of highway in the suffocating heat, and finally the finish line. More uniforms. Their hands presenting medals. Your tired legs, your sweaty body, a lanyard around your neck. The runner next to you uttering two words to the marine in front of him. *Semper fi.*

You do not want him to have any of this. You do not want him to know that one day, should the occasion present itself, you could run.

Not now, though. Your body couldn't do it now. Rule number two of staying alive outside the shed: You will get ready. Until then, you will sit. You will eat. You will watch *Jeopardy!* You will field questions at the dinner table.

With a father and a daughter waiting for your answer, you search your brain for the most plausible lie.

"I had a fitness instructor who used to be a marine," you say. "He taught it to us."

A perplexed father raises an eyebrow. Plays with his pot pie. This is unlike him. He's not a man who hesitates. He eats or he doesn't.

Cecilia leans forward conspiratorially. "He was a marine, too." She points at her dad with her chin. He tries to interject, "Cecilia—" but she continues. "He dropped out of college to serve."

Your fork clinks against your plate.

A marine.

"Wow."

You can't think of anything else to say.

"Hospital corpsman," he mumbles, his voice low. Forced to give you a part of himself. Something he was hoping to keep, like you with the marathon.

You don't know what a hospital corpsman is. You don't know what a hospital corpsman does. He dropped out of college to be one, so presumably being a hospital corpsman doesn't require a medical degree.

A story outlines itself: A man who wanted to be a doctor but couldn't do it. Distracted from his coursework by the thoughts swirling inside his brain, one obsessive circle, a deepening riff inside of him. He didn't drop out *to* serve, like his daughter just said. Rather, he dropped out *and* served. He became a hospital corpsman. He was discharged, honorably or dishonorably—you have no way to know.

Something brought him here, wherever you are. He found a job. He found a wife. He became a man with a family and a house. He became the man you know.

You set your fork down, rest your hand flat on the place mat. *He dropped out to serve.*

Memories: A friend's grandfather, a funeral at Arlington Cemetery. Fourth of July barbecues, your father behind the grill, your mother in a red dress. A country song about the flag, about freedom and revenge. In your class at NYU, a veteran with a service dog who became the class mascot. Words. Five of them. What people said when the time came, in conversation, to acknowledge certain things.

Five words that Cecilia, who grew up hearing the story of how her dad dropped out of college to serve his country, is expecting to hear.

You pick your fork back up. You can't look at him, so you stare above his shoulder as you say it.

"Thank you for your service."

He nods. Your mouth fills with acid.

CHAPTER 19

The woman in the house

The cramps come on a Friday afternoon. You don't get cramps. Haven't in years. At first, you figured your period had stopped because of the stress. He's not a reckless man. He uses condoms. You worried for a while that your cycle would start again. Then, you lost all the weight, and you figured that was that. Perhaps your body knew that life in the shed would be easier that way.

Soon you will bleed. You need pads or tampons, need him to buy them for you. You will have to ask. At this prospect, your insides twist tighter.

You already pissed him off this morning. In the bathroom, as you got dressed, you pointed to the tight waistband of your jeans, the button straining against your abdomen. He has been feeding you, and you have gained weight. "Do you think it would be possible," you tried, then started over. "I'm so sorry. But would it be possible to get the next size up? Whenever you can?" He sighed. Looked at you like you had done it on purpose, to spite him.

You are not in a position to make any more requests. Not for a while.

You try to lie down in a fetal position, head in the crook of your handcuffed arm. Everything about this inconveniences you. The dullness in your abdomen, insistent. Your body testing your limits, daring you to handle more pain.

AT DINNER, HE pulls his phone out of his pocket. This is a thing that happens inside the house: phones appear out of nowhere, the TV chirps to life, a car drives by while you sit in the kitchen. With every occurrence, the tips of your fingers tingle.

"I'm going to the store this weekend." A father looks up at his daughter. "Need anything?"

Cecilia thinks. She mentions a four-color pen, maybe shampoo. He nods and taps on his phone.

"Anything else?"

His gaze is still trained on her. She shakes her head no.

Your lower abdomen is burning. For the entire meal, you've struggled to sit up. The cramps are worse than you remember, pain radiating from the center of you. You clench your jaw. Grind your teeth. Something is coming, and there is nothing you can do to stop it. You need help. You need fucking pads or tampons.

He's about to put the phone back in his pocket when you say it.

"If you're able, actually, tampons or pads would be . . . lovely." You chuckle like someone who still has a private life and just gave a part of it away.

His forehead creases. For a few moments, his fingers hover over the phone. He tries to be nice to you in front of his daughter. He's supposed to. He hands you utensils, sometimes puts food on your plate instead of letting you help yourself. But what you just said—he doesn't like it. He puts his phone back in his pocket without typing, gets up, begins clearing the table. Cecilia goes to help.

"Go upstairs," he tells her. "I've got it."

He listens for her bedroom door, waits until it shuts. Before you can think of stepping out of his reach, his fingers are on you—pulling you by your arm away from the table, pinning you against the kitchen wall. He presses down on your neck, enough to make it hard to swallow. You are back in the shed. Back in a world that belongs entirely to him, where the light doesn't come in. Four walls, no windows. One meal a day. The only world Rachel knew.

"Did you think it was a good idea? Asking me to do your little shopping? Run your errands?"

You try to shake your head no. You can't move. Can't talk. Can't tell him you're sorry, you didn't mean to.

"It's always something. New pants this, tampons that."

Your throat emits a gurgling sound. He lets go with a nudge. You stay still. As much as you want to fall back on your chair, put your head between your knees, search for your breath, you know now's not the time. The man in the kitchen isn't done.

"I'm beginning to think it was a mistake, bringing you in here."

You rub the back of your neck, nod your head yes and shake it no, the same way you used to after a day at the computer.

"I'm sorry," you say. "I wasn't trying to . . . But you're right. You're absolutely right."

He turns to face the window—shades down, always—so his back is to you. He's not scared of the things you could do. Jump him from behind, reach for his neck. This is a man who has no reason to be afraid of you.

"I didn't think," you tell him. "I'm sorry."

You reach for his arm, then take your hand back. Too volatile. The wrong contact at the wrong time, and it will be the end of you.

"Come on," you offer instead. "Let's go upstairs."

He whips around. You take a step back. It only annoys him more.

"Upstairs?" he says. His voice is a furious whisper. His fingers close around your arm again. "Great idea. Just great." You don't understand until he raises his gaze to the ceiling: "She just went upstairs. Fucking genius."

Cecilia. Still wide-awake in her room. This kid. You swear, she'll be the death of you.

He shoves you back onto your chair. "Just sit down and shut up," he tells you. "Can you do that? Can you just shut up for a second?"

You sit, tight-lipped, as he remains leaning over you for a few moments. He straightens his back and stares in the distance as he does it—you can't see but you can feel the explosion of his boot against your calf under the kitchen table, his foot crashing into your leg. You recoil. Bite your lips, hold back a whimper. He's not a man who kicks all that often. He squeezes and twists and pulls and does all manner of things with much more ease. Kicking, that's a card he plays only when he can't think of anything else. Like that time in the beginning, when he found you in the shed and knew—just by looking at you, the guilt in your eyes, the position of your body next to the door— that you had fiddled with the padlock. There was some kicking that evening. A few other times, too. When he strikes, it's always with his feet. Never with his hands.

He heads back to the kitchen counter, his eyes fleeing from yours. There are times when he can't look at you. Times that tell you shame still lives somewhere inside this man. Buried and smothered and ignored, but shame all the same. You like to believe that it takes hold every once in a while. You like to believe that it burns him.

LATER, AFTER HIS daughter falls asleep, he steps into the bedroom. The cramps are still here, but you're not bleeding yet.

After he leaves, a new wave of pain shakes you from within. You hold on to the bed frame like a drowning person clinging to a floating piece of wood.

You bite the inside of your cheeks and taste metal.

Don't fight it. Let the pain take over. Lose yourself in it.

You are here.

You are bleeding.

You are alive.

Once the wave subsides, an impulse from another life: You run your free hand down the back of your calves, the bruised one and the intact one. Feel the bones, unbroken. Start flexing your toes.

CHAPTER 20

Emily

On the day of the 5K, I get up at six and drive my father's old Honda Civic to the start. Eric and Yuwanda sleep in. "I'm way too hungover to watch people run," Eric writes on the group text. "But have fun bb girl. Say hi to the Widower for me."

I stand in the town square. Volunteers showed up at sunrise to set up and clear the course. About a mile in, I'm told, will be the first fluid station and the Garcías' orange slices. Around me, runners in nylon stretch, jog in place, talk about the races they've done and the ones they want to do. Judge Byrne goes around the crowd, greeting everyone.

I twist my fingers in the lining of my pockets to warm them up. My original plan was to set up the hot-cocoa station before the race started, but I, like Eric, had a few drinks last night, and getting out of bed that early was a physical impossibility. And now that I'm here and people are milling about, I might as well hang around and see if I can spot Aidan.

He pulls up in his white pickup truck. Unfairly beautiful, even from afar. Even with his old trapper hat and ski gloves and snow boots. He hasn't zipped his coat all the way up, and it opens on a flannel shirt, his neck exposed. I shiver on his behalf. His kid stands close to him, bundled up in a pastel puffer jacket, white beanie, hands stuffed in her pockets. There's a gravitas to her, something just a bit too heavy. Hard to tell if she's shy, sad, or both. Maybe that's just what teenage girls look like, and I'm only now noticing it. From what I remember, there was nothing easy about being a girl. Especially one who's just lost her mother.

FINALLY, AROUND SEVEN o'clock, Judge Byrne grabs a mic. There's the echo of feedback, scaring birds away from the surrounding trees.

People laugh as the judge struggles to turn the thing off and back on again.

"Good morning, everyone," he says, once he's wrestled the mic into submission. "I want to say a few words to get us started." The crowd goes silent. "We're here today to support a very, very special family. I take great pride in knowing that I'm part of this community. One whose members look out for one another."

There's a round of applause. The judge waits a few seconds to continue. "I want to thank everyone here today. Our volunteers, our spectators, and of course our runners." More applause. Another pause until silence returns. "As you know, this race is a fundraiser. I'm so pleased to announce that, thanks to everyone's generous donations, we've already raised two thousand dollars for our neighbors and friends."

People cheer. I wince. I don't know how Aidan reacts because I can't bring myself to look at him. I don't know who I was kidding, hoping that this town would help without making him feel like a charity case. That we would make this about him, not us.

Judge Byrne looks around. "Now," he says, the mic beginning to moan again. "Where is our guest of honor?"

Oh dear lord.

I have a brief hope that no one will be able to spot him and the judge will move on, but Mrs. Cooper rats him out.

"Right here, Judge!"

Aidan walks up to the judge and takes the mic. No feedback here. Almost like the man knows how to handle electronic equipment.

"I'm not much of a public speaker," he says, in a way that makes me want to hide him under my coat and smuggle him away from the crowd. "But I want to say thank you. And I want to say how grateful we both are, Cecilia and I, for this community. We miss her mom so much. We miss her more every day. She would be so moved by this."

The crowd loses it. There's another round of claps. Aidan says thank you a couple more times, then gives the mic back to Judge Byrne.

The judge clears his throat. "Now, for the not-so-good news: signing up for a race is one thing, but you still have to run it." There are some faint laughs. "Have a safe race. Enjoy this beautiful day. And if you get cold, don't forget there's hot cocoa waiting for you at the finish line."

That would be me.

The judge's nephew, who graduated from the police academy last summer, fires a starter gun. Jakob Dylan's husky voice sputters out of a speaker to sing "One Headlight." The runners set off.

I walk to the restaurant, unlock the front door, flip a light switch, and bring the dining room to life. The place is still, quiet. All mine.

At the back, I dig up the folding table we keep in the pantry for events. The finish line is a block away. I lock up again, then carry the table over and set it farther down from the finish, to give runners time to catch their breath before they reach me.

I'm crouched down, checking the safety mechanism, when I hear it.

"Hi."

My head snaps back up in surprise and hits the side of the table with a bang. A sharp pain radiates from the top of my skull.

Motherfucker.

His fingers brace the point of impact, as if he could retroactively prevent the collision.

"I'm so sorry," he says. "Didn't mean to startle you."

I get up, massaging my head. He takes the side of my arm, helps me steady myself.

"You okay?"

I search the depths of my brain for something, anything, any combination of letters that would do the trick, even vaguely.

"Hi," I manage. "I'm fine. Really." I smile, stop rubbing my scalp, as if to prove something.

He looks over his shoulder. His daughter is standing next to Judge Byrne, who is trying to engage her in conversation—explaining a riveting chapter of our town history, I would assume.

"Thank you for doing this," he tells me, gesturing at what will soon be a hot-cocoa station. "Especially so early on a Saturday morning."

I nod. "It's no trouble. The restaurant is just around the corner."

He places a hand on the folding table. "Let me help. It's the least I can do, after making you bang your head like that."

"You really don't have to."

"Please."

He glances back at the judge briefly. "I'm happy to be here. I am. But . . . how do I put this?"

"You don't love a crowd."

He bites his lip. "I'm that good at hiding it, huh?"

Something flutters in my rib cage.

"Come to think of it," I say, "a sous-chef would be nice. Especially, as you said, given my recent injury."

"Say no more."

His hand lands on the small of my back, ushering me toward the restaurant. "Cece," he says in the direction of his daughter, "I'm going to help out. You're okay to hang out for a bit?" I turn back to see her give him an unconvincing nod.

In front of the restaurant, I search my pocket for the keys, hyper-aware of my movements. The lock gives me trouble. "You got it?" he asks. I tell him yes, fumble for a few more seconds. Finally, the door opens to reveal the empty dining room. The tables are set in preparation for tonight, forks and knives and wineglasses gleaming for an invisible crowd. Saturdays are for dinner service only; brunch is on Sundays.

"Welcome to Amandine: insider edition," I tell him.

He looks around. "So this is what it looks like when all of us have cleared out."

His gaze meets mine. The last time it was just the two of us in a room, this room, actually, I was a teenager and he was married.

"Follow me."

This is my world. He's mine to shepherd, mine to use. We shed our coats and I lead him to the kitchen, switch on the lights to reveal the clean stations, every surface dutifully scrubbed, each utensil in its place, every container labeled and put away. Every parcel of chrome shiny, every tile the purest white. He gives a little whistle.

"Oh, that's right," I say, like it's no big deal. "It's been a while since you were back here."

"No one's invited me in since."

So you were stuck, I want to say, *like a vampire on a doorstep.*

I keep my vampire thoughts to myself.

"It's . . . unbelievably clean," he continues.

I smile like he's just given me an Oscar. "My head chef and I agree on maybe one thing in this world, and it's that you don't go home at the end of a service until your kitchen is as clean as the day it was installed."

He runs a finger on the prep table nearest to him and nods, then looks around again.

"So what can I do?" he asks.

"Well, first, you can wash your hands."

I show him to the sink. We soap our hands in silence, take turns rinsing under the hot stream. I hand him a clean dish towel. He dries his fingers diligently, one by one.

"Now what?"

"This way."

He follows me into the pantry. I gather cocoa powder, vanilla, cinnamon.

"Can you see a plastic jar with a tag on it that says 'granulated sugar'?" I ask. "It should be somewhere near us."

We squint together. "Right here," he says, and reaches for the airtight container on the top shelf. His flannel shirt hikes up his abdomen, the briefest flash of skin in the dark of the pantry. I force myself to look away.

"Excellent."

I say it like I've got it all under control, like I wouldn't give a kidney to be trapped in the pantry with this man forever.

Next step is the walk-in fridge, where I grab a gallon of milk in each hand. He imitates me.

"Look at you," I say. "You're a natural."

He chuckles. It feels like the first bite of a freshly baked chocolate chip cookie, like a warm bath after a rainy day, like the first sip of a dry martini—knowing I made it happen.

We return to the kitchen and put the milk containers down. I pick up the stainless steel dispenser we store in a corner. Aidan leans to help me but I tell him it's okay—the dispenser isn't heavy when it's empty. "When it's full of four gallons of hot cocoa, don't worry— I'll have a job for you." He laughs again. It's almost too easy to be around him, too comfortable, an indictment on how trickily the world behaves the rest of the time.

We work side by side, his gestures mirroring mine. Together, we bring the milk to a simmer in a large pot. We add cocoa powder, sugar, vanilla, cinnamon. I jog back to the pantry. "Smell this," I tell him when I return. He leans in to take a whiff. "Ancho chile powder," I say, and he asks, "Really?" and I tell him yes, my dad insisted on it—it's his recipe, and once you try it, you can never go back.

"I trust you," he says. It moves me more than it should.

He watches as I add a dash of the chile powder to the mix and stir. Just as I'm about to reach for more vanilla, something—a flicker from him to me, a movement in my peripheral vision—stops me.

"What's this?"

His arm extends toward the base of my throat, the small dip where my vocal cords begin. There, his fingers land on the locket I slipped around my neck this morning. An electric current bristles from my neck to my stomach.

"Oh. It was my mom's," I tell him. I hold it up so he can see the design. Three women—three graces is what the jeweler had told her—in flowing dresses, holding hands, one of them pointing to something in the distance. Maybe the sky. In the designer's mind, I think the women were just going on a stroll, but to me, they've always looked like they were performing some kind of ritual. Casting a spell.

"I don't wear it to work because it's a bit . . . much," I tell Aidan. "My mom liked it because it was so different from everything she owned. And I like it because it reminds me she could be fun."

He touches the locket again, picks it up with two fingers as if to feel its weight.

"I think it's a wonderful tribute," he says.

He lets go of the pendant. Our respective ghosts float in the kitchen. I let them haunt us a bit before breaking the silence again: "Do you spend a lot of time in the kitchen? At home? Or are you a takeout guy?"

He tells me he cooks. Nothing fancy, he says. Then, gesturing around the kitchen: "Nothing like what happens here." He's a home cook, a functional one. He wants his daughter to eat well. Not that he minds being in the kitchen. Preparing food relaxes him. "It's always been on my list of chores," he says, "even before—" He stops. The milk bubbles. I stare at the pot's contents, focus on the ladle dipping in and out of the liquid. "Well, you know," he adds.

I look up at him. It costs me a little, shedding a layer of me, allowing him to see whatever's underneath, but it's worth it. A current of knowledge streams between us. The world has given me this gift, this man in this kitchen, all mine for a few minutes. I hope he can hear the things I can't tell him out loud.

Something stings the back of my hand. A droplet of hot cocoa, boiling hot, sputtering out of the pot. "Oops." I bring the heat down, wipe my hand on the towel we used earlier. "I think this is ready."

I turn to him. "Want a taste?"

"Only a fool would say no."

An image flashes in my brain—holding the ladle up to his lips, one hand underneath to catch any drips, tilting the ladle back, watching him drink. Too much. Too on the nose, too risky. I abandon the ladle, retrieve a white coffee cup from the cabinet above the counter. The cocoa is thick, with the perfect color I recognize from my father's batches. We made this. We made this together.

"Here."

His fingers brush against mine as he grabs the cup. My stomach twitches. He takes a sip. I watch in expectation as his eyes close. When he opens them again, there's a sparkle.

"Holy shit," he says. "Sorry. I just didn't know cocoa could taste this way."

He goes back for another sip. I smile. There's nothing to say, nothing to add. This is a perfect moment, and even I know that the only sound thing to do is to stand back and savor it.

HE INSISTS ON washing his empty cup. I tell him I can do it, that I have to clean our utensils anyway. "Don't worry about those," he says, and he scrubs them, too. I put away our dry ingredients, discard the empty containers of milk. Together, we transfer the hot cocoa to the steel dispenser and lift it up. He lets out a grunt.

"See?" I say. "I told you it'd be heavy."

We take careful steps out of the kitchen and into the dining room, our bodies moving with each other. When we reach the door, he leans against it to push it open. A gust of wind tousles his hair and the light hits his face just so.

"There you are!"

Judge Byrne watches as we set the barrel on top of the folding table. I run back to the kitchen for paper cups and napkins. Aidan follows me.

"You didn't have to do that," I say.

"I know. But I'm a part of this cocoa mission now. I'm not going to drop out at the last minute."

When we return to the finish line, Mrs. Cooper is approaching, supple and elegant in her navy-blue leggings and white vest, her pony-tail bouncing with each stride.

I cup my hands around my mouth. "Almost there, Mrs. Cooper!" It feels forced, like a performance I put on. But what happened in the kitchen with Aidan has lifted me up, and I'm willing to play along. Mrs. Cooper gives me a little wave. Less than a minute later, she's the official winner of the first Thomas Family 5K.

Judge Byrne claps and extends congratulations. There are no med-als, no race swag. Just the promise of hot cocoa, which I go to pour into a paper cup.

Aidan materializes at my side. He pushes down on the handle as I position the cup under the spout. Before I can say anything, two more runners show up—Seth, one of the kids from my former high school, and his father, Mr. Roberts, who works in the city. Together, we pour two more cups.

Soon runners are coming in at a steady pace. We find a rhythm. I'm on paper cup duty, he manages the handle. I hand out each cup along with words of admiration—*So well done, you were amazing, I never could have.* Aidan focuses on the task at hand. He fiddles with the stack of cups, checks that the dispenser still feels hot to the touch. This is the man who sits at my bar: allergic to attention, shoulders hunched, eyes trained on anything but your own. His kid sits on a bench on the other side of the road, headphone wires snaking from her pocket to her ears. Her father's daughter.

About forty minutes in, finishers become more spread out. Mrs. Cooper is chatting with Judge Byrne, asking if he could officiate her cousin's wedding in Poughkeepsie three weeks from now. Aidan and I wait for our next runner in silence. The momentum we'd built up at the height of the race has died down. We've run out of tasks to keep our hands busy.

"So how's work?" I try.

He smiles. "Work's good."

"Can I tell you a secret?"

He says of course.

"I don't think I really know what a lineman does. I know it has to do with power lines, obviously. But that's about it."

A laugh. "No one knows what linemen do." He rolls his eyes. "Even some linemen seem confused about that."

Basically, he tells me, their mission is to keep electricity running in people's homes. "That's why you see us up there, fiddling with power lines. We fix the ones that are broken, maintain the ones that aren't. If there's a storm and the lines get knocked down, we work on that. Sometimes we go to people's houses and update their installations."

I nod. "So I take it you're not afraid of heights."

He shakes his head no. "I love it up there. It's so . . . peaceful, if that makes sense?"

I tell him I get it. Working on a project, head literally in the clouds, and no one to bother him: it does sound like his element.

"Besides," he adds, "you get such a good view of everything from up there. The river, the mountains . . . I mean, look what I saw the other day."

He takes his phone out of his pocket and leans toward me. I smell pine needles and laundry detergent and freshly shampooed hair. I want to close my eyes and commit the combination to memory so I can remember it at night, search for him next time I wash my clothes or go for a hike. But there's something he wants to show me, and I must focus. His thumb flicks through a series of images. I catch flashes of hills and rooftops, a screenshot of a recipe for veggie lasagna, his daughter on a trail.

His finger stops on the image he was looking for: a large bird of prey, wings open, gliding over the beech trees behind the church.

"Wow."

It's my turn to get closer. I have an excuse now. I need to see the bird. I can pretend this has nothing to do with the proximity of his body next to mine, his strong arms and taut abdomen and his neck like a swan's, long and slim and graceful and proud.

"It's so . . . majestic," I say.

"That's what I thought, too."

He contemplates the bird, then turns his gaze to me. It's like he's been holding on to this photo for weeks, until he found someone who could appreciate it as much as he does.

"It's a red-tailed hawk," he says. "At least according to the internet."

"He's so big. I bet he could pick up a small dog."

He nods.

I slide two fingers across his phone screen, zoom closer on the hawk.

"Look at it," I say. "Surveying his domain. Hunting for prey. He's so beautiful."

Something hangs between us, a deeper truth that neither of us would know how to put into words.

"Excuse me?"

Bob, Mrs. Cooper's husband, stands in front of the table, paper cup in hand.

"Sorry," I say, and go to pour him some hot cocoa. Aidan puts his phone away.

Runners turn into walkers. A trio of residents from the retirement home cross the finish line together, holding hands. We wait a few more seconds, but Judge Byrne confirms that they were the last participants. There's one last round of congratulations, then people start scattering.

I stack abandoned paper cups, wipe splatters of hot cocoa off the table. Aidan follows me to the restaurant, helps me bring back the dispenser and the folding table. I don't tell him he doesn't have to. I'm done pretending I don't want his help.

Once the dispenser is scrubbed clean and the table tucked back in the pantry, Aidan searches for his words.

"Thanks for letting me keep you company," he says. "It was really . . . Well. I enjoyed it."

"I'm the one who should thank you." The moment is warm, with the lightness of a secret held close for too long and finally released. "I couldn't have asked for a better sous-chef."

He smiles and says he has to go find his kid. I tell him to go, go, go, dismiss him with a wave as if I don't dread his looming absence.

I lock up and walk back to the Civic, where I lay my coat on the backseat. When I look up again, my body tenses. My car keys dig into the palm of my hand. My armpits prickle with sweat.

There is a silhouette on the other side of my car, visible through the passenger-side window. Someone's leaning against the frame. Someone I didn't see or hear when I walked across the parking lot a few seconds ago.

"Sorry. Did I scare you again?"

Every muscle in my body relaxes.

"No," I tell him. "I'm sorry. It's me. I didn't recognize you."

Aidan pulls his phone out of his pocket and gives it a little waggle. "I wanted you to have my number. In case you ever need anything, you know? Shoot me a text. Give me a call."

With the focus of a surgeon opening a patient's chest cavity, I fish my own phone out of the back pocket of my jeans. He waits until I'm ready, screen unlocked, contacts list pulled up, then dictates the string of numbers.

"There you go," he says when I'm done typing.

He goes to step away, then hangs back and eyes the Civic.

"Don't take this the wrong way, but isn't your car older than you?"

His eyes are gleaming, his smile crooked. He's not mocking me. Just teasing.

"Almost," I tell him. "Used to be my father's. Wait until you hear the drive belt squeak. And don't get me started on the transmission."

"Bad?"

"Terrible. And manual."

He scrunches up his nose in sympathy.

"She's not all bad," I say, and pat the Civic's roof. "She's just been through a lot."

He nods. I look down at my phone, where his number is still displayed across the screen, and hit "new contact." By the time I add his name and save, he's gone.

I slip the phone into the front pocket of my jeans. For the entirety of the drive home, the screen stays warm against my thigh.

CHAPTER 21

The woman in the house

The morning after you start bleeding is a Saturday. With the tip of your toes, you nudge your bloodied underwear into a corner of the bathroom. He hands you a new pair. You line it with toilet paper, your best option for now. He watches for a second, then looks away.

At breakfast, Cecilia, between bites of scrambled eggs, asks her dad if the thing is today. He asks if she means the race and she says yes and he says yes, too. She groans.

"It'll be fine," he tells her. "It won't last that long."

After breakfast, he takes you back to the room. He doesn't explain. You don't ask. You wait for him to be gone and curl up into a ball. The pain has begun to dull around the edges of your abdomen, but it is still here. Still bending you in half.

Hours later, the front door opens and slams shut, then immediately opens again.

"Cecilia!"

You smile at his pissed-off yelp. She must have beaten him to the door by a second and slammed it in his face. A daughter openly, explosively, angry at her father.

Furious steps pound up the stairs. Another door bangs, closer to you—Cecilia's room. His own steps—heavy, purposeful, quick but never rushing—follow.

"Cecilia!"

He knocks on her door. A muffled voice tells him to go away. Silence, then a sigh. He makes his way back to the other end of the hallway, then down the stairs.

That kid. His kid. In this moment, you love her so much.

Later in the day, you hear him busy himself in the kitchen. He comes and uncuffs you for dinner. He and Cecilia eat in silence, eyes on their mac and cheese. Halfway through the meal, he makes a new attempt.

"I was helping a friend. That's all."

She keeps chewing her food.

"Cecilia. I'm talking to you."

She looks up, eyes narrowed. "You were ignoring me," she says. "I didn't want to go, but you dragged me to this thing. And then you made us stay the entire morning. And you completely forgot about me."

You assume the thing in question is the race he mentioned at breakfast, the one he promised wouldn't take up too much of their day. Cecilia stabs the contents of her bowl with her fork. You know that combination of facial expressions—gaze down, jaw clenched, brows furrowed. She's holding back tears. You feel an urge to pull her into you, to hold her tight. Rock her back and forth like you hope her mother used to.

"Do you have any idea," she asks him, "how fucking boring that judge guy is?"

He says something about language. She doesn't listen, doesn't apologize. Instead, she pushes her bowl to the side and gets up. He goes to grab her arm, but she swats him away and storms back upstairs. You watch so intently you forget to breathe. He's going to explode, you think. He's going to run after her. He will drag her back to the kitchen by her hair if he must. He will remind her who's in charge.

But he doesn't move. His gaze trails after his daughter and lands on her empty chair. He stares at it for a few moments, then retrieves his phone from his pocket. Unlocks the screen, checks it, and puts the phone back where it came from. A sigh. His leg bobs up and down. He's impatient. Waiting, you would guess, for something that hasn't arrived yet.

He takes you back up after dinner. He'll return in a few hours, once his daughter is asleep and the house quiet. For now, he wants you back where you can't hurt him, in the room, handcuffed to the radiator.

You go first. That's how he prefers it. Always makes you walk in front of him, where he can see you. He opens the door to the room and nudges you in.

Your foot lands on something soft. In the dark, you can't tell what it is, but you know that you don't want him to see.

"What was that?" you ask, tilting your head to the side, as if listening intently. It's not subtle, but it's the only strategy you can think of. He stops, listens up. With your foot, you nudge the soft item in the direction of the bed, pray that your aim is right.

"I can't hear anything," he says.

"Must have been a bird or something. Sorry."

He sighs, resumes motioning you inside, shuts the door. When he switches the light on, the item is nowhere to be seen.

You wait for the post-dinner part of the evening to be over. Some nights, you can hear him and Cecilia downstairs, chatting. Tonight, there is only silence.

You squint, try to peer under the bed, but you can't see. Can't even make out the contours of whatever you just hid there.

You hear water running through pipes, the toilet flushing. Cecilia must be brushing her teeth, getting ready for bed. Her bedroom door shuts for the last time today.

You wait for the world to go still. The doorknob rattles. A father steps in, closes the door behind him. He does to you the things he has decided must be done to somebody.

After, you run through the usual drill: you lie down near the bed, settle for the night. He grabs your arm and handcuffs you to the frame. A couple of tugs on the chain, and he's out.

You wait for him to have gone to bed, too. For his footsteps down the hallway, for his bedroom door snapping shut. And then you wait some more. Finally, when you know you're as safe as you're ever going to be, you wiggle a foot under the bed.

Nothing. You turn your head, squint. You'd need a flashlight. You'd need to not be handcuffed to the bed. You shift your position, angle your hips one way, then another. You put pressure on your rotator cuff. Your body aches and pulls and bends itself into unnatural angles. Finally, you feel it.

You push it toward you with your heel. Move it with your toes. You work silently, take breaks to listen for a stir in his bedroom. The house stays quiet. Finally, your fingers close around it.

You wait for your eyes to absorb the darkness some more. Focus your gaze, implore the pale squares of moonlight around the blackout shades to do their job. Between your fingers: plastic wrappers, what looks like bright green and blue, a geometric pattern. Something pliable, soft, almost bouncy. The outline of a logo you used to see every month.

Sanitary pads. Three, four of them, held together by a rubber band.

At the back of the stack, a piece of paper. Thankfully, she wrote in large, round letters, using a purple marker. You decipher the words one by one. "Hope these help. Let me know if you need more. Cecilia."

She heard. She listened. After dinner, tonight—after she left the table in a huff—she went and took some from her personal stash. She wrote the note, slid the package under your door. Her father must have told her to stay away from your room, but she didn't care. She knows he hasn't gone to the store yet. She knows you need help. She decided she had your back. She chose you over him.

You press the pads against your chest. You won't use them. Can't. He would notice, demand to know where they're from. You will keep lining your underwear with toilet paper until he caves—if he caves—and returns from the store with the cheapest box of tampons.

For now, you feel the pads rise and fall with your rib cage. Someone cares. Someone heard you needed something and went out of their way to give it to you. You bask in that feeling, your first true kindness in five years.

And then—you freeze. Your fingers clutch the plastic wrappers. The cameras. The fucking cameras. The ones he said were everywhere—*in this room, at the front door.* You have to believe what he said. *I'm watching. I'll always be watching.*

You haven't done anything wrong, you tell yourself. But it won't matter. It never does.

There are only bad choices. Leaving the pads out is the worst of all. Then, he would see them for sure. If you hide them, you enter the world of maybe. Maybe he won't watch the video. Maybe he won't find out. Maybe you and Cecilia will get away with it all.

Your books are stacked close to the bed. You reach for the thick *It* paperback. Tuck the pads between two chapters. You slip the note in a different book, your beat-up copy of *A Tree Grows in Brooklyn.* Best to scatter the evidence. The pads would anger him, but the note—he couldn't handle it. His daughter, going behind his back. It would be the end of you. The end of everything.

You do not fall asleep. Not for a while.

You are buzzing with anticipation, overwhelmed with a realization.

I was helping a friend.

That's what he told her.

A friend. A man in society, bonding with others. Holding other people's hearts close to his own.

People say friendship but they mean love. It's all love at the end of the day.

And now, for the first time in years, you know how that feels, too. You know without a doubt. Someone has your back. Someone likes you.

CHAPTER 22

Number three

He was going to be a father. Very soon.

After he found out, at the very beginning of the pregnancy, he stopped drinking.

Cold turkey, he said. Can't walk around getting sloppy. Can't risk saying too much. Not ever, but especially not with a kid in the picture.

Boy or girl, I asked.

Girl, he said.

I thought: One day she'll be my age.

What if I can't do it? he said.

I asked what he meant.

After she's born, he said. What if I can't do it?

I was about to ask if he meant "it" as in being a father or "it" as in what he was about to do to me.

And then I had my response, I suppose, when he did "it." Trying to prove something to himself.

It was the great enigma of his life, what he did to me, and he wasn't done solving it.

If he had let me, I would have told him not to worry. I would have told him that if I had to guess, he would go on doing it for a very long time.

CHAPTER 23

Emily

I wasn't going to text him so soon. I wanted to wait a day or two, maybe three.

Lying on my bed, freshly back from dinner service, I unlocked my phone and looked up facts about red-tailed hawks. Once I found what I was looking for, I started typing. I stopped. Hesitated. I resumed typing.

"Hi! It's Emily (your cocoa conspirator). Thanks again for all your help today. By the way, did you know a red-tailed hawk can lift a dog up to twenty pounds?"

I added a ":O." My thumb hovered over the delete key. Was Aidan an emoticon guy? I had no way of guessing where he fell on that spectrum, and I wasn't prepared to get it wrong. Delete. Delete.

I proofread the message once, then twice, then a couple more times until the words stopped making sense. I changed my "hi" into a "hey"—more casual. I removed "(your cocoa conspirator)." I agonized some more. What if I bothered him? What if giving me his number was nothing more than a business gesture? What if, when he said, "In case you ever need anything," he meant, *If you need your electricity fixed I'll take care of it in exchange for money, as that is my job?*

I closed my eyes. When I opened them back up, I was holding my breath. I kept holding it as I hit "send." The message did a little *woop* as it soared from my phone to his.

It's been fifteen minutes. No answer. No "read." Just a note that the text has been delivered. I don't even know if I regret sending it. My brain is burned out on anxiety.

In the bathroom, I remove my makeup. Take off my uniform, drop my starched button-down and black slacks on the tile. Steam fills the room.

I won't think about him. That's what I tell myself as I step under the stream. As my hands brush my hair back. As my fingers travel over my breasts, down my waist, between my legs. *I won't think about him,* but I do, all the time. I carry a yearning inside me, and sometimes it feels good to let it swallow me.

I rub the places that make me forget everything. In the shower, in this moment, I am not a lovesick puppy. I am a woman who knows her body, knows how to make it feel good. My ribs expand and fall. My palm presses against the wall. The things I see, quick and elusive like moths: his shirt lifting when he reached for the jar of granulated sugar; the place I wanted to kiss, where his neck meets his collarbone; his hands on the table, hovering next to mine; his hands grabbing me, touching me, molding me to his image. My entire self folding into his. I shudder, whisper his name to myself. Somewhere in my brain registers the faint hope that the smacking of the water on the tile will drown me out.

I open my eyes. I'm alone again. I soap myself, wash and rinse my hair, watch the foam trickle into the drain. When I step out, I tell myself I'm going to take my time before I check my phone. I wrap myself in a towel, start combing my hair until I can't stand it any longer. What the fuck am I doing, standing here with my phone just feet away? Trying to play it cool for a nonexistent audience? I stumble out of the bathroom and back into my room. The phone is on my bed, screen down. My palms sweat as I bring it to life, my thumb on the home button.

"Twenty pounds? Whoa! And you're very welcome. Pleasure was all mine."

There's a ":)" followed by his signature, a simple "A."

I go to bed with my heart thrumming in my ears.

CHAPTER 24

The woman in the house

You wait for him to quiz you about the pads. For his hand around your arm, shaking you. For the urgency of his voice demanding answers. He brings you downstairs for breakfast, then for dinner. You wait and you wait and nothing comes.

Does he not know? Did he not see?

Are there no cameras, or did he just not check?

Or is he testing you? Does he know, and is he waiting to unmask you?

But his attention isn't on you. When Cecilia's not looking, and even at times when she is, he keeps taking out his phone and checking it under the table. Every once in a while, he types a few words and puts it away just as quickly.

You're not even halfway through dinner, and already he's done it five times. Right after he placed a roast chicken at the center of the table and called out for his kid. After he carved the bird, meticulously, with a giant fork and knife. After he asked you—made a show of asking you, really—if you preferred a breast or a leg. (You said leg, please. You need all the calories you can get. You have no stomach space to waste on lean protein.) And now, every time Cecilia looks down at her plate, every time she reaches for the water pitcher, his eyes dart to the screen.

After dinner, Cecilia asks if she can watch a movie. He tells her she has to get up for school tomorrow. She begs a bit. She says please, it's still the weekend, and she's done with her homework. He sighs.

Does he know how good he has it? A thirteen-year-old, in this century, whose main demand is a Sunday-night movie? At her age, you were bouncing from one sleepover to the next, negotiating trips to malls across the Hudson, forever expanding the perimeter you were allowed to occupy, parents-free, outside the home.

"Fine," he says. "But be in bed by ten."

She turns to you. "Wanna watch?"

You hold your breath. Give him a few seconds to interject. *Cecilia,* he could say, *I'm sure Rachel is busy tonight.* His pocket buzzes. He takes out his phone, checks the screen, starts typing.

"Sure," you say.

She helps clean the table. After that, you don't know what to do with yourself. Usually, her dad sends her upstairs to brush her teeth, has her riffle through the cupboard to replenish the paper-towel dispenser—whatever he can think of to distract her while he brings you back to the bedroom. But tonight, you are staying. Tonight is movie night. A great unknown, a million opportunities to fuck up along the way.

You follow them to the living room. Hide the twitch in your leg, ignore the burn where he kicked you two days ago. He settles in the armchair. While Cecilia looks around for the remote, he gestures for you to sit on the couch. His daughter curls up on the cushion next to yours. She points the remote at the screen, ignores the live-TV option, and selects a streaming service. You barely recognize the interface, but the logo has remained the same. Back when he took you, the platform was expanding, growing its catalog and beginning to produce its own shows. Now, Cecilia flips through an infinity of TV series and movies—some old, some unknown to you, some with an "original" label.

"This okay?"

The cursor hovers on what the platform describes as a teen rom-com, based on the bestselling young-adult novel series of the same name.

"Looks great," you say.

She leans back with a shy smile. You remember what it was like at her age, being a little ashamed of everything you liked.

You do your best to focus on the screen. It's been so long. All these sounds and colors and people and names. Your brain struggles to keep up. You jump from one subplot to the other, forget what the screenwriters told you five minutes ago. Your heart beats faster. Your fists clench in frustration, maybe panic.

Blue light glows in the corner of your eye. His phone. He's ignoring the movie entirely, neck bent over the small screen, thumb hopping from one corner to the other like a water strider on the surface of a lake.

On the big screen, the love interest says something funny. Cecilia giggles. She catches herself, turns to you as if to check that you, too, appreciate the humor in the scene. A girl, desperate for validation. You think back to the pads, to the note she scribbled in purple ink. *Hope these help. Let me know if you need more.* You do the only human thing. You laugh.

She giggles again and turns her gaze back to the screen. Her position on the couch relaxes, her right side almost leaning into you.

She is here. An ally, a friend. You feel so alone next to her, more than you ever did in the shed.

The love interest makes another wisecrack. Cecilia elbows you. You laugh again. You make yourself. For her.

She has done this to you. Without meaning to, her soft world slipping into yours. Robbing you of the smoothest, toughest parts of you. The ones that helped you survive in the shed. She's stripping them away, replacing them with shades of your former self. The one who loved. The one who opened herself to others.

The vulnerable one. The one who got hurt.

CHAPTER 25

The woman—before the house, before the shed

You write your way through high school. You edit the student paper. You get into colleges. You choose NYU over Columbia. You were born and raised in the city, and you're not tired of it. Your friends leave. They cross the country for California summers, for Silicon Valley, for the good Colorado weed. You stay. You are happy where you are. Happy enough.

You start running, even though you know that it will, over time, ruin your body. Split your bones, stiffen your muscles, gnaw on your tendons. You learn to like it, the fire in your rib cage, your lungs a conduit for the storm raging inside of you. You run, because you only know how to destroy yourself in healthy ways.

Around you, women are writing. It's a time of economic collapse, of odd jobs, of reinvention. The young women write for the best websites and bartend to pay rent. They show up for class tired, their lower backs sore, their eyes dusty with sleep.

Things are happening. There are bylines, summer jobs, internships. Three of your classmates intern at the magazine conglomerate, the one everybody wants to work for. The one that has inspired movies and TV series.

Some place short stories in literary magazines. They win awards and praise from their peers. You try to keep up, but everyone is good. Everyone is better than you. You're just a kid who grew up in New York reading a lot of books. Your grades are fine. Everything about you is just fine.

On the first day of the second semester of your senior year, the news breaks: your classmate got a book deal. There are whispers. Numbers thrown around, five zeros, maybe six. Some find it in themselves to be happy for the classmate. Others pull at the story like a thread until they find things to unravel: the topic of the book is weak, the deal a curse as much as a blessing. A success so great, so visible, and so soon. It's all downhill from here. Can you even imagine?

You can't. From your very fine life, with your very fine grades, your perfectly fine writing. You can't begin to imagine.

There is a website. An online offshoot of a now-defunct teen magazine. The magazine was revolutionary in its time, because it spoke to girls as though they had brains. You like the website. You read it every day. There is a section in it called "I Lived Through It." It's exactly what it sounds like: strangers detailing the crazy things they have lived through. "I Lived Through It: There Was No Pilot on My Plane." "I Lived Through It: I Woke Up from a Two-Year Coma." "I Lived Through It: I Started a Cult."

You read the essays during your lunch breaks. Then you go back to class, where your creative writing professor exhorts you. She's your mother's age, maybe older. Kind in person, ruthless on the page. She has five books and an endless stream of magazine pieces to her name. You look up to her in a way that feels like love.

Your writing is nice, your professor tells you. But it's quiet. It's oddly stiff. You're not like this in real life, your professor says. You're sensitive and funny. You're droll. She calls you droll and it satiates you, just for a second.

I'll work on that, you tell her. I'll work on my voice.

She shakes her head. It's not the voice, she tells you—it's what you write about. You're not writing about what matters. You're hiding. As long as you keep hiding, your reader won't know what to make of you.

You read the women's essays again. "I Lived Through It: My Best Friend Eloped with My Brother." "I Lived Through It: I Was Switched at Birth." "I Lived Through It: My Neighbor Turned Out to Be a Spy."

You think about the things you have lived through. There is only one you can picture on the website. For days, you avoid it, and then one night, you sit and write it all down. The words come to you, bones demanding to be excavated. "I Lived Through It: My Brother Put Me in His Suicide Note."

It doesn't feel like your story to tell. It happened to your brother before it happened to you. He's the one who took the pills, the first time and the second time. He's the one who survived. He's the one who wrote the note.

You weren't supposed to see it. You happened upon it the night of the second time, when you came home and your parents were still at the hospital, filling out paperwork.

"How am I supposed to find my place in the world," your brother wrote, "when everything keeps bringing me back to her?"

He meant you. Your brother, who got in trouble. Who didn't know how to love without losing himself. Whose turbulent adolescence gave you no choice but to become the best kid you could be. You knew how to exist in ways society rewarded and he did not. To you, his mind was a thing of genius, a volcano where precious rocks were made. You thought of yourself as the boring one. It had never occurred to you that your brother might see things differently.

The essay sits in your computer for weeks. You don't know what to do with it. You think about emailing it to your professor but can't bring yourself to hit "send." The writing feels messy, self-centered, immature. It feels like something you might regret one day.

The classmate with the book deal shares a photo on Facebook. It's her, pen in hand, wrist resting on top of a stack of papers. "Amazing news," the classmate writes. "The contract is signed. It's official: THE LITTLE BLUE HOUSE is going to be a movie. Well, maybe! One day! If all goes well! But the rights have been sold and it's a huge first step. I feel so grateful."

Things are happening. You need them to start happening to you. You find the essay on your laptop, type a five-sentence email. Attach. Send.

It runs the following week.

At first, your brother doesn't say anything. Then, one night. A Sunday. The family back at home for roast chicken and lemon potatoes. Your parents in the living room, the two of you in the kitchen, washing dishes.

"You know," your brother says, scrubbing a plate. "I saw it. Your article."

It takes you by surprise. You focus on shining a wineglass with your mother's kitchen towel.

"It's fine," your brother tells you. You consider him: two years older than you, tall but fragile. A delicate child, hypersensitive—that's how your mother described him to a schoolteacher once. Strong jawline, crooked smile. Your father's gait. Your mother's eyes.

He picks up another plate, resumes scrubbing. "Although," he says with a bitterness you recognize from his teenage years, "you kind of proved my point."

Later on, when it's time to put your coats back on and hop on the subway, your brother says goodbye to you. Usually, he would hug you. Your brother, who taught you how to roughhouse. How to run, how to land a punch. Your brother, whose love came out in the breathless mess of playtime. Mud stains on your clothes, blades of grass in your hair. That night, your brother gives you a light, tidy tap on the shoulder.

"Get home safe," he says. Well-adjusted. Free of you.

Your brother waves at you from the other side of the platform, and you know. You know that you have lost him forever.

CHAPTER 26

The woman in the house

You find yourself wanting to repeat the Sunday movie experiment. It's not the film you want, but everything around it. Cecilia next to you on the couch. A change in your itinerary, a stop between the kitchen and the bedroom. A lull between dinner and the silence of the night, the things he does to you.

So when Cecilia starts hovering toward the living area and gives you an interrogating look, you check in her father's direction. He's looking at his phone. You give her a nod. With your silent support secured, she starts negotiating. "It doesn't have to be a full movie," she tells her dad. "It can just be a TV show. Just one episode. Twenty minutes."

You do your best to catch her father's gaze. You glance at his phone, discreetly at first, then without hesitation. A subliminal message. He has to be the one to realize that this could be good for him. That with his daughter's eyes glued to the screen, he'll be free to keep texting.

He caves. One episode, he says. And the deal is sealed.

One evening, while navigating from live TV to the streaming platform, Cecilia pauses on a news segment about a musical. You understand it's about the Founding Fathers. "Are you a fan too?" she asks with an excited smile. On TV, two people talk about the show. You catch the words *history, national tour, masterpiece.* You infer that the musical is important, not only to Cecilia but to the world at large. "Sure," you tell her. "I mean of course."

You used to love theater. The last play you saw was not long before he took you, when your life was beginning to unravel but things still felt salvageable. Julie, your roommate, had tickets for an off-Broadway show. She urged you to come with her. "You haven't left the apartment in three days," she said. "This will be good for you." You caved. It was the right decision.

Cecilia's still raving about her musical. What do you think about the new cast? she wants to know. What are your favorite songs? At this, her father looks up and tells her to press "play" on her TV show already.

Every night he sits in his chair, phone glowing under his fingers. When you're done watching whatever it is you're watching, he tells Cecilia to go get ready for bed. That's your cue to say good night, go back to the room. He comes in a couple of minutes later with the handcuffs. Later on, he returns. Always he returns.

Things start happening later than usual. His nightly visits, the handcuffs clinging to the bed frame. Maybe that's why you start noticing it. You used to be asleep by the time it happened, but now you're awake, and there's no denying it.

Every night, around what you assume are the early hours of the morning, steps creep along the hallway. At first, you think someone is going to the bathroom. But the pattern doesn't match. You listen, night after night. A door opens and shuts. Someone walks from one location to another. There is silence. And then, it happens again. Steps, a door opening and closing.

Theories sprout in your mind. She's scared. She has nightmares, night terrors. He goes to comfort her. But you never hear any voices. No one calling for Dad, no one screaming in their sleep. Just steps, doors, and silence.

You resist thinking it, and then you do. He's going inside her room, night after night. There is an anchor in your stomach. You want to scream, to hurl things at the walls, to set the house on fire. You're going to throw up.

You can't know for sure, but everything about it makes sense to you. You cannot imagine a world where he knows how to love without destroying.

You want to wrap her in your arms and tell her it's all going to be okay. You want to promise her a safe place, a new world. You'll build it for her if you have to, but you'll take her there.

Maybe you're mistaken. Maybe this isn't what you think it is. You lie awake, waiting to be proven wrong. You try to put your faith in other scenarios—maybe she's afraid of the dark and he knows, just knows to go in without her calling out to him. Maybe he is a father, and fathers know when their daughters need them.

But you know the kind of man he is. And you remember things from the world, from before. You know how it's all supposed to go. No matter how hard you search, how far back you look, you can't think of a good reason for a man like him to disappear into his daughter's room every night.

CHAPTER 27

Cecilia

Suddenly, my dad has all these friends.

First, there was Rachel. And that was fine. Rachel, I could understand. She needed somewhere to stay and people to be nice to her.

But this new woman? I don't think so.

I don't even know her name, and I don't want to learn it. I've seen her around town before. She works at that restaurant my dad likes. I guess that's how he knows her. But that still doesn't explain what compelled him to spend the whole morning of that stupid race with her.

I wouldn't have minded so much if he hadn't made me go. But if you tell me I have to attend something, maybe talk to me once or twice while we're there. I feel like maybe that should be a rule.

My dad understands rules. He's always been very into them. *Don't touch other people's stuff, keep out of other people's business.* I don't want to touch your stuff, I used to tell him. No offense, but I don't care about your stuff. But then one day my mom told me he got that from his time in the marines, because no one there had any boundaries and his stuff got stolen all the time, so now he's territorial. Which, you know. Fine. You serve in the marines, you're entitled to some quirks.

But I was still pissed off about the race. And I was mad on Rachel's behalf, too. Which is a bit weird, I know, but I was. If my dad is going to have some weird lady-friend thing going on, well, the position is already taken. By Rachel.

I guess that's why I gave her the pads. My dad has been adamant that under no circumstances should I go anywhere near Rachel's bedroom, but after the race, I didn't care about his rules anymore. I just did what I wanted to do.

Not that she thanked me, mind you. A thank-you would have been nice.

So there's Rachel, and there's Restaurant Woman, and then there's the texting.

People think teenage girls text all the time. They should see what my dad has been up to these past few days. Typing constantly, especially when he thinks I can't see him.

Maybe it's Restaurant Woman. Maybe it's a third one. Who knows, at this point? For fifteen years, my dad only had eyes for my mom. If I were mean, I'd say he's making up for lost time.

But I'm not mean. And I don't really believe that.

I will say, though, that this wasn't the deal. And I don't think my mom would be thrilled with the way he's been acting. It makes me really sad to think it, but it's the truth.

Not long before my mom died, she gave me a little speech. She waited until my dad had gone to talk to some doctor. He spoke to a lot of doctors around that time, not that it changed anything. They had run out of ideas to make her better.

Once it was just the two of us, my mom patted a spot next to her on the bed.

"Come here."

It was weird being so close to her near the end. She didn't feel like herself anymore. She had lost a ton of weight. Her hair grew back after they stopped the chemo, but thinner than before, with gray streaks. Whenever I hugged her, she was all bones under my fingers.

She put an arm around my shoulders and pulled me closer. "I'm not scared," she said. She was looking up at the ceiling, like she was afraid to meet my gaze. "Well, sometimes I am, but not for you. I know I'm leaving you with the best man." She swallowed hard. "I'm so grateful for the time we've had together. All three of us."

This was a goodbye, and I didn't want a goodbye. What I wanted was for my mom to come home. I knew that wasn't possible, but that didn't stop me from wanting it.

The truth was, I didn't want to be a cancer daughter. I didn't want to wake up every day and remember she was gone. This girl at school, Cathy, had a brother who died of leukemia a year ago. She missed a few weeks of classes, and when she came back, everyone treated her like this fragile little thing.

I don't want to be a fragile little thing.

But ready or not, my mom was saying goodbye to me. She hugged me a little tighter and carried on. "At some point it's going to be just the two of you. That's okay. All right? I want you to know that's okay with me. He's going to take such great care of you. And you're going to take such great care of him. We're so lucky to have him."

She rubbed her eyes with the hand that wasn't holding me. I felt like I should have been crying, too, but a lot of sad stuff had happened in a pretty short time, and when a lot of sad stuff happens in a pretty short time, you reach a point where you can't cry anymore.

My mom was still looking at the ceiling. "You two are going to have to stick up for each other. I told him that, too. Okay?" I nodded. "Grandma and Grandpa will be there, too," she said. "I know Dad doesn't always get along with them, but you can count on them. I hope you'll remember that." She stared at me until I nodded again. "But you and Dad, you'll be a team. And you'll always have each other."

I don't know about always. But my mom was right about the other part. Three weeks later, she died, and it was just me and my dad.

Things at home didn't change all that much. I hope that doesn't sound mean. It's just that even when my mom was healthy, he did most of the chores. Cooking, cleaning. Always making us food, taking us places.

So he kept cooking. I helped with the cleaning. He went back to work, and I went back to school. It's early in the year, he said. Getting into a routine might help.

I know he was trying to make things easy for me, but I hated that he held up so well. The house was never messy. After the funeral, people brought casseroles we didn't need. My dad preserved my life as best as he could. It was like he had read a self-help book, something like *Dealing with the Grieving Teenager,* and memorized every chapter.

I wanted him to stop. To let things get messy, to let us be a wreck. It seemed disrespectful to just keep going, like we were coping too well with her absence. I wanted the house to reflect how I felt inside. I wanted chaos.

And then, about a month after she died, he picked me up from school—I tell him all the time that I can take the bus or get a ride, but he never listens—and announced we had to move. My mom's parents were kicking us out. He didn't say it like that, but that was the idea.

I don't get the hype around grandparents. My dad's parents died before I was born, and he's never had anything great to say about them. My mom's parents like me well enough, but they aren't fans of my dad. I'm not sure why. My mom used to joke that they were just mad he took their precious girl away. Sometimes my dad would say it was the money, because my mom had some and he had none. My mom always told him to stop. She'd swat him on the arm and say things like *Come on, they like you just fine, they don't know how to show it—that's all.*

Before my mom died but after she got sick again, I overheard her talking to my dad. I was supposed to be asleep but I went to get a glass of water. Their voices were coming from the kitchen. "I'm not saying we should do it," my mom was saying. "I just wanted you to know they offered. That if you ever feel like you can't . . . on your own . . . they can take her."

My dad got so mad. "I can't fucking believe it," he said. I heard him slam the dining table. The next day, there was a big mark on the wood, next to his spot. "She's my daughter. They visit what, once, twice a year? And they think they can swoop in and take her from us? From me?" He was pacing. I took a couple of steps back to make sure he wouldn't see me. "I know they think I'm some jerk who can't do anything right, but she's my kid. I raised her."

A chair scraped against the kitchen floor. I figured my mom was getting up, putting a hand on his arm, trying to calm him down. "I didn't mean to upset you," she said. "I'm sorry. I just wanted you to know. It's fine. Let's not talk about it anymore."

I don't know what happened after that. The last time I saw my grandparents was at the funeral. They came up to us after the service. My dad was polite, his back straight, his shoulders so stiff I thought they'd never move again. No one said too much, just the things people are expected to say in those circumstances, *How are you holding up* and *She was such a beautiful person* and *I hope she's at peace now.* We had all lost someone we loved very much, but that didn't mean we suddenly liked one another.

So my grandparents made us leave. Maybe they realized in the weeks after the funeral that we would never bond as much as they'd hoped, and it was time to call it quits. Maybe my dad told them to butt out, and to them that meant taking the house back. Not that they wanted to live in it. They have another house far from us, way up north. They just wanted to sell this one. The result was the same. We had to leave the house where I had lived my entire life. The house that held all my memories of my mom.

There, I could still see her. Sitting next to me on the couch when I was a little kid, watching Saturday-morning cartoons. Teaching me how to put my hair in a ponytail in front of the bathroom mirror. Reading the first three *Harry Potter* books to me, and later on, lying down next to me while I read the next four by myself. Singing the *Hamilton* soundtrack in the kitchen, holding a wooden spoon or a spatula as a mic, and seeing which one of us could make it all the way through "My Shot" and "Non-Stop" without messing up the lyrics.

In the new house, my mom is gone. She's not here. She was never here.

Now it's just me and my dad again.

Well, me and my dad, and Rachel, and whoever else might be added to the list next, since my dad is apparently taking applications.

Here's what I think.

I think my dad is a complicated person. He hasn't had an easy life. He never talks about his childhood, and I have to assume that's because it was pretty terrible. He wanted to become a doctor but he became a marine, because he felt a duty to his country but also because . . . I don't know . . . becoming a doctor is hard and the people who manage it tend to have money and good families, and my dad had neither?

Despite all that, he built a nice life for himself. And with my mom, he built a nice life for me, too. Whenever we argued, he and I, and my mom had to bring back the peace, she would tell me, "Your father, he loves being a dad." And he does. I know that. He loves being *my* dad. He drives me around. He buys me clothes. He cooks for me. He cares about what's in my head. He teaches me things. He wants me to know what he knows.

I just feel like I'm not enough, somehow. Like it was supposed to be the two of us, but I failed (at what? I'm not sure), and now he has to recruit all these companions to fill the void.

Maybe that's a fucked-up thing to think. Sorry.

I know he lost her, too.

And so it's me and my dad and his women, and the more people hover around us, the lonelier I feel.

Maybe this is how it's meant to be. Maybe this is what I learn from this. That at the end of the day, the only person you can truly count on is yourself.

CHAPTER 28

Emily

He's a part of my life. I'm not sure how it happened, but he is, and he feels at ease in it.

My message about red-tailed hawks has snowballed in the most beautiful way. We never stopped texting. Now, we talk all day long. At work, I keep my phone in the front pocket of my apron. I check it between customers, under the bar. I check it in the bathroom. I check it in the back of Eric's car. I check it while I brush my teeth, before bed, first thing in the morning. His most recent text replays on a constant loop in the back of my brain.

At first, we graduated from red-tailed hawks to other birds of prey, and eventually the rest of the Hudson Valley fauna. We expanded our horizons to cover work, the town, food, the weather. He sends me pictures of interesting birds. We trade recipes. He asks me how I'm doing every morning, and every evening he says good night. He wants to know how the restaurant treats me. He wants to know how I'm holding up. He's heard the work is brutal. He hopes I'm okay. I tell him about a dream I had, a series of doors down a dark hallway, all locked. He looks up its meaning on the internet. "Closed doors," he says, "apparently mean someone or something is standing in your way. An open door, on the other hand, would signify a new stage in your life, a positive change. Are you sure all those doors were closed?"

He types words in full. No "2" for "two," no "K" for "OK," no "btw" for "by the way." His sentences begin with capital letters and end with periods. His emoticon use is moderate, the rare ":)" loaded with special meaning.

There are things he doesn't bring up, and I know not to ask. His wife. His daughter. I keep my questions vague: "How are you? How was your day?" The door is open. If he wants to talk, he will.

He comes to the bar on Tuesday and Thursday, as usual. I make him virgin old-fashioneds. Whenever I have a moment, we talk. We're less loquacious in person, our bodies catching up with the intimacy we've developed over text.

He's not always quick to text back. An hour, two, three can go by without an answer. In the interim, I reread our messages, search every word for the possibility of a misunderstanding. Right around the time I've convinced myself that I've ruined everything, he writes back. Friendly. Open.

At the restaurant, I run to the kitchen for olives, a clean spoon, a snack, and slow down on the way back. I observe him, the beautiful man on a barstool.

His presence lifts me up. I walk with my head high, my back straighter. My voice rises, self-assured, and dips neatly at the ends of my sentences. I carry it, the certainty of this secret current between us, like a good-luck charm. Nestled against my heart at all times.

AND I NEED IT. This extra pep in my step, this small miracle. I need it so much.

The town is still reeling from the disappearance of the missing woman. She was from the area. Everyone knows someone who knew her. She hasn't been found. No one is saying it, but we know. We just do. We know that when she's found—if she's ever found—she will not be alive.

People have been a bit kinder to one another. On the street, in shops, even at the restaurant. There's a softness in our interactions, though of course it ends where the kitchen begins. But people are trying. Even Nick, in his own way. It helps that we're not too busy. Thanksgiving is almost here, and the town has started to empty. Locals are taking long weekends, traveling to visit family, slipping into their holiday schedules. Soon, the most frantic time of the year will begin, but for now, things are unsettlingly calm. A stillness before the storm.

Tonight, dinner service ends early. I lock the door behind our last table of the evening, parents trying to get their kids in bed before ten. Eric clears the remaining dishes. Already, Cora is setting down clean tablecloths and shining silverware for tomorrow's service. Nick busies himself in the kitchen, gathering dirty pans, tongs, spatulas.

Sophie scrubs a couple of cake pans with all the energy she has left. I go around the dining room to collect used glasses.

A buzz in my apron. I put down a bulbous wineglass and check my phone.

"Did I miss last call? No worries if so. I just didn't want to let a virgin old-fashioned pass me by."

It's Friday. Not Tuesday, not Thursday. He came by yesterday, stuck to his usual schedule. And now he wants more.

I glance toward the kitchen. Eric and Sophie are almost done with the dishes. Nick has picked up a towel and is helping them dry everything off. Cora's counting her tips.

"You did," I type back. "But I might be able to sneak you in. Just give me . . . 20/30 minutes? You can have an after-hour drink."

He replies, "Honored," with a ":)" at the end.

I step into the kitchen, a trident of wineglasses tucked between my fingers.

"Guys." Nick and Eric look up. "I can close up. I still need to shine a bunch of glasses but I don't mind. Save yourselves, everybody."

Fifteen minutes later, I have the place to myself. His truck pulls up outside. My apron buzzes again.

"All clear?"

I take a deep breath before I type back, "All clear." When I go to unlock the door, I find him waiting, hands stuffed in his coat pockets, hair spilling out of his trapper hat. His chin is tucked into a thick wool scarf, poking out just enough to reveal a smile.

"Come on in."

The duffel bag is back, too, bouncing against his hip with each step. He shudders as he unzips his coat, rubs his hands together before he settles on his usual barstool. The duffel rests at his feet like an obedient dog. I start mixing his drink. There is a silence. It's a comfortable one, the kind that blooms between people who don't need to talk each other through every instant.

I give his drink a stir, top it off with a cherry.

"So how was tonight?" he asks.

"Oh, you know. Not too busy. Next week, though—that's when the madness will begin. And then it won't stop until the end of the year."

I slide the glass in his direction. He takes a sip, cocks his head in appreciation.

"Thank you for sneaking me in."

"For our most loyal customers, we'll always find a way."

I put away the bitters, the orange I used for his twist. He gestures at the barstool next to his.

"Why don't you come sit?"

I look around the dining room. Nervous, stupidly so. He licks his lips. "I don't mean to make you break the bartender code. I just—you must have been on your feet all night." He leans in. "And there's no one else here to witness this . . . transgression."

I laugh. I suppose he's right, I tell him. I walk around the bar and hoist myself on the stool next to his. Without our usual setup—him sitting, me standing up, the counter a barrier between our two worlds—we feel closer than ever, thrust into roles we've been inhabiting virtually, but not physically, for almost a week.

He nudges his drink toward me. "Have a sip if you'd like. I feel rude drinking by myself."

I think about saying no thank you. But there's a vulnerability in the way he just extended the offer that makes it impossible to refuse. My fingers brush against his as they wrap around the glass. I tilt my head back, the ice cube knocking against my teeth.

Sitting at a bar, sharing drinks—I've seen this before. In a movie. A spy sipping on a martini, a woman in a cocktail dress plucking the drink from his hand.

"You know," I say, "I've heard that if you drink from someone else's glass, you can read their thoughts. Find out all their secrets."

He chuckles. "Is that so?"

I nod, set the glass down. He considers me. I force myself not to look away.

"Well," he says. "Wouldn't that be something."

A force field grows around us. Pushes us toward each other, into each other. I pull back. Straighten my back, clear my throat, tuck stray hairs behind my ears.

"Are you doing anything nice for the holidays?"

I regret the question as soon as it escapes my lips. So trite. So subpar. And so inappropriate to ask someone who has just experienced a great loss.

He takes a sip from his drink, then shakes his head.

"Not this year. It'll just be me and Cece. We have some relatives out of state, but things are . . . complicated."

"Oh, trust me, I get it."

He swirls the ice cube at the bottom of his glass. "What about you?"

"Working. We're doing three services on Thanksgiving alone."

He winces in solidarity.

"It's all right," I tell him. "I'm not big on the holidays." And then I decide to say it, because when you're grieving, people don't expect you to talk about your dead, but I know he'll get it: "Even when my parents were still around, they weren't really into it. They were always so busy, you know?"

What I don't tell him: my parents weren't neglectful, but I feel like they spent the first ten years of my life waiting to *get* this parenting thing, until one day they had to accept that this was it, that things were as good as they would ever be. My father was a man who loved from the distance of his kitchen, his caring instincts reserved for the strangers who sat in his restaurant. My plan was always to be a bartender, because I thought it would be my chance to love people up close. I didn't realize, of course, that most people want their bartender to leave them the hell alone.

I get up from the barstool and go to collect Aidan's empty glass. He stops me with one hand wrapped around my arm. Softly, he peels my fingers from the glass and laces them with his.

"Sounds like we're both in the same boat, then."

All I can do is nod. His palm is hot against mine, our pulses beating against each other. He uncoils our fingers. Instantly, I miss the contact of his skin. His hand travels up to my face. With three fingers, he brushes away a strand of hair that has escaped from my ponytail.

He raises his eyebrows, as if asking for permission. I nod, and in doing so, bring our faces the slightest bit closer. This is how I will remember it forever: I'm the one who leans in first. I invite him in. For a second I think I've got it completely wrong. That he's going to recoil, drop a twenty on the counter, and leave. Instead, I am rewarded by the softness of his hand cupping my cheek. A microscopic tremor in his thumb as he grazes the corner of my mouth.

Our lips collide. A new world opens underneath my feet. It's a Friday night and I'm kissing Aidan Thomas in the deserted restaurant. This feels like karma, like life making up for all the slights along the way—all forgotten, all forgiven, all worth it, now that I know they were leading up to this moment.

He's still sitting on the barstool. My hands wrap at the back of his neck. His fingers clasp around my waist.

His tongue finds mine. He gives my upper lip the tiniest nibble, sends shivers down my spine, all the way to my ankles. He kisses me like I haven't been kissed since high school, when everything was new and bodies were meant to be explored, every inch of them a mystery to be solved. There is tongue and lips and teeth. It's a little bit messy, a little too hungry. It makes me feel wanted. Celebrated. Loved.

He gets up from the barstool, allowing our bodies to press against each other. We break away from our kiss for a few seconds. Long enough to drink in the moment, to take it all in. He rests his forehead against mine. A sigh travels between us. I can't tell if it's coming from him or me, just that it's warm and trembling and full of longing.

His hands slide down, hover above the small of my back. I'm the one who bridges the gap, who pulls him into me. Closer. Deeper. My body tells him what I could never say out loud: how much I want him, how long I've waited for this, how I've been his this entire time, since before he knew my name or the color of my eyes.

I kiss him, lips swollen, my skin prickling under his facial hair. Our rib cages expand and contract against each other; our hands undo buttons, push fabric out of the way, snake underneath clothes in a desperate search for skin.

I force myself to pull away. Grab his hand. "Over here," I mumble. I lead him through the kitchen, into the pantry.

He doesn't ask questions. He follows me. It's all that matters. It's all that has ever mattered.

Our bodies crash against the shelves, searching for an anchor point. Clumsily, I guide us to a small patch of bare wall. He helps: using the pressure of his body against mine, he pins me against the surface. I keep one foot on the floor and hook my other leg around his waist.

"Look at you," he whispers. "So flexible."

I laugh. He unties my apron. It's the hottest thing anyone has done to me, ever. His hand travels underneath my shirt, applies the slightest amount of pressure against my lower abdomen. I moan and forget to be ashamed.

My fingers search and search and still can't find what they're looking for. He feels me fumbling and comes to my rescue. Finally, I hear it, a door opening onto a new world—the click of his belt buckle opening, the thud of his jeans falling to the floor.

CHAPTER 29

The woman in the house

It's late. Too late. There was no dinner tonight, and now he's MIA. Maybe he has abandoned you again. Maybe he decided it would be good to leave you on your own for a while. Remind you that he's the one who has kept you alive all these years. That without him, you would die. Starve.

Then, the doorknob turns. Here he is. The man who never forgets you.

He uncuffs you. His shoes come off first, then his pants, his sweater, his undershirt. You allow your mind to escape your body. Your brain plays memories of a long-ago train ride, rows and rows of trees flashing against the darkening sky, fading sunlight poking through the branches.

Reality snaps back into place. You are in the room, on the hardwood floor, underneath his body. His left shoulder shifts against your chin, and you see: four red streaks etched into his skin. Half-moons with a scarlet trail. You know these markings. From digging into your own palms, from carving shapes into the pale skin of your legs, the pain temporarily relieving you of something. These are the marks you get when someone digs their nails into the softest parts of you.

It's the first time you've seen these on him. Even after a trip, even after *You know*. He's always returned scratch-free.

After, when he's pulling his pants back up, you study him. He's in no rush to leave. There is an ease about him, a buoyancy. He's in a good mood.

"So," you whisper. "It's later than usual, no?"

The corner of his mouth lifts. "Why? Got somewhere you need to go?"

You force yourself to chuckle. "No. I was just wondering, you know. Where have you been?"

He tilts his head to the side. "Missed me?"

He doesn't wait for your answer, slips his undershirt back on. "Just running some errands," he says, and rubs his nose. "If you must know."

He's lying—of course he's lying—but you can read him. There is no *You know*. No sparkle in his eyes, no electricity coursing through his body.

Whoever scratched his back, you have to believe she is okay. You have to believe she is still alive.

For a second, you are relieved. Then, your throat closes again. If he has her, does he need you? Or is he just playing with his food?

The thought stays with you after he leaves. Scratching a man's back, clinging to his flesh, carving yourself into him, is something you do only in a set of specific circumstances.

You don't like it. You don't like it at all.

You don't like it for her, and you don't like it for you.

There is a stranger outside. A stranger in danger.

And she could be the end of you, too.

Rule number three of staying alive outside the shed: If you have to be in his world, then you must be special. You must be the only one of you.

CHAPTER 30

The woman in the house

It's the morning after the red scratches. Your eyelids are heavy, your head foggy. He, on the other hand, is quick on his feet. His gaze is proud. You could swear his skin is glowing. Maybe he's already killed her, after all?

First comes breakfast. All three of you, quiet. Cecilia's eyes flutter. She pokes at her cereal more than she eats it. He fingers his phone underneath the table. Soon, you're back in the bedroom. He comes in, handcuffs you to the radiator, and leaves. Everything normal. Everything as usual.

The truck departs the driveway. There is a dull pain in your lower back. You adjust your stance to come as close to lying down as possible. That's when you feel it.

The handcuffs. Like gum around your wrist. Useless. You sit up. Brush the metal with your left hand. The loop comes loose, unspools from your arm.

Just like that.

You are free.

Are you free?

There is something. Floating in the air around you, scratching at the back of your brain. It's right here, but you can't reach it. Your legs start shaking. You should unfurl them. Get up. On your feet, start running.

Is this the moment you start running?

You always thought when the moment came you'd know for sure.

Are you afraid?

Are you a coward?

Women like you are supposed to be brave. That's what you used to hear. On the news, in magazine articles. Long profiles of girls who went missing and found their way home. Of women who worked under the tutelage of horrible men and found their way out. *She was so brave.* Like a consolation prize: *Sorry we couldn't save you, but now we'll pretend to worship the ground you walk on.*

You visualize it.

In your head, you stand up. Is this what it feels like to be free? You walk to the bedroom door. It takes courage, but you're a brave woman, remember? You are brave and don't you forget it. In that vision, you open the door and peek outside. He's not here. No one's here. You know that. You know he and his daughter just left. You take a couple of steps down the stairs. Then, something clicks. You start running. You run to the living room, to the front door. You look around one last time and then you do it. You open the door.

And then what?

What happens after you open the door?

Picture it. You are outside. Alone. You don't know where you are, the street, the town, the state. No idea. You don't know where the closest neighbors live, or if they are home. They are strangers. It does not come easily to you—does not occur to you at all, anymore—to trust strangers. Trust them with your life. Trust them to save you.

Forget the neighbors, then. You could keep running, by yourself. To where? A town center? A police station? A grocery store? Those places are full of strangers, too, but at least they're not someone's home. There would be a crowd around you. Witnesses.

And where is he during all this?

Where is his kid?

The cameras.

You remember the cameras.

But he didn't see the pads. Nothing happened then.

Are there cameras?

You can't be sure.

What about his job in the clouds?

Looking down at you.

Ready to swoop down on you.

Maybe you run. You search for someone's home, for a store. An open door. Someone who will listen.

And in the meantime? He gets an alert on his phone. He looks at the livestream on the app. He sees you, hears you. He rushes home. He is furious. You have betrayed him, betrayed his trust. There is no coming back from that.

He finds you before you get to safety. Drives to the woods and does to you what he should have done five years ago. Everything goes black. You can't believe this is how it ends. No one will know you were alive this whole time. No one will understand you could have been saved.

Or he doesn't look at his phone. He comes home and realizes you're gone. He knows what's coming. Police sirens, a capture, a reckoning. He doesn't want to be here for any of it. He lifts his gun to his head and shoots.

Another scenario: He puts his kid in the truck. Tells her they must leave now, no time to pack bags. He drives and drives and drives and is never found. He and Cecilia live on as aged-up composites on the FBI's website.

Or he takes the gun, puts his daughter in the truck, and drives to a remote location. Maybe he kills her before he kills himself. You saw that first night in the house, the terror in his eyes when she called his name, when she almost busted him. You've heard sounds at night, steps down a hallway. The girl, she looks at him like he is a certain kind of man. He will do anything to keep that version of himself alive.

You do not want him to die. It confuses you, but you know that you do not. And you do not want his child to die, either.

You always thought when the moment came you'd know for sure.

If this isn't the moment, what is?

If this isn't it, when do you get out?

Your mother and your father and your brother.

Julie, the friend you never deserved. Matt.

For five years, they have been waiting.

They need you alive.

You need you alive.

You always thought when the moment came you'd know for sure.

This isn't the moment.

You are in the bedroom, sitting cross-legged next to the radiator.

Does this mean you believe a second chance will come? Do you trust you will get another opportunity? A better, safer one?

This is your life. You saved yourself on the first day and you have saved yourself every day since. No one has come to your rescue. You have been doing this alone and you will come out of this alone.

This isn't the moment.

So where does that leave you?

You can't believe yourself. You bite your lips, tug at the delicate skin, bite down harder and harder and harder until something gives. You taste metal. You taste warmth. A fury grows in you, threatens to swallow you. You want to cry, shriek, wail. Conjure up a thunderstorm with the powers of your mind. You want numbness. You want to soar above it all. You want to stop feeling the many parts of you being torn apart.

Another thing.

If he comes home and sees the open handcuffs, he'll realize he's slipping. On the surface, he'll blame you, but deep down he will know. He will stop trusting himself. He will become more vigilant again.

You need him sloppy, distracted. You need his self-confidence intact.

Do it.

It is the greatest betrayal. It is an act of faith.

You don't stand up. Instead, you wrap your fingers around the cuffs and push the metallic ends together.

The mechanism clicks shut.

CHAPTER 31

Number four

His daughter had just taken her first steps.

Soon she won't need me anymore, he said.

What did he want me to do? Swear to him that wasn't true?

I had three of my own.

I could have lied to him about anything, except my babies.

So I told him.

Maybe she won't, I said. Maybe one day she won't need you at all.

It wounded him.

It was the wrong thing to say, obviously. But it was all I had.

He was going to do it no matter what. That, I was sure of. He needed to do it. Even more: he needed to watch himself do it. I saw him, when it was happening. Checking himself out. Catching glimpses of himself in the rearview mirror of my car.

Like he wanted to check that he still could. Like he needed to see it to believe it.

I don't regret what I said about his daughter. It probably shortened my life by an extra minute or so, but I don't regret getting in that one shot.

Like I said, it was all I had.

CHAPTER 32

Emily

They've called off the search for the missing woman. The case is still open, according to the page-four story in the local paper, but we all know what this means. Investigators have run out of places to look, of leads to follow. They've got nothing.

We carry on with our lives. Selfishly. Stupidly. What else can we do? The holidays are around the corner. We're all supposed to be happy.

Thanksgiving is brutal. I prepare for my shift like those kids in *The Hunger Games*, except my weapons are comfortable shoes, an extra hair tie for my ponytail, a generous coating of hair spray, and the matte lipstick that only comes off when rubbed with olive oil.

Despite those precautions, my feet are crying out for a break by the end of the six o'clock service. A glance at the mirror behind the bar informs me that my cheeks are blotchy, my forehead shiny, my perfect hair just a memory. My arms are sore from shaking apple cider martinis and their espresso counterparts. My lower back is heavy. Every time I take a step, a sharp pain flashes up my legs.

The pain is fine. The pain is part of the plan. I took my first steps on the floor of my father's restaurant. I spent my childhood collecting tips, bringing checks, refilling water glasses, burning my hands on hot plates. The pain, I can take.

What breaks me into too many pieces is the rest—the times I mess up, the injustices I allow to happen. Eric fucks up a four-top's appetizers and I can't bring myself to tell him to get his shit together. A sidecar comes back to me, "too weak." And then, there's the Shirley Temple debacle. Nick pitches the recipe to me in the afternoon—*hard seltzer, crème de cassis, a twist, kind of like a Shirley Temple for adults, you know?* I give it a try before the first service. It works. On the menu it goes.

It's not until the second service that Cora speaks up about the drinks, after spotting three of them lined up on the bar.

"It was my idea," she says.

"What?"

"The recipe. I came up with it. Told Nick about it at lunch."

She's not even mad, just stuck somewhere between shock and acceptance. He stole her idea. Like a cartoon villain, like a sitcom bully. He just stole it. And I didn't have a single clue.

"I'm so sorry," I tell her.

"It's fine." It's not fine, but I'm her boss, so she'll pretend it is. She's gone before I can apologize again.

People like to think business is the opposite of personal. Anyone who has ever cared about their work, even just a little bit, will tell you that's bullshit. It's the most personal thing, what we do here. And when I make mistakes, people suffer. It doesn't matter that it's business. At the end of the day, everything metabolizes as sadness.

THANKSGIVING SWALLOWS US like a nuclear mushroom cloud, and then it ends early. It's a family holiday. No one wants to be out after eleven. The restaurant quiets down. For a few minutes, we hover, unsure how to exist in the aftermath of chaos. We sigh. We massage our necks, blow our noses, tilt back bottles of water. Like after a hurricane, the cleanup begins.

"Anybody want to take these home?"

Sophie is holding up a cardboard box filled with bags of cookies—half chocolate truffle, half lavender shortbread. We've been dishing them out all night with the checks. There are about ten left.

No one says anything. We're not shy about freebies, but we've all had enough of the restaurant for one night. No one wants to bring reminders of the evening back into their home.

Sophie surveys the room.

"Come on, people. I'm not letting these go to waste, and I'm not eating them, either."

Her gaze lands on me.

"Boss?"

You don't say no to Sophie.

"Yeah, sure."

I take the box and thank her. When we're done cleaning up, I tell Eric and Yuwanda to go ahead.

"Where the hell are you going?" Yuwanda wants to know. "It's almost midnight."

I make up an errand, something I need to grab from the drugstore. Yuwanda gives me a skeptical glare. I wait for her to keep probing—to point out that the drugstore closes at ten, and that it sure isn't going to be open on Thanksgiving night—but she's too tired for that. She knows, from the period right after my parents died, that sometimes I need to be alone and it doesn't help to question it.

"Just drive safe."

Inside the Civic, I take out my phone. After the night in the pantry, Aidan and I didn't text for twenty-four hours, like we were too stunned to talk. Then, right when I was about to go to bed, he wrote: "Thinking about you :)"

"Oh, yeah?" I texted back. "Yes," he said. I replied "Same :)" and we've been back on our regular texting schedule since. He returned to the restaurant, too, on Tuesday. I spent it in an electric daze, glancing at the door even though I knew it wasn't time yet. When he finally stepped in, my stomach hollowed. His gaze met mine. He smiled. I smiled back. For a few seconds, it was just the two of us. Two happy idiots, sharing the most delicious secret in the world.

We didn't renew our exploits in the pantry. But there were knowing looks, a quick stroke on my wrist when he grabbed the check, a squeeze around my waist when no one was watching. And right before closing time, a miracle: he waited until the dining room was empty, then told me to close my eyes and hold out my hand. When I did, he deposited something cool into my palm and pressed my fist shut. "Go ahead," he said. "Open your eyes. Take a look."

I unfurled my fingers to reveal a small silver necklace. The infinity sign dangling from a thin chain, a pink quartz encased at the back of the pendant. "Oh my God," I whispered. "Where did you get this?"

He didn't say. Told me to turn around.

"Hopefully this one isn't too much to wear to work."

I told him it was perfect. He gathered my hair in a bunch and gently pulled it to the side. I stayed still as he secured the clasp, shivered when his knuckles brushed the nape of my neck.

And now it's my turn. It's not jewelry, but Sophie's cookies are the best thing I have to offer at the moment.

I bring the phone to life and type: "Hey. I've got a surprise for you."

I hit "send" and start the Civic. The judge's house isn't far from the town center, maybe a ten-minute drive from the restaurant, down the main road. Might as well start heading there. About five minutes later, my pocket vibrates. I slow down and check my phone.

"What is it?" he wrote back.

I type one-handed: "You'll know soon enough. I'm making a home delivery :)"

I'm about to give the Honda some gas when my phone buzzes again.

"When?"

"In like . . . two minutes? I'm almost at the end of your street lol."

I consider the message, then erase the "lol" and send it. Immediately, the three typing dots show up.

"OK. Don't move. I'll come to you. Cece's asleep and I don't want her to wake up. First Thanksgiving without Mom, you know?"

My head falls back, hard, against the headrest. How did I not think of this? We texted this morning, just our usual "Hi" and "Have a nice day." After that, the Thanksgiving frenzy kept me too busy to check my phone as often as I wanted. All I managed was a terse—and, I realize now, stupid—"Happy Thanksgiving!" during a bathroom break, while Eric banged on the door yelling something about Grey Goose.

"Of course," I text back. "I'm so sorry for dropping by unannounced. I'll wait around the block."

He doesn't respond. Damn it. What was I thinking, showing up without warning?

It's too late to turn back. He must be on his way already. I drive down the street, make a left, and switch off the engine.

A few seconds later, he jogs toward the Civic. I step out. He's not wearing a coat, just a chunky beige sweater. No hat or gloves, either.

When he catches up with me, I chuckle and gesture at his naked throat, his bare hands. "How quickly did you dash out?"

Before he responds, he looks around, as if to check we're alone. Then, he brings his lips to mine, a gentle peck at first, and then another, longer kiss. "Guess I was in a rush to see you." His hands slip under my coat and find my hips. He presses me against the Honda, softly. I wrap my arms around his shoulders, let myself melt into him.

For a moment, I forget about Thanksgiving. I forget about the restaurant. I forget about margins, weak sidecars, stolen ideas—about the tightening in my throat when I think about the future, frozen water in my lungs when I try to picture myself in five years, ten years, twenty years.

As much as it kills me, I break away long enough to hand him the box of cookies.

"Courtesy of Sophie, for our favorite customer."

He holds one of the bags up into the beam of a streetlight. "Cookies. Well, that's lovely. Thank you. And please tell Sophie I said thanks, too."

I tell him he's welcome and again that I'm sorry, so sorry for turning up like this. That I should have known, that I didn't think, that I really hope I didn't bother him.

"Don't worry about it." He places the box on the roof of the Honda. "I should head back," he says, but he doesn't. Something is holding him here. A temptation. A moment, better than he had imagined, begging to be prolonged.

He touches me again. Cups the back of my head, gives my hair a gentle tug. A quick nibble on my lower lip. Fire in my abdomen.

My breathing deepens. I press him against me, as hard as my sore arms allow. I want him, all of him, and I want him to have all of me. He fumbles with my sweater, with my shirt. Urgent fingers against my skin. His cold against my warmth. I close my eyes.

Maybe he feels it before we hear it. His lips disengage. His hands leave me. Before either of these things can register—before I can begin to miss him—it reaches us.

A scream, so piercing it tears the night in half.

CHAPTER 33

The woman in the house

He tells you how to lie to Cecilia about Thanksgiving. "Tell her you're not seeing your family," he instructs you one night. "Tell her they're traveling. That they worked hard their entire lives and now they spend every holiday on a cruise ship."

Cecilia doesn't care too much about your Thanksgiving plans. She tells you about the things she used to do with her mother at this time of the year. Her dad cooked most nights, but Thanksgiving—that was Mom's thing, she says. There was a specific brine recipe, mashed potatoes with just a little bit of skin left in, toffee chip cookies they baked together and brought to their neighbors.

Her dad grinds his teeth through her reminiscing. There is a stiffness to him, a tension in his shoulders. He is a father. He is a single parent.

The night of, he tries. Sort of. He sets the table, proper napkins instead of the usual paper towels, tucked into turkey-shaped rings Cecilia stapled together a long time ago. Orange candles, golden paper plates with a red rim.

Instead of a turkey, he roasts a goose. A guy at work caught it himself, he says. Froze it and sold it to him a couple of days ago. Bile rises at the back of your throat. You poke at the flesh on your plate, white and patchy. You force yourself to chew and swallow, chew and swallow. It doesn't come naturally to you, feeding on a creature captured in the woods and killed.

Carrots with rosemary. Fingerling potatoes. Cranberry sauce out of a can, just how Cecilia likes it. He is trying. This is his little girl, and he needs her to love him. He needs her obedient, blind, and adoring. He needs her to see everything he's done to make her happy.

After dinner, there is a movie. Cecilia isn't into holiday classics. Neither are you. No one's in the mood for big happy families.

Cecilia flicks through suggestions. She settles on a Christmas rom-com. A young English actress plays a woman who has lost control of her life, stuck at a dead-end job, estranged from her sister. A new guy shows up, clearly an angel back from the dead to rescue her. He takes her on adventures around London, shows her all the quirky, charming things she's missed out on.

"Has anyone ever told you," the young English actress asks as she follows the angel down a dark alley, "that there's something slightly serial killer-y about you?" The handsome angel tells her no, "never more than once, anyway." The line gets a chuckle out of Cecilia. Her father doesn't react. Maybe he didn't even hear. Maybe he's texting. You don't know. You focus on the screen.

Your mind travels back to the first Thanksgiving after he took you. It was around then that you realized you were in this for the long haul. That your time in the shed would be counted in years, not months. You tried not to picture your family—your parents at the dinner table, keeping up appearances. Had your brother visited from Maine, or had he skipped the festivities altogether?

You used to be one part of a bigger whole. So often you held them together, your father, your mother, your brother. Lightening the mood after a fight, bringing home the good grades, the cheerful news, material for the family Christmas card. Did they go on without you? Or has your family split, bonds disintegrating as they often do after a terrible loss?

"Shit."

He looks up from his phone. His eyes narrow.

"I have to run out for a second," he says over the movie. "Stay here."

Ostensibly, he's telling Cecilia, but you know he means you. His phone buzzes. He looks down, then back up again. "I'll be right back. I'm just picking something up."

He types quickly, then sets the phone down on the armrest of his chair to push his feet into his boots. Cecilia pauses the film. "What's going on?"

He gazes up, one boot on, the other in his hand. "Nothing. Just a friend who wants to give me something."

His expression is the same as the night he brought you into the house, when his daughter's voice chimed from the other end of the hallway. It's so rare for you to see him like this. Caught off guard, scrambling to keep his two lives from crashing into each other.

"I'll be right back." He grabs his house keys. "I'm not going far." Slowly, purposely, he adds for your benefit: "I'll be just around the corner." He points to some unknown location west of the house. "I'll only be gone for a few minutes."

Cecilia waves at him briefly, eager to start the movie again. You give her father a slight nod.

He leaps more than he walks to the door and, after one last look back at you, steps out. The lock clicks shut from outside, a useless precaution, keeping intruders at bay but not—you are acutely aware of this—barring anyone from leaving the house.

Your brain churns. Thoughts flutter around you like mosquitoes, whiny, too fast for you. You grab for them, try to bring them into focus one at a time.

He is gone. Not for long, he said, but he is gone. It's just the two of you. You and Cecilia. You shift on the couch, a pressure weighing down your stomach, and that's when you see it.

His phone.

He was in such a rush to get out, he left his phone on the armrest.

You look around. The key to his truck is hanging by the door. But what about him?

Where is he?

If you step out—if you make a run for it—will he see you?

Cecilia curls up against you. You fight to keep your focus. Your brain, wading through cornmeal, swimming through molasses. Can you leave her?

A fist tightens in your rib cage.

You stayed for her. The day he didn't handcuff you properly. You told yourself you were staying because of the cameras. Because you weren't sure. Because you were scared. But you could have been convinced. You could have found the courage.

It was the girl. You stayed for the girl. You know that now.

Whichever way you wiggle out of this, it has to involve her. You want her safe. You want your eyes on her at all times.

Just before he left, her father pointed west. On the first night, when he brought you into the house, you came from the opposite direction. You think. You need to trust your memories of the road, of the tire tracks, of the side you assumed you came from. You could drive east and follow the same roads. He made you close your eyes but you felt them underneath you, the smooth movements of the truck that meant asphalt.

You have been waiting for him to mess up. You have been careful. You have waited to be sure.

This has to be it.

If you don't run now—with him gone, his phone and car key at your disposal, and the contours of an escape plan—then when?

Your ears start buzzing. How much time have you already wasted thinking this through—two minutes, three?

It has to be now.

You could be home by Christmas. That does it. It's the final thought you needed to push you over the edge. You grab the remote and pause the movie. Cecilia raises her eyebrows at you, like *Is there a problem?*

You don't know how to pitch this to her. How to tell her that you both have to go. That there are things you know and she doesn't, and that she needs to trust you.

You have to trust you, too.

"I'm going to go," you tell her. "For a ride."

She frowns. "Now?"

"Yeah." You swallow. You try to speak in the clear, stable tone of someone who goes for rides all the time, who keeps her car parked just around the corner. "I just remembered . . . something. I have to go." It sounds so real in your mouth, *I have to go I have to go I have to go.* "It won't take long."

She shrugs. She's used to this, you realize, adults slipping away at all hours of the night, disappearing for unknown reasons, returning like it's the most natural thing in the world.

Then you tell her.

"You need to come with me."

Her forehead creases. She looks like he does when he's annoyed. When you talk to him, ask him for things. She is Cecilia. She is a father's daughter.

"Just go with me," you say.

She turns to face the screen again. "I can't, really. I'd have to tell my dad. And um, there's the movie."

She's so sweet, so polite. Beating around the bush, sparing your feelings. Making up excuses instead of stating the obvious: *I can't disappear with a stranger at night.*

"It's all right," you say. "Your dad won't mind."

She frowns. You are lying and she knows it.

You insist, "It'll be fine." You don't have any arguments to convince her and no time to think of any. He could be back any minute.

You have to go.

"Come on."

You get up. She doesn't move. She's thirteen. Not ten, not six. She won't follow you just because you said so.

You nudge her. "Let's go."

She recoils slightly. You are annoying her, scaring her. She wants you to leave her alone.

Now's not the time to back down. You will explain later. For now all she needs to know is you're on her side, and life will be better if she follows you.

"There's nothing to be worried about. It's just a ride. Okay? We're just going for a ride."

You want to be reassuring, but there is an edge in your voice that creeps you out. You are losing patience.

Do you make a run for it by yourself?

If she won't let you save her, do you save yourself without looking back?

One last try.

You sit back down next to her. You look into the eyes that are half his.

"Listen." You speak in a low tone, your breath hot and damp, fog on an invisible window. "It's nothing. Just a little trip. It's okay, you know. To spend time without him. It's okay to want that."

She curls into a ball, crosses her arms over her shins. "You don't know what you're talking about."

You do not want to tell her your theories about what goes on at night. You know you might be wrong. You know you know nothing.

You soften your voice as much as possible. "I liked spending time with my parents, too," you say. "When I was your age." Your throat tingles. She is here, anchoring you down like a barnacle on a rock. You need to tear yourself away from this house. Tear her away from him. Shuck her like an oyster, one snap and a shell opening, strands coming lose.

"I loved my parents, too," you tell her. "I still do. I love them, too. But it's okay to be your own person. It's okay to leave him. Just for a little while."

She looks up at you. Her cheeks are red-hot, her eyes black with fury. Daddy's girl.

"You don't understand. You don't understand anything." It costs her, being mean to you. She twists her fingers into anxious knots, white knuckles and scarlet skin. "You have no idea what it's like." She looks up at the ceiling, and your heart breaks into a million shards. She's holding back tears. "No one knows," she says. Her voice shakes like a plane falling from the sky. "No one gets it."

"Listen." You have to say it. You have to go for it. "I know, okay? I know what he does to you."

She looks at you blankly. "What?"

There is nothing else you can do to trick her. This clever girl, fiercely loyal. All she wants is to love and be loved. And you have backed her into a corner. You are making her choose, and she hates you for it. You do not blame her.

Every fiber of you pulls you to the outside world, and every fiber of you pulls you right back to her.

You can't do it. As much as you wish you could, you can't leave without her.

You must choose for her.

"All right." You get up. Clasp her arm and start pulling. "Let's go."

You try to give your voice the weight of authority. You try not to squeeze too hard, to pull in a way that won't tug at her shoulder. You do not want to hurt her. Not now, not ever.

You succeed, partly. She's forced to get up from the couch. But she resists you, pulls in the opposite direction.

"What are you doing?"

Her tone is outraged more than panicked. You grab her other arm with your left hand and double your efforts.

You are stronger than you thought. Maybe it's all the food you've been eating. Maybe your muscles have grown. Maybe you are done being breakable. Most likely it's the adrenaline coursing through your veins and the pull of the night air outside, the call of the asphalt you will soon drive on.

You gather your strength and tug at her arms one more time. Something goes wrong, a miscalculation—her ankle catches on the coffee table with a thud. She gives you a look of such betrayal you have to avert your eyes. You have hurt the girl. The last thing, the very last thing you wanted to do, in this life and all the ones to come.

Before you can apologize, a sound rises through the house, wounded, primal. It's as if your own anger and pain, all five years' worth of them, are passing from your skin to hers like an electric current. She screams and screams and screams. Her mouth is wide and her eyes are wrinkled shut and she does it louder, longer, and with more fury than you've ever heard. You want her to stop and still you are with her, so close to her throughout this moment. When you think she's about to run out of air, something in her opens, a new influx of breath, and she starts over. She screams in a way that frightens you but also secretly, fleetingly, liberates you. She screams enough for the two of you.

CHAPTER 34

Emily

We stand next to each other. For a few instants, all I notice is the absence of his hands in my hair, of his chest against mine, still heaving after we've been torn apart. His breath rises, warm droplets in the icy air.

Reality hits me like a cold shower. That scream. Straight out of a slasher film, when the curtain slides to reveal a dark silhouette, the glimmer of a butcher knife.

We're standing in the middle of an empty street. Whatever caused that scream can't be more than five hundred feet away. I freeze.

"What was that?"

My voice shakes. His body has shifted toward the scream, which I now realize came from his house. His face tenses up. Then he seems to process something, and his features relax.

"That would be my daughter."

I frown. How is this good news?

"She has nightmares. Night terrors. She was asleep when you texted me, remember?"

Of course. I lean against the Honda, my legs shaky with relief. His thirteen-year-old daughter, woken up by a bad dream.

"I'll go check on her," he says.

I'm so relieved, I suppress a giggle, my heart as light as a helium balloon in my chest.

"Of course," I say, my tone serious again. "Go."

I unlock the car and slip into the driver's seat. He waits until the door slams shut, then gives me a quick wave and starts jogging back to the house. I watch him in the rearview mirror, his stride escalating into a full-blown sprint. A father on a mission.

I back up quickly. There's a thud. I hit the brake pedal, my heart in my throat again. Did I just hit something? I didn't see anything, but a squirrel, maybe?

Or a person?

Did I just hit someone? The roads are so fucking dark around here. Even the judge is always complaining about it, begging the city council to splurge on a few more streetlamps.

I stop, ready to puke, and check my front tires.

Another wave of relief washes over me. It's the box of cookies, the same one he placed on the roof of my car and forgot in his haste.

I keep driving. Even though I know the scream was nothing, I'm not in the mood to stop on a dark stretch of road by myself. I drive straight home.

CHAPTER 35

The woman in the house

The moment Cecilia starts to scream, you let go. Open your fingers. Release her into the wild. You plead with her to stop, to just shhhh shhhh shhhh, but it's too late. She screams until he comes in, a furious blur heading straight for the two of you.

This is the biggest mistake you have made in five years. You know this immediately, with blinding clarity.

What he sees: his wailing kid, his precious child, his only daughter, who suddenly stops yelling, and you, hunched next to her, imploring arms raised in vain.

The door slams behind him. One, two, three strides are enough. He steps between you and his child, grabs one of your wrists and one of hers.

Cecilia tries to explain, her words stumbling into one another. It's okay, she says, it's all right, I just thought I saw something, I got spooked so I screamed but it was nothing, I'm not hurt, no one's hurt, Dad, Rachel was just trying, she was just trying to help.

Intuitively, she knows to do it. She lies in hopes of saving you.

He lets out a long exhale. Lets go of Cecilia's arm and yours. His chest moves up and down, up and down, as he tries to slow his breath.

He smiles. This is all for show. You can still feel it, the fury pulsing underneath. His nostrils are flared, his eyes unfocused.

"You okay?" he asks in a calm voice. A dad's voice.

She nods.

He turns to you, as if waiting for you to answer the same question. All an act. All for her benefit.

You nod, too.

He brings his attention back to his daughter.

"Why don't you go to your room for a bit?"

She says okay, scampers without a look back. She has done what she could.

Upstairs, the door to Cecilia's room shuts.

"I'm sorry," you whisper. "It's like she said, she thought she saw something and she got scared and—"

"Shut up."

"I'm sorry," you tell him, and again: "I'm so sorry."

He does not hear you.

"What the fuck did you do?"

His hands are on you. Grabbing you, shaking you. Before him, you didn't know—never fully grasped the concept, the devastating simplicity of someone with more physical strength than you. You had never been reduced to nothing by another person's clenched fists. Never had your shoulders shaken so hard you could feel the whiplash take hold of your neck in real time.

"It was a misunderstanding," you say. "I was only trying to—"

"I said shut up."

He nudges you against the wall, silent, deadly.

If you could, you would run up to your bedroom like Cecilia. You would disappear from his life, allow him to forget you for a moment. But you can't, because the room belongs to him and the world belongs to him, and he wants you gone but he also wants you here, right here, where he can see you.

His arm digs into your throat. Pushes and pushes and pushes until black dots start dancing in front of your eyes.

He has done this before, but he has always let go at the last moment. This time, he doesn't.

You cannot breathe. It's like you never knew how. You try and try and try but the walls of your trachea have collapsed and nothing can pass through.

Alarming sounds come out of you. Gurgles. Attempts at whining. Last-moment sounds. Dying sounds.

Ten seconds. You heard that on a podcast one time. You have ten seconds until you lose consciousness. Until your body slips away from you forever and you lose any chance to save it.

You do not ask your arms to move, nor your legs. They just do it. You do not understand until you feel his grasp loosen, ever so briefly.

You hear yourself gasp before you can feel the air, finally, clearing your windpipe. You cough. You choke. You take another breath.

You are so focused on bringing yourself back to life that you forget, for a second or so, that he is here.

He reminds you.

You pushed him away, just now. You fought back, just a little. And he didn't like it. He didn't like it one bit.

He finds you again. An arm around your waist, a hand on your mouth and nose. Silencing your cough. Stealing the air from you once more.

"Shut the fuck up," he whispers in your ear. He is behind you, his full weight on your back. "Just shut. The fuck. Up."

All this man wants, all this man has ever wanted, is for you to stop talking. To stop moving. He just wants you to stop.

Rule number four of staying alive outside the shed:

You don't know.

Whatever it is, you just violated it.

With great effort, you jerk your head a couple of inches to the left. Your gaze meets his for a second. This man. He should have killed you a long time ago. He sees that now, and you see it, too. So obvious, so undeniable. You have been nothing but trouble.

His left arm wraps around your neck. There is a pressure at the back of your head—his right hand, you presume. A choke hold. He has you in a choke hold.

You cannot move. You can barely think.

You don't know if you're breathing. That knowledge does not belong to you. What belongs to you is your blurring vision and your weakening limbs and the pulsing in your ears—your blood, each contraction of your heart like a strum on a guitar.

The sound fills you.

It slows down.

One beat after the other, farther apart.

There is one last try, a surge of brightness rocking your spine against his chest.

And then nothing.

Everything goes black.

CHAPTER 36

Cecilia

When I was little, my dad taught me how to read. Every night, he would quiz me: What sound do an *i* and an *n* make, strung together? What about a double *o*? And a double *e*? Later on, he taught me words. Food words, nature words, plant words. Construction words, medical words, electricity words. One time we drove past a bunch of turkeys on the side of the road—I must have been six or seven—and he told me that was called a gang, a gang of turkeys.

I became obsessed. I went through a whole phase of wanting to know what different groups of animals were called. A swarm of bees, a quiver of cobras. He printed a list off the internet and every day he taught me a new one. A colony of bats, or a camp, or a cloud. A sloth of bears. A caravan of camels. A shadow of jaguars. We made a game of it, anytime he drove me anywhere. He'd say falcons and I'd say cast, a cast of falcons. Crocodiles? A bask of crocodiles. Rhinos? A crash. Lemurs? A conspiracy. Crows? A murder. That was my favorite one. A murder of crows. Crows are so goth. It had to be a murder.

We fight, my dad and I.

Of course we fight. He's my dad. But I know he loves me.

Some daughters won't ever know what it feels like to be loved this way. I hear people at school. In the stories of their lives, their dads are always in the background, working late, showing up for games and holidays like guests instead of actual parents.

Me, I'll always know. Sometimes I think it's the only thing I'll know for sure in my entire life. No matter what, if I die old or young, sick or healthy, happy or miserable, married or not. If anyone asks—like if I become famous and suddenly everyone wants to know what it was like to be me before they knew my name—there's one thing I'll be able to say with certainty.

I will tell the world my father loved me.

CHAPTER 37

The woman in danger

He takes you to the woods.

Here's how it happens: he lets your body slide, rag-doll-limp, to the living room floor. Hurt, but breathing. That's the thing with you: you never stop breathing.

He slides one arm under your back, wraps the other behind your knees. Maybe that's how he carries you to the truck. Or maybe he slings you over his shoulder, potato-sack style. You're not some delicate little thing. You know what you are: A chore to be checked off. A problem to solve.

Or perhaps he nudges you and you open your eyes, not really conscious but awake enough to be lifted up. Maybe the both of you hobble to the truck together, your arm over his shoulder, his fingers tight on your wrist, one hand around your waist. Maybe you look like friends after a night out—you sloppily drunk, and he bringing you to safety.

A door opens. Cold air on your face. You hear the rustle of the wind in tree branches, but you can't see anything. Not a single leaf. Someone has turned the lights off in your head, your brain a mess of broken bulbs. You cry silent sobs. If you're about to go, you need to see the trees one last time. You need their roots to steady you, the sweet sway of their leaves to lull you to sleep.

He sits you down on the passenger seat. Your head rolls against the window, the glass like an icicle against your skin. He holds you upright to wrap the seat belt around your chest. What does it matter? you want to ask. Who cares if the truck skids off the road and you go flying through the windshield? You'd be gone, and he wouldn't have to lift a finger.

But he's not a man who leaves things up to fate. He slams your door shut and walks to the other side.

If this is it, then he will be the last person to see you alive. The last person to see you blink, swallow. The last one to watch your chest rise and fall like a metronome.

If you choose to speak, he will be the last person to hear the sound of your voice.

Is there anything you need to get off your chest? Anything you need someone to hear before it's too late?

He starts the truck.

I had a mother, you could tell him. *I had a father. Like your daughter. I had a father. I had a brother. I was born on a stormy summer night. My mother was so done being pregnant. She was relieved I finally came into the world. Happy, too, but mainly relieved. My birth marked the end of a period of great unpleasantness.*

You never saw it, but I used to love my life. It wasn't perfect. It was comfortable, but it wasn't always easy. My first boyfriend hurt me and I hurt him back, one voice mail on his answering machine, a furious exclamation mark bringing young love to an end. My brother hurt himself, twice, and then I hurt him, too.

I searched for my place in the world. Sometimes I felt I had found it, but then I worried it would be taken from me. A stranger hurt me—not you, another one before. You weren't the only one. You don't know this. You never asked and I never told you. But I knew what it was like, before you found me. I knew what it was like when someone you don't know, someone you have never met, decides a part of you will forever belong to them.

That was your one mistake, the day I met you. You thought you would surprise me. You thought you would be the first bad thing to ever happen to me. But I knew how it worked. I was born in the city that killed Kitty Genovese; some people heard her scream but were scared of speaking to the police, or they were confused, or they didn't think calling would do any good. What Kitty Genovese taught me: when the world doesn't look out for you, you can't look out for others.

I took my first steps in a park where, one morning in August of 1986, the body of an eighteen-year-old girl was found, hours after she'd left a bar with a boy she knew. Across the street from the same park was where the singer was gunned down in 1980, by a man who had in his pocket a paperback of my favorite novel when I was a teen.

So no, when you found me, it didn't surprise me. Of course you found me. You had to happen to someone, and you happened to me.

The truck comes to a halt. The engine stops.

The year of my birth: 1991. I looked it up on Wikipedia one day, the things that happened that year. Like a horoscope. I wanted to know under what auspices I had been born.

Maybe you remember. The Giants won the Super Bowl. Dick Cheney canceled a fifty-seven-billion-dollar contract for some type of military aircraft. A killer jet, a stealth bomber, a machine designed to annihilate. Do you see where I'm going with this?

That year, the woman—you know the one: Charlize Theron played her in a movie—confessed to killing seven men. They beat her, she said. They tried to rape her. She had no choice.

It was a time of turmoil. Operation Desert Storm in the background. A grand jury indicted Mike Tyson. The police arrested Jeffrey Dahmer. In Europe, the Soviet Union ended.

The world, it was so wretched. So chaotic. I loved it then and I love it now. That's the one thing you never took from me. I stopped loving others. I stopped loving myself. I stopped loving my family when loving them became too much. But I never stopped loving this big, absurd, beautiful ensemble we all form together.

I don't know why you took it so personally, like an offense to you and your beliefs—the statistical improbability of human life on earth.

There is a sigh and the click of his seat belt. Footsteps outside, going around the truck. The passenger door opens. He frees you from the vehicle. You can't see, but you remember the woods—your favorite spot before he took you, the tallest trees, the softest grass.

This ground isn't soft. You land on it with a thud. Your skull explodes against something—roots, a tree stump, maybe a rock. All you know is your head is burning and your scalp is gushing and it all hurts so much.

It seems unnecessary, to make it hurt this way.

But you don't make the rules. Never have.

This is where you end up, a quivering shape on the ground. Soon it will all be over. He will do what he has to do and then you will go. Finally.

You never realized until now how much energy it takes to stay alive. How tired you are from clinging to your beating heart, your breathing lungs, when the elements keep conspiring against you.

It's time to go.

You hear the click of a gun. The grass ruffles next to you. His hand cradles the back of your head. You feel the warmth of his body next to yours, a cold rim of metal against your temple.

Is this how it happens? You always thought the gun was for show. You figured he did it with his hands, pressing down, waiting, watching, listening for gasps, the hissing sound of air leaving a body, never to return.

Maybe you've angered him so much he doesn't have the patience for that. Maybe he, too, wants this to be over as fast as possible.

He shifts. His breath finds your ear, hot and frazzled. He whispers something you can't hear. You wait for it. You imagine a bang, fireworks behind your eyelids, a flash of pain shattering your skull in half. You wait and you wait and it doesn't come.

There is a thud. Both of his hands are on you.

A thought pushes through you.

Did he just drop the gun?

His fingers run across the back of your scalp, where your skull has split open. A blast of pain bursts through your brain. It radiates across your body, brings chills and nausea and a moan, and you can't feel your toes and you can't feel your hands and you can't feel your arms and then nothing.

You are lost in darkness.

CHAPTER 38

The woman, a long time ago

After your brother shuns you, you take a psychology class. Your professor used to treat veterans with PTSD. One day, he explains that trauma is what happens after you see yourself die. You witness the story of your own death, and it rings so true you're never the same again.

You don't get it, until you do.

One Saturday evening, Julie convinces you to go out. She has a new girlfriend. On the dance floor, she kisses her in front of you. For the first time, your friend—your best friend, the only person you could imagine living with—is in love. You welcome that knowledge like a precious gift.

Your fingers go numb. You don't realize immediately what's happening. This is how it works: you're slipping but you don't realize it, and by the time you catch up, it's too late. An odd calm envelops you. You float above the dance floor, separated from the crowd by an invisible veil. Blue halos undulate around every light. For a few minutes, you feel at peace, and then you feel strange.

You slip away from the dance floor. Put your drink down on the nearest table. Your drink—you never left it unattended. But you didn't keep your palm over it at all times. The glass didn't have a lid. You were dancing. You left the door open a crack, the tiniest crack through which a stranger could slip in to hurt you.

You step outside. What you need is a cold gust of wind, a blast of Arctic air to snap you out of it. The nor'easter nibbling at your cheeks, reminding you that you're alive. But the air that night is warm and sticky, and your head fills with syrup.

You hail a taxi. It both shocks and relieves you that you are able to do so.

Inside the cab, you drift in and out of consciousness. Nothing hurts, but everything is wrong. "Sir," you tell the driver. "Please, sir."

He glances at you in the rearview mirror. You don't remember his face. You will never remember his face.

You ask him, Please, sir, can you call my friend—I think someone put something in my drink. You can't believe your own words. The cabdriver pulls over—you think he does. He hands you his phone.

You type Julie's phone number as fast as you can, before it falls out of your brain forever. *Quick,* your body tells you, *you have to get all the numbers out before I shut down.* You think, *Shut down,* and your body says, *Yes, shut d*— and everything goes dark.

You wake up, medical-drama style, on a bed in the ER. Julie's concerned face floats above yours. "Can you hear me?" she asks, and it turns out you've been awake in some capacity for some time, you just can't remember it. There is a black hole where memories should be. It will never fill up. In the great movie of your life, the screen stays black for several minutes. You feel robbed, like something of great value has been taken from you.

Gloved hands tug at your shoulder. You have to sit up. You have to pull your shirt up so they can stick electrodes to your chest. You have to hold out your arm for blood tests. "I don't want blood tests," you tell them. "Even on a good day, I faint when people draw blood from me." They insist, and the more you tell them no, the less they listen. You were brought unconscious on a stretcher with alcohol on your breath. Nothing you say matters. "I don't consent," you say. "I don't consent to these tests." A man in scrubs rolls his eyes at you.

You tell Julie you're going to throw up. A plastic pouch materializes. It's half full already; you must have been puking earlier. You hurl a string of bile. Your stomach is empty but the muscles in your abdomen keep clenching. Terrible sounds come out of you, all throat, no voice. You throw up so hard your abs will be sore the next day.

In between gags, you explain what happened. You phrase it in different ways. *I was drugged. My drink was spiked. Someone put something in my drink.* Several hours later, when you're ready to get discharged, a diagnosis sheet is handed to you. It says, will always say, "alcohol poisoning."

No one believes you.

Julie calls an Uber. Back in the apartment, she says you'll feel better after a shower. "Get the ER off you," she says. You wash your body, but you're too tired to tackle your hair.

"Tomorrow," you tell Julie. "I'll do it tomorrow."

Your head touches the pillow. Here, a dissonance—everything normal, everything exceptional. You are so lucky to be alive. So lucky to be sleeping in your own bed.

The next day is a blur. You wake up with a headache. Chew on a bagel. Go for a walk. There is a great divide between you and the world. It's here but you can't touch it. You are not sure how to exist in it anymore.

You don't know it yet, but pieces of you are broken that will never feel whole again.

You don't know it yet, but this isn't the great tragedy of your life.

This is the part he didn't anticipate. That day near the woods, he needed you to be surprised, shocked by the very possibility that someone might want to harm you.

What happened at the club, it changed you. By the time he found you, the only part left of you was the one that knew how to survive.

CHAPTER 39

The woman in the house

A cold, hard surface against your back. A faint rattle of metal above your head. The back of your skull burns. Your eyelids are heavy. Your body is one large wound.

Everything is a blur. Dark walls and darker shapes—furniture? Boxes.

Piles of boxes. The outline of a chair. What you think is a workbench, a pegboard with tools.

Sounds coming from above—a voice, then another.

You are in the house. The bowels of it.

The basement. That has to be it.

You shift the slightest bit and wince. Everything hurts.

But you are alive.

CHAPTER 40

The woman in the house

You don't know how many days go by. You don't know what he tells his kid. It's not your job to know. You are so tired of carrying yourself through everything. Of bolstering his lies, of playing along.

This is the most honest the two of you have ever been with each other.

He comes in and doesn't say a word. He brings you water, sometimes soup. He feeds you. Lifts cups of water and spoonfuls of chicken broth to your lips. He props you up in the crook of his elbow. When you choke, he pats you on the back, between your shoulder blades.

Sometimes you think that's all he wants. To possess someone, fully and absolutely. For someone to need him, only him.

That must be why he didn't do it. In the woods. He saw something in you that was more interesting than death. Pain, and your endless ability to feel it, to demonstrate it. He will entertain the possibility of you being whole again, as long as he's the one who gets to put you back together.

Rule number five of staying alive outside the shed: He must need you at least as much as you need him.

One morning, after Cecilia leaves for school, he brings you to the bathroom and leans you over the tub. Water cascades onto your head, into your ears and mouth. You taste blood. He shampoos your hair, gentle strokes against your scalp. Still, it burns. You wince, and he says, Don't move, don't move—it will go faster if you stay still.

After, you throw up. He grabs you by the shoulders, directs you over the toilet. He gathers your hair in one hand and holds it back, like you're hungover and he's your friend, like you're sick and he's your mother. Your stomach muscles clench so tightly you get out of breath. You keep retching even when there's nothing left, noisy, painful gags echoing down the toilet bowl. You grab his hand. It's a reflex. You don't know you're doing it until he gives you a soft squeeze back.

You get through it together.

He takes you back to the bedroom, lays you down on the bed. No more hardwood floor. You let yourself sink into the mattress, the sheets soft against your cheeks. If it must, the comforter will swallow you. The room will collapse on top of you. You will let it all happen to you.

You are done fighting.

He rests his palm against your forehead. You've spiked a fever. Your vision blurs. Every time you try to sit up, the ground opens underneath you. You tell him you need to see someone, a doctor, anyone. He tells you not to worry. It will all be okay, he says, as long as you calm down.

Your brain is on fire. You are wounded and he's here and you feel cold, so cold, even as he piles a new blanket on top of you. Sorrow freezes you from inside. You start weeping. You cry for yourself, for Cecilia, for her dead mom, for the women he is now after. It all crashes into you, one sadness after the other, until he asks what's going on.

"Your wife," you say between sobs. "Your poor wife." It's all you can muster. He pauses and looks sharply at you.

"What about my wife?"

You try to explain, to drag him under your own tidal wave of pain. "She was so young," you tell him. "They both were. Your wife and your kid. I'm just so sorry for your kid." And you mean it. You feel her loss as acutely as you feel the absence of your own mother. Do you even still have a mother? And if she's alive, does she still hold out hope that you are, too?

"Cancer," he says. "Nasty stuff."

Cancer, you want to say. *Really?*

Through the haze of your fever, you squint at him. You thought maybe he'd done it. Maybe he'd been the one to kill her. But he's telling the truth. The two of you have never been so close, so direct with each other.

He smooths the blanket over your legs. "Sometimes it's just bad luck," he says. "She kicked it once, but it came back five years ago."

YOU STOP BEING afraid. You are so sick of scheming, of plotting your way through another day.

And so you tell him. Later that night, when he returns, you tell him.

"You did it wrong. The other day. You didn't check the handcuffs."

He's sitting on the bed next to you. The bottle of Tylenol rattles between his hands.

"They were open," you continue. "Just wide open. I could have left, you know. But I didn't."

He puts down the Tylenol. He sighs—his breath on your face, on your neck, on your chest. He leans over you and whispers in your ear.

"I know."

For a brief second, you see the light. A tragic thought pierces you, entry wound, exit wound. It jolts you awake. It undoes you, the entire geometry of you, your straight lines and your bends and angles clattering to the ground.

He didn't mess up.

SHE KICKED IT once, but it came back five years ago.

The information travels through you in the night.

It takes its time to reach you, but once it finds you, it spreads to your entire self like an infection.

Five years.

You think.

This is when he found you.

He was going to kill you, but he didn't.

Things were happening to him. Things he couldn't stop.

Death was happening to him, to the family he had built. And there was nothing he could do about it.

It must have unmoored him.

He needed control. This is what it's about for him. Deciding where a woman begins and where she ends. Deciding everything, and getting away with it.

He got you. You were in the truck.

He was going to kill you, but he didn't.

CHAPTER 41

The woman without a number

You look for him. The person who roofied you. You assume it's a guy. What are the odds? You try to find out. You grab your laptop and look up "drink spiking statistics," "drink spiking perpetrators," "people who roofie other people." You can't find what you're looking for. People like you don't report what happened to them.

Everyone on the street is a suspect. The guy in front of you at the coffee shop. The yoga instructor, the bus driver, your professors. No one above suspicion.

You stop sleeping through the night. Every evening around seven, a shadow descends upon you. Before bed, you check that the door is locked. Check, and check again. You look inside closets. You check the bathroom. Check under your bed. You search and search and search for the threat following you like a shadow.

You listen to the stories. You read them. There are podcasts, online threads unraveling the mysteries for you. You learn about the student who went out with friends and never came home. The wife who went missing and her husband definitely did it, but they didn't catch him. The girl who went on spring break. The woman who crashed her car and vanished before dispatchers arrived at the scene.

Perhaps you absorbed so many stories they ended up absorbing you.

You lose the ability to focus. Your professors' lectures fade into the background. You fall asleep in class and stare at the ceiling at night. Your grades plummet. You stop drinking, cold turkey. You stop seeing friends. You stop texting Matt, your almost-boyfriend. You just stop.

After a while it's just you, Julie, and the ghosts. Julie never gives up on you. "I worry about you," she says after you get kicked out of Media Law for snoozing at your seat.

"I'm okay," you tell her.

"No, you're not," she says. "It's fine."

"I think I just need a break," you say.

Julie tells you that's fine, too. So you take a break. You speak to your academic adviser and go online searching for trees, air, and silence. For the opposite of the city.

THE CABIN IS small. Ranch-style, one bedroom. Crucially, it belongs to a European woman who has installed shutters on all the windows. The woman believes in locks, in a robust security system. There, you will be safe.

The shuttered house is two hours out of Manhattan. You drain what's left of your meager savings—four years' worth of summer jobs, of internships fetching coffee and groceries for editors who don't bother learning your name—to rent a car. One Sunday evening, you pack a suitcase full of leggings, soft sweaters, and quirky little books. You drive upstate. You put your clothes in the European lady's drawers. Finally, you take a breath.

Leaving the city is like a massage for your brain. That week, you go to bed early and get up whenever the birds start singing. You keep up with schoolwork to a degree, but mostly you drink tea and read your funny little books and nap a lot. You find a nature book and study birdsong. You start believing in a new world.

THERE IS A place you like. In the woods. Not too far off the main road. You walk there in the morning, after the sun rises but before it starts giving off any warmth.

Your place is a clearing, of sorts. Grass surrounded by trees. Trees in a circle. Your place is green, then brown, then green again, and then blue. It's always quiet, except for the softest sounds. Wind whooshing in tree leaves, swirling through blades of grass. Woodpeckers and squirrels. Birds you can't identify despite your best efforts.

You like to sit down and close your eyes. Feel the humidity seeping through your leggings and let the ground hold you up. Tune out the world to feel yourself exist in it.

One morning, you are walking home from the clearing. You are not in the woods, exactly, but you are not in the town center, either.

It's a country road. Not enough traffic to justify a sidewalk. It's a place where no one sees you. If you were to scream—this has occurred to you a few times—no one would hear you.

That day, there is a car. It puts its siren on. A Pavlovian response ticks through you—you hear a siren, you think the person at the wheel is in charge.

You glance behind your shoulder. It's not a cop car. It's a white pickup truck. Cops do that, you think. They drive unmarked cars all the time.

Through the windshield, the man behind the wheel motions for you to stop on the side of the road. You stop. A safety rule drilled into you since childhood resurfaces: you remain at a distance from the truck.

The man steps out. You take him in. Your brain sizes him up. Friend or foe, ally or attacker? Shake his hand or run?

The man looks clean. He smiles. Lines crinkle at the corners of his eyes. White teeth, parka, jeans. The hair, freshly cut. The hands, clean.

In this moment, you are ready to trust him. In this moment, you do not fear.

THE MAN STEPS closer. He smells nice, too. You never expect evil to smell nice. What kind of devil wears cologne?

Later on, you think about carnivorous plants. How they glow to attract insects. How they trick them with tantalizing nectars before feasting on them.

It takes you a second to see the gun, black pistol, black silencer. You see it, and then you feel it. For the first time in your life, a weapon digging into your shoulder blade.

"Don't move," he tells you. "If you try to run, I will hurt you. Do you understand?"

You nod your head yes.

"Wallet? Phone?"

You surrender your possessions to him. You have thought about what you'd do if you were robbed at gunpoint, and promised yourself you would give everything in exchange for your life.

"Gun? Pepper spray? Knife?"

You shake your head no.

"I'm going to check, and if I find out you lied to me, I won't be happy."

He pats you down. You stand still. This is the first test, and you pass. You haven't lied to him.

"Jewelry?"

"Just what I'm wearing."

He waits for you to remove your necklace, slips it into his pocket. In another timeline, this is where it ends. This is where he returns to the truck and you walk away slowly, then run, back to the house and back to the city. This is where you find people and tell them what happened.

In your timeline, the man with the gun throws your phone to the ground and smashes it with his boot. He waves the gun in the direction of the truck.

"Get in," he says.

Here is what it feels like, the moment your life becomes a tragedy. The moment you've anticipated. When your life stops being yours and turns into a crime story.

It feels like your legs are turning to lead, your rib cage is freezing into place, your brain skimming through a list of possibilities—run, scream, comply. But mainly, it feels like nothing. The earth doesn't split open. You are still you. It's the world around you that changes. Everything changes but you.

Run, scream, comply. Running is out of the question. You could beat him, but you don't run from the man with the gun. Not if there's any chance he'll catch you. Scream? Only scream if you know you'll be heard. You are on a quiet road with no one else in sight. You do not scream.

Comply. You do not know, at this point, what the man wants. If you comply, there is a chance he will let you go.

You get into the truck.

He walks back to the driver's side. Calm and smooth. The soft focus of a man used to the world obeying him.

He tucks the gun into what you guess is a holster strapped around his hips. You do not look at him directly; eye contact feels like a lethal idea. You stare straight ahead through the windshield. As you try to focus on your surroundings, something stirs in the back of your brain. You saw something. Just a few seconds ago, as you were leaning to get inside the truck. Your gaze caught on the backseat and you saw. A shovel, rope, handcuffs. A roll of trash bags.

The man presses a button. Doors lock on both sides.

All the hopeful parts of you die together.

He keeps quiet, eyes on the road. Focused. A man inhabiting a routine. Someone who has done this before.

Talk. The only thing you can do. You can't run, you can't scream. But you can talk. You think you can talk.

You swallow. Search for words, bland but personal. A bridge from you to him. An escape trail under a bed of leaves.

"Are you from around here?"

It's the best you've got, and it gets nothing out of him.

You detach your gaze from the road and look at him. *Young,* you think. *Not bad-looking.* A man you could have met at the grocery store, in line at a coffee shop.

"You know," you say, "you don't have to do this."

He ignores you still.

"Look at you," you insist. Then, timidly, your voice fading: "Look at me."

He doesn't look.

You think about the stories. The podcasts. The news articles. The tabloid headlines, long and convoluted, with the most outrageous WORDS in all caps. Some of the stories came with tips. *Humanize yourself to your captor. Hold your keys between your fingers and use them as a weapon. Jab them in his eyes. Hit him in the nose. Kick him in the nuts. Scream. Don't scream. Surprise him. Don't surprise him.*

What the stories never said: at the end of the day, if a man wants to kill you, he kills you. It's not on you to convince him not to.

You look out the window. You think: *Almost. Something bad happened to me, and I thought I was going to die but I didn't, and I almost made it. It just wasn't meant to be.*

You don't want to die, but death makes sense to you.

Something surges through you. Maybe you stop being afraid. Maybe you're more terrified than ever, and it unlocks the reckless parts of you. You keep talking. You say a bunch of bullshit, like you don't care anymore. Talking is the only thing that belongs to you, and you're going to use it for all it's worth.

"The weather is so nice up here," you say. "I watched a movie the other night and I expected it to end well but it didn't. Don't you hate when that happens?"

He raises an eyebrow at you, just barely.

"I don't even watch that many movies," you continue, "precisely for that reason. I don't like investing two, three hours of my time only to end up disappointed. Or sad."

His fingers flick an invisible speck of dust off the steering wheel. Long fingers, strong hands. Bad news everywhere.

"Shut up," he says.

Or else? You'll kill me?

You stare back outside. He's driving down a stretch of road you don't recognize, trees and mud as far as you can see.

Then, a deer. He sees it coming from afar and slows down, waits for it to cross. A responsible driver. Now's not the time to crash or stall out. What would he do, call AAA? How would he explain the quivering girl in the passenger seat, and all that stuff in the back?

You watch as the deer gets away. She's not coming to save you. But behind her, you spot them: black birds, at least ten of them, pecking at a tree trunk.

"It's called a murder," you say.

The truck rolls past the birds. They turn their beady eyes up to you, like your presence compels them to believe in something.

He takes his foot off the gas pedal. The truck stops. He turns to look at you. Really look at you, for the first time.

Blue eyes, you think. *How dare you have blue eyes? How dare you ruin that for everybody?*

"What did you just say?" he asks.

You tilt your head toward the birds.

"That's what they call a group of crows. Not a flock or a fleet or anything. A murder of crows."

His Adam's apple bobs up and down. What you just said, it must mean something to him. You don't know if it's good or bad. You don't know if it's anything of value.

You don't know it yet, but this man has a family. A daughter and a wife, whose cancer has just returned.

You don't know it yet, but this man has trouble believing in anything. For the first time since he started killing, he has trouble believing in himself.

He turns to face the road. His fingers grip the steering wheel, white knuckles on black polyurethane.

Outside the truck, a crow flies away.

The truck starts again. He gives it some gas, then veers to the right. The truck comes to a halt. He steers the other way, across the road, and hits the gas pedal. Your body shifts against the seat, rocked by his maneuvering.

A U-turn.

A fucking U-turn.

You have no idea what this means.

He takes one hand off the wheel and shuffles around the glove compartment until he finds a bandanna.

"Put this on," he says.

You don't move.

"Over your eyes," he says impatiently, like *Don't make me change my mind.*

You bandanna yourself blind.

He drives and drives and drives. It could be forty minutes or sixty or two hundred. You hear his breath, slow, with the occasional sigh. The tap of his fingers on the wheel. Pedals groaning underneath his feet.

Some jerks, followed by a never-ending straight line. The truck slows down. You hear the brakes, the gearshift squeaking this way and that. The engine goes quiet.

A tug at the back of your head. The bandanna slips off your face. You try to look around, but he grabs your chin so you're forced to focus on him.

"We're going to do this quickly," he tells you. He's holding the gun again, waving it in your face. "We're going to get out of here and walk together."

Then, the rules. "If you try anything—anything at all, we're going back to the truck." He waits, like *Did you hear what I just said?*

You nod. He steps out of the truck, grabs a couple of items from the backseat—the handcuffs and the rope, from what you can see—and collects you on the other side. "Don't look around," he says, "just keep your eyes on the ground." His hand clasps your left arm, so tight you feel bruises forming.

He walks you away from his truck and down a long, winding dirt path. You sneak glances. Already, you are learning to take what you can. You catch a flash of the house and the matching buildings surrounding it on the property. No neighbors. His garden, lovely and well tended. You want to cling to it all, but he is a man with a purpose, climbing a hill. He is a man taking you to a shed.

The door shuts behind you. You don't know it yet, but this is when it happens. This is when your world freezes into a new shape.

At this point in time, the shed is a work in progress. Tools strewn across the floor, a bag of fertilizer in a corner. Foldable chair and table, a pile of magazines—porn or guns, you can't tell for sure. Probably a mix of both.

This is his space. You will find out later on that he has started preparing it for the faint, distant, entirely theoretical possibility of someone like you. Someone he might like to keep. He has soundproofed it. Padded the floor with a rubber mat, run his hands on the walls and plugged every last gap with caulk. It's not done, though. You are not the one he meant to keep. You are a spur-of-the-moment decision, an impulse buy.

He will return the next day to finish the job. He will nail a chain to the wall. He will remove his stuff, clear the space. He will make it yours. For now, he brings your hands behind your back and handcuffs you. Ties the rope around your ankles, knots it around the door handle.

"I need to go to the house for a minute," he says. "I'm the only one home. If you scream, I'm the only one who will hear you, and I won't be happy. Believe me."

You believe him.

As soon as the door shuts behind him, you try. You wriggle your wrists, twist your ankles, reach for tools. But he knows how to handcuff someone. He knows how to tie a knot. And he knows to move his tools out of reach from the woman he just tied up in his garden shed.

You need to trust that people will look for you. Your photo will circulate on social media. Your parents and Julie—your throat closes at the thought of them—will put up posters. They will give interviews, plead for your safe return.

You need to trust that this is temporary, and one day the world will find you.

But there are things you know that he doesn't. Things that will work to his advantage. Anyone who knows you will say that you haven't been yourself. That prior to your disappearance, you became withdrawn. You fell asleep in class. Your grades suffered. You packed your belongings, left the city you loved and the people you knew.

A new story will emerge. Days will go by, weeks, months. People will say it to themselves at first, and then, as they get more comfortable, to one another: Maybe you went missing on purpose. Maybe you drove somewhere and allowed yourself to slip out of existence. You jumped into a ravine, fell into water. Maybe you started over somewhere else. Maybe you are free, finally, of your demons.

No one waits for their dead to come back to life.

Eventually, people will stop looking for you. They will stop showing your picture. They will let you fade away. They will stop telling your story, until one day you're the only one left to remember it.

CHAPTER 42

The woman in the house

The fever goes down. You stop throwing up. He keeps bringing you food, but he doesn't watch over you. His interest is dwindling.

The world comes back into focus. The indentations at the back of your head even out. The wounds begin to heal. When you wake up, your pillow isn't caked with blood.

One evening, he shows up empty-handed. It's time to go back downstairs, he tells you. Dinner's ready.

You pull yourself up. The floor is water. The floor is the rowdy sea. You are on a ship, swaying. He says, Come on, come on. You steady yourself, one hand against the wall. *I don't know if I'm ready,* you want to tell him. *I've lost weight. I'm still so tired.* But he knows what he wants. Your sea legs will have to carry you downstairs.

She's here.

Cecilia.

She attempts a smile, shyly. She must be wondering where things stand between you two. Maybe she has a sense that she got you into some kind of trouble. She must remember as well as you do your last moments together, before her father tore into the living room.

What did he tell her? You feel around for it, a narrative of confusion. He heard her scream. He thought she was scared, or hurt. He wanted to get to her as quickly as possible. And so he put himself between the two of you. He grabbed her and he grabbed you. She didn't see the next part. But she saw something, and she has to find a way to make sense of it.

He hid his anger from her. Tried to. Even if she sensed it, you could see her being used to it—his temper, its unpredictable flare-ups. And then, everything de-escalating as quickly as it started. Just wait for it to be over, and he returns. The father she knows. The dad she trusts.

She was angry at you, too. Before he barged in. But now she is trying to make amends, a smile like an extended hand from the other end of the table. She's too lonely to be mad at you for long.

But you do not smile back. Can't bring yourself to.

You could have left.

The thought clings to you as you go through the motions. You could have left. You could have run away, you could have saved yourself. Your body was getting stronger. And now this.

You convinced yourself you couldn't leave without her, but she wouldn't let herself be saved. She ruined it. She ruined everything for you.

And now you hate her.

It takes you by surprise, this torrent of hostility, but it's here. A kind of hatred that rages inside you like wildfire. You feel it rise and rise and you worry he's going to notice. He's sitting right next to you. How can he not feel this new force, this heat radiating from every inch of you?

The most terrible thoughts cross your mind. It feels unnatural, hating a girl. In your previous life, you gave women and girls the benefit of the doubt, always. You made a point of it. Even when it came to the objectively reprehensible ones, you could never bring yourself to join the pile-on. You could never say *What a bitch, what a cunt, what a fucking whore.* There was something unholy about those words. You didn't want them in your mouth.

But now you see her, his kid. You'd be out of here if it weren't for her. You would have made it out. You would have started the truck. He would have heard the engine, but it would have been too late. You would have driven and driven and driven until you found something, anything—a convenience store, a gas station, somewhere with security cameras and witnesses.

At the dinner table, Cecilia reaches for the salt. It's only a couple of inches to the left of your hand, but you don't move. She doesn't dare ask. There is spectacular cruelty, and then there is this: small gestures, rife with plausible deniability, so minimal that if she were to say anything, she would sound crazy. Paranoid. Self-centered. But you know and she knows, and it feels good, good to make her feel small, good to let her know how much she has disappointed you, how little she means to you now.

She gets up to retrieve the salt, eyes on the table.

You stare at your soup. You are aware that you share some energies with her father. That a part of you takes pleasure, occasionally, in hurting others.

You never said you were perfect.

She pokes at her soup for a while, until finally she sets her spoon down, turns to her father, and asks if she can go back to her room. She's not hungry, she says. She doesn't feel very well. He nods. You watch her go up the stairs, one heavy step after the other. No movie tonight. No couch. No love lost.

The house. Closing around you like a wolf trap. In this narrative, from this point of view, you will be the wolf.

AT NIGHT, YOU don't sleep. Your own anger turns against you.

You decided you couldn't leave without her. You got distracted. You betrayed them, everyone you left behind. Your mother. Your father. Your brother. Julie. Matt. You are one big question mark in their lives and you had a chance to bring it all to an end. The doubt, the not knowing. The empty seat at the table, the extra space under the Christmas tree.

You imagine they have found ways to move on. No one puts their lives on hold forever. But it must tug at them still. The thoughts must take them by surprise on a hot Monday morning, waiting to cross the street in front of the office. Saturday night at the movies, fingers in a buttery bucket of popcorn. Trying to go about their lives, trying to enjoy their time on earth, and always that question gnawing at a corner of their brains: *What happened to her?*

They must think you're dead. They must think, inevitably, that you did it to yourself. Whenever you consider this, a silent scream tears through you. They are, relatively speaking, maddeningly close to you—all on the same planet, same country, same plane of existence. And still, you are lost. You are Ulysses. You were working through some stuff. You went on a journey, and now you can't get home.

You could be telling them the truth right now. They wouldn't understand—not all of it, not right away. You know how these things happen. You've read articles and books. You've watched movies. You know it's not easy, going back into the world. People ask the wrong questions. They have no idea. But people try.

You could all be doing the work together, at this very moment, if it weren't for this girl. If it weren't for you, and this kid, and your heart. Your tender, stupid heart, that, after all this—after all five years of this—saw a girl and told you, *We are not leaving without her.*

THE NEXT EVENING, he brings you downstairs again. The words find you at the table. Two words he has never told you.

He goes to sit and gets back up again, pulls the envelope from the back of his jeans. Drops it on the table and sits.

Immediately, you scan it. He needs only a second to realize his mistake—maybe he didn't think you'd dare, maybe he forgot, maybe he thought you were still too slow, too injured. He takes the envelope back and stuffs it in his front pocket.

You couldn't get the address, the name of the town. But you got something else.

It fills your brain like water gushing out of a fire hydrant. Shiny, new information. A world to explore. A father's name.

Aidan Thomas.

He never said. You never asked. It went without saying that he didn't want to tell you. What good would it have done, in the shed, a name? But now. Now you are in the house and the man who keeps you has a name.

Aidan Thomas.

Later, in the dark, you form the syllables with your lips, silently. Ai-dan Tho-mas. A-i-d-a-n-T-h-o-m-a-s. You taste it. Tap your fingers against the floor, once per letter. It's a beginning and an end. A birth and a death. The final word of a myth. The first word of a true story.

Back in your previous life, when you listened to podcasts and trawled online forums, when you were the weird crime friend, you learned the details, the theories, the nicknames. You knew about the Golden State Killer. The Unabomber. Son of Sam. The Grim Sleeper, the Green River Killer, the Butcher Baker. Always the same story: men without a name, without a face. Until they got caught. Until they got names and jobs and biographies. Until cops handed them boards scribbled with the date and place and snapped their mug shots.

The name was always the first thing to pin them down to reality.

You hold on to two words, eleven letters, like a buoy. Aidan Thomas.

The man in the shed, he began and ended with you. But for years, Aidan Thomas has existed without you. On credit cards, tax forms, Social Security cards. On his marriage license, on his daughter's birth certificate. He made his way into the world, and it had nothing to do with you.

One day, Aidan Thomas will exist without you again.

CHAPTER 43

Emily

The day after the scream, I texted him. "Hope everything's all right"—I hesitated, then added a ":)." *It's what we do,* I told myself. *We kiss. We put our hands on each other. We exchange secret presents. We put smiley faces at the end of our messages.*

I tucked the phone into my apron, snug against my thigh. All through service, I waited for it to vibrate. Nothing. Bargaining: *After I make one drink, he'll text back. After I make two drinks. After I make five. If I take a bathroom break, things will reset and he'll text back. If I stop looking at my phone for five minutes. Maybe ten. If I switch my phone off and then back on.*

He didn't text back.

He always texts back.

Men do this, I told myself. *People do this. He's busy. He works. Maybe a power line collapsed. Hundreds of people in a nearby town without electricity, and I'm worried about a text. Maybe his daughter needs him. Maybe she's sick. Maybe he's sick. Bottom line is, people don't answer texts sometimes and it doesn't mean anything's wrong. Life just happens.*

Not with him, though. With him, it was special—*is* special.

It's been almost a week. I haven't seen him at the restaurant or in town.

I know what happened. His hands on my skin, his breath in my mouth. The silver chain, cold around my neck. The present he gave me. That was real. I have proof.

DINNER SERVICE. IT'S a Thursday. I watch out for him. Any second now, he'll show up. He'll smile at me from across the room and my worries will dissolve. He'll have a perfectly valid explanation. I won't even have to ask. You won't believe what happened, he'll say.

My truck broke down. My phone was stolen. It broke. Fell into the toilet. You didn't try to text me, did you?

The door opens and shuts. It's Judge Byrne. It's Mrs. Cooper. It's my former schoolteacher. It's everyone but him and the night is stupid busy and I tell myself that at least I'm paying less attention to my phone and that's bound to compel it to buzz.

It doesn't buzz.

Eric drives us home. He adjusts the rearview mirror to catch a glance of me in the back. "What's wrong, baby girl?" he asks. "You've been quiet all night."

"Just tired." I give him a pinched-lip smile, mime sleeping on the back of my hand. He nods and gets his eyes back on the road.

I lean my forehead against the window. It's so cold that it hurts, and I press harder, harder until my skin goes numb. I welcome the pain and the emptiness that follows.

We're a couple of streets from Aidan's house. How I wish I could tell Eric to drive there and drop me off. I would knock or ring the doorbell. He'd pull back the shade, glance outside. His face would light up. "I'm so happy you came by," he'd say. He'd wrap his arms around me and I'd breathe in his smell, my whole body a celebration.

At home, I tell Eric and Yuwanda I'm going to bed. It's the holidays, I say. I always get so exhausted around the holidays. More like holidaze, am I right?

Under the comforter, I take out my phone. Still nothing. I slam it down against the mattress. Sigh. Then, I pick the phone back up and read his most recent message. "OK. Don't move. I'll come to you. Cece's asleep and I don't want her to wake up. First Thanksgiving without Mom, you know?"

It wasn't even a good one. No ":)," no *Good night,* no *Good morning,* no *I'll be thinking about you today.* No *I hope your shift went well, I hope you have sweet dreams, I hope you're doing OK.*

I scroll through our text exchange, all the way up to our very first messages, to "Hey! It's Emily. Thanks again for all your help today." To our conversations about red-tailed hawks and nightmares about closed doors and dark hallways.

It was real. I have it all here, all of our history. He likes me. He made room for me even when his life was in turmoil.

I could text him. I don't need to wait for him to contact me. I know that. I've tried, but every attempt at composing the perfect message has ended with me hitting the delete key. *How are you d*—delete. *Just wanted to make sure everything's*—delete. *Don't mean to bother you, but I just hope t*—delete, delete, delete.

I bring my hand to the silver necklace, close my fist around the pendant, hold still until the metal reaches the temperature of my skin.

I saw it. I lived it. He gave me all these things and no one forced him to do it. He did it because he wanted to.

He did it because he likes me.

FRIDAY AT THE Hairy Spider. I make myself go. For the team, I tell myself. As if they care.

Still no sign of him.

If he wanted to do it on purpose—if he wanted to make me crazy, this is how he would do it.

Just one drink tonight. I knew Eric would want to stay out, and I knew I wouldn't be in the mood, so I drove myself.

On the way back to the Civic, a hallucination.

And yet, I swear I see it. His white truck, parked at the back of a side street, glimmering ever so faintly through the Hairy Spider's bushes.

I look around, glance at the entrance of the bar.

He's not here.

Another check. No dice.

I start the Honda, adjust my mirrors, go to pull out of my spot, and—

It's gone.

His truck is gone.

My shoulders tense up. I look through my windows. Turn in my seat, head on a swivel. Peer at the bushes. Nothing.

What the . . . ?

Like he was waiting for something, saw it, and left. I laugh to myself, at myself, because the concept is so ridiculous, and yet that's what it looks like.

Like he was waiting to see me, and drove away as soon as he did.

CHAPTER 44

The woman in the house

You get used to this furnace inside your chest, sucking up all the oxygen. It consumes you. It will engulf you—you, him, his kid—if you don't get it under control. You will make mistakes. If there is one thing he has taught you, it's that people make mistakes when they let the furnace take over.

Rule number six of staying alive outside the shed: You cannot burn yourself to the ground.

At dinner, you hear a sound. He notices it first. He is a man attuned to his surroundings, eyes and ears everywhere, always. You catch up, then Cecilia. The three of you sit with your heads cocked toward the back door, brows furrowed. A scraping, something—someone—whining.

Cecilia points in the direction of the sound. "It's coming from outside."

"Must be a critter," he says.

She shakes her head and gets up. With two fingers, she draws a shade back.

"Cecilia, don't—"

Before he can tell her to sit back down, she's at the door, twisting the knob open. For a brief moment, it's you and him and the open door, cold wind swirling between your bodies. He shoots you a look. *Give me a break,* you want to tell him. *Do you really think I'm going to run? Here? Now? I can still feel the scar tissue, tender and thick at the back of my head. I can still feel what you did to me the last time.*

Cecilia returns. You swallow a gasp. Her shirt—it's bleeding red. She holds her arms out in front of her. Against her chest is a quivering black mass.

Her father recoils. "Cecilia, what the f—" Here, he remembers he's not a man who swears, at least not in front of people who are not you, and certainly not in front of his child. "What are you doing?"

She crouches and delicately places the ball of black fur on the kitchen floor. It's a dog. A wounded dog with a large, open gash on its left leg, blood gushing onto the tile.

Your face heats up. You lose feeling in your fingers. You used to love dogs. You had one, growing up—a Newfie-and-Bernese-mountain-dog mix. Absolutely enormous. All love, all slobber, all the time.

This dog is small. If it could stand, you figure it would be about a foot tall. You make out pointy ears, a long snout. A little terrier, panting, big brown eyes bouncing frantically from one end of the kitchen to the other.

"Cecilia, the door."

He rushes to close it. His first order of business, always—shielding you from the world. Then he kneels next to his daughter, leans over the dog.

His kid looks up at him. The gaze of a little child, round eyes and a boundless faith in her father's ability to make everything better.

"We have to help her," she says.

You get up, too, walk to the other side of the kitchen table. He raises an eyebrow at you, like *That's enough—you can stop now.*

You cross your arms over your chest. Cecilia insists. "We have to help her. Maybe she got hit by a car. Someone must have left her on the side of the highway." A jolt of electricity in your brain. *The highway?* Cecilia's voice quavers. "Come on. She must have walked miles to get here. We have to do something."

Miles. How many? Five? Ten? Thirteen? Is it a walkable distance? Is it runnable?

To your right, a father sighs, pinches his temples between his thumb and middle finger. "I'm not sure there's anything we can do."

She shakes her head. "We can help her. Take her to a vet. She doesn't have a collar." The tremble in her voice again: "No one wants her. We can't leave her like this."

He rubs his hand over his face. The dog is still oozing blood. Some of it gets on the soles of his boots. He'll scrub them later. He must be good at it, getting that stuff off his clothes, off his skin, off every particle of him. He has to be.

"Cecilia."

He looks down at the dog. That's how they get started, you remember. People like him. You heard it on TV as a kid, in podcasts as an adult. It begins when they're children, sometimes teens. Somewhere around his daughter's age, between childhood and adulthood. A child traps butterflies in an airless box. Family pets go missing. Squirrels turn up dead at the bottom of a tree. That's how they practice. How they test the waters, toe the darkness below.

"It's too late," he tells her.

She says it's not, it's not too late, look, the dog's still breathing. But he doesn't listen. He gets up, brings a hand to his waistband. You hadn't noticed it there—the gun in its holster. He doesn't usually carry it around the house. It must be a new precaution, one he decided on after your close call in the living room.

Cecilia looks up. "What are you doing?"

The same question is lodged in your throat. He can't possibly be considering it. In front of you, he'd do it. But in front of his kid?

He wraps his fingers around the gun. Every muscle in your body tenses. "Sometimes it's the humane thing to do," he says. "The dog's suffering. There's no way it can be helped."

She puts her hands on the animal. With her bare palms, she applies pressure to the wound. So much blood—on her hands, underneath her fingers, up to her elbows. "She's still breathing," she says, and the dog's rib cage expands as if to confirm. "Please, Dad. Please."

A tear rolls down her cheek. She wipes it immediately. Blood at the corner of her eye, blood on her chin.

He sighs again, hand still on the gun. "I don't want to do this any more than you do," he says. "But look. This is what happens when an animal gets hurt. I know it doesn't seem like it, but it's the kind thing to do."

He kneels at his daughter's side. "Let me take it outside."

Is this really going to happen? And are you going to let it? Are you going to watch as this dog—this cute dog, with a round belly, white teeth, and the tiniest paws—is shot dead?

Cecilia picks up the dog again. The pup lets out a whimper, as if begging you to intervene.

"Put it down, Cecilia." His voice comes out low. It's the same growl, almost like a purr, that he used the day he took you.

Perhaps that's what spurs you into action. Perhaps you take it personally, the idea that this—any part of this—could compare to what he felt when he thought he was about to kill you.

"She's still breathing."

His head jerks up in your direction. He gives you a look of intense focus, like *How dare you.* You shrug. *I'm just saying.* He fiddles with the holster.

You insist, "She's not dead."

Cecilia looks up at you. It's the first time your eyes have met since the night in the living room. Since you tried to save her, and all she gave you in return was a scream. Something grabs you by the throat—a girl, fierce and afraid and resolute. Bent against the will of her father.

Shame rises in your stomach, thick and hot. You forgot. You have been so busy hating her, despising every cell of her, that you forgot everything you know about her and her dad. Footsteps down the hallway at night. His iron grip on her life. Everything he does, everything he hides from her.

And now here she is, crouched on the kitchen tiles with a bloodied animal in her arms, and she's thirteen and sweet and kind and she wants to rescue this dog. Her mom died just a few months ago, her life's been turned upside down, and still this girl wants to do good. Maybe she wants something to love. She's been lonely. You know she has. Maybe she wants a companion, something to hold. Something that will love her back. Something that won't hurt her.

You step forward, wedge yourself between Cecilia and her father. Let your gaze meet his, *Easy now.* You lower yourself to take a closer look at the wound. It's nasty. Can a dog even survive this much blood loss? You're not sure. But it's worth a shot.

Something ignites within you. You need it, desperately, the possibility of a rebirth in this house. Proof that the wounded can come back to life within these walls.

The wheels in your brain turn furiously, trying to twist this into a situation that lets him emerge as the winner.

"You could help her," you say.

He glares at you. He thinks you're being defiant, reckless. But you know where you're going with this.

"Didn't you learn what to do in these situations?" you continue.

He frowns. He's close, so close to having a bit of fun, and you keep getting in the way. But to your left, Cecilia gets animated. She looks up at him again, eyes wide with purpose.

"Yes, Dad," she says. "When you were in the marines?"

He rolls his eyes, still unconvinced.

As discreetly as possible, you catch his glance, then tilt your head toward his daughter. Your gaze travels to the dog, then back to him. *This is your chance,* you want to tell him. *Remember those fights you've been having, those stormy dinners and her furious steps up the staircase? Your little girl is growing up, but you still need her to regard you as a hero.*

Save the dog. Be a hero. Don't do it for her. Don't do it for the dog. Do it for yourself.

He bends down. You can barely believe it. With his free hand, he opens a cabinet under the sink and rummages inside, pulls out a first aid kit. Then he gestures for Cecilia to place the dog back onto the floor. He lets go of the holster. Cecilia releases the dog. With precise, quick gestures, her father opens the kit and takes out a bottle of disinfectant.

A nudge against your leg. "Put one hand underneath its jaw. The other on its hip. Make sure it stays still." You hesitate a second, then place your hands on the dog as directed. He shakes the disinfectant bottle. "Above all, make sure it doesn't bite me."

Tempting, you think, but you are rooting for the dog, for Cecilia, for yourself, for the three of you to stay out of trouble. There is a slight tremor in his fingers as they approach the dog and spray the wound. He winces, dabs the torn flesh with a compress. "Put your hand here," he tells you. You apply pressure to the gash. Together, the three of you wait for the bleeding to stop. Cecilia gestures to help, but he tells her to stay away.

You will the dog to life underneath your palms, persuade yourself you can perform miracles. The kid is watching. You won't let the dog die in front of her. You will never let her down again.

The bleeding slows. You wait some more and, when it has mostly stopped, he starts dressing the wound, tapes the bandage into place. The dog pants. She is in pain, surely, but she is alive. She is alive.

Cecilia volunteers to retrieve an old pillow from downstairs. The dog can use it as a bed, she says. Her father tells her to stay here, that he'll go get it.

Downstairs.

Where he took you after the woods. Where his tools live. Where, judging by how quickly he springs to his feet, he really doesn't want his daughter to go.

You stay in the kitchen with his kid, the two of you hovering over the dog. She looks at you and bites her lip, like she has something to say but isn't quite sure how. Before you can think of a way to articulate your own thoughts, her dad is back with what looks like an old couch pillow. He sets it on the ground, in a corner of the kitchen. Cecilia picks up the dog again and gently lays her down. The dog lets out a moan, then a long exhale. Finally, she settles, front paws on each side of her snout.

He sighs. "We'll see if she makes it through the night," he says. Cecilia goes to pat the dog's head, then decides against it. "We could . . ." she starts. The rest of her sentence goes unsaid. She was probably going to suggest taking her to the vet, now that the bleeding is controlled. See if there's anything an actual pro can do. Stitches might be a start. But she knows her dad. She knows to take her victory and leave the rest.

He gets up, puts the disinfectant and the leftover gauze back in the first aid kit, and starts cleaning up.

Behind his back, a hand wraps around yours. You hold your breath. She squeezes gently around your fingers. *Thank you.* A silent gesture, loud as a drum to you. *Thank you.*

You wait for her dad to busy himself with a mop and a bucket. A father, focused and matter-of-fact, casually cleaning blood off his kitchen floor.

Cecilia's pulse beats faintly against your wrist. You stand still for a few seconds, then give her fingers a squeeze back.

CHAPTER 45

The woman on the move

He walks into the room, uncuffs you, and says, "Let's go."

"What?" you ask.

He urges you with a wave. "Come on," he says. "I don't have all day."

You get up—slowly, in case you are misunderstanding. But he doesn't freak out. If anything, he wants you to go faster. He pulls you by the wrist, hurries you down the stairs.

It's the middle of the day. A Monday. Cecilia's at school. He's supposed to be at work. You weren't expecting him back until dinnertime at the earliest.

The dog. He had to come back to check on her. And while he was at it, he decided to do . . . whatever this is, too.

He lifts the bottom of his sweater, shows you the gun in the holster. Waits for you to nod, then opens the door.

"To the truck," he says.

He has eyes everywhere—on you, on the pickup, on your surroundings, on the trees and houses and birds. His arm wraps snugly around your shoulder. He guides you to the truck, opens and shuts the passenger door, jogs to the other side. You can feel the atmosphere shift, his relief once you're both inside.

"What's going on?"

He clicks his tongue like the answer is obvious. "We're going for a ride."

Your stomach contracts. You have no idea what he means. He turns the key in the ignition, focuses on pulling out of the driveway. His face is blank, undecipherable.

Fuck.

He doesn't tell you to close your eyes. You wait until the truck is on the road—a country road, trees on each side and houses, actual damn houses, but no one in sight—to ask.

"Can I . . . can I look?"

"You can do what you want," he says, as if that's not the biggest fucking lie to ever come out of his mouth.

Your eyes are glued to the window. Focus. Everything—every leaf, every window—is a vital clue. Since that night in the living room, processing information has been like pedaling in dry rice, nothing sticking, everything slipping through, but you must try.

You must try.

He drives slowly, passing house after house. The neighborhood is a residential cluster, the opposite of his former home—that large property hidden in the woods, no one else around, acres of land shielding him from view.

This isn't a natural environment for him. So exposed, so intrusive. You put a man like this in a place like that, he's bound to turn into a powder keg.

There are trees and power lines and not much else. No one in the front yards. The grown-ups are at work, the kids at school. You pass a herd of cows on the right. A meat plant is advertised a few feet farther, the Butcher Bros. Next to the billboard, an old well—rusty, creepy. The kind of well you read about in fairy tales from another century.

Focus.

So far, he's gone left, left, and right. Left, left, and right. You hold on to it like a cheat code. Left, left, right, and straight ahead past the Butcher Bros.' cattle.

A bed-and-breakfast on the left. To your right, a library. And, suddenly—open, available, free for the taking, right in front of you—a town center.

You must be hallucinating.

He drives down what you assume is Main Street. It's too much, way too much to take in all at once—a sandwich shop and a bookstore and a coffee place and a bakery and a liquor store and a hair salon and a yoga studio and a drugstore. Around a corner, a restaurant called Amandine. It's closed. Restaurants, you remember, often close on Mondays.

It feels so normal. Like you could step out of the car and do things again—grab a latte, catch a vinyasa class, shop for a new lipstick.

You turn to look at him. His eyes gleam, translucent in the winter sun. His palms whoosh on the steering wheel. So basic. The bookstore in the background. Hands in the ten-and-two position. A guy running errands. A dad about town. A well-respected man, living a respectable life in a respectable town.

He pulls over by the bakery. Parks behind a silver BMW, puts the engine in idle.

"So what do you think?" he asks.

You have no clue what he expects from you. You risk a glance to the side. Shouldn't he be worried? Someone could see you. Any second now. He has spent five years hiding you, pulling shades down, locking doors behind you. What is he doing?

"It's . . . lovely," you try.

A small laugh. "That's a good word for it," he says. "The people are *lovely*, too." He glances outside. "Speaking of . . ."

You follow his gaze. A man walks out of the bakery. He's hunched over, wrapped in a gray coat, a paper bag under his arm. The man spots the truck and changes his trajectory.

He heads toward you.

As he gets closer, you can see the details of him: balding hair, brown spots lining the base of his scalp, silver band on his left ring finger. You cling to every element, captivated by his completely average physique. Five years without new faces has done this to you.

The man waves in the direction of the truck. "Aidan!"

This is it. He's going to pull out the gun, and it will be the end of the man in the gray coat. You grip the passenger seat. Your jaws lock. Your teeth squeak against one another, a record scratch echoing through your brain.

A sound on your right. You risk a glimpse.

The window on the passenger side is going down.

What the fuck is happening?

"Good afternoon, Judge."

His voice is warm and polite and syrupy. On his face is the simple, believable pleasure of running into an old pal on the street.

Now your window is fully down. The man in the gray coat leans against the truck and says hello again.

"How's everything?" he asks. "No work today?"

The man on your left laughs, taps his fingers on the steering wheel.

"Just on a break, Judge. You know how these things go. Boss never lets me out of his sight for too long."

The man chuckles, too. Sure, he says, don't I know it. "Call me Francis," he says, "I've told you a hundred times. No need to be so formal."

"If you insist." Then, in a joking tone: "Judge."

You raise your gaze to the man in the gray coat, stare as intensely as you can without arousing suspicion from the driver's seat. Your eyes water. Your face is burning. *Look at me. Hear my thoughts. Look at me, you fucking fucker. Do you know who I am?*

There must have been posters. After he took you. That was somewhere else, but it couldn't have been that far away. If you were a judge in a nearby town, wouldn't you have heard? Wouldn't you remember? Wouldn't the faces of the missing be etched in your brain forever?

The man's gaze lands on you. Finally. For a few moments, you think it has happened. The man has recognized you. This man will save you. Then, he shifts his focus to the driver's seat, lifts his eyebrows in a silent question, *And this is . . . ?*

Your brain tries to yell it. The answer, the correct one. Your brain tries to scream your name, but nothing comes out. Like a body weighed down. Nothing will budge.

From the left, a hand on your shoulder. "This is my cousin," he says. "Came to visit over the holidays."

What you know: On your first day inside the house, you saw a woman in the bathroom mirror. She looked nothing like you. White streaks in her hair, sunken cheeks. Five years older. No makeup. You used to wear so much makeup. Eyeliner, foundation, every shade of lipstick. And now look at you. How could anyone recognize you, unless they were your mother and father, searching for your face in every stranger on the street?

You can't even say your fucking name. Not even in your fucking head.

The judge nods in appreciation. He turns to you. "And where are you visiting from?"

Your tongue sticks to the roof of your mouth. Are you supposed to lie? Name a random place? What if the judge has follow-up questions? Or could you tell the truth? Could you plant a seed, say the name of the town you were taken from?

Before you can decide, the man in the driver's seat answers for you. "Raiford, Florida. Just north of Gainesville. Whole family's from there originally."

The judge cracks a joke, something about coming here for the weather, enough of that Florida sunshine?

You think: Raiford, Florida? How it rolled off his tongue. What have you heard about skilled liars? That they wrap every falsehood in a thin layer of truth?

This must be where he's from, you decide. Raiford, Florida. You picture a boy baking in the heat, humidity curling his hair, shirt sticking to his shoulders. Mosquitoes and baby alligators and knotty oak trees. Inside his head, a storm brewing.

The judge taps your side of the car.

"Well, I won't keep you." He nods in your direction. "Very nice to meet you. I hope you enjoy your stay. Apologies about the bitter cold. It's a local specialty."

A silence hangs in the air, until you remember how these conversations are supposed to go. You smile at the man. Articulate a thank-you. It sets fire to your tongue.

Don't you recognize me? Can you really slip away from the world, like falling through the surface of a frozen lake, and no one even remembers to look for you?

The window on the passenger side slides back up. He waits for the judge to trot back to his own car, then merges back onto the road. With a final wave at his old friend, he begins the drive out of town.

You stay quiet as the scenery changes back to trees, brush, and power lines. You are grieving for a lost opportunity. For a man who could have saved you. For the person you used to look like, the one they have stopped searching for.

"Nice man, the judge." His elbow rests against the driver's-side window, left hand hanging in the air, the other on the wheel. "People around here are like that. Very nice. Very trusting."

He glances at the clock on the dashboard. Inside your brain, pieces click into place: He wanted this. He wanted to run into the judge. He knew when and where to expect him. He made sure to get there on time.

He smiles at nothing in particular, takes a long, peaceful breath in. A man whose plan has just worked out perfectly.

He wanted you to see. This prison he has built for you—it's not just about walls or roofs or cameras. It's about the world he has created, and how you have faded from it.

CHAPTER 46

Emily

I won't stay long. That's what I tell myself. I'll just take a peek.

I drive there after my shift. I give Eric and Yuwanda the same drugstore excuse as the other day. They know I'm lying. They're being good friends, giving me the space I need.

I hate lying to them. I'm terrible at it. But I have no other choice.

When I get there, his truck is parked in the driveway. He's here. He's right here.

I watch from the road, about a hundred feet away, where the trees are thick and the weeds high. What would I do if he saw me? Maybe I'd tell him my car stalled and I was about to call for help. He'd tell me not to move. He'd run to the house, then back to me, holding up a pair of jumper cables.

It wouldn't be the worst thing in the world, if he saw me.

Still, I turn the engine off. My lights, too. The shades inside his house are drawn but I can tell the lights are on downstairs, and in two rooms upstairs.

I picture him sitting in the living room, reading, watching TV. Maybe he's lying down, scrolling through old photos of his wife on his phone, telling himself he'll go to sleep after one more, just one more.

My muscles relax. My back settles against the driver's seat. Even from afar, the knowledge of him soothes me. It's not enough, but it's something.

He's here. He's real. That makes me feel real, too.

A bang breaks the silence from the other side of the street. I jump, then peer through the trees. Mr. Gonzalez steps out of his house holding a garbage bag. On his way back from the trash can, he stops to adjust the string lights on the side of his house, red and yellow bulbs tracing the outline of the structure. The Gonzalezes have gone all out this year. A red-nosed reindeer grazes in the front yard. An inflatable Santa stages a break-in through a first-floor window. A large wreath hangs from the door. The house itself has been turned into one huge wrapped-up present, by way of a large red ribbon twinkling above the garage.

It's not just the Gonzalezes. The houses nearby are all done up, blinking gold and red and green. Aidan's home is the only one on the street without decorations.

Every December, he and his wife used to host a holiday party. My parents let me go with friends a couple of times, and I'll never forget the lights—hanging from the roof to the ground, cascading from the gutters, aligned in neat rows, wrapping around trees, wreaths, every bush in a half-mile radius. People couldn't stop complimenting him. He waved away their praise. "I work with electricity," I heard him say. "It'd be embarrassing, really, if I didn't know my way around a few string lights."

His heart isn't into it this year. *Of course.* I tug at a piece of dry skin on my lower lip. *Of course* his heart isn't into it this year. *The man's wife died, Emily.* Obviously, he doesn't want to screw around with string lights. Obviously, he's not feeling the Christmas spirit.

All this time, I thought something was wrong with us, with me. I didn't stop to think that perhaps he was just sad. Grieving.

I gaze at the windows again.

Maybe he doesn't know how to ask for help. Maybe he's waiting for someone. A person, intuitive and stubborn, who will knock at his door again and again and again, until he has no choice but to let her in.

CHAPTER 47

The woman in the house

It is long after dinner, after the house has gone quiet. Silence, then he's here. Sigh, zippers. You always find yourselves back to the same place, the two of you, like magnets facing opposing directions.

After, he lingers, sits next to you.

"Listen," he says.

You listen.

"I need you to do something."

You give yourself a few seconds. "Tell me."

He bites the inside of his cheek. "It's Cecilia."

Your stomach contracts. "What about her?"

"Christmas break is starting soon." He waits for you to react, but you've got nothing, so he continues. "I need you to keep an eye on her."

You frown. "Keep an eye on her?"

He explains pointedly, like this is all very obvious and you're making things harder, for no reason. "She's not going to be in school. She'll be home all day. She's a grown kid. She doesn't need someone to look after her or anything like that. Just . . . someone to be around. Know what she's up to."

He looks up at the ceiling. "Usually she'd spend time with her mom this time of year, but, you know. And I have to work, so."

Cecilia. His kid who never gets a minute to herself. Who never has sleepovers, never spends time at a friend's. Who gets ferried to and from the house the minute her classes begin and the second they end. Who spends her weekends with her dad and her evenings in front of the television.

If she had a minute to herself, she might start to think. About her father and the things he does.

"Sure," you say. "I'll do it."

He smiles out of the corner of his mouth. "Well, thank you," he says, the irony biting at you. He wasn't really asking. You never had a choice.

"Two more things," he says.

You nod.

"The dog. I told her to let her out every day at noon. She'll do it. Don't even think about it."

What it sounds like: *Don't worry about it, she's taking care of it.* What he means: *You don't touch the doorknob, not even for the dog. You don't use her as an excuse. You don't try anything.*

He reaches into his pocket. "And this is the final thing."

He opens his fingers to reveal a plastic wristband with a metallic attachment. "Know what this is?"

You used to have one of those. You wore it on runs to track your mileage around Washington Square Park.

"GPS tracker?"

You say it like a question, to give him the satisfaction of explaining it to you.

"Correct." He turns the band over to reveal a black shiny strip underneath the white plastic. Not part of the original design, you can tell. His personal addition.

"And do you know what this is?"

You shake your head no.

"Strip steel. Very resistant. You can't cut it with scissors. So don't try, okay? Don't mess with it. If anything happens to it, I'll notice."

You nod. He sets the band aside and takes out his phone, taps an icon that brings up a map with a blue dot blinking at its center. Your eyes bounce across the screen—everything is knowledge, everything is a clue—but before you can see anything of note, he presses a button and the phone goes dark again.

"The tracker links to an app," he says. "I can see where you are. Always." Technology, too, has kept going without you. He has learned how to deploy it, how to use it in his favor. "If you try anything, I'll find out," he says. "I won't be far." A pause. "Remember what I do for a living?" He points toward the sky.

You tell him you do.

He gestures for you to hand him your wrist.

The band is cold against your skin. He disregards the clasp and instead pulls the straps on top of each other, so tight your skin starts creasing.

"Don't move," he says. He reaches into his pocket again, takes out a tool you can't identify. The thing clicks a couple of times before a flame rises. It's a butane torch, but tiny, snug against his palm like the grip of a gun. Still holding your wrist, he brings the torch toward your skin. You recoil. He bites his lip. "I said don't move."

The flame licks the wristband. Together, you watch as the plastic melts, sealing both ends together.

"There."

The torch switches off. You lose him for a second, your eyes no longer adjusted to the dark.

He finds you, handcuffs you to the bed. You sleep on the mattress now. Have done so ever since your recovery from the woods. The plastic pulses against your wrist, hot, a spirit clinging to you as his footsteps fade away.

SOMETHING DOESN'T MAKE sense to you. Why let you roam around the house at all? Sure, he has the assurances of the GPS tracker around your wrist, the constant threat of his gaze on you even from afar. But why burden himself with your moving presence at all?

After he's gone, you lie in the dark, eyes open. You become the ceiling, a boring white expanse, flat and forgotten. You wouldn't look at it twice, but if you removed it, the house would collapse. Everything would go wrong.

Cecilia.

What did she do, the girl who reads, the girl who says please and thank you, the girl who looks at him with so much love? The girl who wouldn't dream of causing trouble, studious and disciplined and sweet and loyal?

What did you do, sweet summer child, that he's terrified of leaving you out of anyone's sight for even a few hours?

CHAPTER 48

Cecilia

He asked her to keep tabs on me. That's obvious. I don't blame her for doing it, and I don't really blame him for asking. He's a worrier, my dad. He's even started wearing his gun indoors. "No gun in the house," my mom used to tell him. But she's not here to tame his paranoia anymore, so here we are.

Maybe I'd do the same if I were him. Ask someone to keep an eye on my kid, I mean. My mom used to tell me all the time, *When you have kids, you'll understand.*

I wish he'd believe me when I say it was just that one time.

It was after my mom died. I went back to school something like three days later. People kept looking at me. They thought they were being discreet but it was impossible not to notice them whispering, stepping out of my path as if bumping into me would trigger some sort of large-scale disaster.

I hate this school. I transferred two years ago, and I've never felt comfortable there. The only good thing about it is it has longer vacations than where I used to go. Everything was going well at my previous one, until my dad came home from a parent-teacher conference in a huff one evening. He asked me all kinds of questions about my math teacher, Ms. Rollins. It turned out she had asked *him* all kinds of questions about us, about what my dad called our "home life" and whatnot. That was before my mom died, but after she got sick again. "Maybe that's what she meant," my mom said. "Maybe she was concerned." But my dad said there was a fine line between concerned and nosy, and Ms. Rollins had crossed it. His mind was made up: I had to transfer. He found me a spot somewhere else—at a charter school in the next town over, where we didn't know anyone—within a week.

So anyway, I went back to school after my mom died, and things got weird. I wanted to go home. But home meant Dad, and I didn't want to be around him. For just a few hours, I wanted to be by myself.

I love him. Of course I do. It's just that in front of him, I felt like I had to hold it together. And I didn't have it in me to do that any longer.

I waited until after third period. Then, instead of going to Algebra, I walked out. No one saw me. I kept going until I reached the train station. No one stopped me, so I bought a ticket from the machine and boarded the Amtrak.

I rested my forehead against the window. My head tapped on the cold glass at every jerk, the vibrations of the train resonating through my body. After a few minutes, I could feel myself breathe again.

I'm not an idiot. I knew he'd freak out. That's why I got off at Poughkeepsie. The plan was to buy another ticket and go back before anyone noticed. But while I was in line for the machine, someone came running. He put his hands on my shoulders and spun me around. My chin bumped against his chest; I bit my lip but he didn't realize. He was too busy holding me tight, pushing me away to look at my face, then pulling me back in.

"What happened," he said. It wasn't a question. More like a lamentation. "What did you do. Why. Why would you do something like this."

I was surprised to see him, but it also made sense that he'd found me. He's always been like that—*eyes at the back of his head,* my mom always said, especially for anything having to do with me.

We walked to the truck together, his hand on my back. Like he was afraid I'd make a run for it if he let go.

He wasn't mad. Too relieved to muster up the anger, probably. He made us shepherd's pie for dinner. We ate in silence. It wasn't until later, at night, that he found the words.

We were in the living room, watching a movie. He paused it and shifted in his armchair to look at me.

"You can't do that again," he said. His elbows were propped up on his knees, his hands in prayer position under his chin. "Never again. You hear me?"

I nodded, hoping he'd stop there, but he carried on. "You have no idea what it felt like, when people told me. The school called. They were this close to alerting the police."

There was one thing I couldn't figure out.

"How did you know where I was?"

"Your phone," he said. "It's trackable."

That made sense to me. People at school are always dropping pins to each other instead of explaining where they are, even though there's a total of maybe three meeting places in town.

My dad wasn't done. "You have no idea what could have happened," he said. His voice was low, his breath short and quick. "You could have been gone forever. Someone could have . . . and then what?"

I tried to interject, "Dad—" but it was like he couldn't hear me.

"They would have searched for you. They would have searched the house. My stuff. Your stuff. They would have looked everywhere for you."

He rubbed his temples and said it again. "You have no idea what could have happened."

That was the only day I saw it. That was the day I brought fear into my father's eyes.

CHAPTER 49

The woman in the house, so very close to a girl

You think he's not going to go through with it. Too risky. But this is the man who left the handcuffs open. This is the man who drove you into town. This is the man who trusts the walls he has built around you.

He lets himself into the room, frees you from the bed, motions for you to follow him downstairs. Breakfast with him and Cecilia—no school chatter today, no inquiries about tests or grades or notes to such-and-such teacher.

Christmas break has begun.

You finish your toast. He gets up and so does his kid. Today, she has time to help clean up. She doesn't have to rush upstairs and brush her teeth, doesn't need to hurry back downstairs, backpack thumping against her hips.

You help, too, in silence. After the last coffee mug is tucked into the dishwasher, he snaps the appliance shut and turns to his daughter.

"Don't forget to let the dog out at noon," he tells her. "Don't go far." He looks at you over her shoulder. "I'll drop by if I can."

She holds back a sigh. "Dad," she reminds him, "I'm thirteen, not three. I won't set the house on fire, I promise."

Finally, he leaves. You hear the truck start and pull away. For the first time, it's just you and Cecilia.

In the parallel universe he has created for her benefit, you're taking time off work, having a staycation. It has been established by now that Rachel, your alter ego, doesn't have a close relationship with her family. She's staying put. Taking a breather.

Cecilia shifts to face you. Too polite to ignore you, too shy not to feel awkward around you.

"So . . . what are you up to?" she asks.

You think for a second. What *is* Rachel up to?

"Not much," you say. "Just chilling."

A silence, then she goes again: "You're not super social, are you?"

She frowns like she just said the quiet part out loud, like she's worried she's offended you. A memory hangs in the air, her sneer the night you tried to pull her away from this house. *You don't understand. You don't understand anything.*

"I don't mean that in a bad way," she says, too fast. "Just—I don't know. It's fine. It's all fine."

One-half of you wants to shake her by the shoulders and tell her everything, *Don't you see, you have to help me, this is all a charade, your father, he did this to me, you have to call someone, you have to get me out of here.* And then there's the other half. The one that remembers the last time you tried to get her to follow you. The one that has learned, a pattern in your neural pathways, that Cecilia is a child and there are things she's not ready to hear, parts of her world she's not ready to let unravel. If you try to push her, she'll get defensive. She'll get you into trouble.

Rule number seven of staying alive outside the shed: You do not ask the girl to save you.

And so you say, gentle, teasing, "I could tell you the same thing, you know. You're not exactly a social butterfly."

Something in her dims. "Yeah. I guess me and my dad . . . we've been sticking together."

You imagine her as a child, years ago. When her family was still intact. The beginning of a string of pearls: her, her mother, her father. Each of them linked to the other two. How disorienting it must have been, half of the rug pulled from under her feet, only one person left to care for her.

"I get it," you say. "People are complicated. Trust me, I know. Sometimes it's easier to keep to yourself."

She nods gravely, like you've touched on a deep truth.

"So . . . TV?"

You follow her to the living room. She brings the dog between the two of you on the couch. Rosa. She named her three days after the rescue, when her father caved and agreed to let her stay. They got her a collar and a tag. Rosa, Cecilia explained, like Rosa Bonheur, the French painter of animals. She'd learned about her in her art class. Her father nodded. That's a nice name, he said. Very grown-up.

And now, you feel his presence around you. Eyes peering through the bookshelves, an eagle stalking his domain from up high.

For all you know, he could be right outside, ready to catch you.

Years ago, you read the story of a girl, somewhere in Europe. Eight years in a cellar, and one day she saw her chance. She ran. Ran and ran and ran until she found people. Not people—just one person. She asked for help. Finally she was heard, by an old neighbor who called the police.

Another tale of escape: three women trapped in a man's house in Ohio. You read the headlines, back when you were still outside. He left a door unlocked; one of the women thought it was a test but she went for it anyway. Another door, locked, this time. The woman caught a neighbor's attention. She got out, used someone's phone to call 911. The police got there in time. They found the other two alive.

Each time, a mess. Uncertainty. The need for someone to see, to hear.

What if no one ever hears you?

In the living room, Cecilia curls up against you, dog in her lap. A quiet friendship, officially mended.

You will run one day. When you're certain.

CHAPTER 50

Number five

It didn't go the way he wanted.

He was always going to do it, but not so soon.

Something happened. I was too fast for him, too slippery. It scared him.

He only meant for me to calm down, but he went too far.

He had done it before. For sure.

The only reason I almost got away was that I knew the woods better than he did. My theory: he had to change his turf every once in a while. If he didn't, people might see him. They might start recognizing him.

He knew the area. That, he told me. But he didn't know these specific woods and the specific bend at the end of the road and the dip in the ground that looked like a ditch but was actually just a dip.

A dip that could serve as a shortcut if you were trying to run.

So I ran. Just for a minute or so. I saw the light. I saw life, or the possibility of it.

And then he caught me.

He was out of breath, his eyes like they would never focus again. Looking everywhere. Straight from the beginning to the end of me.

He was angry. And he was terrified.

I suppose it had gone better with the others.

Before he did it, he told me his wife was sick.

I told him I was sorry.

Don't be, he told me. The doctors say she's going to be fine.

CHAPTER 51

Emily

I lie in bed and queue up an old Belle & Sebastian album, search for the girl in me. The one who believed in love and friendship. Who waited, faithfully, for someone to unlock the remote corners of her heart.

Stuart Murdoch barely gets through the first sentence of the chorus before I make him stop.

My hand falls back on the comforter. I wish I could fall asleep. But there's a current pulsing through me. The impulse, directionless but pressing, to do something.

Anything.

I get up. My eyeballs are dry, gummy. The skin on my hands is rough. Today is Monday, a rare day off. I check the time on my phone. It's one in the afternoon.

I want to see him.

No. This isn't want. This is need.

I need to see him.

I've tried, okay? I've tried giving him space. I've tried forgetting. I've tried trusting that he'll come back to me. I've tried convincing myself that maybe, when he's done hibernating, I could be his friend.

It hasn't worked.

Every night, I dream of him. Every morning, I feel the void of his absence all over again. I think about him. I think about his dark house and its lack of Christmas lights. How my brain feels like that sometimes—dim, closed in on itself, not a glimmer of light poking through.

In those moments, I would give anything for someone to barge in.

I get to work. Laundry is overdue, two weeks' worth of button-down shirts oozing out of the hamper. At the back of a drawer, a coral wool sweater saves me. The silver necklace falls in the V-shaped neckline, between my collarbones. I rescue a pair of decently clean jeans from the pile of clothes at the foot of my bed. Power up the blow-dryer, run a brush through my hair. Concealer, blush, powder, mascara. Lip gloss. Lip gloss?

I pause, the sparkly wand inches from my face.

No.

No lip gloss. Too girly. The man I'm looking for—he's a real man. A father. Not some creep with a Lolita complex.

Lipstick, I decide. Blotted onto my lips with the tips of my fingers. A discreet hue, like I've bitten into a cherry or sipped dark-red wine.

I lace my snow boots with shaky fingers. Something like excitement constricts my chest.

I will wait, however long it takes. He will come home and I will be there—well, not *there* there, I'm not completely crazy. I will be in the neighborhood, doing errands. We'll run into each other by chance. He'll provide an explanation for his silence and I'll say, *Tsssk, don't even mention it. Life happens. We've all been busy.*

You have to make things happen for yourself. That's what everyone says—magazines, life coaches in morning-show interviews, every dude ever. *So-and-so stole your idea? Grabbed your ass on his way to the walk-in? Toughen up. Don't go to HR. Only trouble goes to HR. Ignore them. Ignore the surge of anxiety that wrings your intestines every day when you show up for work. Keep working. Be better than them. That's the best kind of revenge.*

Be bold. Be brave. Make them see you. Make them listen.

I zip up my coat, grab my car keys, and head downstairs, the echo of my feet on the steps like a declaration of faith.

CHAPTER 52

The woman in the house, always in the house

The house is begging you to do it. It wants to tell you everything, if only you would let it.

It has to be safe. Something that could be explained away if he saw it on the screen of his phone.

Rule number eight of staying alive outside the shed: Know the things you can get away with.

Without meaning to, he has taught you how to recognize them. The shape of them. The feel of them. They are lazy things, treacherous things. Things that look like nothing. Things that hide their importance.

It has to be, you have decided, the bookshelf.

Once Cecilia is upstairs, you approach. Bring your hand up to the row of books. The paperbacks, the medical thrillers. His stuff or his dead wife's stuff. Either way, something you're not supposed to touch.

You think of a rose under a bell jar, of a villager locked up in a castle by a beast. You think of a man named Bluebeard and the wives he kept killing because they wouldn't stay away from his secret room. You think of the last woman. Bluebeard went after her, too. It was her sister Anne who saved her, you remember from a book of fairy tales.

You do not have a sister Anne.

You raise your arm and, with the tip of a finger, tilt the spine of the nearest book toward you.

What you see: a title, *Coma,* and a body floating in midair, held up by ropes. What you see: his things, disturbed by you.

And then, a rattle.

Your body stiffens. You push the book back into its rightful spot, jump to the couch. It must be him. Who else? His daughter is upstairs. They don't have visitors, ever.

You prepare your excuses. *I was just looking for something to read. I promise. What kind of trouble was I going to get into with a book? I'm sorry. It's a paperback. I'm sorry. You can't hurt anyone with a paperback. I'm sorry. I'm sorry. I'm sorry.*

But—the doorbell. Once, twice.

It's not him.

Right?

Or is this some kind of game? Does he want to see what you'll do?

Three thumps on the front door. You jump with each of them, *knock, knock, knock.* You think: *Someone is here.* You think: *He sees everything.*

From a corner of the living room, the dog barks, alerting you to the presence of a stranger outside. You shush her, implore her to stop, in a whisper. What about Cecilia? You listen for her footsteps down the staircase, but nothing comes. She must have headphones on. It is just the three of you, then—you, whoever is at the door, and the man with eyes everywhere.

You hear a rasp. A key sliding into a lock, a door pushed open.

Someone is here.

CHAPTER 53

Emily

My chest swells with renewed hope as I drive from my house to his. I'm not even tempted to put music on. The moment is hopeful, comfortable enough that I can sit with it in silence.

I park on a nearby street and walk the last bit.

His truck isn't in the driveway. It's the middle of the afternoon on a weekday. He's probably at work. But he could come by to check on something. His daughter—aren't kids on break this time of year? Or he could drive by, on his way from one job to the other.

It doesn't matter. He's bound to show up at some point. I have time. I have all the time in the world.

I walk around a bit. Take a few steps down the street, turn back, go across to the other end. There are neighbors, people who will talk if they see me loitering.

Before I can stop myself, I'm stepping away from the tree, advancing toward his house. This is as close as I've ever been to it. Inventory: white wooden slats and gray shingles and a small, well-tended yard with wrought iron patio furniture. Front door, back door. Both locked.

Doorbell.

I press it once, twice. Nothing happens. I listen for a minute or so but hear only silence.

Not too surprising. He's clearly not home. But I don't hate the idea of being here without him. Rehearsing, exploring his territory. I try knocking, three short raps on the wooden frame. More silence, then—was that a bark?

He never said anything about a dog.

Okay, maybe he just got a dog. Or maybe he had a secret dog this entire time. Maybe I don't know him as well as I think I do.

No one shows. I think about trying again, but I don't want the dog to freak out.

My ears perk up. Is that . . . ?

I think I hear something. A hissing sound. It's faint, but it's here. Someone going, *Shhhh, shhhh.* Trying to evade detection.

My hands get to work before I can think about what to do next. I'm searching. For what? A visual, a key, a door opening to reveal his world.

Answers. I'm searching for answers.

I lift the welcome mat. Nothing. Run my hand over the top of the doorframe. Nothing there, either.

Potted plants—there's a variety of them, scattered around the deck. None of them are blooming right now, not in the middle of winter. No specks of red, pink, or white. Just greenish stems rising lazily from beds of dirt.

Those plants shouldn't be outside. Not if their real purpose is to bloom. Not unless they're hiding something.

I lift one pot, two, three. Bingo.

The key is under the most damaged of them, frost-burned, brown, dead. That plant will never blossom again.

The key leaves indents on my skin where the metal presses into my palm.

Am I really doing this?

There's someone inside. Someone who's not him. Someone who didn't come to the door.

I hold my breath as the key slips into the lock. One last moment of hesitation—a story, I need a story. What's it going to be? *I thought I smelled smoke and wanted to make sure everything was all right?*

Sure, why not. That'll do.

The world stops spinning. I push the door open.

CHAPTER 54

The woman in the house

A woman stands in the doorway.

She's young. Your age, maybe, or the age you were when you went missing. It's all so hard to tell, how old you currently look, how old you would look if he hadn't happened to you.

She's pretty. That, you know for sure. Glossy hair, glowing cheeks, tweezed eyebrows and—is that lipstick?

The dog goes to greet her, but you hold on to the collar.

"She'll run out," you say, bent in half. "She doesn't know her name yet."

The woman steps in and shuts the door behind her. As soon as you let go, the dog leaps. She sniffs the stranger's coat, tongue out, tail wagging.

I'm so dead, you think. His phone must be buzzing like crazy.

For fuck's sake, you tell her inside your head. *Do you have any idea what I've done to stay alive all this time? Of course you don't. It doesn't matter, now that you've wasted it all away. Now that he's going to kill us both.*

The stranger gives the dog a distracted pat on the head, then focuses on you.

"I'm a friend," she says.

Should you warn her? Push her outside and tell her to run, run and never return?

She continues, answering questions you didn't ask. "I thought I heard . . . I thought I smelled smoke. I'm off work today, so I was just . . . killing time, walking around. I smelled smoke and wanted to make sure the house wasn't burning down."

She holds out her hand. "Anyway, I'm Emily."

Her palm is soft against yours. She is a visitor from another world, one with nightstands and tubes of cream, nightly rituals. You used to lather your hands and feet, too, every night before sleep.

She—Emily, she's Emily now—holds on to your hand a bit longer than necessary. She is waiting, you realize, for you to say your name back.

Maybe *this* is the test. Maybe he sent her to see how you'd react.

Do you trust this woman you know nothing about, except that she just lied—very obviously so—about smelling smoke?

You think about cameras, about microphones. You think about the house and all the ways it whispers your secrets to him.

Your name is Rachel. You will act naturally.

If he can hear you, and you stick to the plan, maybe there's a chance. A chance for you, and a chance for the stranger.

"I'm Rachel," you tell her. "I'm a . . . friend." You remember the story he told the judge back in the truck. A lie for strangers, different from the lie he crafted for his kid. "Well, a relative. A relative who is friendly." You chuckle, or try to. "Cousin. Visiting from Florida. I just arrived for the holidays."

If she can tell you're lying, she doesn't show it. She smiles and gathers her shiny brown hair on one side of her neck, and that's when you see it.

The necklace.

It looks just like—no.

But could it be?

She follows your confused stare.

"Sorry," you say. "It's just—your necklace. It's . . . it's so pretty."

She smiles. "Thanks so much," she says, and she lifts it up to give you a better look.

It's a silver infinity symbol dangling from a chain.

You know that chain.

It's the same delicate chain you wore the day he took you.

Wallet? Phone? he said. Then: *Gun? Pepper spray? Knife? I'm going to check, and if I find out you lied to me, I won't be happy.*

You told him the truth. Nothing in your pockets, nothing up your sleeves.

Jewelry?

Just what I'm wearing, you told him.

Julie bought you the necklace for your nineteenth birthday. She used to make fun of your fascination with the little blue boxes, the white ribbons. So girly, so basic. It didn't match the rest of your personality. *There's just one thing,* she said as you unwrapped it. *I couldn't let you walk around looking like an extra from* The Hills. *So I added a little something.*

She fiddled with the chain to reveal an extra trinket—a pink quartz in a silver casing, which she had somehow attached to the infinity symbol.

It's so great, you told her. *I love it. You're such a good friend.*

I know, she said.

You wore the necklace every day until he took it from you.

And now it's here.

Your necklace—unique, the only bespoke piece of jewelry you have ever owned—has found you again.

Emily releases the pendant. It lands at the base of her neck with a delicate thud.

You force yourself to swallow.

"Really nice," you tell her in what you hope passes for a casual tone. "Where did you get it, if you don't mind me asking?"

She smiles. Is she blushing? "Oh," she says. "It was a gift. From a . . . friend."

Her cheeks are flushed, glistening. She opens her coat. "Sorry," she says, fanning her face with her hand. "You know how it goes. You bundle up and you're still cold outside, but the minute you step inside, you're boiling."

Actually, I don't know, you want to say. *It's been five years since I've had a good coat. Ask your friend—he'll tell you all about it.*

She considers you. She wants things from you that you cannot give her. Conversation, small talk. Answers.

"So," she asks. "When did you say you got here?"

I didn't, you think. You try to figure it out—what would he like you to say? What answer will keep you out of trouble?

"Oh, just the other day," you tell her.

Her smile pinches. You are frustrating her. You are in this man's house. Incongruous, stupid. And she can't get anything out of you.

You are sorry. You are so sorry. You want to fall into her arms and tell her everything. You want to tell her that it's not—really, really not—what she thinks.

"Well," she says, and she doesn't bother holding back a sigh. "I should go."

An impulse rises through you. To hold her back. To clasp your fingers around the fabric of her coat and never let go. To start talking and never shut up.

She turns away, walks to the door.

"Bye," she says, and barely turns to give you one last look.

You are going to do it. You are going to tell her all the things and you are going to trust her because she is your only chance, and—

The door shuts behind her, right in your face.

Like it was never an option. Like she knew, knew from the start, you weren't going to do it.

CHAPTER 55

Emily

I put the key back where I found it. My breath beatboxes up and down my trachea as I go back to the car. I sit behind the wheel, bury my face in my hands.

Well.

Now I know.

She's beautiful in that raw, earthy way that's the opposite of pretty. No makeup. Natural hair. Doesn't give a shit about her clothes, clearly. Why would she?

If I had her bone structure, I wouldn't care, either.

A giggle comes out of me like a hiccup. My rib cage quivers. Something like sobs, but not really.

She said she was a friend, then that she was his cousin. It was a lie. An obvious one.

All I know is there's a woman in his house, and she's definitely not his cousin.

CHAPTER 56

The woman in the house

You return to the bedroom, as if it could keep you safe.

Any minute now, the tires of his truck will screech outside. He'll climb up the stairs, the furious *tap-tap-tap* of his boots a prelude to his anger.

He'll materialize, a blur in the doorframe, and deal with you.

What about her?

What will he do to her?

It had to be her. The stranger who left those marks on his back. Who dug her fingernails into his flesh—a mark of pleasure, you know that now.

Who the fuck are you, Emily, and what did you want?

And you—you, you. How could you let her go?

How could you not tell her anything?

How could you not fucking warn her?

You wrap your arms around your legs. Cecilia is still in her room, quiet. Good. *Stay out of it, kid. Keep yourself out of this mess and maybe you'll grow up to see a better world.*

Truck. The roar of the engine, then silence. *Snap, snap*—the door on the driver's side opens and shuts. Front door.

A brief silence. The thud of his steps. Remote, then close, and then even closer.

The door opens.

"What are you doing in here?"

He looks at you, folded into a ball by the heater, where you don't have to be.

"I was just . . . resting," you tell him. Should you start explaining right away, or wait for him to ask?

He's decided not to care. "She in her bedroom?"

He means his daughter. You tell him yes. Does he want to know if the coast is clear? If he can drag you down the stairs undetected?

"Okay," he says. "Well. I'll be in the kitchen. Why don't you stay here until dinner, since you like it so much."

He closes the door softly.

Your throat tightens. You have no idea what he's up to. You can't get a read on him. Your ability to stay alive has depended on this, above all else, his thoughts like a knot you could work on until it unraveled.

Cooking smells rise through the house. He calls from the kitchen. You and Cecilia run into each other at the top of the stairs. She gestures for you to go first.

Her father deposits a steaming pan of mac and cheese at the center of the table and hands you a serving spoon. It's torture, at this point. His calm manners, something an outsider would mistake for politeness.

Just let me have it, you think. *Say something. Anything.*

But he sits down, asks his daughter about her day. While they talk, you take a better look at him. You search for signs—a pep in his posture, a glimmer in his eyes, adrenaline coursing through his body like it always does after a kill.

Nothing.

You move the mac and cheese around your plate until he and Cecilia are done. You follow along with their motions, cleanup, couch, TV. Still, you wait for a snag that doesn't come.

As the house settles for the night, he handcuffs you to the radiator. That part hasn't changed with Christmas break.

You lie awake until he returns. *This is it,* you think. You await instructions. *Get up,* he'll say, and then he'll take you to the truck and drive away.

A sigh. Little smile. He gets to work on his belt, slides off his jeans.

It all happens as usual.

Afterward, he puts his clothes back on, runs a hand over his face, suppresses a yawn.

With a calm assurance, he brings your arm above your head, wraps one end of the cuffs around your wrist, the other around the bed frame. Routine gestures. Everything normal.

The door shuts behind him. You lie, eyes open. Ears ringing.

He doesn't know.

A woman came into his house, stood in his living room. Stole his key. Invaded his domain. And he has no idea.

She did it all under the gaze of his cameras. The ones that don't miss anything. The ones that keep him informed via phone of your slightest movements.

His alleged cameras. The ones he made up. The ones that exist only in your head.

CHAPTER 57

Number seven

He was so careful.

He had made mistakes, he said. The two previous times.

On one occasion, he was too fast, and on the other, he was too nice. He let the girl live.

With me, he needed everything to be perfect.

He had a daughter, he told me, and a sick wife.

She was supposed to get better, and then she didn't.

And now she was dying.

Soon, he'd be the only one left to take care of his kid.

He couldn't afford to make mistakes.

He had to be there for her, he told me. She was such a smart kid. It was unbelievable, what a great kid she was.

She deserved to have one parent left to take care of her.

So things with me had to work out. There would be no messing up, with me.

I think he'd tell you it all went according to plan.

CHAPTER 58

The woman in the house

Your brain must work to accept this new reality. No cameras. No one watching.

You try the most obvious thing. In the kitchen, first with scissors, then with a knife. You strain to get the blade between your skin and the plastic band, careful not to nick yourself. You wriggle and rub and apply pressure, but he didn't lie: strip steel cannot be cut. Not with scissors, and not with kitchen knives.

You look for tools, but of course there's no trace of the mini butane torch. No circular saw, no special blade. What do you think he is? An idiot?

And so the GPS tracker stays on. Your dot blinks on his phone. He holds you in the palm of his hand, trapped in a virtual map.

You cannot leave. Not yet. But you can move around. There are places to explore, doors to open. Rule number nine of staying alive outside the shed: Find out what you can. Wear his secrets like diamonds around your neck.

You start in the safest spot. The bedroom. Your bedroom. There, you practice poking around. Run your hands over the surfaces you've never been able to touch. The desk that's just a decoy, the chest of drawers, every corner of the bed.

Nothing happens. This is a new world, one where you don't have to weigh every action based on his expected reaction.

You step into the hallway. Cecilia's bedroom—she's in there, but even if she weren't, you'd steer clear. This is her world, and you're not violating it. The bathroom? He's never let you in there unsupervised. Told you not to go during the day. Told you to keep to your bedroom, the kitchen, the living room. You know what this means: there are things in there he doesn't want you to access when he's not around. Nail clippers, razor blades, pill bottles?

Time to find out.

With trepidation, you step into the bathroom. You are here, without him. Without his eyes watching you undress, his gaze sticking to you as you stand in the shower.

You open the medicine cabinet. Aftershave, mouthwash, deodorant, toothbrush, comb, pomade, floss. Pieces of him, like a theater dressing room.

In the cabinet underneath the sink, you find Drano and toilet cleaner with bleach. Extra soap bars, Windex, a small stack of clean rags. His other life—the clean one, the organized one. The bathroom of a single father with a firm handle on his household.

No time to waste. You step back into the hallway. His bedroom— you hesitate. Wrap your hand around the knob and twist it open. Push the door open—no. Yes. No. Yes. *Yes.*

You hover at the entrance. His bedroom. Where he lies at night, defenseless, unaware of the world around him. Thick green carpet on the floor. A queen-size bed, impeccably made, not a wrinkle on the flannel sheets.

You tiptoe inside. He has a nightstand—bedside lamp, a paperback next to it. You can't see clearly from here, but you think you recognize one of the thrillers from downstairs. The nightstand has a drawer. Shut, of course. Full of possibilities. What does he keep in there? Reading glasses? Sleep aids? A gun?

The ground comes alive underneath you. Your skin burns as if you're standing on a pile of toxic waste. What if your feet betray you? Leave traces on the carpet? What if he can tell somehow—what if he can smell you, feel your presence lingering in his corner of the world?

This isn't worth it. You exit in one long step, check that the carpet won't give away your intrusion.

You must carry on.

Just as you head downstairs, Cecilia materializes behind you. She settles on the couch and buries herself in a book. The living area will have to wait. You give the downstairs bathroom a cursory sweep— extra towels, toilet paper, more soap bars, more bleach.

That leaves the kitchen. With Cecilia a few feet away, you do your best to be discreet. Open the cabinets, peer inside the drawers. You've never been able to memorize their contents, not in his presence. Now you can take inventory. On the counter, the block of knives. Last drawer before the sink: long scissors, roll of tape, pens, a couple of takeout menus. Under the sink: cleaning products, disinfecting wipes, bleach, bleach, bleach.

In the cabinets, no surprise: plates, coffee mugs. An old toaster, possibly broken. Mismatched glasses.

She was right here. In this house. The woman who was wearing your necklace.

That necklace. You haven't stopped thinking about it.

He keeps memories. Treasures. Some of them, he has given to you. Your necklace, though? He kept it for himself, until he decided he wanted to see it on someone else.

He must have kept other things. Where does he stash them? In his bedroom? Something tells you no. It's so clean, so staged. That's not where he lets loose. In there, he still pretends.

Where, then?

You sit on the couch. Cecilia gives you a quick look, then goes back to her book.

The door underneath the staircase.

Leading somewhere. Downstairs.

What you know of downstairs: a workbench, the floor beneath your body. Piles of boxes.

Downstairs is where he took you in your darkest hour. Downstairs is a place you remember as being all his.

You have to check.

But you can't go in there with Cecilia watching. You need her to leave.

You peer over her shoulder.

"What are you reading?"

She shuts the paperback so you can see the cover, a microscope slide dotted with drops of blood. "It's one of my dad's," she says. "It's okay. I've already guessed the ending. I'm just waiting for the detective to catch up."

With the tip of your finger, you lift the volume as if to look at the back cover. If you keep badgering her, maybe she'll go to her room.

"What's it about?"

She shoots you an amused look, her eyebrow a suspicious arch. "You bored or something?"

She gets it from him. Questioning other people's motives, trying to see through them. You'd be like that, too, if he had raised you.

"Just curious," you tell her.

"It's about a doctor," she says. "A surgeon who keeps killing his patients. No one stops him, because people can't tell if he's evil or just really bad at his job."

You tell her that sounds like something. She nods and starts reading again.

Get up, you want to tell her. *Go to your room. Go to your damn room already.*

You go back upstairs and bring down your own book. You are not ready to borrow one of his, dog-ear the pages, bend the spine. You go back to *Loves Music, Loves to Dance* and keep Cecilia in the corner of your eye.

A little later, she gets up. Could she be? No. Bathroom break. False alarm. It's not until late in the afternoon, when the rectangles of light around the shades have begun to fade, that she shuts the book for good and heads upstairs.

You wait a couple of minutes. Listen for the sound of her door opening and shutting, the *tap-tap-tap* of her feet on the floor.

Silence.

The coast is as clear as it will ever be.

You wrap your hand around the doorknob.

It doesn't turn.

Shit.

It's locked.

YOU SEARCH. WITH your eyes and your hands. You see potential keys everywhere.

It's the same type of doorknob as the one on your bedroom door, round with a lock at the center. You try a fork. You try a knife. You try a pen. You try the fucking corner of a picture frame, as if that could do anything.

Nothing works.

Your fingers shake. You have worked so hard. You have done so much. You cannot catch a break, and it angers you.

It was your necklace. Your own fucking necklace. The one your friend customized for you, because she loved you.

You need to keep trying.

You need a room that hasn't been staged, a place he couldn't sanitize.

You need his daughter's bedroom.

CHAPTER 59

The woman in the house

You knock on Cecilia's door. She opens it with a *Seriously?* written all across her face.

"How's it going?" you ask.

She frowns, then catches herself. Sweet kid. You don't know what her father has told her about you, but he has convinced her to humor you, always.

"Did you need something?"

You do, but you don't know what. You will know it when you see it.

If only she could let you in.

"Do you have a . . ."

You peer over her shoulder. Her room is purple and blue and something you think is called teal. There is a twin bed. There is a small desk from the Swedish furniture store. Fingers around your throat: you used to have that desk. You used to have a computer and you used to have access to paper and . . .

"Pens."

"You want a pen?"

You do not want a pen. You already tried a pen, and it didn't work. But if a pen gets you inside her room, then so be it.

"If you can spare one? Please?"

She tells you, Of course, and ushers you in. Her room, the world shaped by her eyes: art on the walls, pictures she liked and must have printed at school. Andy Warhol's cans of soup, Banksy's rats, more Keith Haring. She walks to her desk to retrieve a pen.

Think. Now. You need to hurry the hell up and figure something out.

At the foot of her desk, abandoned for Christmas break, her backpack. The design is basic, purple cotton, a couple of zippers, a logo you don't recognize. But Cecilia, this artsy kid, this crafty kid, has made it her own. She has drawn on it with markers, a tree branch down the side, a large rose at the top. And at the front, two letters, c c, rendered—you squint—in safety pins. She did things well, made sure the letters were symmetrical, doubled the rows so people could see them from afar.

"This is cute," you say, and you point toward her bag.

You think about Matt, your almost-boyfriend, who knew how to pick locks. An array of tools strewn over his coffee table, his fingers bending as he slid metal rods into holes, held one into place, and jiggled the other, until something clicked.

A safety pin could do the trick, you decide. A safety pin would be worth a shot.

"Thanks." Cecilia gives the bag an uninterested glance, goes back to the pens. "Blue ink okay?"

You tell her it is. "Did you do it yourself?" You kneel by the backpack, run your fingers over the design.

"I did." She shrugs. "It's nothing fancy, you know. Just some pins."

She hands you a pen. You barely look at it and stuff it in your pocket. "What a great idea," you tell her. "So pretty."

She shifts her weight from one foot to the other. You are trying her patience.

Good.

This is her time to herself, and you are stealing it from her. She will do anything to have it back.

"Do you want one?"

Yes.

"Oh, I couldn't," you tell her. "I don't want the letters to be ruined."

She kneels next to you. "I'll just get more and replace this one. It will take ten seconds."

Before you can say anything else, she removes a pin from the first c and hands it to you.

"Thank you," you tell her. "Thank you so much."

You get back up, gesture around the room. "I'll leave you to it."

She nods. Then, because she cannot help herself, because she is sweet and accommodating and if she kills you, it will be with kindness: "Let me know if the pen doesn't work. I'll give you a different one."

You tell her you will. Cecilia's door shuts behind you.

Downstairs, you search the forgotten confines of your brain.

Matt ordered the lock-picking kit online after getting laid off from his job at a tech start-up. "It's not that hard when you know what you're doing," he said. The way he told it, all you had to do was put the thing in another thing and twist this way and that, and *poof,* the world opened like an oyster, soft and briny in the palm of your hand.

He showed you a video on YouTube, on a channel called—you had to read the name three times to make sure—*Essential Skills for Men*. A dude demonstrated how to insert one tool vertically first, how to apply the right amount of pressure, how to insert another tool perpendicular to the first one, and how to work both tools against each other until the lock gave.

"It's a matter of pressure and counterpressure," the man said.

What you made of it: at the end of the day, it's the magic of two opposing forces that sets you free.

In front of the door under the stairs, you bend the safety pin until it breaks into two pieces: the sharp one and the curvy one.

You insert the curvy one, then the sharp one. Work slowly. Softly. Everything hinges on this, the pressure of your fingers against metal. The right amount. Enough, but not too much.

It takes time. You need to practice. Like speaking a foreign language, like learning a new dance: each attempt gets you a little closer. You keep one eye on the lock, one on the disappearing rectangles of light around the drawn shades. You do not have all day.

Think. Remember. It doesn't come easy to your brain, remembering. You have allowed parts of yourself to fade away. You had to.

And now you need them back.

Those round locks, Matt used to tell you. Those round locks are among the easiest to pick. It was all so straightforward in theory: apply pressure, wriggle, find your way around the mechanism. Listen for a click. The most important part, Matt used to say, was to secure the right tool. It had to be tiny but sturdy. Inconspicuous but deadly. If you knew where you were going, your fingers would figure out how to get you there.

Where you are going: his brain, his mind. The pounding force of him, locked and hidden away.

There is a series of clicks, and the lock turns.

You put the safety pin, both parts of it, in the pocket of your hoodie, with Cecilia's pen.

Try the doorknob again.

It works.

Do it.

You open the door underneath the stairs. It creaks to reveal a flight of concrete steps.

Down you go.

CHAPTER 60

The woman, descending

Darkness envelops you. Blood pulsing in your ears, you feel for a light switch. You can't afford to trip, to scrape your knee. Can't afford so much as an unexpected bruise on your shin.

At the bottom of the stairs, your fingers bump into what you've been searching for. A click, and the yellow light of a bare lightbulb reveals your surroundings.

It's the basement. He's using it as some sort of man cave–storage unit hybrid. A patio chair next to a small folding table. A reusable water bottle, a flashlight. Stacks of cardboard boxes against the back wall. To the side, the workbench. His tools: pliers, hammer, zip ties.

The air in here smells like him. Like the woods, like oranges, something outdoorsy and prickly. A smell you wouldn't fear unless you really knew him.

This is where he comes to be alone. To hear himself think. It's a meditation room, a place where he can be himself.

Your hand hovers above his tools. The pliers: Do you pick them up, try to slide them between your skin and the plastic band?

These aren't ordinary pliers. They are his. They have traveled with him, done his bidding.

You take your hand back.

Focus. You didn't come here for pliers. You came here for secrets and stolen goods. You came here for the hidden corners of his heart.

You step closer to the boxes. They have words scribbled on them: KITCHEN STUFF, CLOTHES, BOOKS, and so on. Leftover items he couldn't fit in the new house but decided to hold on to.

Some of the boxes say CAROLINE.

Aidan, Cecilia, and Caroline. The mother who gave her daughter her own initial.

You reach for the nearest Caroline box. It's taped shut. You can't open it—can't risk ripping the cardboard, messing up the tape. What would you even hope to find? A voice? A spirit?

Caroline. She must not have known. You saw him outside. You saw how he inhabited the world, his effect on the judge that one day. You saw him charming and polite and friendly. She must have left in peace, knowing that if her daughter fell, he would be the one to catch her.

Opening the boxes is a no-go, but you can move them around. Take them down one by one, memorizing the order in which they were piled up so you can restack them properly when you're done. You want to read the scribbles on each of them, weigh their contents between your hands. Stick your ear against the cardboard and hope that whatever's inside will speak to you.

A film of sweat coats your face. Your arms hurt, your legs, too. You keep going, the fuzzy power of adrenaline coursing through you.

You need to see. You need to know. It's been five years. You need to see him, all of him.

CAROLINE, CAROLINE, CAMPING STUFF. Then, all the way at the back, a row of MISCELLANEOUS.

You lean against the nearest pile of boxes. Your chest rises and falls.

MISCELLANEOUS. Banal boxes, the same dirty-beige cardboard as the rest, his writing in black marker on the front.

Except—a quick look around to confirm—the miscellaneous boxes have humidity stains. All of them, and only them. Abstract shapes like maps of foreign lands, spreading on the top left corner of one, the bottom half of another.

Miscellaneous.

Another look around—there are no pipes here. Not at the right place, not where they'd need to be to cause that kind of damage. The stains are old, prominent. Not a light drizzle of rain on moving day.

These stains have been here for a long time.

The boxes were stored somewhere else before. In a different room—a cellar, maybe, in an old house with leaky pipes. Not the best place to keep them, but they were hidden from view. No one would want to go poke under the leaky pipes.

And now, they are hidden again. Not as skillfully—there is less room in the new house, fewer nooks and crannies—but still. They are relegated behind all the other boxes, almost buried under them. You wouldn't find them unless you were looking.

Your hand, shaking as it approaches the box. The first of three that he piled on top of one another. The cardboard must be fragile, ready to tear at the first sharp tug. You must proceed gently.

The box slides into your arms, then onto the floor. Its top is folded shut, not taped.

Good.

You can almost hear it rattle inside. His soul, the abyss of him. A portal for you to fall into.

Fear knots around your rib cage. It's just things, you tell yourself. Things that belonged to you and people like you.

What else did he keep? The sweater you wore that day? Underwear? Wallet, driver's license, credit card?

Trophies. Evidence. Proof of who you are.

Are you ready to see her again—the younger you, the one who slipped through your fingers, the one you couldn't save, not really, not entirely?

What about the others?

Are you ready to see them? To meet them?

You pinch one of the top flaps between two fingers. Pry it to the side slowly, always slowly. Another flap. The rustling of cardboard against cardboard. Something giving in, a treasure chest creaking open.

THE BOX OPENS in a whiff of mildew. Its contents—no one really wants to know what's inside. No one really, truly wants to hold that information in their heart, carry it with them forever. But someone has to do it.

You bear the weight so others won't have to.

First, you see the photos. Polaroids. Makes sense: no memory cards, no film to develop. Most of them taken from afar. Silhouettes. Clothing styles from different times, beginning, you would say, in the 1990s.

The photos are divided with rubber bands into nine small stacks. Bile burns the back of your throat. Do you look?

Of course you look. Someone must see them. Take in their faces, their smiles, their postures, the color of their hair. Missing women, missing people. Stories that ended, and no one has any idea how. Except him, and now you.

You will remember.

You see the first and you see the second and the third and the fourth and the fifth—and then you. A you that feels more like a her, so different from the person you are now.

Your knees quiver. You swallow, or try to. Your tongue rubs, dry, against the roof of your mouth.

Slide down on the concrete floor, cold and hard under your flesh, all the soft parts that are left of you.

You have to get to know her all over again. The younger you.

Black hair, freshly cut, brushing against her shoulders. Big, round eyes. Plump lips. The clothes you had packed for your trip upstate— leggings and loose sweaters and duck boots. Makeup. You wore a lot of it, all the time, even by yourself. You liked it. Red lipstick and winged black eyeliner and pale foundation, rosy powder on your cheekbones.

So young. A woman with traces of girl left in her. More future ahead of her than past behind her.

She just wanted a break. The young woman in the Polaroids. Just needed to catch her breath. To sleep through the night. To slow down.

You're on the go in every photo. Stepping in and out of your rental car, driving to town, coming out of the drugstore.

A wave of nausea shakes you from deep within. Your lips twitch.

He watched you.

You always wondered how he had found you. If he knew you'd be there, or if he had run into you by chance and seen an opportunity. Now you know. The photos confirm it. For days before, he trailed you. Studied you. Picked you. Prepared for you.

Your stomach roils. Breathe. You can't be sick. Not now, and definitely not here. It's just pictures. It's just faces.

Look at number seven, eight, nine. The ones who came after you. The ones you couldn't save.

I'm sorry. I'm so fucking sorry.

It's not just pictures and it's not just faces. Deeper in the box, you dig up a soft navy sweater. A bottle of nail polish, red and crusty. A straw hat. A silver ring. A single sneaker, the sole caked with dry mud. Sunglasses you recognize from the shed, the same pair he handed to you and immediately took back. Treasures. Memories. Things. Their things.

You hold each item for a few seconds. *It's all I can do,* you tell them. *Look at your pictures and hold your things and try to match them to the silhouettes on the photos. I don't know your stories. I don't even know your names.*

Pack everything back up—this is the most important—the way you found it. Check, check, and check again. Pull out box number two. There are no more photos, thankfully. Just more stuff.

Jeans, stained with grass. Yellow stilettos with red soles. A gray cashmere sweater—*your* gray cashmere sweater. The one you put on the final morning, before you set out on your usual walk in the woods. You didn't wear a coat. You weren't planning to stay out long.

You bring the fabric up to your face. Search for the scent of the other woman, the former you. All you get is the smell of mold.

More things. A bra, pearl earrings, a silk scarf. None of these are yours. He didn't keep anything more of you, just the sweater and the necklace he ended up giving to Emily. The rest—your wallet, your cards—he must have disposed of.

That leaves box number three.

You bring it to the top of the pile, peel it open.

It's not memories. It's not sweaters or bras or makeup.

It's tools.

Tools of a different kind. Handcuffs, similar to the ones he uses with you. Binoculars. The Polaroid camera.

Toughness wrapped in softness. Metal that comes tumbling out of a dirty rag. A gun.

Not the one you're familiar with. This one is light gray with a black grip. No silencer.

You pick it up with trembling fingers, lay it flat on your palm.

A sound nudges you out of your daze. Even in the basement, it reaches you. First a purr, then a growl, and then a roar.

The full, open-throated roar of his truck in the driveway.

CHAPTER 61

Emily

He owes me an explanation. At least a lie. I want to watch him squirm, stumble over his words, look at his feet. I want him embarrassed and I want him sorry.

I keep my eyes peeled. At the grocery store, at the coffee shop. This isn't a bustling metropolis where people go unnoticed. He's bound to show up somewhere.

Around lunchtime, I drive into town. Check the sandwich place, the drugstore. Nothing. I look for his truck on Main Street, but still no dice.

My luck turns at sunset. I'm not even looking for him at this point, but we run out of Angostura bitters and I have to go borrow some from the competition.

He steps out of the shadows.

It takes me a second to notice him emerge from the back of the alley, behind the restaurant.

"Hey!"

I try to keep my tone casual, like I'm just pleased to see him. His head turns. I think I see him frown—is he surprised to see me here? Right outside my own restaurant?—but his face relaxes as he steps in my direction. Tall and beautiful and quiet, one thumb tucked under the strap of his duffel bag.

"Hey," he says back. "Sorry, I was just trying to take a shortcut to . . ."

He gestures toward Main Street.

"Don't worry about it," I tell him. "The one thing I'm not okay with is when kids get high behind the dumpster. So as long as you weren't doing that, well, we're fine."

He laughs. This is me: A pop of color in his life, a touch of absurdity to liven things up. A pretty thing he can pick up when he wants to and leave when he's done with it.

It's not enough, and it's not okay, but—and it kills me, it kills me to think that, but I do think it—I'll take it any day over nothing.

Aidan slips his duffel off his shoulder and drops it at his feet. With both hands free, he crosses his arms over his chest, eyes me up and down.

"No coat?"

I stare at my white button-down, black slacks, crimson apron. "I'm not going far."

I wasn't cold until he said anything, but now all I can think about is the December wind on my skin, so chilly it almost burns.

"Hold on."

He unties his thick wool scarf and gives me a look, a silent request for permission to approach. When I don't say anything, he steps closer and wraps it around my neck.

"There," he says.

I smell pine needles. I smell bay leaves.

"Better?"

I blink myself back to earth.

"Yes," I tell him. "Thank you. I . . ."

What did I want to discuss again?

Oh. Right. The woman in his house.

Before I can find the right words, he interjects, "So how have you been?"

It's like dancing with someone who's always half a step ahead. I tell him I've been fine.

"Just working. The usual."

He nods.

"You?" I ask.

"Same," he says. "Work has been busy. Lots to do at home, too."

A silence.

"I'm so sorry I never wrote back," he says.

He's looking into my eyes, his forehead creased, his neck bare against the biting cold, an earnestness that pierces my heart. Something deflates inside my chest. I came prepared for battle, and he just wrestled the knife out of my hand.

"It's okay," I tell him, but he shakes his head.

"No. It's not. You were—you are—perfect. It's just . . . There's a lot going on, you know? At home, and—"

Oh my God.

I want to wrap him in my arms. I want to tell him *he's* perfect and I'm an idiot. I want to tell him I have no idea what it feels like, losing your person, watching their body disappear into the ground. I want to tell him it's okay. This is what I want more than anything: for him to know it will all be okay.

"I understand," I say. "I mean, I don't. But it's fine. Really."

He gives me a shy smile. "I hope we can still . . . I hope I can do better. In the future."

I nod. What does "better" mean? Does it mean friendship? Texting? Kissing? Sex?

His scarf scratches my chin. I go to adjust it, and in doing so, unearth a patch of bare skin between two folds of wool. He reaches for my neck.

"You're wearing it."

His fingers brush against my throat, drop down to the necklace he gave me.

"Of course I'm wearing it," I tell him. "I—"

I can't say it, can't say *I love it,* because it's too close, way too dangerously close to *I love you,* and I am not going anywhere near that mess.

"It's so beautiful," I say instead.

He nods vaguely. His eyes are on my neck, his thumb on the pendant. His other fingers slip under the scarf and settle around the curve of my shoulder.

I don't know what's going on. What I know is his fingers are on me and they are warm and I am cold and it feels good, I think, good and a little bit weird, to be touched like this after weeks of missing him. It feels like us finding each other again. A reminder that we know each other. That we can talk.

"I have a confession," I tell him. His hand falls. His gaze bounces from my collarbones to my face. "I thought . . . I thought I smelled smoke the other day. In your house." He cocks his head. "I let myself in, just to check everything was okay, and—"

"You went inside?"

My face prickles. "I . . . I didn't mean to intrude. I just wanted to make sure nothing was burning." A memory, a sentence uttered by the town real estate agent one evening at the bar: "That's the thing with those beautiful wooden houses. They look great, but they disappear like that."

I snap my fingers on the *that*. He fiddles with the zipper on his coat pocket, snippy little *zip-zip-zips*, like he's stressed or—worse—annoyed.

"Everything was fine," I say. I laugh, a dig at my past self's paranoia. "All quiet on the Western Front."

Okay, stop talking now.

"Well, that's good to know," he says, and nudges the duffel with the tip of his boot. In passing, a question: "Who let you in? My daughter?"

A new wave of shame crashes into me. "No one was coming to the door. And the smell was just really strong." I can hear the derailment in my voice, the blatant lie I can't quite pull off. "I had to use your spare key."

That's it. He's going to call the cops, request a restraining order. But if anything, he sounds amused. "You found it, huh? Guess I should think of a better hiding spot."

I hear myself giggle. "Under the plant. Very cunning. Must have taken me at least . . . twenty seconds to find it."

He laughs with me. For a second, we're back to being us—two people, two friends. Two souls that have interlocked with each other.

His face falls. He's serious again. "Did you see anyone inside?"

"I did," I tell him. "I met your . . . cousin. She seems great."

Around us, the streets are empty. It's too cold for people to linger.

"You met her, huh?" he says. He thinks. "Good." Clicks his tongue, and again: "Good."

There's still a trace of worry on his face, a tension in his upper body.

"Could I ask you," he starts. "It's my truck. There's something—I can't start it. That's why I was cutting through here in the first place. I was trying to get help."

How much does he think I know about trucks?

He must see the confusion on my face, because he adds: "I think it's the battery. You got cables?"

I do. Borrowed from Eric and never returned.

"Sure," I tell him.

He says great. He says he saw my car parked on the street and his truck isn't far.

I say great, too. He picks up the duffel, lifts it back onto his shoulder, and starts toward the sidewalk. I follow him.

We're about to exit the alley when the back door of the restaurant opens.

Yuwanda leans outside. "Everything okay back here?" She sees Aidan next to me, represses a smile. "Hi there. Sorry." Then, to me: "Didn't realize you had company."

At this, she smiles frankly. A cat that got the cream, a sommelier who just scored some gossip.

"Did you need anything?" I ask.

She shakes her head, leans against the doorframe. "Nope. I just saw you out there and wanted to make sure you were all right." Her gaze travels to Aidan. "But I see you're in good hands."

Before I can widen my eyes at her, she's gone again. A burst of laughter travels to us as the door slams shut behind her.

I won't ever be able to look him in the eyes again.

"Sorry about that," I tell the ground.

"It's okay."

But it doesn't sound okay when he says it. His voice is faint, distant. His eyes are nowhere to be found.

I take a couple more steps in the direction of the street, but he doesn't move.

"You know what," he says. "Don't worry about it. You're busy."

Oh, come on.

"I really don't mind," I tell him. "I'll just—"

"It's fine."

"But your truck?"

So lame. A plea more than a question.

"I'll figure something out."

There's a brief silence. Nothing to add.

I begin to untie his scarf, but he stops me with a raised hand. "I'll get it back another day."

There's no time to ask if he's sure, to assure him I won't be outside long. A wave goodbye and he disappears from the alley, his duffel clicking at his side.

Back in the restaurant, Yuwanda grabs me on my way to the bar. "Hope I didn't interrupt anything."

She nudges me. Playful, happy, in a way that eludes me.

I should mirror her, be more like her. There is so much I have to learn.

I nudge her back. She gets a smile out of me, even as I tell her to stop it.

CHAPTER 62

The woman in the house

Outside, a door opens and snaps shut. He's out of the truck.

You haven't moved this fast in five years. A final glance to make sure everything is back where you found it. Switch the light off, then carelessly, recklessly bound up the stairs. Turn the button at the back of the doorknob. Shut the door behind you, make sure it's locked. Curl up on the couch just as the keyhole starts rattling. Open *Loves Music, Loves to Dance* at a random page.

He steps in. *I was reading, just reading. Definitely not snooping. I definitely wasn't about to plunge my hands into your chest cavity and pull out your beating heart.*

He hangs the key to his truck by the door, surveys the room. You hold your breath so he won't notice your rib cage expanding and collapsing, your body recuperating from your sprint up the stairs.

A frown. *What? What is it?* He looks you up and down. *Shit.* You forgot to take a look at yourself on the way back up. You were so focused on leaving the basement in pristine condition that you neglected to check for red blotches on your skin, a telltale smear of dust on your forehead.

Shitshitshitshitshit.

"She upstairs?" he asks. You tell him yes. In a low voice, like you're on the same team and his daughter is the outsider, you add: "She spent most of the afternoon down here, but she went to her room a little while ago."

His eyes dart around the living room. There is a heaviness to him, like gravity is keeping him tethered to the ground more firmly than usual.

He takes a step toward the door under the staircase.

Something has happened. He needs to go downstairs. He needs silence, a place that belongs only to him. He needs the space you invaded just minutes ago.

He can't go. Not yet. It's too soon. If he goes, he'll know. He'll see your ghost in the room, your shadow on the walls.

"I can help with dinner," you say.

He looks at you like he's forgotten what dinner means, then comes back to reality.

Tonight's prep work consists only in reheating two cans of chili. No cornbread, no butter. He calls for Cecilia. She skips the TV and settles in to eat quietly, diligently, like she knows this is one of those nights she needs to stay out of his way.

This man, shaken, unnerved. Something has happened that he didn't plan for. The world slipped out of his control, and now he's wrestling it back, adjusting his grip.

LATER, WHEN HE slides into your room, he's somber. You kick your hoodie under the bed, pray he doesn't notice the safety pin still tucked in your pocket, next to his daughter's pen. Tomorrow, when he's gone, you will hide them in the chest of drawers. He has never looked there, and you have to believe he's not about to start.

If he does, you will lie. You will say you don't know anything about the chest of drawers or the things it might be concealing.

He doesn't notice. This man has things to worry about other than the secrets lurking in your pockets. Tonight, his hands linger around your neck. He's all nails and teeth and bones, all tough parts digging into your flesh. A soldier going to war. A man with something to prove.

She must have spoken. Emily. The woman who found the key to his house, walked into his living room.

And now he knows.

CHAPTER 63

Cecilia

The thing about my dad: he's nice, but I've always been . . . I don't know. *Scared* isn't the right word. It's just easy to get on his wrong side, and then good luck to you. It's because we're too similar, my mom used to say. Two strong personalities. Both of us with our likes and dislikes and no room for compromise.

I don't know why my mom thought that. I compromise all the freaking time.

I guess it was nice of him to let me keep the dog, though. We don't have all that much money anymore. And he doesn't have all that much free time. It was a nice thing he did, and he did it for me. Thanks to Rachel.

Rachel.

Okay, so, Rachel is super weird. But I like her.

This sounds so lame. But she's kind of a . . . friend?

She has all sorts of ideas about me and my life and my dad, that's for sure. But at the end of the day, she's not bad. She's just been through some stuff, I guess, and when you go through some stuff, you're allowed to be a little weird. And she saved Rosa. I'll never forget that.

So I gave her one of my pins. It was nothing, but she liked the pins, and that was something I could give her. Plus I wanted her to get out of my room. I knew if I gave her the pin, she'd leave.

I like Rachel, but sometimes I also like to be alone. My mom used to tell me that was okay. She used to tell me it was another thing me and my dad have in common.

It's nice to have a friend—if I can call Rachel that, and I'm not totally sure I can, because honestly, she's kind of old—but it's also a problem.

It makes me feel like I can talk to her.

It makes me *want* to talk to her.

It makes me want to tell her things I haven't told anyone else.

CHAPTER 64

The woman under the house

You cannot leave. You're not strong enough to run. But you can move, around the house and in the bedroom. You can do things when his daughter's not looking. You can get ready.

What do you remember about moving your body? You search for memories from the times you were outside, running. Training plans, speed work on weekdays and long runs on weekends. Useless. What you need is the other part, the one you skipped so often because you were young and your body convinced you you didn't need it. Cross-training. Movements that strengthened your legs, your back, your abdomen.

In the bedroom, once he's gone, you try. The easiest things you remember: squats. One, two, three, ten. It's a foreign sensation, the pulsing in your thighs, a burning at the back of your calves. Calves—calf raises. You try those, too. Your heart beats faster. For the first time in years, not in fear or anticipation. Your heart beats faster because the rest of your body tells it to.

Everything about this belongs to you. Your limbs and the things you make them do. The curve of your lower back against the floor as you lie down for crunches. The soreness in your biceps when you hold the paperback of *It* at arm's length—it's the thickest in your collection and still it doesn't weigh much, but you hold the position long enough to start a fire in your shoulders. Also yours: the pain in your wrists when you try a push-up. The dryness inside your mouth, the stickiness at the back of your neck.

By the time he returns, sweat will have dried off your clothes. Heat will have cooled off your cheeks. He will not know. Even if you do it again the next day and the one after that. This will remain yours and yours alone.

———

WHEN YOUR ARMS start shaking and your legs beg you for a break, you go back to the basement. Jimmy the lock with the safety pin. A million times, you expect it to fail you. A million times, the safety pin proves you wrong. You put it in your back pocket and carry on.

You find the gun. You can't tell if it's loaded. You don't know where the safety is. Should you be able to tell? You have no idea. All you know about guns is what you learned from movies, but even you know movies get it all wrong. In real life, you'll miss your target if you're out of practice; in real life, you have no idea what you're doing.

You riffle through the box, move a hammer out of the way, a hunting knife, ski gloves, a length of rope. You find stubby rectangles of black metal, one, two, three. Magazines. Bullets gleaming at the top, through holes on the sides. You can't tell if it's a lot of ammo or a little. All you can do is hope it'll be enough for whatever you end up doing.

If you had a phone or a laptop, you'd look everything up. In the span of a video tutorial or two, you'd learn how to load the gun. Could probably learn to shoot, too, how to aim and when to pull the trigger and how to steel yourself against the recoil.

You'll have to learn by yourself. You know nothing, but it's a gun, not quantum physics. You'll have to come back and figure things out.

In a paper bag, more photos. Polaroids, too, separate from the first stack but similar in style. Taken from afar, the subject unaware. You shuffle through them. Brown hair and pale skin. White coat. Mundane moments: stepping in and out of a Honda Civic, going inside a restaurant. The shots are blurry, but you make out a silhouette and a bar and a crimson apron.

One neat photo, like an asteroid falling to earth. Her face. Her pretty face. You know her. Of course you know her. You met her right here in this house.

She is the woman from the living room. The one who wore your necklace.

She is a project. A target.

Stacked with the Polaroids, a cardboard disc with the word *Amandine* written in loopy cursive. Amandine, like the restaurant you saw the day he took you out for a drive. A coaster. He must have gone there, slipped it into his pocket. A piece of her world, smuggled into his. Like the trinkets he plucked from the other women and gave to you. Your books, the empty wallet, the stress ball. All stolen.

You must keep going. For her, for you, for all the ones like you.

At the bottom of the box, stacked in a corner, you find three little books. Guidebooks, you realize. *Secrets of the Hudson Valley, Beyond the Hudson, Hidden Upstate Gems.* In all three of them, the same chapter, dog-eared and highlighted.

The name of a town. Seven letters, a *gh*—silent, according to the guides. This has to be it. The town, his town. This town.

A map. A few scribbles, nothing dramatic. No *X* marking the new house, no *x* marking the former one. No code signaling his victims or geometric shape connecting his kills. Just roads and clusters, expanses of green and trickles of blue.

Near the center, almost hidden in the fold, a tiny white shape—the symbol for a local landmark, says the key in the bottom left corner. You squint. How long has it been since your last eye exam? How long has your body been drifting, every part of you aging faster than normal?

THE WISHING WELL. That's what it says in small black letters, next to a page number for more information. You flip to that location. Next to the history of the well—built centuries ago, visited by families wishing for good crops and healthy babies—are photos.

Splintering stones. A rusty chain. Moss wherever it can grow, and even in places it shouldn't be able to.

It's the well. The one you passed that day in the truck, from the house to downtown and back. Right next to the cows. Right next to the Butcher Bros.

Focus. Search for the map's scale. Find it. Do the math. Faster. Come on, now. Could you run that far? Maybe. You have no idea what your body is capable of.

Focus. Look at the map. You have to learn this. Now. Quick. Remember the twists and turns, *left, left, right, and straight ahead past the Butcher Bros.' cattle.* Reverse. Apply to the map. Zoom out, zoom back in. This is where you are.

Now you know. You know for sure.

Something else. At the back of one of the guides, *Secrets of the*

Hudson Valley. A list scribbled on a sheet of paper, folded, hidden away. Names. Addresses. Times. Job titles. The paper is thick and yellow, the ink purple. He wrote on it a long time ago. When he moved here, probably, with his wife and maybe his kid. When he made the town his project, when he turned it into his playground. A space where he'd live above suspicion, a world tailored to his needs.

He's been watching, studying everything and everyone for so long. Creating a place where he could get away with things.

You've reached the bottom of the box.

Put everything back the way you found it. Check, check again.

A sound comes from upstairs. A voice.

"Rachel?"

Shit. *Shit.* If it's not the father, it's the daughter. Stay still. She doesn't know where you are. What if she comes looking for you? Slide the boxes back on top of one another. Wipe your hands on your jeans. Look around and find something—an excuse, an idea, anything.

The door at the top of the stairs opens. In a few seconds, she's downstairs, next to you.

Can she feel them, her dad's secrets floating like vapor in the air? Can she hear the women's voices whispering in the dark, begging you, begging her, begging anyone who will listen not to forget about them?

"Hey," she says, "I was looking for you."

Well, you found me, you want to tell her, but you can't speak.

"Do you want to come walk the dog with me?" she asks. "I was just about to leave. Not going far, just to the water and back."

The water. You assume she means the Hudson, if the guidebooks and the map are to be trusted. The same river you used to run by in the city.

"Oh, thanks," you tell her, "but I can't. I have to, um, get some work done. Upstairs."

"Okay," she says. "No worries."

She goes quiet. Looks around.

"Were you looking for something?"

You think. "Yes," you tell her. "I needed . . . batteries, and I couldn't find any, so I figured I'd check here. But it's okay. It's fine. Not urgent. No need to worry about it."

She leans against the patio chair.

"I come down here, too, you know."

Her voice is a whisper.

"Do you really?" you ask.

"Yeah. At night. I just—we keep some of my mom's things down here."

Don't say anything. Let her talk. She needs someone to listen.

"It's stupid," she says. "But I miss her smell. Other things, too, but we have pictures and videos. Her smell, though, that's harder to find. So sometimes I come down here and I take out one of her old sweaters and I just . . . sit with it for a bit." She looks up at you. "Pretty dumb, huh?"

"I don't think so," you tell her. "You just miss her."

What you don't say: in the days after her dad took you, you couldn't think about your mom without forgetting how to breathe. You had to stop thinking about your family altogether because it hurt too much, and you couldn't afford to fall apart.

"My dad can't know," she says. "He wouldn't understand. Or maybe he would, but it would hurt him. So I come down here at night, when he's asleep."

"At night?" you ask.

"Yeah," she says, eyes on the ground. "I wait for him—for everyone to be asleep. Then, I go. I try to be quiet but I know he's heard me a couple times. He asked about it once. I told him I was going to the bathroom."

The words pour out of her, like this has been weighing on her conscience for a while.

"I have to steal the key," she tells you, her voice so low you have to hold your breath to hear her. "Every time." She shakes her head. "I don't like doing it, but he leaves it in his coat pocket at night. He doesn't know I know. He hates it when people touch his stuff."

Before you can open your mouth, a question: "How did you get in?"

You reach for the easiest lie. "It was unlocked," you say. "I guess he forgot."

You hold your breath for a second. Maybe the lie is too big. Maybe she'll call you out. But she rolls her eyes. "Wow. Seriously?" You nod, poker-faced. "Guess he's been distracted," she says. You're about to say yes, that's true, her father is a busy man, he can't possibly remember every little thing, but Cecilia speaks again. She has things to say, confessions to unload, more pressing issues than locks and whether her father remembers to use them.

"I have to replace the tape," she tells you. "On the boxes. Every time. I throw out the old pieces at school so he doesn't see them."

You want to tell her it's fine—the key, the tape, everything. You want to ask her more about keys and the places her father hides them. But she's not done.

"I don't want to hurt him," she tells you.

"You mean your dad?"

"Yeah."

You consider what she just said. She goes at night, when everyone is asleep—or so she thinks. When she believes no one can hear her.

The steps. In the hallway, at night. You thought it was him. Hurting her. It made sense for it to be him. You believed he broke everything he touched.

Did you think wrong? Has it been her all along, a girl visiting her mother's ghost in the basement?

"You're really close to him, aren't you?" you ask. "I mean, you two seem to have a strong kind of bond. If that makes sense."

She nods. Still won't look at you. "Yeah," she says. "It's just the two of us now. He's not perfect, but neither am I. And he tries. He tries so hard to be enough, you know?"

You nod.

There is something here. As real as your old cashmere sweater under your fingers, as blunt and heavy as the gun in the palm of your hand.

It's more than loyalty, more than the sense of obligation children feel toward their parents.

It's strong, and you couldn't break it even if you wanted to.

CHAPTER 65

Emily

He comes back to the restaurant. A Thursday, like before. He smiles at me. When I hand him back his credit card, his fingers brush against mine. But they're cold. Dead. Like they will never hold on to me again, grip me like I'm the most tantalizing, the most beloved creature in the world.

On Friday evening, the judge comes in for dinner. He sits at the bar, his preferred spot. It's more casual this way, he says. He can mingle. Plus he'd feel self-conscious, all by himself at a table.

The idea is here. In my mind. It has the air of generosity, but there's a toxicity to it. It feels interesting and a little bit dangerous.

Aidan won't like it at first, but—if I play my cards right—he'll come around to it.

"We should do more."

The judge looks up like he's just noticed my presence.

"For the family," I tell him. "They've been through so much. I can't imagine what it's been like for his daughter."

He stares at something above my shoulder, considering it. Judge Byrne. Three decades on the bench. Every four years, his name on the ballot. Every four years, his future in the hands of the town. How it matters to him, not only being liked, but for people to know he likes them back.

"You're right," he says. "You're absolutely right."

Okay. There's no turning back now. We're doing this. I'm doing this.

"If I were her," I tell the judge, "I'd want a little party. Christmas break, you miss your friends, right?" A brief nod. "I would never admit it, of course. Teenagers . . ." The judge and I roll our eyes together as if we both know, as if he remembers as well as I do what it's like to be a thirteen-year-old girl.

Eric deposits a plate of mushroom risotto in front of the judge. I pour him an Irish coffee on the house, and we keep talking.

The easiest thing, I supply, would be to do it at their house.

The judge isn't so sure. "Won't we be imposing?"

"It's your house, Judge."

"I know, I know," he says. "But Aidan's renting it. I'm not sure I want to be that kind of landlord."

I lean over the bar. *Stay with me, Judge.* "We could have it outside the house. The yard is so nice." The judge tilts his head. "We can use the space heaters from the restaurant patio," I tell him. "Hang Christmas lights. I'll make mulled wine. We'll take care of everything. It'll be beautiful."

He thinks it over.

"Have you seen the house?" I ask. "It could be so pretty, but right now it's just sad. It's the only one on the street without any lights. I'm not blaming anyone, mind you. They moved here at the worst time in their lives. But I think they need a little help making it feel like home. They need to start making nice memories there."

This time, the judge smiles. He's in. "All right," he says. "That's not a bad idea. I'll speak to Aidan, let him know he won't have to lift a finger."

"Great." Then, with a grin: "He'll probably have a hard time with that, though. You know how he gets. Can't ever stay still. Always has to help with everything."

The judge chuckles, like *Don't I know it.* I top up his Irish coffee, and he raises his cup to our dear friend.

"It should be soon," I say as I screw the cap back on the bottle of Jameson. "It should be before Christmas."

The judge nods.

After he leaves, I rest my hands on the counter and consider what just happened. A little dizzy, a little out of breath.

Aidan.

His house, his home.

We will be there, together. And I will get to him. I will get right to the heart of him.

CHAPTER 66

The woman in the house

You always knew the kind of man he was. You knew what he did, and you knew when he did it. But you had never seen their faces. You had never summoned the women's ghosts, held the remnants of their lives in your hands.

At night, they visit you. *You let us die,* they say. The ones that came after you. *You should have stopped him by now. What are you doing? Why haven't you run away? Why aren't you telling the world about him?*

You tell them you're sorry. You tell them it's complicated. You try to get them to see things from your point of view: *You know how he is. I have to do things right. You take one wrong step with him, you die.*

Oh, so now it's our fault, the women say. *You must think you're so smart, whereas us—we're the idiots who died?*

You try to explain. *That's not what I meant. I would never say that. Don't you know I'm on your side?*

After a while, the women stop responding. Even after they leave, you can't sleep.

So that's you. Cecilia, though—what's her excuse? Why so crestfallen?

At dinner, she waits until her plate is empty and turns to her dad.

"Is there really no way we can get out of it?" she asks.

He sighs like it's not the first time they've had this conversation.

"It's a nice thing, Cecilia. Sometimes people try to do nice things for you, and it's polite to let them."

"But it's Christmas break," she insists. "They can't leave us alone during Christmas break?"

He frowns. "Listen," he says. *Such a dad.* "I worked all day. I'm tired. I don't want to do this again. People like you. And they like me. They think we're nice, and they've decided they want to throw us a party. I'm not thrilled about it, either. But that's how life works."

Cecilia looks away. He knows, she knows, you all know he's won, but he carries on anyway. "You remember how we got the house?" he asks her. "It was the judge. He pulled some strings for us, because he likes us. It's easier to go through life if people like you."

"It's just . . ." she mutters. "Do they have to do it right here? In the yard?"

He shrugs. "That's what they want to do. Let's just go along with it."

The yard?

You try to make sense of it.

This man, in this town? Letting people in so close, into the orbit of his darkest secrets?

He's planning something.

He would have found a way out of it otherwise. This is a man who does what he wants, for the reasons he wants.

He's planning something.

Rule number ten of staying alive outside the shed: You can learn from him. You can plan things, too.

YOU LIE AWAKE through another night. Force yourself to remain lying down, pin your back to the mattress. An electric current pulses through your legs; a restlessness tickles the inside of your chest. You did your exercises earlier, while he was away. Tired your calves, your arms. It's not your body keeping you awake. It's your mind, like a broken compass, spinning and spinning in vain.

A party. There's going to be a party. People—lots of people. *Right here. In the yard.*

He will be busy, so busy keeping track of it all. Focused on making sure people stay where he needs them to be. Focused on making sure his plan, whatever it might be, unfolds as he wants it to.

And there will be eyes. Eyes everywhere.

Your brain thinks, thinks, thinks itself into overdrive. Like your brother's Lego when the two of you were kids—try it this way and that. Put two things together and break them apart. Build and build and watch it all collapse and start building anew.

She wore your necklace.

Emily. Her name rises through you, over the buzz in your ears.

It's her. It has to be her. The object of the party, the reason he's letting everyone in. He has been circling her, casing her like a bank to be robbed.

The women in the boxes start clamoring. *You know what you have to do,* they say. *Are you going to let her die, too?* You want to tell them, *Please stop, just for a second—let me think,* but you can't, you can't because your fingers are burning and your throat is burning and there is a woman out there and she was in the living room and you saw her, you met her and she seemed nice, and even if she's not, she should still live. She should still live for as long as possible.

You roll onto your side and bring the pillow over your head. With your free hand you push, apply pressure until you can barely breathe, until there's nothing in your ears but the pulsing of blood and the faint rush of oxygen at the back of your trachea. You open your mouth, teeth against the sheet, and bury a silent scream into the mattress.

CHAPTER 67

Number eight

His wife was dying. Again.

So was I.

When the doctors told me, I thought of only one place.

The cove by the Hudson, hidden from the rest of the world by rows and rows of trees. You had to know it was there. If you did, then you had the keys to heaven.

There was a NO SWIMMING sign, but no one listened. This was a place to dive underwater. This was a place for sand and kayaks and coolers full of beer.

It was where I wanted to spend the time I had left, wearing nothing but a bathing suit and a straw hat.

He found me one evening.

I was focused on other things. I was dying, and I was trying to come to terms with that.

I didn't expect a man like him would take matters into his own hands.

I know. I know. I was always going to die sooner than most.

Still, it matters, what he took from me.

After a lifetime of running around, trying to please other people, this was my last chance.

It was supposed to be my time.

CHAPTER 68

The woman in the house

You can't explain. You can't tell her anything.

You have to trust that she will get it.

"I wish this party thing didn't have to happen right here," Cecilia tells you the next afternoon, when it's just the two of you.

I know, you tell her in your head. *But if only you knew. It's going to be magnificent.*

You let her speak. "Kinda wish it didn't have to happen at all. I know people are trying to be nice, but . . ."

Her voice trails off.

"I get it," you tell her. "I don't love crowds, either."

She nods. "Honestly, I think I'll slip back to my room whenever I can. Take a break, you know?"

It's your turn to nod.

I get it, kiddo. I remember what it's like to need a break.

YOU GO BACK downstairs. Don't look at the photos—they'll suck the life out of you, and you have none left to waste.

It's the gun you're interested in. Pick it up. Feel the weight of it in your hand. Get used to it. Try to insert a magazine. Get it wrong. Try again. You've never done this before, but no one has to know.

With the gun nestled against your palm, a power rises through you. You could do so many things. Sneak up on him in his sleep. Aim and pull the trigger. How many bullets would it take? One, if it lands correctly. Two, three, five. You have no idea.

That is not what you want. Blood on the bedsheets. Brain matter on his pillow. Cecilia running from the other end of the hallway, tripping over herself, sleepy, startled. A sight she would never forget—her father's body and the pistol still warm in your hand. And you? You would just go to jail. Trapped again.

You know what the world has to offer to people like you. The best you can hope for: Him, alive, in an orange jumpsuit. A courthouse, chains around his wrists and ankles. Newspaper headlines telling the world what he did. It's not quite right, and you're not sure you want any of it. But it's the only option, and you will have to take it.

Here, in the house, for the first time—for the only time—you get to decide for yourself.

What you want: A way to exist in the world, after. A life that doesn't involve waking up every night, haunted by the memory of the man you killed. Because it would haunt you, to kill him. You are not him. You will never be him.

HE HAS SHAPED his daughter's life so that it revolves around him, and one day he will be taken from her. The life he has given her is built on shallow graves, and the dead will rise and turn the ground under her feet upside down.

At dinner, she is happy. Happy enough. She spent most of the day reading. She taught Rosa a new trick. So far, she has scored five correct answers on *Jeopardy!* Maybe tonight gives her hope. Maybe tonight tells her that life will one day be joyful again.

At the dinner table, she turns to you. Something in her dims. Ashamed, you would guess, of her own buoyancy.

It's okay, you want to tell her. *You should be happy. You deserve to be happy. You're just a kid. You've done nothing wrong.*

You deserve to grow up without having to think about any of this. You are a girl. Life will teach you about bad guys soon enough.

One day, you will learn your father was one of them.

She will need someone to blame. Because she will hurt, and when you hurt it helps to know who did it. If you had known, that night at the club, maybe you would have been able to stay in the city. If you had been given a face and a name. A singular person instead of a hostile world. You would have healed, and you would never have met her dad. Your life would still be your own.

She will need someone to blame, and if it's not him, then it will have to be you.

Cecilia. I'm so sorry for what I'm about to do to you.
I'm so sorry for what I'm about to do to your life.
Maybe one day you'll understand.
I hope you'll know I did it all for you.

THAT NIGHT, YOU plan to do what you always do. You plan to wait for him to be done. You plan to be Rachel. You plan to do the things that keep you alive.

And you try. But he finds you in the dark and you think about the women downstairs. You think about his daughter. You think about you and the ones like you.

You have never let yourself feel this. You knew that it would be dangerous. That this wasn't a type of anger that could be meted out in drops, only tsunamis.

He goes to handcuff you to the bed frame and misses. The metal nicks your skin. You pull your wrist back—it's instinct, what people do when someone hurts them. He clasps your arm and holds it in place. This, too, is instinct. Putting your body, all the moving parts of it, in the places where he wants them.

The wise thing would be to let him. He's going to handcuff you anyway, so what does it matter? But tonight, it matters. Tonight, you get onto your knees and give another tug. Your wrist slips out of his grasp. Immediately, his hand is on you, grabbing for your elbow, your shoulder, any part of you he can use as an anchor. You resist him. Slide out of his reach, stand up, swat his palm away. Your movements surprise you—so quick, so precise. Muscle memory. Your body, brought out of a long hibernation by your secret exercise sessions.

He comes at you with both hands and you forget to be scared. You are only angry.

It's a silent tussle, reckless, desperate. Your hand makes contact with his chest. You push—it's a light shove and it barely shakes him, this immovable force of a man. It barely does anything but it means everything, everything to you.

He regains control—of course he does. He is him and you are you. He grabs your arm and twists it and the other one too, puts his weight on you until you crumple like a shriveled leaf onto the floor. But his breath is heavy and his heart beats against your back, fast and loud and panicky, and you did that, you got away from him for a few seconds, and it scared him.

You have terrified this man. You have made his pulse race.

"What the fuck," he whispers, furious breath between gritted teeth, "do you think you're doing?"

He twists your arms tighter. You surrender to it. Now you can. You must.

"I'm sorry," you tell him. You don't mean a word of it. It's a password, a conduit to another day.

Your own breath settles. You realize what you've done, how close to the sun you just flew. Foolishly, without a thought for your wings and the wax holding them together. "I'm sorry," you say again, and a dash of truth: "I don't know what I was thinking."

He regains control over the handcuffs and chains you to the bed frame.

So strong, this body of yours. You didn't know you had it in you. To push him like that. To fight back.

He runs his fingers over the back of your head, gathers your hair in a tight fistful, and pulls. Your head snaps back. He brings his face close to yours.

"You have some fucking nerve, you know that?"

Don't try to nod. Don't try to explain. Just let him speak.

"You were lost. You were so fucking alone. I found you." A tug. "I'm the only reason you're alive. You know what you'd be, without me?"

Nothing. You recite the words in your head so they won't touch you when he says them. *You'd be dead.*

"Nothing. You'd be dead."

Do not listen to him. Do not let him inside your brain.

He lets go of your hair with a nudge.

"I'm sorry," you say again. You could say it five hundred times if he needed you to. *Sorry* costs you nothing.

"Shut up. Can you do that? Can you just stop talking for one fucking second?"

You settle against the bed frame. He shakes his head at you.

He has plans beyond you. You have seen the photos. The Polaroids of Emily in his basement, the tools in his boxes and on his workbench.

It was a mistake, shoving him. Scaring him like that. You do not regret it, not completely. But you must be careful.

You are so close.

CHAPTER 69

The woman in the house

He explains things to you.

"There's going to be a party," he says, as if he and Cecilia haven't already discussed it in front of you. As if you can hear things only when he wants you to hear them.

You nod.

"People are going to come. Here. In the front yard. They're not going to go inside. You hear me?"

You tell him you do.

"You'll be here," he says, meaning the bedroom.

No surprise there, you want to say, but instead you nod again.

"We'll do things as usual."

"Got it," you say.

He fingers the handcuffs.

"Tell me your name."

You think, *This again?* but your brain knows what to do. Words have a special power when they keep you alive.

You are Rachel. He found you.

"My name is Rachel," you tell him, and a weight lifts from your chest. Like you have been lying and just now came back to the truth.

All you know is what he has taught you. All you have is what he has given you.

He doesn't need to ask for the rest.

"I moved here recently. I needed somewhere to stay, and you offered me a room."

He nods. Grabs you by the shoulders, fingers drilling into your skin, pushing against the muscles underneath. Embedding himself into you.

"You will not scream," he tells you. "You will not say or do anything. If you do, I'll take you to the woods. This will end for good."

"I understand," you say.

"Good." Then, just to make sure the message is clear: "You will be quiet. You will not make a sound."

You nod one more time.

You're not lying. He's right.

You won't.

CHAPTER 70

Number nine

He had the gall to look scared of me.

Him. Scared. Of *me*.

I don't know what he was expecting.

Maybe he thought I'd be older. Or younger.

Who knows?

Not me.

I made him work for it. I fought. I didn't know I had those reflexes. They just found me when I needed them. When he leaned over me and my elbow had a clear path to his nose.

I went for it.

He ducked before my bones could make contact with his. But the sway it had over him, this one tiny thing. The spark of life on the other end.

He was *rattled*.

I think he was mad at himself more than me. I have a daughter, he told me. I have a—I have a someone. A tenant. I have a life.

He told me he had a life. I didn't say I did, too.

He knew.

And then he did it. I fought, and at the end of it all, he still did it.

Like he had decided I was a force of evil and he needed to end me.

The last thing I remember: him, staring at my face like it was an abyss.

Clinging to my body like it was the end of everything.

CHAPTER 71

Emily

The house looks beautiful. Finally. Sophie and I came around earlier today and put up some string lights in the yard, around his plants and in the sole tree. We switched on the restaurant's heaters, tall flames inside steel cages. It snowed last night, barely an inch, but some of it stuck to the ground.

I take it all in, and my mood lifts a little.

He's at the door. Instructing people on where to park, directing them to the mulled wine Sophie and I brought over. Everyone joyful, everyone bundled up. That includes him, parka zipped up to his ears, and always that gray trapper hat.

I can't look at him for too long.

There was the question of whether to wear his scarf. I didn't want to be too obvious. Then again, he gave it to me. And it's a good scarf. The kind that actually keeps you warm. I figured if I wore it, people would see. They might recognize it, his scarf around my neck, and connect some dots.

Plus, he said he would get it back at some point. Maybe that point is today. Maybe if I wore it, he'd talk to me.

I decided to go with the scarf.

I'm wearing it now, with my white down coat and the good snow boots. Earmuffs to avoid messing up my hair with a hat. Some makeup—enough to feel put together, not enough to look like I tried.

When Sophie and I arrived, he hugged me hello. "Glad you could make it," he said. I want to believe his hands lingered a little longer than necessary around my arms, but I don't know.

Everyone's here, from the judge to Mr. Gonzalez. Even Eric and Yuwanda made it. ("Party at the Widower's?" Eric said on the group text. "Wouldn't miss it for the world.")

The daughter's here. Wrapped in her purple puffer jacket, white scarf covering the bottom half of her face. She has that long reddish hair like her mother's. Her mom's freckles, too. Sometimes it's hard to see him in her. In other circumstances—if he were a different kind of man, if he and his wife had formed a different kind of couple—you might wonder if she's actually his.

She's standing in a corner, next to some kids I've seen around town. Not really mingling. She's shy, like I imagine he was at her age. Like he can still be, at times.

If you observe him closely, you'll notice. How he takes little breaks to collect himself. How he ends a conversation, retreats into a corner, and pinches his temples for a second, before he's ready to go again.

We're not supposed to go inside. That was the only condition, related to us in a group email. "Aidan kindly requested that we keep the party to the front yard," the judge wrote. "I do hope we can all oblige. We're all very busy with the holiday season, and we don't want to create more work than necessary for anyone."

And so we've been staying outside. All of us except him.

He thinks he's being discreet, but I've noticed.

In addition to the short breaks, to the pinched temples, he has slipped inside twice already. He locked the door each time he came back out. I wouldn't have paid it much attention if he had done, well, anything. If he had returned with a stack of paper cups or a pile of napkins. Maybe a sweater to lend a guest.

But I saw through a window, that little gap between the glass and the shade. He went in, and he just stood there. Still, at the bottom of the staircase. Head tilted toward the upper floor. Listening.

For what?

I think about his house and the people who inhabit it. About his cousin who's not his cousin. About this woman who is currently nowhere to be seen.

I wait until the judge drags him into a conversation with a couple he married last summer. No one's watching.

I walk to the house. He hasn't made good on his plan to find a new hiding place for his spare key. Not yet.

Like he's not afraid of me. Like he's not worried about what I might do with this knowledge.

I let myself in.

CHAPTER 72

The woman in the house

Every step is improv. Every step is a question mark, heavy with the possibility of a momentous fuckup.

Tonight is the party. He came earlier, handcuffed you to the radiator, put the key in his pocket like Cinderella's stepmother the night of the ball.

"Remember what we discussed," he said.

"Yep," you told him. "Got it."

He thought for a brief moment. "There will be music. Outside. People will be socializing. Talking and eating, that kind of stuff. They'll be busy."

I know, you wanted to say. *You don't have to tell me that no one's coming to get me.*

You wait for the sounds of cars down the road. For voices and greetings. For music. You wait for guests with expectant eyes and bleeding hearts, ready to shower him and his daughter with their affection.

First, there's the safety pin. Retrieved from the chest of drawers in the afternoon while he was away, and hidden in the padding of your sports bra. For years, you rolled your eyes at padded bras, and look at you now.

You always thought when the moment came you'd know for sure.

Tonight, there are things you know with certainty. What he's done, and to whom. Where he keeps his spare gun.

You know, and he doesn't, that his daughter came to you. That she gave you pads and a pin.

What he doesn't realize: That you know, now, that the world isn't just a place where things happen to you. That you can happen to the world too.

You haven't heard him come inside, but you have to assume it's a possibility. You have to work cautiously, confidently.

On the handcuffs, there are two locks. You only need to open one. The one closest to you. The one keeping one end of the cuffs tethered to your wrist.

Insert the pin into the lock.

Conjure up the spirits you need. Matt. The YouTube man. Everything they taught you about locks. Everything you remembered while working on the door under the stairs.

This is a different kind of lock. But there is a universality to these mechanisms: pieces of metal that interlock to trap people places. You know all about those.

Wedge your handcuffed wrist against the wall for a better grip.

Focus.

The truth is, neither your almost-boyfriend nor the YouTube man did a great job at explaining how locks work. In their demonstrations, there always came a point when they had to surrender to the mystery of it. Magical thinking at play. Put the tools into place with your rational mind, then let your heart take over.

You have to work on the lock like someone might work on a person. Getting to know it, getting it to open bit by bit.

No turning back. No setbacks. Every inch, every victory, has to be won forever.

Something inside the handcuffs almost yields. Your heart races. You breathe. Keep working.

The cuff slips from your wrist.

You catch it before it clangs against the radiator.

You will be quiet. You will not make a sound.

This is when you leave the room. This is when you start doing things that will one day make people say, *She was so brave.*

A peek through the window, one finger peeling away the blinds. People below. Stomping on his grass, invading his domain. He's at the center of it all. He's got his back to you but you can see his hands moving animatedly, his body bending at the pace of his words. A man putting on a show.

Cecilia. You can't look at her. She's a blur of lavender in a corner. A pastel blob in a sea of black and gray. A bird about to fall from the nest.

This is when you unlock the bedroom door from inside, wrap your fingers around the knob, and turn.

This is when you start to believe. That his guests will keep to themselves. That you will go where you need to go, on schedule and undisturbed.

You shut the door on your way out.

This is very easy. You've done it dozens of times. Pad down the hallway. No one's here. You know no one's here. Then, the staircase: one step down, then another, then another. Hunch your back as if you could make yourself invisible.

Be quick. That's the most important thing here. If you're quick, you won't be seen. Not really. You will be a ghost. *I thought I saw,* people will say, *but no, it was nothing.*

You know the drill. You have been a ghost for five years.

You make it to the living room. Your head is spinning. No time to steady yourself. No time to think about what you're doing. It has to be now, all of it.

One more floor. Work the safety pin. Open the door. This is the last time. If all goes according to plan, and even if it doesn't. Last time in the basement. Last time in the house.

Take only what you need.

The gun, for a start. Tucked at the front of your waistband, nestled between denim and skin. The magazines. You know what to do. Load it.

No.

Your hand stops.

Because Cecilia is a lavender blob in a dark sea, and she doesn't deserve what's coming for her.

Because you won't raise a loaded gun in front of a girl.

You need to come out of this alive. Inside and out. Inhabit your own skin, show your face to the world.

Take the gun. Not the magazines. Take the Polaroids. Rectangles at the back of your pants, underneath the gray hoodie, concealed, like the gun. Insurance. Just in case.

This is where you say goodbye to him.

Farewell. Stay alive. I need you alive.

Put the boxes away, go back up the stairs. Push the door open and—

Fuck.

Someone's here.

Shut the door. Open it again, just a crack. Just enough to peer.

It's her.

Goddamn it, Emily. God fucking damn it.

She's snooping. Of course she is.

The gun weighs heavily against your waistband. You can feel it leaving indents in your abdomen, metal carving itself into flesh.

If she's snooping, then she's bound to leave soon. People who snoop can't afford to linger.

She runs her fingers against the back of the couch. Lifts a paperback from the coffee table and puts it back. She's all glossy hair and reddening cheeks, getting warm, you assume, in her white down coat.

Finally, she steps in the direction of the bathroom.

Just as she's about to disappear, the front door opens. Shit. Shit. *Shit.*

Your mind leaps to the boxes downstairs, to the magazines you left behind. To your unloaded gun. Is it too late to go back for bullets?

A pulse in your throat. Your hands, damp. Slippery. You can't do this with slippery hands. Maybe you can't do this at all.

A gust of cold air. A breath held and released.

It's Cecilia.

Emily jumps. Cecilia, too. They've startled each other, just like they've startled you. All three of you in places you're not supposed to be.

"Oh," Cecilia says. "Hi."

Emily says hi back. "I was just going to the bathroom," she says, the tone of an apology.

Cecilia nods. "Cool. I . . ." She hesitates. "I just needed a break."

This is good for you. You didn't expect her to slip away from the party so soon. You were going to wait, back in the bedroom, gun in hand. But now. Now she's here. Now you can proceed.

There is the thump of Cecilia's steps as she goes upstairs, then nothing. You listen more, an undetected silhouette through a cracked door, a ghost in a haunted house.

Inside, silence. Outside, the muffled echo of voices, the thrum of a pop song.

Time to come out.

You shut the door but do not lock it. It is an act of faith, sowing the seed of disturbance in his world. A reckoning, too: You do not need to leave his things how you found them. You are not coming back, no matter how this ends.

One, two, three steps, then a force—a burning regret, an invisible elastic pulling you back to the basement, making you wish you'd never stepped from behind the door.

You have made a mistake. You miscalculated. You misheard. You messed up. She's still here, in the living room. Illicit and alive and pretty, with two eyes that land on you and widen slightly.

"Oh. Hey," she says.

You give her a "Hey" back, because what else is there to say?

"I was just looking for the bathroom," she tells you.

You point at the door behind her.

"Right there."

She looks back. Smacks her lips. "Right. Thank you."

She turns around, one, two, three steps just like you, then stops and doubles back.

"Listen," she says. "I'm not really supposed to be in here. No one was supposed to come in. I just"—she thinks. Trying to decide, probably, how to best lie to you. "I had too much to drink." She bites her rosy lips, rolls her own eyes at herself. "I just couldn't hold it anymore."

You stare, each of you both the deer and the headlights.

She's waiting for you to say something.

"Understandable," you tell her.

"Right," she says. "So please, if you could not tell him you saw me in here? It's no big deal, really, I don't think, but I don't want him to . . . I'd rather he didn't know."

You blink.

"I won't tell," you say. An idea, a bargain. "Actually, I'm not really supposed to be here, either. It's—it's complicated."

You're his cousin, you remember. *In her head, you're his cousin. His loner cousin, who decided, for reasons unknown to the world, not to attend the party in the yard. You are busy. Shy. The kind of person who'd rather keep to herself.*

"We're a complicated family," you tell her.

She smiles. "What family isn't?"

You nod in agreement.

The shadow of a frown on her beautiful face. "Is everything okay, though?"

You swallow. "Everything's fine. All good. It's just, you know. Family stuff."

She nods.

"I should probably let you use the bathroom now," you say.

"Right."

She lingers a brief moment, then turns back to face the door behind her.

Two women keeping each other's secrets. Two women, silently agreeing to leave each other alone.

Maybe she'll get it, too. Maybe she'll know you did it all for her, too.

But now comes the part that will ruin you forever.

This is the part you can only experience from outside your body. This is when you shut down all the places in you that feel pain, sadness, anything.

This is the part where you learn from him. A soldier. Someone who sticks to the plan.

There is a key hanging by the door, in its usual place. Grab it.

Climb the stairs.

Knock on Cecilia's door.

She doesn't tell you to come in. Instead, she opens the door for you. She welcomes you in. The dog is napping, crated in a corner of the room. Away from the guests and the chatter.

This is when you shed a part of yourself, trap it within the walls of this house forever. Maybe people will hear it, years from now. It will come out at night asking for forgiveness, begging to be loved.

"I didn't realize you were here," she says. "My dad said you'd be away tonight."

You shut the door behind you.

This is the part where you start pretending. It has to look real, or it won't work. It has to look real, or you all die.

"Don't scream," you say.

She gives you a look, then spots the gun in your hand. Her body recoils. She takes a step back. When she gazes at you again, she's a beam of fear and confusion.

Maybe part of her knew. Maybe she could feel it, running in the pipes like hot steam, snaking through the foundations of the house. The prospect of violence.

Maybe part of her expected it, but she never saw it coming from you.

"If you scream, I won't be happy," you say. The words, his, like dirt in your mouth. You have to wrestle them off your tongue, every part of your body fighting back.

"What's going on?" she asks, a whimper.

I can't say, you think. You feel yourself beginning to give in, a tenderness in your stomach, words crowding the back of your throat. You want to tell her everything. You want her to understand. You want her to know that you would never—

No.

"We're going to go for a ride," you tell her. Not a question. Not a request. Someone looking into the future.

She nods. Is it that easy? You point a gun at people and they do as you tell them?

"You won't make a sound," you say. "You won't run. You won't scream."

Then, the one truth you have to offer: "Just do exactly as I say, and everything will be all right."

Another nod.

What you don't tell her: That this is the only way to make sure she's safe. To have eyes on her at all times.

Later, when she thinks about tonight, here's what you hope she'll remember: A great commotion. You doing something bad, and her father slipping away from her.

She will think herself the victim of a great injustice. She won't be wrong about that part. One day, she will get the full story. One day, she will find out. But not now.

You gesture toward the door with your free hand.

"Let's go," you say.

Her eyes travel to the dog. You prepare to tell her again: *I said, Let's go.* But she thinks better of it, steels herself on her own.

What you don't tell her: *I wish the dog could come, too. I hope she finds her way back to you.*

She goes down the stairs, and you don't even have to rush her. Don't have to pull or tug, don't have to press the gun at her side. She's thirteen and you're an adult with a gun and it breaks you, it destroys you one step after the other, how easy it is with her.

"Stop," you say.

A break halfway down the stairs to peer into the living room.

It's empty.

"Let's go," you say.

You make it to the back door.

"Here's how it's going to happen," you tell her. Whispering, hunching your shoulders, disappearing. He could be anywhere. "We're going to go to the truck. You will follow me. Do not try anything, okay?"

There is an undertone of supplication in your voice. None of this comes naturally to you.

"I trust you," you say.

She whines. Tears roll down her cheeks. *It's okay, you want to tell her. Honestly, I'm surprised it took you this long.*

Instead, you tell her to be strong. "I need you to be brave. Do you understand?"

She wipes her cheeks with the back of her hands and nods.

You clutch the gun tighter. A quick look outside the window. Nothing. Everyone's in the front yard, partying, oblivious to the great escape unfolding inside.

Let's keep it that way.

This is the part where you jump.

This is the part where nothing is for certain.

This is the part where the planets align, and you go free.

CHAPTER 73

Emily

I take a look around the bathroom—the soap, a supermarket brand, the towels, freshly cleaned. In a cabinet under the sink, bottles of bleach. He likes his house as clean as I like my kitchen.

I step back out.

She's gone. I'm alone again.

The door under the staircase. She was coming from there.

What was she doing?

I open it and find a flight of concrete steps.

At the bottom of the stairs, a light switch. I flick it.

It's a basement. Clean but ugly, folding furniture and a flashlight.

It smells nice. Like his scarf, like the crook of his neck. It smells like him.

There's a workbench, his duffel tucked underneath it. There are boxes. Stacks of them, piled up at the back of the room. Left over from the move, I suppose.

With the tip of a finger, I follow the large, woozy letters he scribbled in a hurry. KITCHEN STUFF, BOOKS, and, like an incantation, CAROLINE, CAROLINE, CAROLINE.

His wife. The one he was supposed to end up with. The one who took a vow and received one in return. The one who bore their child, who gave him what I imagine were the happiest days of his life. The one who—

A sound behind me. A scraping—soles on concrete.

Shit.

I didn't hear him open the door. Didn't hear him going down the stairs. But he's here, right here, inches from me, his beautiful gaze so piercing I want to tell him to look away, to leave me alone. But I can't, because I'm the trespasser. I ignored his request. I went where I wasn't supposed to go, and I've lost all bargaining power.

"How did you end up down here?" he asks.

He's calm. There's the hint of a smile on his face. He's curious, I tell myself, just curious to know what on earth I'm doing here.

"I was looking for the bathroom," I lie.

"And you thought you'd find it in the basement?"

A silence hangs between us. Then, the most beautiful sound: he laughs and I laugh, too, at myself, at my obvious lie, at the wonderful sense of relief warming me from head to toe.

"Busted," I say.

He cocks his head. Studies me as if he's never seen me before, like I'm a statue at a museum and he wants to memorize all my indentations and crevices. Like he wants to find out, and never forget, which parts of me give off light and which are pure shade.

I shift under his gaze. "I'm sorry," I tell him. Serious again.

He opens his mouth, perhaps to reassure me that it's okay, that he didn't want the whole party to come inside but there's no harm if it's just one person, no harm if it's just me, but—

His eyes are unsettled. They bounce from me to something above my right shoulder. Back to me, back to the thing. I trace his gaze from my coat sleeve to . . .

The piles of boxes?

It's a reflex. An instinct left over from childhood, when the kid next to me at school shielded their test sheet from view and it made me want to peek even more.

My body moves before I tell it to. An imperceptible shift—my back twisting ever so slightly, rib cage turning, neck craning in the direction of the boxes behind us.

A hand clasps my arm. He's grabbing on to me. Not the way he once did, the delicacy of affection, the urgency of passion. This is a tight grasp, somewhere between strength and panic. This is control.

I trace an invisible line with my eyes from his hand, veinous and white-knuckled around my coat sleeve, to his face. The handsome face I cradled that night at the restaurant. The lips I nibbled on, the nose I kissed swiftly, shyly, when it was all over.

There's something I don't recognize. A toughness, a void. An abyss opening underneath our feet. The sudden awareness that I don't know him. Not really. That we've never stayed up all night talking.

That he's never told me about his childhood, his parents, his hopes and dreams and how they turned out.

He's a man who hides things in his basement.

There's an infinite range of possibilities, from the most innocent to the most embarrassing.

It's okay, I want to tell him. *We all have secrets. The truth is I hated my parents—no, wait, even that's not true. The truth—the truth is that no one has ever loved me unconditionally. No one ever paid attention to me before you did, and I thought I was fine alone in my corner but I'm not. I'm really not.*

The truth is I haven't been fine in a long time.

The truth is I want to take up room. I want to be at the center of a person's life. Adored, celebrated. The truth is I want someone to laugh at my jokes, especially the stupid ones, and I want someone who will see me and not run the other way.

The truth, I want to tell him, *the truth is I would follow you anywhere.*

He blinks. His grasp relaxes around my arm. He lets go, slowly, as if he's only just realized he grabbed me in the first place.

He clears his throat. "I'm sorry. I—" He makes a humming sound and says it again, like a prayer he learned by heart: "I'm sorry."

I touch the skin underneath my coat and sweater, still hot from being squeezed, slightly painful to the touch.

"It's fine," I tell him.

My own hand reaches out and hovers awkwardly as I can't decide what to do—a hug, a tap, a fucking handshake?

"Come over here," he says. "Let me show you something."

He points to the workbench. To the shadowy end of the basement, where the light of the bare lightbulb doesn't quite reach.

I would follow you anywhere.

"It's just something I've been working on," he tells me, his hand beckoning me to join him.

Then, a thud, actually more like a slam coming from upstairs, and an engine like a clap of thunder. Close to us. Right outside the house, if I had to guess. Where only his truck is parked. Everyone else found spots down the street.

His head, his entire body turning in the direction of the sound. A blur—I watch as his silhouette bolts, then disappears up the concrete steps.

For the briefest moment, I am alone again. In his basement, in the belly of his house. Hands shaking. Ears ringing.

Outside, the rumble of the engine. His voice rising over it.

Finally, my body remembers.

I run. I run after him.

CHAPTER 74

The woman in the truck

You don't make a sound. Except for the soft whimpers coming out of Cecilia, except for the padding of your feet on the grass—yours bare, hers in sneakers. None of it is enough to give you away. There is a party. People are busy, blinded by string lights, brains hazy from what smells like mulled wine.

You can't see him anywhere. Ideally, you would have wanted him in the corner of your eye, accounted for in the distance. But this will have to do.

You open the passenger door to his truck.

"Get in," you tell his daughter.

You know how to do this.

She gives you this look as she slips onto the seat, the barrel of the gun inches from her. Wounded. The look of a girl who will never forgive you. She doesn't know that the pistol isn't loaded. That this is killing you maybe as much as it's killing her.

You shut her door as quietly as possible. Somewhere, before he can even realize it, his ears perk up. A disturbance in the universe. Something happening that he didn't plan for.

He doesn't know it yet, but in a few instants he'll be after you.

You go around to the driver's side. These are the seconds of danger. This is a situation you wouldn't be able to explain, your fingers around a gun that doesn't belong to you, a trapped girl who doesn't belong to you, either.

This is the moment that will kill you if it goes wrong.

You are in a vehicle. You are in the driver's seat.

"Seat belt."

Cecilia shoots you a look of incomprehension.

"Seat belt," you say again, and wave the gun around.

She buckles up. You tuck the gun back in your waistband.

The truck shudders to life.

Focus.

The way you make it out of here is by existing only in this moment, in the compartment, with your hands on the wheel. Think only what you need to think, see only what you need to see. Maneuver the truck away from the driveway. You think you hear things—someone yelling in the distance, confusion, the beginning of a commotion.

Focus.

Press the gas pedal.

What happens at the house is no longer your problem.

CHAPTER 75

Emily

He panics. Runs outside, looks around the yard. Wild. Frantic. "She's not here," he says. He goes back inside, doesn't bother shutting the front door, climbs the staircase two, three steps at a time. Doors open upstairs and slam against walls. He comes back out of breath.

"Cece's not here."

He's telling me and the people who have started gathering in the living room and at the entrance of the house, alarmed. This is the first time I've seen him like this. A father, wounded, something vital pried away from him.

"She's got my kid," he says. "In the truck."

No one understands what he means exactly, but we get the essential. The truck has driven away with the girl in it. The bones of his bones, the flesh of his flesh.

"I need a car," he says.

People search their pockets, but I'm faster. I jog up to him, press the keys to the Civic into his hand.

He runs to the car without looking at me.

I slip into the passenger seat. This is my car, my world. I don't need an invitation.

He twists the key in the ignition. People clear the way. The Civic's engine roars. Its tires squeak against the asphalt.

We pull away from the house.

CHAPTER 76

The woman on the move

You are on the road. You *are* the road. Eyes on it, steadfast grasp on the wheel. You drive. You drive like him that day, when he plucked you from a patch of grass, when he removed you from the world.

He has taught you well.

A sob reaches you from the passenger side. One glance—she's still where she's supposed to be. Still going along with this.

It will all be okay, you want to tell her. *This is all for show, but the fear is real, and for that I'll never stop being sorry.*

Left, left, right. It's not a long drive, but time slips away from you. Maybe you drive for ten minutes and maybe you drive for a whole year. Maybe you and Cecilia take a road trip, a woman and a girl in a post-apocalyptic movie, roaming America in search of a better life, a new life, any life at all.

Just as you're about to pass the Butcher Bros. and their cows, something in the rearview mirror. A glimmer, a Honda logo heading for you. You press harder on the gas pedal. You expect the Honda to fade into the background but it sticks to you. Soon it's riding your bumper. You can't shake it, like a bee on the rim of a soda can in the summer.

In the mirror, a flash of white. It's her. Sitting in her down coat on the passenger side of the Honda. If she's not driving, then it must be him. Coming for you, following you. Claiming back what is rightfully his.

After the cows, straight down. Bed-and-breakfast on the left. Library to your right. And the heart of it all, one building after the other. The town center.

You must get there. Even with the Honda on your back. You can't let him catch you.

Cecilia sobs. She can feel his presence, so near, calling her back to the world she knows, to everything you just took from her. You take one hand off the wheel and feel around for hers. Press gently like you did in the kitchen, when you saved her dog—when you saved her together, the two of you against him.

"Shhhh," you tell her. A calming intonation you learned from your mother as a girl, when the world wronged you and you collapsed into her arms. "Shhhh."

Keep your eyes on the road. You must go as fast as you can without losing control. You must drive like you have never driven before.

You try. You try to do it right. The pressure of your right foot on the gas pedal, the vital grip of your hands on the steering wheel.

The Honda starts fading away. You manage, somehow, to put distance between you and him.

But it has been five years. And even before that, you weren't a great driver. You were a city kid. You didn't know the names of trees, the sounds of birds. You learned how to drive in Manhattan, at twenty miles per hour.

Something catches your eye. A shape heading for you, darting across your window.

You swerve. You don't want to—it is the very last thing you want to do—but in this moment you do not control your hands.

It was a bird, your brain tells you, and you see it flying away. Some type of bird of prey, hooked claws, a beak like a can opener. Flying too close to you, too close to the truck. And still, unscathed.

Who cares about the bird?

The truck is drifting. In the passenger seat, Cecilia shrieks. Her hand searches for a handle, for any surface she can hold on to.

You try to take back control, to get back on the road, but the truck is no longer listening to you. Like it has remembered, finally, that you are not its rightful owner. That it was never meant to serve you.

There is a drop. You, the girl, and the truck, falling together. In this moment, you belong only to the laws of physics, to the forces that pull you to the ground and the ones that let you sink.

You open your eyes. When did you close them?

You don't know. What you do know is you never told them to close.

What you do know: That you, the girl, and the truck are no longer moving. That you are in a ditch.

What you do know: That he is out here. Chasing you.

CHAPTER 77

Emily

He drives like a madman. Like a father chasing after his daughter.

The Civic obeys him until it doesn't. He presses the gas pedal, but the car struggles to keep up. There's a buzzing sound.

The transmission.

He grabs for the gearshift, tries to jerk it into fourth.

It's stuck.

The car crawls to a stop. Ahead of us, the truck speeds away.

"Fuck!"

He wrenches the gearshift left and right. Doesn't know the secrets of the Civic, of its manual transmission.

He tries one more time to force it, but the car doesn't budge.

"Fuck!"

His fist slams against the dashboard.

"That bitch," he says in a voice I don't recognize. "I should have killed her a long time ago."

Before I can ask. Before I can formulate a single thought. Before my stomach can tighten. Before I can even think of feeling nauseous, of questioning everything I thought I knew, of hearing the air rush out of my lungs like they will never, ever inflate again, he's gone.

He leaps out of the car and runs.

After her is all I can think.

After the woman I saw.

And his daughter.

It's the anchor of hope, the possibility of a misunderstanding.

We all say things, right? In the heat of the moment. Things we don't mean. Things we regret.

He runs after her, I decide.

He runs after his daughter.

CHAPTER 78

The woman, almost there

"We have to go."

Your neck hurts. Pain pulses at the back of your head. Shit. It must have happened during the drop, when you went careening into the ditch.

You do not have time to hurt. You do not have time to check that your body still works as expected.

"We have to go now," you tell her.

The pistol. You still have the pistol. You reach for it under your sweater. Your face hardens.

In a few seconds, he'll catch up with you.

"Get out," you say.

She listens. You have the gun, so she listens.

You step out. It's frigid outside. Here you are—outside, without him. Gun in hand. A brief inventory: ice on the road, icicles dripping from the trees that line it.

Your bare feet burn against the frozen ground. You can't slip. Can't fall. A fall would bring this whole enterprise to a tragic end.

Hurry up.

You link your fingers around the girl's wrist. The two of you, one.

"Come on."

There is no time, no time at all. You climb out of the ditch, pull her after you, onto the asphalt.

One stride, then two.

You find your pace. You urge her forward and she follows, smooth and malleable, not because she trusts you but because you have a gun and she is a girl in a body, tender and exposed.

Soon you're running. Your body propels the both of you. With every step, the town gets closer.

Search. You saw it in the guidebooks. On the map. A small icon like an officer's badge. In the basement, you followed the road with your finger, from the Butcher Bros. to the Wishing Well to the town center. You have to trust you got it right.

Somewhere in the distance, the Honda screeches. Doors slam. A scream. His voice. He found you, just like he promised he would.

You run for you and you run for her and it has to be enough. Maybe she looks back. Maybe she tries to reverse course, every fiber of her pulling her back to the truck, back to him. Back to the hands that held her when she was born and fed her when she was hungry, to the eyes that watched her on the playground and the ears that listened for her cries in the night.

We gravitate toward the bodies that keep us alive.

He calls for her. You recognize the syllables, her name in his mouth, and this is bad news. If you can make out what he's saying, then he is too close.

Something gives in. There is a lightness to your left, the same place where you felt his daughter pulling just moments ago.

You have lost her. He must have caught up with you, snatched her back from you.

So close.

You clutch the gun, think of the bullets you left back in the house, the magazines in the cardboard box. You regret not loading the pistol. You regret everything.

No.

She's still here. By your side, where she's supposed to be.

No longer tugging, no longer resisting. Her stride mirroring yours.

She turns her head back. You don't know what she sees. Your best guess: her father, furious, his face a mask of betrayal. A man she knows but doesn't recognize.

This is the part only she understands.

For reasons that belong to her alone, she does it. Her father's footsteps close in on you. And the girl, she runs. She runs with you.

CHAPTER 79

Emily

I start the Honda again.

He's fast. The fastest runner I've ever seen.

He finds them. The woman and his girl, running from him. Together.

I'm about thirty feet away when it happens. It unfolds in the beam of the Honda's headlights.

First, the girl. He reaches for her, snatches her back.

This is it, I tell myself. This is when he stops and holds her tight and tells her how worried he was, so scared he almost died, so terrified he almost killed.

But he leaves her.

After he's taken her back, yanked her by the wrist, detached her from the woman, he starts again.

Like a man who will never hear another sound. Like a man who will never think another thought.

He runs after this woman like she's the only thing that matters.

I stop the Honda.

"Aidan!"

I'm standing outside the car. Yelling his name with the entire force of my lungs, straining my vocal cords.

"Aidan!"

He turns around. First his face, then his upper body.

"Aidan, get back here!"

It doesn't matter what I'm saying, only that I'm saying it.

He slows down, then stops. The briefest moment, but enough. Enough to wonder. Enough to consider me.

My breath catches. I'm gasping for air even though I didn't run. It's the terror of it, the gaping abyss of it.

The hope is that he will turn around. That he will stop chasing her.

The hope, I realize, is that he will start chasing me.

His legs twitch. The shadow of a sprint, the start of a Plan B. The first word of a story in which he changes his mind. Where he just goes for it. Me. Where he just goes for me.

Reality pulls him back in. Or is it hope? Hope that he will catch her? That he will stop her, wherever she's headed?

I'm not the one he wants. Not the one he's after.

But I've bought her some time. Whoever she is, I've bought her a few feet between him and her.

He turns his back to me and starts running again.

CHAPTER 80

The woman, running

After everything, it comes down to two bodies.

Yours and his.

You run.

This isn't about running fast. This is beyond fast.

You run like you ran back in your former life, when you yearned to feel your legs dissolve underneath you. When you craved the pounding in your rib cage, the blaze of your lungs searching for air.

You run to it. A small, stand-alone building. So plebeian under the starlit sky. Right here, maybe one hundred meters away.

You can run one hundred meters. You have prepared for this. Felt the muscles in your legs, the strain in your thighs, the toughness of your calves.

You do it and you do not look back and he is right behind you and you can hear him and you can feel him, feel him in your bones and in your brain and underneath your skin and behind your eyes and in every corner of you, every crevice of the world.

And so you run.

The ultimate rule of staying alive: You run, because it is how you have always saved yourself.

CHAPTER 81

The woman at the police station

It's the end of the world. A chaos so big you can't expect the planets to ever align again.

What you know: You are still breathing. You are a body, two arms and two legs, a head and a torso.

What you left outside: cold, ice, and snow. The gun, tossed at the last second. The Stars and Stripes flapping meekly in the December wind. A building made of brick and glass. You are inside now, at the heart of it. A lab rat under fluorescent lights. Too much noise, too many voices.

Your head is full. All you can hear is your heart pounding in your chest, the pulse of blood in your ears.

It isn't over. He's here. The righteous father. The man everyone trusts. The man who knows the world has his back. The one who can only fail up.

"She took my kid," he says, over and over again. "She took my kid."

This man. You go places and he finds you. He is a hotel you can never check out of.

And his daughter. Cecilia. She is here, too. You lost her, and she found you.

Him, you realize. She found him.

It is always about him.

You are standing a few feet inside the police station. He is at the entrance. A man in blue stands between the two of you.

"Aidan," the man in blue says. "Aidan, we know. Calm down."

He doesn't calm down.

"She took my kid." His voice ricochets across the room. It bounces on the walls, high-pitched and plaintive.

Once. Just once, you took something of his.

He wants them to know. Before you can say anything. He wants to get there first, make sure his voice is heard so yours vanishes forever.

It's not just the voice. There's his body, too, tall and lean and trying to push past the man in blue.

The man in blue turns halfway to face you. A cop. Young, all baby fat and bouncy cheeks. An officer. Two ears and a brain. You must get to him.

"Aidan," the young cop says, a plea for reason.

He doesn't listen. "She took my kid." The outrage of it. The sheer disbelief.

Cecilia raises an arm. "Dad," she says, an echo to his litany. "Dad. Dad."

Maybe it's her voice, years of parenting having predisposed him to leap at that word, *Dad, Dad, Dad*. The most essential part of her, waking up the most essential part of him.

"Let me through," he says, trying to step toward you. The young cop stays where he is.

"Aidan," the cop tries, "calm down, I don't want to have t—"

A scuffle. Voices rising, bodies colliding. Your eyes shut, a reflex. You squeeze your hands into fists. *Breathe. Inhale, exhale. Stay alive.*

"I'm so sorry, Aidan," the cop says. There's the click of metal, handcuffs zipping shut. When you open your eyes again, Cecilia's father is standing with his arms behind his back, wrists crossed, head bowed. Silent. Finally.

"You, too," the cop says. He reaches for something, and your shoulders are burning. Hands on your back, cold metal against your skin. Again. Maybe this is your life forever. Wherever you go, a man will be waiting with handcuffs, demanding you hold out your wrists.

"All right," the officer announces. "Now we can talk."

Another silhouette in blue approaches. "You take her, I'll take him," she tells the young cop. He nods and nudges you away.

You look back. Cecilia. You need to know what they're going to do with her.

From the corner of your eye, you see her try to follow her dad. A third officer—older, almost too old to be her father—stops her. "Hang back here," he says, and you think you hear *sweetie*. You hear *dad,* you hear *a few questions.* Cecilia nods as the older cop gestures toward an empty chair.

From the other side of the room, he looks back, too. The father. The man in handcuffs.

His gaze catches yours.

There is a recognition here, an air of *Of course.* Like he was expecting this. Like he was waiting for you to betray him all along.

This is how it had to end, you want to tell him.

Both of us chained to ourselves and, in the middle, the girl. Free.

CHAPTER 82

The woman with a name

The room is small and windowless. A desk, fluorescent lights, a manila folder. Lingering smells of sweat and instant coffee.

You love it. All of it. A room where the air doesn't belong to him.

"Sit," the cop says.

You sit.

"I need to tell you," you say, and he interrupts.

"What happened out there?" he wants to know. "Who are you? How do you know Aidan?"

You take a breath. Your skin prickles. *I'm trying,* you want to say. *I'm trying to tell you. I've been sitting on this for five years and now it's time and you have to listen to me.*

You have to believe me.

Promise you'll believe me, you want to say. *Promise that after I tell you this, it will all be over.*

The way he said his name just now. The way he apologized as he put him in handcuffs. *I'm so sorry, Aidan.* Buddies. Two men who have known each other for a while.

Aidan Thomas? the young cop will say on TV. *He was just a very nice guy. The type of person everyone likes. Polite. If your car broke down, he was there with jumper cables. We never had any issues with him. He got along with everybody.*

You take a gulp of stale air. *Listen,* you want to say. *Let's make a deal. I will give you the case of a century. I will change your life, as long as you change mine.*

Look at him. The words that follow are words you need to say with your back straight, your head held high. No hesitation. You have waited five years for this. For a room devoid of his presence, for a pair of ears to listen, for your voice in the middle of it all.

"Officer," you start. Your voice thick like syrup, your jaw working its way heavily through each syllable.

You have to say it.

Remember it. The sound, the feeling of it in your mouth.

Your name.

Illicit, like a curse word.

For five years, you have not spoken it.

Even thinking it felt wrong. In the shed. Anytime he was around. You worried he might hear the syllables in your head. That he would feel your deception, a part of yourself kept out of his reach.

"My name," you say. Start over. You can't fuck it up.

It has to be perfect.

When you say these words, you have to give them the power to unlock doors and keep them open forever.

"Officer," you say again, and this time you don't stop. "My name is May Mitchell."

CHAPTER 83

Emily

Everywhere I go, he stares at me.

Abandoned on park benches. Next to the registers at the drugstore. At home, on the living room table, where Eric abandoned a copy of the newspaper yesterday. I came back before Yuwanda could tell him to put it away.

Most papers have been using his mug shot. Two of them, tabloids from the city, got their hands on a couple of family photos. One was taken years ago at a Halloween party, when his daughter was a little kid. He's wearing a plushy gray sweater, holding on to her waist as she bobs for apples in the town square, her face pixelated. The invisible child of the most visible man.

The other photo is even older. He's young, posing next to his wife in front of their former house, the big one in the woods. Both of them smile at the camera. She's resting her head on his shoulder; he has one arm around her. It was taken, I imagine, around the time they moved here. Back when they looked into the future together and liked what they saw.

It's been ten days. No one believed anything at first. The news articles kept coming, and people kept shaking their heads. Then he confessed. Some of it, not all. But enough.

The cops tried to ask me questions the first night. At first, I waited outside in my car. Nothing happened. I went in and couldn't see him anywhere. The kid was by herself, sitting on a chair. I motioned toward her but an officer stopped me. She took me to a separate room. "Do you know this girl's father?" she asked. "Do you know Aidan Thomas?"

And then she said words that didn't make sense to me. Still don't. She kept probing, but I was useless. Confused. Cold. She gave up and told me to go home, that she'd come by the next day.

"Can I come in instead?" I asked. I didn't want her inside our house. Didn't want to drag Eric and Yuwanda into any of this. The officer said sure.

I kept my promise. I returned the following day. By then, the FBI had arrived. The fucking FBI. They were helping with the investigation, the officer said. Could I speak to them?

I told the officer okay. It didn't matter who I told. She introduced me to Agent Something. I didn't catch her name when she first said it and then it was too late to ask.

It doesn't matter what her name is. It only matters what I told her, and those facts will remain the same. They will remain the same forever.

In a small room with the heating set too high, I sat with Agent Something and surrendered everything that used to be ours, every sentence a betrayal. The texts. That night in the pantry. I chose my words carefully, but there are things that don't sound pretty, no matter how hard you think about your words.

Agent Something took notes. My phone had to stay, she said. Ditto the necklace. She took the scarf, too. "It's just a scarf," I told her. "What difference does it make?"

She shook her head. "We don't know," she told me. "That's why we have to check. It could be evidence. Anything could be."

I removed the scarf and gave it to her. A draft snaked down my neck. "Something else," she said. "We searched his house overnight. We found some items pertaining to you."

That was news to me. I never gave him anything aside from a box of cookies.

Agent Something leaned over the table that separated us. "Would you like to know?" she asked.

It was my turn to shake my head. "It doesn't matter now," I said.

She gave me a nod and turned a page on her notebook. Scanned it like she was searching for something, but wasn't sure what.

"Listen," she said, her hand falling back onto the page. "Maybe you can help me understand. Every person we've spoken to so far says this man was beloved. Or at least very well liked by all those who knew him. No one can remember a single argument, not one unpleasant interaction. And it's my understanding that you were . . . very attached to him."

She waited. I didn't say anything.

"It seems to me," she continued, "that people loved and trusted him because he was a normal man. Because he was a father who took his daughter to school and clothed and fed her and helped people around town." She shifted in her seat, adjusted the service weapon hanging from her waistband. "I don't know that a woman in the same situation would have scored as many sympathy points. That's all."

You have no idea, I wanted to tell her. *You have no idea, because you didn't know him like we did, and now you never will. He didn't lay his eyes on you and make you feel like you'd never be alone again. You've never felt warmed by his laugh, comforted by the heat of his skin against yours.*

You've never loved him, and so you'll never know. You'll never understand how he could be.

"I guess you're right," I told her. She let out a brief sigh and told me I was free to go.

Right before she opened the door to let me out, she paused, her hand on the doorknob. "Would it be okay if we contacted you further down the road?" she asked. I nodded.

Cooperating. That's what I've been doing. Telling them everything I know. Showing them everything they can see.

I know what they're thinking. That I must have known. How could I not have known? How could I have looked into his eyes, how could I have held him so close, and not known?

They want to believe I knew. They need to tell themselves I did, because if I didn't, it means they wouldn't have known, either.

FOR THREE DAYS, I hide. I don't go to the restaurant. I don't open. I don't close. No one asks. No one wants to come near me.

On the third day, Yuwanda walks into my bedroom, carrying a cup of tea and a mug of coffee. "I didn't know which one you'd prefer," she says. "I feel like there's a lot about you I don't know." I wince. She says sorry. I tell her it's okay.

We talk. Just a bit. Eric joins us and sits on the edge of the bed. They don't want to ask too much, and I don't have many answers to give. I tell them about the texts. I tell them Aidan and I had been seeing each other. They don't ask what it means, exactly, seeing each other.

One day, the police report will become public. They will read it. People I've never met—hundreds of them—will read it.

None of this belongs to me anymore.

Yuwanda shakes her head. "You were alone with him," she says. "I can't believe you were alone with him, all these times, and we had no idea."

I raise my hand. She stops. I don't want to talk about him. I don't want to talk about why I don't want to talk about him. I don't want to try to explain.

I can't explain.

Eric changes the topic.

"The restaurant," he says. "Any idea what's going to happen with that?"

I've thought about it for three days. But before I make a decision, I need to give it one last shot.

It was my father's restaurant. It was home, sort of. It was imperfect, and I resented it often, and still it was home.

On the fourth night, I put on a fresh button-down and my crimson apron and drive myself downtown.

I pretend not to notice the lingering looks as I step behind the bar. Eric and Yuwanda hover around me like bodyguards. Gestures I remember: peeling a twist off a lemon, stuffing olives with blue cheese and stabbing them with a cocktail pick. What I want: To disappear into my work. Become so focused that I forget to hear the whispers, fail to notice the abnormal number of customers requesting to dine at the bar tonight. Trying to get a better look at me. Searching for clues, anything in the way I carry myself that would explain why he picked me.

The air is thick. My button-down sticks to my back, slick with sweat. I meet Cora's gaze as I hand her two old-fashioneds—regular, not virgin. No one orders those anymore. Cora thanks me. She walks away from the bar faster, I think, than necessary.

Everything a question. Every detail weighed down by suspicion.

I carry on. Trudge through dinner service. I have a right to be here. This part of the world was mine long, long before it was his.

But then. I run out of lemons. I run out of oranges. I run out of Maraschino cherries. That means two things: For citrus, the walk-in. For the jarred cherries, the pantry.

I tell myself it's nothing. My back straightens. One of my front teeth sinks into my bottom lip. I force myself to relax. Step inside the pantry like it's just another room. I must do it. I must do it all, as if nothing ever happened.

The jar is on the top shelf. I lift my arm and the button-down spills out of the waistband of my slacks.

I am him. I am his silhouette that day, the day of the 5K, the day of the hot cocoa. When he grabbed the sugar from this very shelf, flannel shirt slipping up to reveal his abdomen.

When I became his, and he became a little bit mine.

The words I read in the newspapers come back to me. Victims. Body count. Stalking. Murder. Serial.

The ground shifts. I haven't slept in days. Maybe I'll never sleep again.

I'm going to be sick.

I'M NOT SICK.

I get out of the pantry and finish my service. The next morning, my choice is made.

That was my last shift.

I don't know the first thing about selling a restaurant. My parents never taught me that part. Only how to run one.

The internet tells me selling a restaurant requires strategy, cautious thinking, and detailed planning.

A restaurateur from the city tells me he wants to buy the place. His price doesn't sound like a complete insult.

I take his offer.

I STILL NEED to work. To pay my bills while the money moves around. And even after it arrives, a restaurant sale isn't a trust fund.

I need to work.

Yuwanda calls a friend who calls a cousin whose brother needs a bartender. The job is in the city, the restaurant on a cross street off Union Square. Shitty pay, shittier hours. I take it on the spot.

I've never dreamed of the city, but now it's a thing that is happening to me. I find a sublet in Harlem, tour it on Skype. The room is small, with just one tiny window. Rent will eat up more than half my paycheck. I sign a virtual contract and wire my new landlord the deposit.

This will be me. This job, this room. I will take the subway to work, wander around the buildings while I wait for my shift to start. If I'm lucky, the city won't care about me. I will disappear.

FINDING THE ADDRESS wasn't easy. The media was barred from giving it away. Ditto the cops. But a friend of the family stopped for dinner one night on their way to delivering a care package. Yuwanda overheard enough. She relayed the information to me the next morning.

"Do with it what you want," she said. "I just thought you might want to know. Apparently her parents moved there after she went missing. It's close to where she was last seen. They never stopped looking for her."

It's only in the next town over—restaurants and convenience stores and coffee shops, the kind of place you visit only if you know people there. The house is nice enough. It sits at the bottom of a hill, modern, with floor-to-ceiling windows, the kind of porch furniture you can't get at Walmart. A house inhabited by loss and tragedy, yet so tasteful.

What was it like for them to learn they'd been just a few miles apart? So close, this entire time?

I park around the corner and walk to the end of the driveway. It's lined with pebbles, carefully raked.

One step, then two. I force myself to keep walking until I reach the front door. It's now. It has to be.

My fingers hover over the doorbell. Before I can press it, the door cracks open. A woman, old enough to be my mother, peers at me.

"Can I help you?"

In the background, a flash of colors, jeans and a black sweater and that hair, long and clean and streaked with white. Her round eyes catch mine even from a distance.

"It's okay, Mom," she says. "Let her in."

The woman glances back behind her shoulder, then reluctantly does as she's told. I step in with an apologetic smile, to which she doesn't respond.

"I'm so sorry to come by unannounced," I say. "I'm on my way out. Of town, I mean. I'm leaving."

What am I doing here? Bothering these strangers with my little life plans when they have so much healing to do, so much to rebuild?

I search for the gaze of the person I came to see.

"I think I wanted to say goodbye." My words, heavy and uncertain. "And sorry."

My voice quavers. I hate it, the sound of it. What right do I have to be the traumatized one? I'm fine. He didn't hurt me. He liked me, maybe, in the strange way he might have been capable of.

She steps toward me. The memory of our last moments together hangs in the air. The urgency of the situation, her in his house, on her way out, and me, blind as Oedipus jabbing golden brooches into his eyes.

"You didn't know," she says. "You had no idea."

It's not entirely exculpatory in her mouth. Just a truth: I didn't know, and I acted like it.

"I'm so sorry," I repeat.

Something glistens in her eyes. I wish we had more time. I wish it were just the two of us and we could talk for hours. I wish she could tell me all her stuff and I could tell her mine. I wish we could combine our powers, mesh into one unstoppable force.

"I don't suppose—" I stand at the edge of stupidity. What do I have to lose? What credibility do I have left? What dignity, what privacy? And if I've been stripped of all that, then isn't it fair to at least try to wrap myself in something else? "I don't suppose you'd let me . . . hug you goodbye?"

There's a silence. The echo of my words, grotesque, crashing against the walls of the vestibule. A console to my left, a mirror, a ceramic bowl of odds and ends, keys, buttons, folded pieces of paper.

"It's fine if not," I tell her. "I completely understand. I know it's weird. I just . . ."

Then the woman speaks, the older one who can only be her mother. "My daughter," she says. She speaks with difficulty, like she doesn't know exactly how to explain. "My daughter doesn't—"

But she cuts her off. May. I read her name in the paper. It rang a vague bell—distant memories from news reports, maybe a missing-person poster at the gas station. Hard to tell how much I actually remember, and how much of it is my brain filling in the blanks.

May leans against the console next to me. Her eyes, ringed with shadows, piercing in the daylight. Searching for something in me. If I knew what it was, I'd give it to her instantly.

"Mom," she says. "It's fine."

CHAPTER 84

May Mitchell

She steps in, and you can tell she's been destroyed. Like submarines on each other's radars, you recognize each other. The ones who have lived through things.

For days, the world has grabbed onto you. Welcoming you back. Hands reaching out to you, arms pulling you in. Throats sobbing against your temples. Voices, hoarse, telling you how much you've been missed. A new house. Not in the city. Not yet. Some items from the past. More voices—in person, over the phone, recorded memos and video calls and postcards and care packages.

Your mother, your father. Your brother. Julie. Even Matt emailed, your almost-boyfriend. "I hope you're doing okay," he wrote. "Well, as okay as possible. I'm sorry if this sounds dumb."

No one has any idea how to navigate this, and everyone is sorry.

At night, the voices go away. You lie in a bed your mother says is yours. You listen for steps down the hallway, but there's only silence. Still, you listen, always you listen, ready for something to pierce the quiet. You doze off only in the mornings, when your family awakens and the smell of coffee fills the house and the world starts standing guard.

Cecilia.

You think about her all the time. The newspapers assure you she's fine, "safe and in the care of relatives." The cops, too. Every day you call and every day they tell you the same thing.

Did she get the dog back? you asked on the third day. They said yes. An officer found the crate during a search of the house. They gave the dog to the girl's grandparents.

She's staying with them, the officer said. She's not alone. She's going to be okay.

She's going to be okay.

You need them to keep saying it. If you hear it enough times, maybe one day you'll believe it.

And now, the other woman is here. The woman from the living room. The one who wore your necklace. Emily.

She stands in the new house, and maybe she's the only one who understands. What it was like to live in a world where he was the center of everything.

She doesn't know how to exist. How to stand, how to speak. How to look at your mother. How to look at you.

She wants a hug.

Your mother tries to step in. She knows you're weird about that stuff now, that you struggle to let yourself be touched. That you don't like people sneaking up on you. That you can't handle being held too tight or for too long. That sometimes you need time alone and there's nothing to do but wait it out.

What your mother doesn't know: that this woman in her house is the only person who's seemed familiar to you in days. That she means something to you. That you saw her then and you see her now. That this woman is like you, her body a bridge between two worlds.

You wish you could keep her close forever. You wish she could stay and the two of you could talk about everything or sit next to each other for hours saying nothing.

People have been trying to understand. Journalists have asked questions and relayed the answers. Cops, too. They're compiling evidence, digging into his past, searching for motives and methods, retracing his steps, trying to name the women in the basement.

Everyone scrambling for every little piece, but they'll never know.

Her, you, and his daughter. The three of you. Your stories combined. That's the closest anyone will ever get to the truth.

"Mom," you say. "It's fine."

Your mother steps aside. It doesn't come naturally to her, these days, leaving you at the mercy of the world.

The other woman waits, wrapped in the puffy white coat that threatens to swallow her, jeans and snow boots peeking out, brown hair stuffed under a trapper hat. Brand-new. Recently purchased, probably. A new item for a new life.

She wants a hug. She has asked and now she stands, hands at her sides, already an air of regret on her face.

You open your arms.

ACKNOWLEDGMENTS

I (a French person) started playing with the idea of maybe one day writing a novel in English when I was nineteen. It took me a decade to get there—a decade during which U.S. publishing seemed to me a bright, impossibly distant wonder. What I'm trying to say is: I can't believe I'm here. Sorry, I know I'm supposed to play it cool, but I truly can't.

In the making of this novel, I have been incredibly lucky to work with people who are not only disturbingly good at their jobs but who understood what I was trying to do with this story—and, even better, who loved it. This means more to me than I can put into words. (Even though putting things into words is my literal job.) And so, I extend my most heartfelt thanks to:

Reagan Arthur, my editor: You have edited and published some of my very favorite books, books that made me a writer. Thank you for your kindness, your keen eye, your energy, and your generosity. Tim O'Connell, my acquiring editor on this book, for the first round of edits, and for telling me early on that this is supposed to be fun. Reagan, Tim: I don't think it's easy to make a writer feel completely safe on the page, but you both did. Thank you.

Stephen Barbara, whom I am so lucky to call my agent, for supporting this novel from the very first moments, for your tireless work, and for your friendship. I don't mean to sound dramatic, but your belief in my work changed my life. Thank you for everything.

The dream team at Knopf: Jordan Pavlin, my friend Abby Endler, Rita Madrigal, Isabel Yao Meyers, Rob Shapiro, Maria Carella, Kelsey Manning, Zachary Lutz, Sara Eagle, John Gall, and Michael Windsor.

The dream team at InkWell Management: Alexis Hurley, for taking this book quite literally around the world, Maria Whelan, Hannah Lehmkuhl, Jessie Thorsted, Lyndsey Blessing, and Laura Hill.

And to Ryan Wilson at Anonymous Content for his work on screen rights.

To Clare Smith from Little, Brown UK, for bringing this book across the Atlantic, for her endless enthusiasm, and for her ever-helpful notes. Thank you, Clare. Special thanks also to Éléonore Delair at Fayard/Mazarine, and to the editors around the world who have loved this book.

To Paul Bogaards, a very special publicist who makes everything fun and easy (and who brings the best surprise guests to coffee). I'm so honored you love my work. And to Stephanie Kloss and Stephanie Hauer from Bogaards PR.

It is a truth universally acknowledged that writers want to be loved, but I think a lot of us underestimate how much the love of a good scout can change a life. Heartfelt thanks to the scouts who supported this book.

To Tyler Daniels, my husband. Thank you for believing in me, for reading my drafts, for finding the title of this novel, and for talking through plot points. I'm so lucky to have you in my life and to be in yours. And thank you for being an amazing dad to our dog, Claudine.

To my parents, Jean-Jacques and Anne-France Michallon, respectively for teaching me there's nothing wrong with chasing slightly absurd goals (such as writing novels in English when your first language is French), and for enabling my immense love of books (and kick-starting my, um, interest in serial killers). To my grandmother Arlette Pennequin, who heard about this novel before it became a book and learned everything there was to learn about U.S. publishing. I think she might be the French grandmother with the most thorough knowledge of the industry.

To my in-laws, Tom and Donna Daniels: I started writing this novel while staying in a house with you in the Hudson Valley. And then I used this house (your house) as the model for Aidan's in this book. And I told you only *after* I'd finished the book and gotten a publishing deal for it. And you weren't even mad. In fact, you were so happy and proud. Thank you for your love and support, which mean so much to me.

To Holly Baxter, for her faith in this novel before it was even completed. Your enthusiasm got me over the finish line, as did your wise advice. (First draft first, existential crisis later.)

To my French friends, for being amazing and witty and so very supportive and, let's face it, extremely good-looking: Morgane Giuliani, Clara Chevassut, Lucie Ronfaut-Hazard, Ines Zallouz, Camille Jacques, Xavier Eutrope, Geoffroy Husson, Swann Ménage.

To Christine Opperman, an amazing friend and generous reader whose notes somehow always match those later given to me by editors. Thank you so much for taking the time to read my work, and for talking some sense into me when necessary.

To my dear friend Nathan McDermott, the best friend a writer (or, really, any person) could want. Thank you for your support and praise, and for everything else.

To my therapist, whom I can't name for obvious reasons, who read an early draft of this novel. (How awesome is that?) Thank you for literally keeping me sane.

The movie quote in chapter 33 is from the lovely *Last Christmas* starring Emilia Clarke and Henry Golding. I've often wondered what it's like for people who are somehow related to serial killers (or, you know, *are* serial killers) to hear serial killer jokes in movies or on television. There we have it.

In chapter 25, May contributes an essay to a section of a website called "I Lived Through It." It's inspired by the "It Happened to Me" essays run by the now-defunct xoJane from, I believe, the website's inception in 2011 to its closing in 2016. Those pieces were my introduction to personal essays back when I was attending college in France. They captivated me. I'm happy I got to experience a version of that era, vicariously, through this novel, many years later.

And finally, a world of thanks to the other people who made me a writer: Madame Sultan, the high school teacher who told me when I was a teenager: "Do not stop writing. Otherwise, you'll let yourself get taken by life . . ." (I didn't stop writing.) Monsieur Chaumié, who read my short stories before they were ready to be read. Arlaina Tibensky, who embraced my messy ideas. And Karen Stabiner, who taught me I had to love this more than anything else.

A Note About the Author

Clémence Michallon was born and raised near Paris. She studied journalism at City, University of London, received an MS in journalism from Columbia University, and started working as a journalist for *The Independent* in 2018.

At *The Independent*, she has interviewed artists from Judd Apatow to Ben Platt and authors such as Rumaan Alam, Taylor Jenkins Reid, and Curtis Sittenfeld. Her essays and features have covered true crime, celebrity culture, and literature.

She moved to New York City in 2014 and became a U.S. citizen in 2022. She now divides her time between New York City and Rhinebeck, New York, with her husband and their dog, Claudine. She has been a fan of crime novels ever since she started stealing her mother's mass-market paperbacks as a teen. *The Quiet Tenant* is her debut thriller.

You can find her on Instagram @Clemencemichallon, where she often posts about crime novels, mysteries, and thrillers, and on Twitter @Clemence_Mcl.